The Saint and the Fasting Girl

Anna Richenda

Anna Richenda

iUniverse, Inc.
New York Bloomington

The Saint and the Fasting Girl

Copyright © 2009 Anna Richenda

All rights reserved. No part of this book may be used or reproduced by any means, graphic, electronic, or mechanical, including photocopying, recording, taping or by any information storage retrieval system without the written permission of the publisher except in the case of brief quotations embodied in critical articles and reviews.

This is a work of fiction. All of the characters, names, incidents, organizations, and dialogue in this novel are either the products of the author's imagination or are used fictitiously.

iUniverse books may be ordered through booksellers or by contacting:

iUniverse
1663 Liberty Drive
Bloomington, IN 47403
www.iuniverse.com
1-800-Authors (1-800-288-4677)

Because of the dynamic nature of the Internet, any Web addresses or links contained in this book may have changed since publication and may no longer be valid. The views expressed in this work are solely those of the author and do not necessarily reflect the views of the publisher, and the publisher hereby disclaims any responsibility for them.

ISBN: 978-1-4401-3241-4 (pbk)
ISBN: 978-1-4401-3243-8 (cloth)
ISBN: 978-1-4401-3242-1 (ebk)

Printed in the United States of America

Library of Congress Control Number: 2009925104

iUniverse rev. date: 6/4/2009

For Georgia

BOOK ONE

*I will tell you of the promise,
of Isela, of the ghost-clay,
of the red furrowed land.
You will know my presence
as a pledge remade
at the crossroads of delivery,
when the flame of the Bearer
shall flicker and renew,
when the sown breath
harrows a flock to stir the wind.
Such is that day! When
from the earth shall rise
a fountain, a gift! Nonna,
I tell you that as my death,
so is my life,
so steps my footprint
trailing the blood
of the birth-promise.
For the saints and angels
will cry not louder
for a scattered clan
than we who keen for Saint Isela
when the Chooser comes.*

CHAPTER 1:
Omens

She should be tucked into goose down and woolen blankets, Georgia thought. She should be sleeping. Instead, she was staggering in the dark beneath an armload of fire logs. *Mater Dei,* the kitchen latch was difficult to get free in the dark. She pressed down on the handful of kindling she had tucked under her chin, trying to keep it from falling off the top of her load and spilling under her feet. The whole cold-slicked pile of it smelled like ice from the duck pond.

Why, she wondered, had no one thought to stock wood by the hearth to dry out for the morning? She had given the servants leave to go for the night, but she did not mean they could shirk their duties and leave yet another thing to worry her. What she really needed was a little rest. She laughed and almost dropped the load. Another lifetime, perhaps. The world was far too big and far too unhappy. For instance, here she was, as usual, struggling to complete yet another task in the dark.

At least she needn't worry about setting the logs down quietly, she thought as she staggered to the hearth and let the logs tumble to the floor. There were no servants asleep on the floor tonight. And though they forgot to stock for morning, it was right that she had sent them home. It had been three long days of mourning, prayer, and fasting for them as for everyone. They would return tomorrow refreshed.

Her load deposited, she stood and shook out the stiffness in her shoulders and back, flinging off bits of bark into the darkness. The ache of her shoulders was as always, but she could not remember when her knees were last so painful. Three days of kneeling on the cold stone floor of the church had done it, and the chill lingered.

Taking up the fire poker, she tossed her handful of kindling onto the ashes of the hearth, stirring them into the embers on one side so that they flared brightly. As the flame burst out she wondered, was a little light and warmth too much to ask? The earl had been another impediment, yet another to claim what was theirs. Was it wrong for her to be happy that the earl was dead? Was it wrong for her to hope that perhaps, with his final gift, that they were one step closer to the fulfillment of the promise?

She made the sign of the cross over her heart. Saint Isela had died so long ago. Too often when hope surged, things fell apart. And it was too much to think about tonight.

Right now, she needed relief from her aches, and for that she needed warmed beer and medicine. She took a jug and filled it, and then sprinkled in some of Sister Mendaline's sweet-black powder, stirring after. In addition to the ache of her knees, her courses had come early. This particular powder was the only thing that soothed the cramping. It would soothe her stomach and her back so she could sleep.

She poked the flaming pile of kindling again, breaking up the embers, before setting the jug into the center to warm. She sat gingerly back on the little hearth stool to wait, stretching out her legs. The toes of her leather shoes poked out under her heavy skirts and petticoats as she smoothed the black monks-cloth overskirt and the blue undergown beneath.

Sleep or no, there was something to be said for the solitude of this peaceful hour. All slept while she did not, perhaps. But the quiet was rest in its own way, for there was no one here to bother her with chores to be done and the demands of the day.

It was, praise Isela, wonderful. Perhaps it was even the perfect opportunity to risk hope. Even to gloat. The earl was dead! Everything was, finally, as it should be.

She sat back to allow the heat to work into her bones. She closed her eyes, but the room seemed colder than before. Georgia pulled her toes underneath her skirt for heat. It should be warming, yet the chill sprang up and with it the smell of ore. Georgia shivered as the fire flickered. The cold drained away her sense of peace. And then she heard a noise.

Something moved outside.

Georgia sat up. She'd left the door open! She jumped to close it, to close the cold outside and away. But first she checked the path. In the rough moonlight, she could see along between the buttery and the corner of the stable. Nothing stirred there. The only sounds were familiar ones—horses' hooves scraping through straw, the goatherd snoring, the echo of the Bilsdale River rolling through the hills.

She closed the door and scooted back toward the fire. She should try to warm herself. It was foolish to let the cold crawl along her neck and frighten her.

Yet the noise began again, lingering this time. There was a note of desolation in it, like wind in a graveyard, or as if long bones rubbed together. Georgia wished she had made an enormous fire now. Though perhaps darkness was useful in its way, like a blanket she could hide in. She kicked ashes over the burning kindling so that the flames retreated. The kitchen went dark.

She could hear it louder now. Whatever it was, it scratched along the outer wall. Would it come? It was before cockcrow, she thought, and the worst time to be about. Georgia took hold of the rendering spoon—the one Sister Thomasine used to terrorize the servants and sisters alike—and held it up. If this noise was only one of the servants drunk, then the spoon would serve well for a good trouncing. But if the noise was something else—she tightened her grip on the handle and crept toward the door. They had interred the earl today, she thought. Spirits were known to walk on the day a man was buried.

She waited, listening. From in the stable, the goatherd snorted but resumed snoring. Georgia pulled the door open to the moonlight, just a bit. There, emerging from the dark, was something naked and bone white. It stepped to the end of the path and stopped.

"*O Jesu!*" Georgia made a sign of warding, but it sprung. The door flung open, and she tumbled out, mashing into the corner of the outside wall, waving the spoon as if to fight.

The thing bashed into her, but fled. It tore along the path, barefoot, its arms notched red, its feet seeming not to touch the ground. Behind it trailed a flapping stream that looked like swaddling come undone. Or hanging flesh. Georgia stayed against the wall, holding the spoon over her head. She would let it run.

But it ran to the end of the path and turned toward the courtyard. It was heading for the dorter, the dormitory where all the sisters slept. The fires would be low. Georgia could not remember if she had locked the door to the dorter after midnight prayers—after Sister Mendaline had been called away to tend a birthing in the village. She grasped the copper key at her belt. Had she locked it?

Whatever this apparition was—demon, human, or ghost—it could not be allowed to come upon the sisters as they slept.

Georgia followed, running low, her skirts a jumble under her feet. There were simply too many of them—an over skirt, undergown, and numerous petticoats. She almost tripped where the vegetable garden intersected with the orchard and cemetery. She stopped there, in the dark, catching her breath in the damp early morning. When would the first cock crow and disperse the spirits?

At least from here she could see the dorter. It looked undisturbed; in fact, all seemed well again. The courtyard was absolutely still. From the cemetery ahead, she could smell the ripeness of the fruit, as apples and pears hung heavily and swept low over the graves.

In the daylight, the orchard was beautiful, the unordered shrines and monuments of stone many hundreds of years old. But in the darkness, the rot of overripe quinces caught her breath. Shadows seemed clustered under the trees, and the mist rising from the stones obscured the ground. Her knees resumed their aching. She should have heeded the ironmonger and built an iron gate around the graves to keep the spirits in. This one, certainly, had not stayed put.

But now, she did not know where it had gone. She would have to check the dorter. She would have to pass the cemetery to do it, but if all was well, she could run inside and lock the door behind her. If there was a ghost with a mind to wander this night, perhaps a ghost made restless by the earl's death or even the ghost of the earl himself—*Mater Dei*! Georgia made another sign of warding—if so, let God will it that it should leave them all in peace.

She trained her gaze forward. Whatever it was, she did not want to see it again. She shuddered remembering it had touched her. She would not have it touch her again.

She quickened her pace. The dorter was just ahead, a low stone building in the center of the priory. Its doors were closed. Had she locked it? She rummaged for the key in case she might have to unlock the door quickly to get inside. She passed the stones, the graves, the reeking fruit trees.

Something flew at her. A bone white figure raised itself as if from the dark behind a stone. Its skin hung off it in great shreds. It lunged, grasping Georgia by the wrist with a grip like iron needles.

Georgia screamed. The muscles in her cheeks spasmed, and her lungs collapsed as every ounce of breath was forced out.

The apparition wailed in return. It threw back its body as if to break its back and shrieked like a demon.

The shriek stilled her. It was a cry Georgia had heard before, and she stopped screaming. This demonic wail, loud and piercing as it was, was as familiar to her as all the other noises of the night. This was no ghost. This was Sister Agnes.

Sister Agnes the possessed, the seer, the anchorite who shrieked all the days and nights so that the sisters grew used to the noise and slept in spite of it. But tonight Sister Agnes was somehow out of her cell. And she would not let go her tormenting grip.

Sister Agnes lived in a small bricked cell, a tiny room, attached to the outer wall of the church. In living like this, she was like other anchorites who built small rooms for themselves adjoining churches in which they could seek isolation from the world. The life of an anchorite was severe. But Sister Agnes had chosen to make her life more severe still. For her cell was barely large enough to move or stand in. She had built it herself, cementing it brick by brick, until she had sealed herself into it. The only opening was a small window into the church itself through which she could chant the offices, be confessed, and take communion.

Yet tonight Agnes was outside. She was loose and almost naked. Her clothes hung around her like curled cloth or matted hair. Her skin was marked over with red lines and splotches. Her hands and feet looked blue from cold, as did her lips and the fissures under her eyes.

Georgia set the rendering spoon against a stone. It would be of no use against Agnes. She tried to dislodge her wrist from the anchorite's needle grip. It was a puzzle. Agnes never left her cell, never that Georgia had ever known.

Inside her cell there was some containment for her rages, and Georgia could soothe her if she took too wild a fit. But in the cemetery and in the dark, Agnes's frenzy seemed without boundary. She would not be still. She spat and shrieked, hopping on first one foot and then another, all the time pulling sharply on Georgia's wrist.

Georgia turned to scolding. "Sister Agnes, pray, still yourself!"

"I have been searching," Agnes held up a rectangle of bed linen, retted and mucked as if it had been dragged through the stable and the ponds. "Your bed was empty."

"You took my bedsheet?"

Agnes dug her bare heels into the earth, leaning backward between gravestones. She shook the sheet in a balled fist. "Woman's blood!"

"My courses, yes, yes," Georgia said. "It is not amiss."

"There is no child, no child!" Agnes wailed as if her heart would split. "And now too late! Too late!"

Agnes began a crazed trot through the cemetery. She did not release her grip. Georgia tumbled along, trying to think what to do. Perhaps Agnes was taken with fever. She needed blankets and a fire. She had left beer warming in the kitchen. Angelica steeped in beer might calm her, if she could get Agnes to drink it.

"Come, Agnes, to the kitchen where it is warm. Celebrate with me, for now the earl is dead, and the priory belongs to us alone."

"Too late, too late!"

Agnes stopped and threw down Georgia's wrist as if she were forever done with it. Georgia rubbed her wrist, oily now and cold to the touch, as Agnes began to writhe. Agnes stamped her feet on the earth and shook her shoulders, her head falling side to side. "The maw! The maw! It opens its jaw!"

"Hush, Agnes. Hush. I'll fetch a blanket."

"I must know the answer."

"Come into the kitchen," Georgia said. "I will tell you everything."

"No!" Agnes backed further into the cemetery, the smell of rot deepening as a quince burst open under her toes. The shadows of the gravestones seemed to close around her.

This would not do. Georgia tried a stern tone. "If you will not come, I will fetch Sister Thomasine. You know how cross she gets with your howling."

Agnes flinched but did not retreat. "I needed holy water for the charm," she said. She stamped her foot, splattering liquid quince. "And a cross. And a cross. The signs must be known. Do you feel nothing?"

Georgia rubbed her wrist. Nothing besides a broken wrist and her stomach cramping. And cold. The night looked like it might collapse under shadows. It would seem a lot less frightening if she were in the kitchen. She would throw some good dry logs on the fire at once to make it flare large and bright.

Georgia tried wheedling. "There's bread in the kitchen, Agnes. And if you come, I will make you a sop with honey and grains of paradise."

Agnes backed away. "But I cannot wield it!" She spun and resumed wailing, throwing herself first onto one stone and then another. She flung her arms wide and released from her hand an orb of red-gold glass, a jewel, a fist-sized beauty encased in a fiery bronze halo. It swung on a silver chain.

The relic! It was the relic of Saint Isela! The relic that Georgia alone could touch. Agnes must have stolen it from the west altar.

"Agnes! What have you done in your madness? Dare you touch that? Dare you anger the saint? Give the relic to me."

Agnes held it away. "You must come."

"I mean it, Agnes, now. This is no small matter. Madness cannot excuse it."

"You must come."

Agnes turned and ran. Georgia flinched as the relic swung wide over a gravestone. She grabbed her skirts up to pursue. If Agnes took the relic back into her cell, Georgia would have to tear the mortar down to get it back.

☙

But Agnes did not go to her cell. She pitched from stone to stone until she reached the sepulchre in the center of the orchard. In it were the bones of the Holy Martyr Gotesind, the founder of the priory. Agnes flung herself at the large square tomb, leaping at the last so that she sprang to the top and crouched there, like a maddened death crow glowing white.

Georgia lunged but grabbed only a few shreds of cloth as Agnes leapt away.

Agnes waved the relic at her and shrieked, "What do you see?" She kicked a bowl of water at her feet. It clattered against the stone top of the sepulchre.

"Agnes!" Georgia stepped back. "Is that the altar basin? The holy water? *Ave Maria*! What else have you stolen this night?"

Agnes splashed the relic into the bowl of water. Then, gripping the bowl along the widened lip, she took careful aim and threw the water into Georgia's face. Frozen cold soaked Georgia's headdress and partlet, the wool sucking in every drop and spreading ice across her skin.

Agnes shrieked again. "What do you see?"

The ground seemed to open under Georgia's feet. A wash of warmth spilled up, the warmth of the relic so close to her, calling to her, a river of prayer. The dark water brightened, and light swept in. A woman appeared, a woman in a green dress. It was Isela, her hair undone and shimmering. She turned and whispered, *Safeguard the child*. And she was gone.

The vision faded.

Agnes jumped up and down on the tomb. The bowl clattered, and she threw the bowl aside. Georgia dived to catch it before it smashed on the stones.

"What did you, what did you see—see—see?" Agnes screamed as if her bony chest would split along the seams where her ribs lined side by side. "Tell me what you know!"

"Give me the relic and I will say." Georgia made her voice even and cool. For all Agnes's fits, she was not violent. She was a seer. And this vision spoke of the promise. Georgia held out her hand. "Agnes. I am the Bearer. Isela's relic belongs to me. I won't say what I have seen unless you give it back to me. *Now*."

Agnes swallowed hard in her chest. She hunched down over the tomb, drawing up her knees like a gargoyle readying to spring. But she stayed put, rocking a little just on the edge. Then she held out the relic, and Georgia took it.

"Tell me," Agnes said, her voice quiet, rasping.

Georgia couldn't help smiling. At the touch of the relic, she felt the surety of the saint and the vision. "Victory." Georgia tucked the relic under her skirt. "I have seen victory, Agnes. Praise Isela! We have waited—I have waited—so very long."

Agnes stilled her rocking. "You gloat over much."

"I am happy, Agnes. It is done!" And then, there it was—the first cock's crow of morning. Loud and triumphant, the sound echoed across the priory and bounced back and forth between the stones. The worst of the night was over.

"Agnes," Georgia felt like shouting. "A new day!"

Agnes stood up. She towered at that height, the shreds of her gown blown wide. She began to spin, and the world seemed dark again. "We have sought our time. Yes." Agnes said, "But in the crux, they will seek their time, too."

"Agnes!"

"It comes." Agnes shrieked and jumped and ran to the church, rounding the building to where her cell bulged out from the church wall. "It comes. It comes. It comes!"

A band of gray pressed in from behind the wooded outline of the hills. Soon the bell would ring for prime, for the first prayer service of the morning.

And Agnes was loose again.

Georgia ran after her. "Agnes! It is not too late for you to come with me into the kitchen. I have yet time to make a sop for you before prayers."

Agnes ran to her cell, then fell to her knees, and scrabbled at the ground. The cell seemed pronounced in the first filters of dawn light, a rounded blister of home-baked bricks and straw mortar. Crude, but thick and strong. At the bottom of the outer wall, a foundation stone had been pulled out. Agnes scrabbled at it and then wriggled through the tiny hole to get back inside.

"Wait!" Georgia grabbed Agnes's foot. Agnes kicked her and disappeared. Georgia crouched to peer into the cell. Inside was wholly dark, but she could hear Agnes as she threw herself against the wall, slapping the sides of the cell, and all the while shrieking.

"Agnes! Come out again if you like. I'll make you a lovely sop. Or I could bring one if you wish. With honey. You like honey."

Agnes shot her bloodied hand out of the cell, and Georgia jumped back. She grabbed at a cluster of weeds, a late jump-up and a dandelion, pulling them inside. She then pushed the stone back into the opening, sealing it completely.

"Wait!" Georgia pushed against it, but the stone laid in and would not budge. "At least let me tend you. Your hands bleed. Or let me fetch a blanket."

"Mercy! Mercy!" Agnes screamed. "I have seen it!"

"All things are well, Sister. Please, heed me."

"No—no—no!" Agnes resumed spinning in the cell, slapping the stones in rhythm to her chanting. "Death. It will come today!"

Georgia sat back on her heels. At least if Agnes were back in her cell, she could not harm herself further. Or anyone else. And the day was lightening. It would be no worse, then, than any other day. Georgia stood, smoothing her veil back down over her sodden overdress, which hung with wet. She would need a change of clothes.

She thought to head back to the dorter but stopped. There was a smell on the wind. Was it smoke?

Georgia walked along the outer wall of the church toward the main path. As Agnes's cries receded, Georgia tried to place the unusual smell. It was smoke, yes. But not a smell like the fire of the cotter's hearth or the blacksmith or the tanner. This was the smell of a burning roof, of thatch.

The rising hue and cry that rose up from below confirmed it. There was fire in the village.

CHAPTER 2:
Outlaws

A FIRE BEGUN AT NIGHT WAS DEADLY, for the sleepers may be overcome before they can escape. Or fire can spread quickly, moving from roof to roof before any cry of warning can be made.

Georgia hurried around the church and to the top of the main path. From there, with the doors of the church behind her, the Yorkshire landscape of the lower dales opened to a wide view. Immediately below, the croft village of Attewater looked restless but sound. But beyond, across the Bilsdale River, there the fire burned. Next to the little town of Bilsdale, a field was alight, and the house next to it as well. The fire spread even as she watched. Another house flared up, and then a third caught flame.

Someone must raise the alarm! The villagers would need help to fight the fire. The folk of Bilsdale would need buckets, as many as could be carried, and wet sacking to beat the flames. Saint Anthony, let no one perish! May all below live to be a hundred.

Georgia turned and hurried back to the priory, taking the entry path in through the main gate. The church was across from the dorter, and she rushed in through the sacristy door and into the central nave. The bells must ring a warning. And the church, too, must be put right. Prayers must be said. Blessings must be made. The altar basin must be fetched, and the relic restored to its rightful place. Fortune must be preserved. Above all, Georgia crossed herself, the omens must stay favorable.

The priory bells rang: the morning call to prayer. Yes, prayers must be said. The able must fight the fire, and the infirm must stay and chant the office. They must make a plea to Saint Ursula, whose day it was, and to the eleven thousand virgins—a plea for mercy.

The relic bumped against her, still suspended underneath her skirts. As the Bearer, she could carry it if she wished. It was better, though, to keep the relic at the altar where others could come to see it, to pray, to plead, or to be healed. She unhooked the chain and grasped the round glass orb. It felt warm, soothing even, a contrast to the silver chain that slid cool across her fingers. She drew the relic out from her skirts to kiss it. But as the orb emerged it shone out, an orange-red glow that seemed to ignite the darkness of the church.

"*Mater Dei*!" Georgia stopped short and almost collided with the stone corner of the altar table. She grasped the corner stone, fumbling for a handhold, sending the embroidered linen frontlet sliding to the floor. She began a prayer, "*Queen of Heaven—Mistress of the Angels—Light of the Earth—Lady most comely—*" The orb neither flickered nor deepened. Its glow was silken, an ember red, muted as if smoldering. For all the years that had passed, for all the toil, Georgia could not remember that the relic ever glowed. Agnes! She thought, what have you done?

The door to the sacristy banged open. Sister Elizabeth sped into the church, her yellow veil hastily drawn over her blue cap with the linen wrinkled and crooked over her brow. More wrongness, Georgia thought.

Elizabeth almost slipped on the fallen frontlet, but caught herself, flipping her body in a sharp twist such as only the young could do. She didn't even lose her breath. "Domina, we will all be killed! Sister Thomasine has said it!"

Georgia shoved the relic back under her skirt to hide it. There was no need to cause further alarm. "The fire is a mile west. Sister Thomasine will know what to do. Go, fetch the altar basin. It was moved in the night. It is now near Gotesind's tomb. Bring it quickly." A blessing, perhaps, would cool the orb. She would need holy water.

Elizabeth curtseyed, but stayed where she was. "Y-yes—but, Domina, there are men below. Marauders."

The bells in the village began to ring. Georgia held up a hand for quiet and listened. Though distant, the bells of Saint Mark's in the village rang discordant and strong. Their notes pealed unmistakable. Though it was prime, Saint Mark's did not ring a call to prayer; it rang a call to arms. Elizabeth spoke the truth.

Georgia strode down the center of the church and forced open the heavy oak doors. She walked out again to the top of the path. The oncoming sun threw a dewy prism of slanted light across the dale, gold and green and blue. The morning promised to be beautiful. Why this on such a day?

Sister Elizabeth let out a cry, "There, Domina, look!"

Men, perhaps fifteen of them, some carrying torches, streamed across the river and into Bilsdale. One of them ignited the roof of a house as he passed by.

"*O Jesu!*" Georgia crossed herself.

Behind her, the main priory gate burst open, and Sister Thomasine strode out, puffing loudly. "There you are! By Saint Agricola, Sister! Do you not see the—"

Georgia turned and stared at her levelly. "Do I see what, Sister? Storks?" The last thing she needed was for Sister Thomasine to drive everyone to panic. They needed action, thought, care, but not panic. "Yes, I see them, Sister. The earl died without an heir. No doubt these few think this part of Yorkshire is now lawless. They are mistaken."

Yet Georgia shivered, cold cramped into her belly, and her feet were sticky in her shoes. Her headdress and partlet were still wet from when Sister Agnes had soaked her. She rested her hand over her chest to warm the cloth. Wool grew warmer when wet, but not when the wind blew.

Sister Thomasine stood squarely, her feet wide to balance her large form. "Do not stand there like one of the Four Innocents! The store rooms are filled with barley and flax. The meat from the salting is sitting out across the racks, in plain sight for any thief! And I found *this*—" She shook the rendering spoon accusingly, the one Georgia had left near the cemetery. "—in the orchard covered in apple skins!"

Georgia thought again of the glow of the relic. "Something has happened."

Elizabeth's breath left her all at once, and her cheeks purpled. "I will fight."

"So will I." Georgia turned to look at the priory church behind her, at its mossy, lumpy stone walls and heavy thatch roof. It could be defended from anything but fire. Would they have to defend it? She took Elizabeth's elbow and steered her quickly back through the priory gate and into the courtyard.

"Sister Elizabeth, fetch Sister Catherine—"

"Oh! Domina," Elizabeth blushed. "Sister Catherine is—is—"

"Hold!" Georgia shook her head. "Spare the telling of it. Fetch Sister Joan instead. Have her bring the bows up from the cellar, all that are stocked there. We must be ready."

Elizabeth nodded.

"All who seek it must have sanctuary. And, Sister, the herdsmen must drive the remaining stock into the high pasture—sheep, goats, geese, and pigs, all. Do not leave an ox in the stables. Mind, do not waver from what I have said. Go. Go!"

Elizabeth ran, then, remembering to curtsey, turned and tripped over her skirts before getting up again and disappearing through the orchard.

It was maddening. Their troubles should be over. The earl had died without an heir. His widow now lived at the priory, and she was a great lady, a countess! The rank entitled her to be their prioress. There were no other claimants to the earl's property. Except one perhaps—but no, Georgia shook her head. It was not possible. The priory now belonged to them.

"Sister Thomasine, I pray you. If we lose the salted meat, it will be a small thing in comparison to what else might be lost this day. Hide the stores and prepare our defense. I must look to the prioress, Dame Marjorie."

A little of Sister Thomasine's bluster left her. Real fear crept into her eyes. "They will come for her, then?"

"I fear so, yes."

"And what of us?"

"It will pass. It must," Georgia said. "Today, we will seek sanctuary in the church." She ran her fingers along her prayer beads, *Saint Bertilla pray for us, Saint Cecilia pray for us, Saint Margaret, and Saint Ursula pray for us.*

The bells of the priory church rang loud, echoing the call of the Bilsdale church below. To arms! To arms! A resounding ring.

With one last look down the hill at the swirling smoke, Georgia turned away and headed back through the gate.

Sister Thomasine was already headed to the kitchen, bellowing. A pair of waiting servants scattered in opposite directions.

"Sister," Georgia hurried to catch up. Panic was an enemy. "Sister, you must calm yourself!"

Thomasine turned. "Saint Jude! Even now the rogues clamber up our very hills. We will all be slaughtered on our feet!"

"They will find me harder to kill than most, Sister. Mark me, this is *not* Saint Jude's fight, for the hopeless, but Saint Sebastian's, with his bow."

"Saint Sebastian died of a great clubbing! And we, a pack of women."

"Peace! If we do not get the cellar bolted, we will lose our food stores until Lent. You must spread earth over the cellar doors to hide them. You are kitchener. You are hearty, Sister, and hale! *Mater Dei*, you must see to this." Sister Thomasine pushed her sleeves up over thick elbows as Georgia continued, "I will see to the prioress and Sister Mendaline. For she must gather medicines for the sick—"

Sister Thomasine puffed out her cheeks. She pointed her spoon down the hill toward the fire and the smoke. "Sister Mendaline is in Attewater at a birthing."

Georgia felt pulled bodily from one direction to another. Of course, how had she forgotten? "She was called in the night."

"Saint Fool, that is what I said!" Sister Thomasine smacked the spoon against her skirts. "You bade her Godspeed yourself."

The dizziness subsided, but the center of her gut ached. Everything moved too quickly. Too many things at once. What was it Agnes had said? *Death*. Yet the time was ripe, overripe! And now the orb glowed. And her vision at Gotesind's tomb, what was said?

Safeguard the child.

For the space of an *Ave Maria*, Georgia thought she might be sick. She placed her hand over the orb under her skirts, and its warmth pushed back at her through the woolen monks cloth.

Sister Thomasine pointed the spoon like a practiced scold. "I'll know your mind. You have that look about you."

"Sister, pray you, *you* must see Dame Marjorie to sanctuary, for I cannot. I must go to Attewater."

"You jest."

"The child, this child, it must be brought to sanctuary, and Johanna too. *O clement, O pious, O sweet Virgin Mary.*"

"You cannot go down into Attewater!"

Georgia stamped her foot onto the courtyard brick. She wanted to run; her legs tensed and cramped. "I beg you, Sister, abide me."

"Go then. Leave with it all on my hands. If I am alive at your return, and am not burnt to death, I will say a thousand paternosters at vespers." Sister Thomasine crossed herself, turned squarely on her heel, and headed to the kitchen.

Georgia ran back through the gates and to the top of the path. The first folk from Attewater crested the hill. They clutched sacks, dragged goats, and hefted pots over their shoulders.

Georgia looked out over Yorkshire as before, but now Bilsdale was lost in smoke. She could no longer see how many men crossed into the village with ill intent, but no marauders had yet begun the climb over the dale to the upper village of Attewater. And John and Johanna's croft was on the priory side of Attewater. She could make it.

She took up handfuls of her skirt and underskirts, her legs and shift slick with the blood from her courses. Yet modesty was nothing. She would need her full stride to gain the village and bring Sister Mendaline and the mother and child back to the priory.

She sucked in a breath and ran headlong down the hill.

CHAPTER 3:
Leeches

As she ran, she focused on each step, recalling the curves of the road and where a runner could cut over the way weeds. She passed the lye pits and retting ponds newly stocked with flax. Often the ponds stank of rot, but today the world smelled only of smoke. By the time she came upon the low stone wall that marked the edge of Attewater, all of the lower village of Bilsdale seemed to blaze.

A low wall stretched along the path, which meandered its way through the center of the village. Once near John and Johanna's house, Georgia jumped over the stones and into the tiny poultry yard without waiting to gain the gate. The house was small and tidy, with a stripe of new thatch showing tawny yellow along the roof. John stood guard at the door, his eyes ringed with tiredness. He clasped an iron-tipped shovel with both hands. A curved knife hung from his belt.

He startled as Georgia jumped the wall. Then he nodded. "My wife is—" He broke off. A knot appeared along his jaw.

She wanted to reassure him that all would be well, but her throat was raw and she was out of breath. Instead she only returned his nod. As he stepped away from the door, she opened it and hurried through.

The open door brought in the morning sunlight, bright enough to extinguish the fire glow inside. More smoke, as thick as any, filled the small croft house. It spewed from overstoked coals in the fat brick hearth.

Mendaline's prized bronze pot steamed by the fire with the smell of barley and retting wafting out from it.

There was no time for greetings. "Sister Mendaline, the baby! Where is it?"

In the streaming light, Sister Mendaline looked up, squinting. Her look was hard; the deep furrows that usually stood out softly from her forehead and along her nose were now ridged with shadows. Even as the door slowly closed and the sun-edged shadows faded, the hardness stayed on her, lancing across her face and over the folds of her kyrtle, which was bunched and tied firmly under a spattered apron.

She looked away. "The babe is not delivered yet."

"Not yet?" The door closed, and the last of the sunlight went out.

Mendaline stayed at her work, her sleeves unbuttoned and set aside, the embroidered Spanish work on her cuffs darkened with whirls of fresh blood. "If you have a mind to do something, cinch the pouches." Mendaline nudged the well-worn satchel next to her with her foot. The stoppered bottles of herbs and oils and salts jumbled together. It looked like someone had rummaged through the satchel in a hurry.

As her eyes adjusted, Georgia could see that the laboring mother, Johanna, was on the other side of the fire, a squarish lump under a dirty blanket. Johanna sighed, a long, low moan, followed with a grunt, and a fit of coughing.

No baby yet! Georgia thought. She stooped to cinch oily pouches. Her fingers were clumsy, the ties stiff. How much longer? "We must go, Sister. Now."

"Be still!" Mendaline swung around, shaking the wrung cloth with vigor, so that the last drops sprinkled across her cheek. "If her husband can bide, by Saint Catherine so can you."

Georgia grabbed a blanket from where it warmed by the fire. Baby or no baby, they had to take Johanna and go. They would have to carry her, though she looked pitiful. Georgia placed her hand over the relic under her gown. How warm it felt. She crossed herself. *Isela have mercy on us.*

Johanna knelt on all fours over crushed straw, her kyrtle up over her belly, which was distended and lined from where she had been lying on the hay. Streaks of red coated her thighs. Her eyes were shut tight and her lips cracked.

Georgia placed her hand across Johanna's forehead. She was even warmer than the relic. "Sister, please. Perhaps you don't understand how desperate this is. The outlaws will not stop in Bilsdale. Even now they will be moving up to this village."

"Stand by then, and be ready. But hear me. If Johanna dies on the path, it will not be better."

Mendaline knelt, and wiped Johanna's face. She made the sign of the cross over Johanna's belly, punctuating each touch with a pleading prayer. "*Infinite Father, Uncreated Father, Eternal Father—little innocent, come out.*"

The door burst open, and Georgia fell back against the beam. She expected John with an alarm, or worse, men armed with torches. Her fall shook spiders' eggs and dust from the thatch roof. But it was Alice, not John, who burst in, stout and steadfast Alice, who attended all the births and passings in Attewater. She made a quick curtsey, and her girdle jangled with knives, a wooden cup, and prayer beads.

"I have a handcart," she said.

Mendaline frowned. "In the time you have spent, you could have reared a mule to cart it."

Alice waved a misshapen bunch of sticks and kissed it. "I fetched my cross. I carved it during mass on the feast of Corpus Christi," she said. "Nothing can harm us now."

Georgia rubbed her neck; she had no doubt earned a bruise when she fell. "What of the raiders, Alice? Is there fire yet in Attewater?"

"Enough!" Mendaline snatched the steaming cloth from the pot. "Sister Georgia, speak the birth charm."

Georgia pulled the relic out from under her skirts. If anything it glowed brighter. She crossed herself and hid it back away. If Mendaline saw it, she would know it was amiss. And there was no time for that discussion now. She began the prayer. "*Anna bore Samuel, Elizabeth bore John, Anne bore Mary, Mary bore—*"

Steam from the pot filled the house with the weedy smell of simmering beer, decomposing herbs, and an oily meat. Mendaline dipped her cloth into the center of it. "Hold her steady."

Alice put a sturdy arm around Johanna, turning her onto her side easily as Mendaline daubed a bluish oil onto the now saturated cloth, then smeared Johanna's legs and underbelly. When she was done, she tied the corners over Johanna's thigh to hold the cloth secure.

There were shouts outside. Georgia stopped chanting. "Mendaline! This is madness! We must get to the church!"

"Yes. Now we go. Robe—"

Georgia snatched a coarse wool robe, heavily patched, from a peg near the door. She helped Alice to lift and wrap Johanna, who was exhausted and of little help. Still, her eyes were watchful. Georgia felt better to see it. Perhaps this would be no worse than any other difficult first birthing.

"Let us go!"

"Wait." Mendaline scooped Alice's wooden cup into the pot.

Georgia strained, listening for more shouts, for more commotion outside.

How could she safeguard anyone or anything? "Sister, please! There is not time—"

Mendaline glared. "I'll dare you to mention that again." She handed the cup to Johanna. "Drink."

"It's Saint Ulric's cup," Alice said, her voice certain. "It will ease the pains—you can be sure of it."

Johanna bent her head obediently, but the beer was hot.

Mendaline was merciless. "Be quick."

Johanna gulped miserably and burped after.

Satisfied, Mendaline stuck a leaf in Johanna's mouth. "Chew this, go on."

As Johanna bit down, her expression changed. She gagged, and her eyes watered.

Mendaline nodded to Georgia. "That leaf tastes of pig's dung. But now something other than pain will occupy her mind." She stood back and raised her arms. "And it will wake her. Heave! Let us be off."

Georgia shoved her shoulder under Johanna's armpit as did Alice on the other side. Mendaline circled to push Johanna from behind. Johanna, chewing, mouth open and wild-eyed, managed to walk.

Georgia kicked open the door, and John jumped back. The relief on his face to see his wife walking touched Georgia's heart. She sent a look sidewise at Mendaline. What had the leaf been for, she wondered, to give Johanna vigor or to give John hope?

There were more shouts. By the sound of it, the raiders had gained the lower village. John would need hope, then, for he would need the strength to fight.

At least John would not have to fight alone. As he stepped away to let them pass, Georgia saw that Robert was with him. The men were oath-sworn brothers, pledged to aid in each other's care and defense. Robert had a reputation as a good fighter. He looked away as the women struggled out, directing his gaze back along the village lane.

Alice shoved as they hurried Johanna through the poultry yard, pulling her over the low stone wall and placing her into the cart. Each step felt agonizingly slow. They had been in Attewater too long. A prickling foreboding crawled over Georgia's skin as new smoke rose into the morning. The outlying homes leading up to the village were now burning.

"Go! Go!" Alice took the handcart, but Georgia pushed in so they could each take a handle and so go faster. They broke into a run.

Johanna mewed fitfully, her mouth still open and her eyes wide. Ahead, the hill that on every other day seemed to be an easy slope now loomed like the mountains to Jerusalem.

Johanna screamed and rolled sideways in the cart, which almost upended as Alice struggled to right it.

"Hold!" Mendaline said. "If she thrashes, it will be worse."

Georgia pushed with all she had, her feet slipping inside the leather of her shoes. "We must not hold! There will be no end to our loss if we delay." A cramp cinched under Georgia's belly and down her thigh like knotted strings tightening. They were too exposed. There was nothing but tall weeds on either side to block them.

"Ave Maria, gratia plena ..." she pleaded for pity and protection. John and Robert were just behind, but they could not mount a stand here, in the middle of the path, with a laboring woman at their feet.

She called to Isela. She could feel the relic now even through her layers of petticoats. The warmth intruded—a reminder, perhaps, that she must stay focused on her task. That this child—

Johanna gave another cry, and a little black fluid flowed from her, smearing the side of the cart and dripping down her leg into the dirt. As Mendaline noted it, her jaw locked tight.

Safeguard the child. Safeguard the child. Georgia put her head down and pushed all the harder, so that now, even Alice made a gasp to keep up. *Sweet Isela*! Georgia pleaded. If you would have me do this, then give me what I need to complete the task.

Alice was now wheezing and snorting. Johanna fought again to curl herself forward. Georgia had to twist backward to keep from spilling her out.

As she twisted, Robert called out a warning. The outlaws were now on the path. Mendaline muttered a hasty prayer between her teeth, and Georgia joined it. John would lay down his life for his wife and child—Georgia knew it of him—but she prayed to God to spare him that sacrifice today.

The clash of metal on splintering wood sounded behind them.

Georgia glanced back. John and Robert had turned to fight. Though they were farmers, they stood their ground, as practiced with hand-to-hand combat as any soldier, for the king insisted every man in England learn to fight.

The priory was just ahead. The shouts behind them grew louder. How many men were fighting now, Georgia couldn't tell. She didn't dare look back again.

There was a cry of pain behind, followed by a second, and then hoots of triumph. Robert or John had gone down in the fighting. *Lord, have mercy on us.*

As they crested the hill, the outlaws were in pursuit.

Mendaline gripped the side of the handcart and headed straight for the church. Alice pulled the cart toward the gates, toward the infirmary, and Georgia was pulled both ways at once.

It would be an abomination to take Johanna into the church. A laboring woman existed in a world outside life and death. While in the throes of childbirth, it was not known if she would be delivered or she would die. Her baby also neither lived nor didn't live, but was instead on the verge of life. In this state of babies not yet born and of mothers in both life and death at once, the priests had looked away from the miraculous and instead called the women unclean. By the law, Joanna was banned from entering the church.

If Johanna lived, it would be forty days before she could go inside. Even then a priest must perform the churching at the church door. Only after the ritual could she enter. The church fathers had even declared Mary unclean. Her churching, forty days after Christ's birth, was celebrated each year as the holiday Candlemas.

Mendaline, however, held steadfast toward the doors of the church. Alice quickly righted and returned to speed, Georgia with her. The church was the closest, safest place to go. And this was Saint Isela's church. Her church. Any other action was monstrous.

They cleared the threshold, and all within seemed ready. Georgia released the cart and yelled to the archers at the windows. "Bar the doors! Bar the doors!"

Mendaline yelled orders as she forced her way through the nave, now crowded with villagers, chickens, goats. "I need clean straw, water, ale, and blankets!" She clapped her hands at two boys who squatted near a writhing sack of rabbits. "Go on! Don't wait 'til lambing!" The boys jumped up. "And that screen too. Move that, here, now!"

The archers pushed the heavy doors to close them, barking at the crowding children to clear the way.

Sister Thomasine's voice rose over the creak of hinges and the scraping of the doors against the paving stones. "Sister Georgia!" Sister Thomasine's face was red now from yelling and pushing through the throng. Several children scrambled to move away. "Sister, I tried! By Saint Ursula I did. But Dame Marjorie will not come. *Sweet Mary in heaven.* You'd think she was the only widow in Yorkshire!"

The archers gained momentum, and the doors began to close. Sister Thomasine shoved a sack out of her way and dodged a retreating child. "Did you hear me, Sister? Dame Marjorie declares she'll stay right where she is and burn if she likes."

Georgia stopped; her heart still pounded from the trip up the hill. She could feel slime on her hands. "Dame Marjorie is where?"

"In her chambers. Praying, just as you please."

Georgia wished to pitch her head back and scream as Agnes had done in the night. She had dragged a laboring woman from fire and men bent on mayhem. Could she not return to sanctuary herself and see some kind of safety? How could she defend the church and priory both? The church doors would be enough, for even a madman would think twice before burning a church and people in it. But Dame Marjorie was not within them. The dorter and kitchens, the prioress's chamber—all of it was easily accessed by anyone who skirted the gates.

The sunlight slivered as the doors narrowed to close. One thing was certain now; the raiders must not skirt the gates. Somehow, she must turn them back. Georgia grabbed an arrow from the nearest archer. "Bar the door," she said, "and *saints preserve us*." She charged through the doors as they swung closed behind her. The bolts slid down, and the doors locked. With a resounding snap, she was locked out.

A triumphant, goading shout came from the raiders just behind her. Clutching the arrow, she turned to face them.

CHAPTER 4:
Curses

THERE WERE FIVE OF THEM, OUTLAWS, BORDER men perhaps. One, barefoot, looked to be Burgundian, in torn hose and a dirty jerkin. The looks on their gaunt faces mixed the glint of sudden greed with long-term deprivation.

That they were all strangers did not surprise her. No ruffian living near the priory would dare incite violence. The sisters were too well thought of, too vital to the village. These men had been condemned, likely, all of them, to hang. They had somehow escaped that fate and now wandered the countryside, masterless, with a low price for their allegiance. A little loot, perhaps, was all they wanted, and a chance to avenge their misfortunes.

Behind her, within the church and behind the gate, she could hear the villagers ready the priory defense. One of them, an archer, launched a bodkin from the church. The Burgundian dodged, shielding himself with a sack of loot. The arrow glanced off something in the sack, tore a great hole, and sunk deep into the leg of the man behind. That man cried in pain and rage.

"Hold!" Georgia tightened her grip around her arrow and held it up. If pressed, the raiders would certainly charge. No. They must be held here, and turned back here. She wanted no bloodshed and no killing. The priory was sacred ground.

"Archers, hold!" She cried out again and held the arrow high. Then, grasping it with two hands, she brought it down fast and broke it over her knee. She flung the pieces toward the men. The shaft landed close, while the bodkin blade fell just short of the nearest man.

She smoothed her kyrtle; she was splattered with mud and filth. The side rolls of her hair spilled out from under her cap and headdress. She likely looked anything but dignified, and certainly devoid of any ecclesiastic authority. But perhaps she could use that to her advantage.

Georgia held her head high and walked a few paces out along the path. She chose a place and planted her feet and stood immobile. As a rock. Or a wraith. The coarse fabric of her skirts caught the wind and napped, bristling. Her black veil, half undone, flapped against the blue cap underneath. Yet she ignored it, and lifting her arms became as a pillar, or as a forfending witch, and forbade them to pass.

"Before you is the Sacred Priory of Saint Isela." She circled her arms and then bent to scoop a handful of soil. Clenching the dirt, she waved her fist at the men, glaring at each one in turn. "You may not pass!" She let the words hang in the smoky air. "You may not trespass here. The Holy Martyr Gotesind protects this ground. She will blind all trespassers! You will writhe as snakes in the fire, as helpless as newborns on the very coals of hell."

Georgia paused. The men did not flee, but neither did they goad or jest.

Shaking both fists now, she stretched her arms over her head and recited Latin, the language of the Psalter and of curses. She knew the words of the Psalms by heart, though she did not know the meaning. Still, the sounds of the words themselves drew power.

"*Et iter impiorum peribit,*" she said, the words gurgling from deep in her throat. "*Flumina praeparavit eum.*"

The men exchanged glances. The Burgundian jeered.

She focused her strength. Stepping rapidly forward, she made herself as large and menacing as she could. Let them think she would run them all into the ground!

"*Flumina eum*—be gone! You will be struck down! Your eyes will foam and your beards will rot. The very reeds of Moses will rise up from the ground to whip you."

She ended this declaration with a high, keening wail. It was not enough.

One of the group mocked her. "Ad diddum diddum dee," he said, and he gyrated his hips in a show of bravado.

Still, he did not move forward.

Georgia tightened her gut hard across her belly and used the tension to anchor her. If she failed, they would lose the stores and the tithe barns, and all that would see the whole village through winter.

She raised her voice. "Leave God's house or I will curse you—now." She flung her handfuls of dirt toward them and up into the air. "*In loco sancto! In loco sancto! In loco sancto!*" Three times she spun, and then she fell forward and bit the dirt—a behavior expected for curses. They would not mistake the action.

Two of the raiders broke and ran. Their leader fidgeted but did not break, and Georgia saw in the yellowed shadow of his cheeks that he starved. A curse was no match for a crawling stomach. Perhaps her tact had been the wrong one. Perhaps she should instead have fed them, brought them bread and meat. No, she shook her head. These men knew only violence.

She raised her hands, preparing another curse. She opened her mouth to scream—and then there came a noise as if purgatory had split wide open. From her cell in the church, Agnes had unleashed a demonic wail that surprised even Georgia, so that she froze with her mouth gaping. The sound burst over the priory like dwarf echo, like rabbits skinned and roasted alive.

The men called to Saint Machudd and threw their hands over their faces in warding. When the sound came again, they fled. Georgia jumped after them. She wanted to grab Agnes by her bony shoulders and kiss her filthy cheek.

"Already the madness takes you!" she yelled after the men as they fled. "Already you feel the wrath of the holy martyr!"

God bless Agnes and her madness and her shrieking! Georgia thought. She watched them run, and her whole body twitched with the fight she had not had to give them. It had almost been too easy! Isela bless this day. And bless Johanna. *Sweet Anne, bless Johanna.* Georgia crossed herself. May Johanna be safely delivered.

The sound of a sharp clang echoed behind her. It would be the archers, she thought, unlatching the church doors. Georgia turned back toward the doors of the church. She could take her place at Johanna's side. If this child was the one, she would be needed.

But as she turned, the sound shifted. Another clang resounded, but it only bounced from the great doors of the church, it did not come from them. More clanging rang out, and bells, and the clop-clop of horses. The sound was of riders on the path, of yeomen and knights, with their horses decked with clackers and bells, the favorite noisemakers of men-at-arms. She turned back to face them. Yes, it had been too easy.

Three horsed men crested the path. Two of these were trained fighting men who wore mail shirts with liveried hose and tunics. They were helmeted and carried spiked bills. Following were more raiders, ten perhaps, on foot. But leading the party, front and center, rode the man Georgia had hoped not to see. Like a peacock on a perch, he clung to the saddle bar, bobbing like the failed knight he was. By blood he was the earl's son. Yet Horley Romsfeld was a bastard.

Georgia backed slowly toward the church. So then, she thought, worse had come to be.

But she could not back far enough, for Romsfeld had crested the hill and brought his mount to within a foot of where she stood. The palfrey's breath was hot on her face and wet with droplets of foam.

She stood without flinching; she must show strength.

Romsfeld swiveled in the saddle and spoke to the men behind him. "Well, what is it, knaves? A witch perhaps?" He unsheathed his sword as he turned back to face her. He raised the weapon and made a motion to slash her across her gut from her armpit down into her hip.

"I have granted the men the right of firebote," he smiled nastily. "They needed a little firewood. Don't send them away before the burning."

Georgia remained silent. He would enjoy burning her as a witch, and covered as she was in dirt with her clothes askew, she looked the part too well.

Romsfeld spoke louder, leaning forward in the saddle and shouting. "Can she hear me, or has the dirt in her mouth clogged her ears? Tell me, witch, are you deaf with frenzy?"

Georgia held her tongue and struggled to put the pieces together. The earl was dead. Romsfeld was a bastard; he could not inherit the earl's title or his lands. While it was true the earl had shown him favor, and that Romsfeld had even been raised in the earl's household, he was still illegitimate. Even now he wore the clothes of a yeoman, not a lord. Though they were costly all the same, a lawn shirt and a sparkling white tunic with his father's crest blazoned across it. It was a crest he had no right to, except as livery like any other servant.

He was a bastard, a man-at-arms, and legally nothing more. And though for this misfortune he blamed everyone, yet so it was. In a final petition to the king, he had asked to be legitimized as his father's heir. But his bid had failed. Or had it? Had there been some last minute trick? Did she now face the new earl?

He kept the sword pointed at her. Whatever he was, she could not frighten him with threats or curses. If she challenged him, he would probably attack. Yet as he aspired to power, perhaps she could shame him. She brushed the earth from her mouth and straightened herself, clasping her hands neatly, devoutly.

"I am no witch, good sir," she said. "I am but a nun."

Romsfeld stared as if incredulous, but he withdrew his sword. Then, with an apprising glance at the priory, he spurred his horse toward the gate.

Georgia started—she'd given him the wrong message! He thought she had given up. She jumped and threw herself bodily in his way. The palfrey thrashed its legs but stopped short.

Romsfeld grabbed wildly for the saddle bar and teetered in his seat.

Let him teeter, Georgia thought. Let him fall! "We are simple religious women," she said, seeking a firmer tone now. "You may pass only with my leave."

As Romsfeld steadied in the saddle, he regained some color, but he looked angrier than before. He raised his voice again. "Is this not a church, witch? Am I not a pilgrim led here to erase heresy? Step aside."

She held her place; he had said "pilgrim" and not "lord." That was a good sign. She raised her voice. "Pilgrims do not approach with drawn swords. If you are a gentleman and a pilgrim, dismount in courtesy."

"Courtesy," Romsfeld scowled. "Courtesy is nothing to me." He threw back his head and addressed the windows all along the length of the priory. "There is a new master here," he paused, and his voice filled with contempt. "Our great and noble king has named the bishop of London, the Marquess Philip SeVerde, rightful lord and master of all these lands." The palfrey pawed at the ground and sidled left. Romsfeld wobbled, but steadied himself. He spoke directly to Georgia. "I am his lordship's steward," he paused again. "*I* am the law here. I will decide how the law is carried out! And I demand to see the widow countess." He waited in the saddle until the horse quieted. Only then, with an elaborate affectation of manner, did he dismount.

Yet he was not an earl! The relief of it left her tired. Her feet hurt, and her legs shook. Romsfeld was only a steward. A steward took charge in the lord's absence, supervised the household, settled disputes, collected the rents, and brought in the harvest. While a steward had authority, he was subject and not lord. Romsfeld must do as he was bid.

And she could best him.

"Dame Marjorie the countess is ill," she said. "She is in mourning for her husband."

"I do not care."

"And," Georgia added, "she has sought sanctuary."

"Haul her out!"

"I cannot."

The corner of Romsfeld's mouth twitched up over a yellow tooth. "Then I will burn this priory to the ground."

Georgia curtseyed. She looked quickly over her shoulder at the church, then back at Romsfeld. He bluffed, she thought. To burn a church was desecration of the worst kind. He'd never dare to do it. Yet—much in the valley below was now ablaze. What would keep him from launching a flaming arrow now to the church?

He scowled so that she thought he might spit on her.

She cleared her throat. "Perhaps, good sir, if Dame Marjorie is in private prayer, I could escort you to meet with her. Alone. But arms are forbidden in the priory."

Romsfeld bowed, sneering. "We are, of course, your guests," he eyed the bristling church walls and indicated for his men-at-arms to lower their weapons, although they stayed mounted.

Georgia tucked her veil into her cap. She would act her part then and make sure he did the same. But the raiders must be kept back from the gate.

She kept her gaze on Romsfeld. She needed someone who could stand guard without the risk of inciting a fight. "Sister Maud!" she called out. "I have need of you."

Maud came quickly through the gate, clutching a rust-pitted hayfork in her hand. Stitch-eyed and almost toothless, with a knack for terrifying animals and small boys, Maud would make a perfect chaperone for the gate.

"Shall I keep my good eye on them, Sister Georgia?"

"Yes. Thank you."

Maud arched a pig-bristled brow, picked up a large rock, and rested it on her knee. She jutted her chin, and the whiskers there stood out like scotch broom. The men exchanged glances, and even Romsfeld skirted her as he walked by.

"Ha!" Maud shook the fork at him and hissed.

Ha, indeed, Georgia thought. Let Maud frighten them and keep them busy for a while.

As for herself, Georgia grasped her prayer beads and held them tightly; she must lead a bastard through the gate.

CHAPTER 5:
Bastards

GEORGIA FOLDED HER HANDS, AND AS SHE walked, she felt the gentle motion of the relic as it moved from side to side under her skirts. She doubted the new lord, this Philip SeVerde, had ordered the burning and looting. The town of Bilsdale belonged to him, and burning it only destroyed his own property.

It was far more likely that Romsfeld saw an opportunity for revenge and had taken it. Perhaps he sought to settle old grudges while the transition was still new. He could blame the violence on quelling resistance and establishing control. He probably also wished to demonstrate just how far he was willing to go in exercising his new power. For this new lord, this bishop far away, would likely remain in his diocese in London. Romsfeld, then, could assert power in Yorkshire virtually unchecked.

For the moment, that meant she must lead Romsfeld through the gate. She could hear his throaty breathing too close behind her. The hair on the back of her neck prickled, and all the layers of her dress—linen, wool, and silk—did not feel enough to protect her from his predation.

She guarded her own breath, matching it to her step, taking note of each doorway, and where there were archers behind the priory walls. She noted the iron pick and trowels in the cloister garden as they passed. If she needed a weapon, she thought, she would snatch what was nearest to hand.

Whatever his intent, Dame Marjorie must be protected. While the priory had been given over to the sisters, as long as the countess lived, the property deed belonged to her. The priory was her dowry, to formally be relinquished only at her death, thus ensuring she would be well provided for during the remainder of her life. Yet this meant that if Dame Marjorie were removed from the priory, even by force, the deed went with her. If Romsfeld seized or arrested her or forced her to return with him, ownership of the land could be lost—again.

Georgia came to the door of the prioress's rooms with Romsfeld close behind her. He kicked his boot against her heel, shoving past her to the door. But Georgia sidestepped, turning squarely to block him. She pushed tight into the doorframe.

"I will announce you," she said. She held there and then turned, thinking he would wait. He did not. As soon as she moved, he pushed again. This time he succeeded. The chambermaid rushed forward only to cower as Romsfeld swept into the room.

The sudden heat and darkness dulled Georgia's senses. The fire flared in the hearth, fed by the new, raw current of air. Dame Marjorie's terriers barked. Romsfeld kicked the smallest one, sending her skidding across the plank floor, yelping.

Georgia bit the inside of her cheek against a sharp rebuke, reminding herself that her goal was courtesy. She must keep the social rules, for he must do so as well. And here, it was he who must bow to precedence. For though a widow and a nun, Dame Marjorie was still a countess, and she ranked far above him.

As the light rushed over the room, the dame rose gracefully. Shrouded in black, she stepped up from a silk prayer pillow near a small altar in the corner of the room. The woolen mourning robe she wore slopped heavily around her, and a full hood hid her face from the onrushing light.

Georgia curtsied, and Romsfeld gave a sharp, perfunctory bow. Dame Marjorie eased the hood back over her headdress, appraising him as if he were only of polite concern. In her eyes there was the sign of weeping, but also a steady gaze. The tightness in Georgia's stomach eased to see it.

"Dame," Georgia began, but Dame Marjorie lifted a hand to quiet her. Georgia checked herself. She, too, must bow to precedence. Yet she distrusted Romsfeld and crept forward, stopping just behind him at the shoulder. From there, she could intervene. There was a spine-tipped distaff against the wall; she could use it, if she needed, as a pike.

Near the bed the chambermaid tucked behind a small ornate table of heavy oak and gathered the terriers, shushing them. The dogs would not hush, however, until Dame Marjorie turned toward them with a sharp, "Pity's sake!"

She then moved toward the only chair in the room. With a wary glance at Romsfeld, Georgia took the prioress's arm, supporting her up onto the dais and arranging her robe. All the while, Georgia noted Romsfeld's impatience and estimated his level of control.

Dame Marjorie settled in the chair. "To what may I credit the honor of your company?"

"I am named master steward to the new lord, the bishop of London and Marquess Philip SeVerde." Romsfeld made a curt bow. "I am charged with overseeing his lordship's Yorkshire rights and properties, including ensuring that his lands remain intact and that all whores and nuns under his domain submit forthwith to orthodoxy and reform. This priory now belongs to Lord SeVerde. You will surrender your accounts to me and submit to be cloistered. All of your affairs are ended, save what purpose you can best find in prayer."

He bowed again after his speech, and Georgia detected triumph in his gaze. He handed a letter to Dame Marjorie with a sarcastic flip. "But I am sure you can read the declaration for yourself, Dame."

Dame Marjorie could not read. It was no secret, nor uncommon, yet it was an insult to draw attention to that fact, especially as it called into question her fitness to serve as prioress. Lady Marjorie rose above the offense by refusing to take the letter. Romsfeld gave it instead to Georgia, though he did so with a sneer.

Georgia examined the seal. The formal address was written in Latin, and she could read only a little. It was a writ perhaps, *Anno Domini MDXXIV*— the year of Our Lord, 1524.

Few nuns now knew the art of reading. While monks still enjoyed education and self-rule, few nuns enjoyed the same. Nuns must be as conquered wives with the church a great father to manage and enclose their persons, their possessions, and their dowries. Men who sought the power to silence them did not understand the calling of a woman to be a nun.

A wave of fatigue left her dizzy and teased her balance. A small amount of blood gushed from between her legs and trickled down her thigh and past her knee. Her courses were yet another burden on this day. She longed to close her eyes and open them again with the world put right.

Romsfeld cleared his throat and repeated his ultimatum. "Perhaps, Dame, I have not spoken simply enough. Please allow me to repeat. You are to surrender the seal of this priory to me, forthwith, return the surrounding land wrongly severed from the lord's estate, and submit yourselves to reform without further curses, spells, sorcery, or women's tricks."

More silence followed. When the prioress spoke, her words were clear and even. "You have no authority here, Master Steward. Still, I thank you for safe delivery of this letter and your assessment of its contents. Please be assured that we will pray for your continued good health and for the health of the new lord."

It was a dismissal, and Romsfeld rasped. His face purpled as he choked out an angry reply that set the dogs to barking again. "I assure you, madam, that I have full authority. And, should you doubt it, know that I can enforce the letter of this law. I will have the priory seal. Today is, most assuredly, the day of your reform."

Georgia lost her control. "The devil!" Why had the Lord made so many rotten men, she thought. And why did he not silence this one?

"Hold your tongue, nun." Romsfeld said, "I'll have no curses struck against me."

Georgia raised her fists. "So spoken by he who opens the hell gates onto our land! *A porta inferi.*"

"Master Steward," Dame Marjorie said, "if you think to cow God's will before you like a common thing, you are mistaken. You are standing on the premises of the Priory of Saint Isela and in her house. These are matters of decorum even you should tend to."

Romsfeld looked as if he might spit into the fire. "You are not so mighty to God. I think his lordship SeVerde, the bishop, more on the course of what the matters of God shall be." He finished with a quiet tone, his face lined in resentment. "You flaunt yourself, Dame."

"Are you still so angry, Horley?" Dame Marjorie said.

Romsfeld answered with a squeak. "You do not have leave to call me by my given name."

Dame Marjorie offered a conciliatory sigh. "Good Master Steward, pray accept my apology if I have offended." She regarded him, and her eyes glazed into memory. "Yet, Horley, do you remember so little of your boyhood? Do you choose only to be angry, to forget—"

"I am not a boy, my lady, unbreeched and ignorant of the price of cake and silly women's games. You retreat into senile narratives, but you will not find me there."

"But was I not a mother to you? Did I not encourage you? See to your education? Did I not embrace you, in spite of—"

"In spite of what I was?" Romsfeld whispered it as if it were a curse. He took a step toward her, his whole manner wrapped in accusation. "What were you to me but a barren, dried up hag. *My* mother died. Where was your love for *her*? It was my lord father who schooled me, my lord father who brought me into his household. But you! A little pretended fawning and a few sweetmeats cannot turn one thing into another."

"I did love you, Horley."

"You loved me? You loved me so much so that God grew my father's seed inside another! You chose not to be a wife to my father. You chose this," he waved his arms to indicate the nunnery. "This! You abandoned him to serving girls and chambermaids. You denied him the legitimacy of a true heir."

"Your father was content."

"Content? Is that what you call this—him—me?"

"My lord husband took mistresses well before we swore between us an oath of chastity," Dame Marjorie said. "He was my husband, he loved me, and he choose to honor my wishes and endow me with this gift." She paused. "To save his soul, I expect."

"That oath and these lands you gained through witchcraft," Romsfeld crowed. "Sorceress!"

Georgia's grip on courtliness fell away. Shoving the letter into her belt, she slapped Romsfeld full on the face.

"Bastard!"

He lunged for her, and she ducked behind the bed. Snatching the distaff from the wall, she planted her feet and held the point at the ready. From behind her, silver bowls and a bronze goblet clattered to the floor as the chambermaid rose with the side table and raised it in readiness for a blow. The dogs darted out from her skirts and skittered, barking, across the floor, the smallest one attacking.

Romsfeld glared, but he retreated. He brushed savagely at the dog where it latched onto his riding cloak.

"Rollie!" Dame Marjorie clapped her hands together, and the dog hid under the bed.

Romsfeld pressed a gloved hand high on his cheek where Georgia struck him; his eyes closed while the ringing, clattering bowl settled into stillness. When he spoke, his body seemed to tremble. "Speak it. Speak how you bewitched my father, how you sinned against me, his only son."

"Of course he loved you, Horley. Yet your ambition turned him away." Dame Marjorie seemed to weigh her words gently. "And you were not his *only* son, Horley. There were others like you, born of desire but not control. Though they were not so favored, perhaps."

Romsfeld charged at her, but Georgia was quicker and still armed. She brought the sharp top of the distaff under his chin.

He twisted the staff from her hands and threw it aside. But the chambermaid held the table high, and Romsfeld retreated, rocking his anger near the fire of the hearth. Abused by the grudge that nursed him.

Dame Marjorie stepped off the dais, her huge black robe deflating a little, giving away some of her frailty beneath.

"I do have regrets. I regret that God did not see fit to give me a living son. You think I did not want a son, for his sake, for myself? But for some things there are no answers. It was God's will, Horley, God's will."

Romsfeld blinked, wiping his eyes with the sleeve of his tunic. "Dare you not imagine God's will. There is nothing of God's will in this. I am the earl's only son! My lord father raised me, taught me, wanted to—wanted to—give it all to me."

Silence filled the chamber once again. The prioress fingered the line of prayer beads at her waist. "I did what I could. I was a good wife to him."

This time Romsfeld did spit into the fire. He spit his helplessness and slammed his fist in the oak beam set above the stone hearth.

Tears rolled down his cheeks. "You were no man's wife and no man's mother." His voice filled with both craving and hatred. "I am the son. I am the rightful heir. All that should be mine is lost to me. Mine! For things were not supposed to be as they were. Your filthy, barren nature forced what should have been—" he choked, then roared so loudly the goblet on the floor rang with the vibration, "—what should have been my fortune into a shape it could not be. You closed your legs and suffocated my birth. For I, lady, I—I should have been *your son*."

He turned heel and flung himself against the door, rending it open, leaving it shuddering against the force of his exit. The daylight flooded in, and Georgia blinked as the sun caught him, reducing him to shadow and escorting him around the walls of the dorter and out of sight.

The door swung back, shutting out the residual burst that had burned through the room. It was as if the door had breached, releasing a small, unpapered tyrant into the world.

CHAPTER 6:
Saints

As the door swung shut, the fire flared, and the warmth of it pushed heat against Georgia's cheeks. The warmth reassured, but she still felt cold to her fingertips.

"Hold, Sister," Dame Marjorie said, and Georgia stopped short, tripping over the prioress's black robes. She curtsied a quick apology as she realized she had been dragging the prioress bodily toward the door. "Pray pardon, Dame, yet we must get to sanctuary still. And Sister Maud stands at the gate." Georgia doubted Romsfeld was finished with them, but what he would do next, she did not know.

"You presume, Sister." The prioress settled down onto the prayer cushion. "Your worries will not serve you. Go, if that is your wish, but Horley is a coward still. A pity."

The chambermaid gathered the pottery shards from the floor. She scooped the spill of herbs from the planks, returning the clumped powder to a small pouch. The smell of peppermint cooled the heavy heat of fire and exhalation.

Georgia tried to mask her urgency. "Dame, do you understand why you, especially, must seek sanctuary?"

"Everyone always worries so about Horley. But he is a child."

"He is a man, my lady. You must see this. He is a man, fully grown and denied his ambition. And he bears you this grudge. And he blames Isela's for this thing. You must seek sanctuary. Our danger has not passed."

There was a loud knock. Georgia placed herself bodily in front of the prioress as a stout servant came into the room, a woman, red faced, who bobbed curtsey after curtsey.

"Please you, milady. Sorry, milady, but Sister Joan, milady, sent me directly to fetch you. Me and William, so sorry—please you."

"Romsfeld?" Georgia said.

"No, Domina. He's rode off. But he's left his—"

"—his men—"

The servant bobbed another curtsey. "Yes, Domina, milady."

Georgia knelt and took Dame Marjorie's hand. "I beseech you. If we do not quiet this trouble, I fear that we will lose our home." Georgia thought of the relic, warm under her skirts, and of Johanna and the child. "Something has begun. Though I scarcely dare hope at what it might be. Come to sanctuary. If prayer calls you, then it is there, if anywhere, that your prayers are most urgently needed." Georgia swept her gaze around the room, over the new afternoon shadows, and the two serving women whose faces now showed an anxious worry. "We are all in danger here."

Dame Marjorie frowned. "To the church, then, you must go." She gestured to the chambermaid. "And you also if you wish it. But I will stay here."

Georgia almost laughed. Agnes's words ran over each other in her thoughts, "quickly, quickly." The plank under her foot squealed. How could she do what was impossible? To place guards at the prioress's door, it seemed, was all the best she could make of it.

☙

The courtyard path led between the dormitory and the orchard, and Georgia ran across it. Next to her, the ravens, unconcerned with the smoke, ripped into the pears and speared the quinces, their stabbing beaks slimed with the half-rotted ooze within.

Maud was still at the gate.

"Blackguards. Dogs!" Maud's shouts carried through the courtyard. A shard of limestone hurtled over the gate and sunk into the garden earth.

Georgia quickened her step.

Georgia opened the gate, and Maud was crouched just ahead, glaring at the raiders, two of whom stood just out of the range of the hayfork. These two gave a bellowing cry and charged. Maud jabbed the fork at them. A few arrows volleyed from the walls of the church, but the angle was bad, and the arrows missed. Maud, however, did not miss, and the men repeated yelping, each nursing a sizable gash.

Georgia jumped out just far enough to pull Maud back through the gate.

She brought down the spar to lock it behind them. The gate vibrated under a barrage of stones as the outlaws unloaded their slings. Maud shook her fist. Picking up a stone, she hurled it back over the gate.

"Lawless wretches, ha!" Maud waved a fist. "And I've seen the little one before." With a wink, she pinched Georgia on the cheek. "We won't die, though. We're fit as cabbages."

Georgia took Maud by the elbow. Leaving the village men to watch the gate, she steered back through the sacristy into the church. The outlaws continued throwing stones, but she ignored them. Let them throw all the limestone they could find; it would keep them busy. From that, at least, the gate would hold.

❧

Returning to the sanctuary brought darkness again, for the sanctuary was lit only by a few open lamps. The afternoon light that would usually come through the windows was blocked by strips of leather, upturned benches, and wooden planking—whatever covering material the villagers had found quick to hand.

Sister Thomasine stood at the lectern, leading the sisters through the Psalter. She could not read, but that did not matter. She could recite every psalm. Whether the hymn was of penance, prayer, or deliverance mattered less to her than the performance and zeal with which she rolled the Latin over her tongue.

The women were anything but silent. Their musical chanting mingled their voices, prickled at the back of Georgia's neck, and pierced her body. The immediacy of the chant flowed right through her. And the relic under her skirt warmed with an onrushing heat as wide as a river.

She almost surrendered to such a powerful call to prayer. But instead she stepped away and aside as if to outmaneuver it. Prayer was too all encompassing. She must find the chill and maintain wakefulness. She must focus on her task.

Sister Joan hurried toward her with singular purpose, her robes immaculate and her headdress perfectly in place. Quick and efficient, Sister Joan served as treasurer, tallying each item in and out of the priory. Only the small blotches of ink on the tally margins betrayed her nervous disposition.

"I had to keep things here without you. There were screams outside—"

"You did well, Sister." Georgia glanced toward Isela's altar and to where Mendaline had set up a small infirmary space. Johanna seemed no better.

"Have John or Robert returned?" Georgia asked.

"No."

Georgia crossed herself. There must be justice, some protection. "Can you send a few out to search for them, a few who are quick and quiet? See to it, Sister, quickly. For I must speak to Mendaline about the child."

A young boy ran into the church, and Sister Joan spoke quickly with him.

"Sister Georgia," Sister Joan motioned the boy to wait. "Sister, the outlaws have left the gate. They have gone around by way of the latrine. They'll be into the kitchen and the brewhouse next."

"And the buttery, and the cellar, and the byre—" Georgia thought of the thin, sunken faces of the mercenaries, how hungry they looked. "Sister, tell the village men to let the outlaws into the kitchen and the buttery. Send the boy with that basket of bread from the dais, and bacon. Perhaps, if the raiders can fill their bellies it will slow them."

Georgia smoothed her palms over her skirt, and pain caught underneath her fingernail. The letter was still tucked into her belt; she had forgotten it. It must be read, for Romsfeld could not be trusted to speak the truth of it. Yet none of the villagers, and no sister, could read.

The nun's devotions shifted to a keening prayer, with a sweet, soft alto voice at its center. Sister Catherine brought a reedy richness to their song. Sister Joan had begun to turn away, but Georgia stopped her as she gazed at Sister Catherine in the choir. "Wait, Sister. One thing more. I need you to fetch someone who may be hiding in the byre."

Catherine was the only sister without her gaze cast downward as the prayer concluded. Georgia stared pointedly at her and indicated for her to come down from the choir stands. Catherine flushed. Her sanguine look, which likely came from her shame at being caught inattentive, reddened her cheeks and brightened her eyes, and only made her even more vibrantly lovely.

A woman of one and twenty, Sister Catherine was not only robustly pretty, but she was one of the few at Saint Isela's who did not choose the religious life for herself. Her younger brother had sent her to Saint Isela's rather than pay twice more the dowry he would need to secure her a worthy husband. She was a fine girl, but ill suited for the religious life. She was prone to naive notions about men and love and fortune. She visited the alehouses in Bilsdale and flirted outright, even laughing at the lewd humor of the merchants. No amount of penance seemed to cure her.

"Yes, Domina?" Sister Catherine made a small curtsey, her gaze flicking quickly up then back to the floor again.

Georgia spoke quietly. "Sister Catherine, would there be a monk hiding in the byre, perchance?"

Catherine flushed more deeply, and Georgia thought perhaps a small amount of shame finally showed through. Or at least concern. Certainly not surprise. It was well-known that Catherine's monk visited from *LeRouge* monastery—some twenty miles south—with regularity. It was a relationship that had been ongoing despite all Georgia's best efforts.

Sister Catherine fidgeted. "Domina, I will—I do—I did not mean to—"

Georgia held up a hand to quiet her. "The outlaws have moved toward the brewhouse and the cellar. From there, they will go straight around to the byre."

Catherine looked up again, true alarm in her expression. "Please, sister, I am, I am—" She focused her gaze on the door and then whispered, "I can fetch him."

Georgia shook her head. "No. You will ask Sister Joan to send a man for him. But know this. Today, I have need of him."

☙

A pungent bitterness wafted across the church, the scent of birthing weed. Birthing weed was only used in childbirth when the mother faded. Its sharp scent was thought to anchor her spirit lest it slip away.

Georgia turned away from Sisters Catherine and Joan and moved through the piles of cloth, straw, and miscellany that littered the church floor to where Mendaline worked with Johanna behind the screens. The faded gilt of the nearest screen showed Saint Mary as a child with an open prayer book. Mary's mother, Saint Anne, was painted there as well, teaching her daughter to read.

Behind the saints, Mendaline crouched over Johanna, coaxing her to drink candle-warmed beer foamed black with herbs ground fine, particle to particle, for the best healing effect. The rich brew could only do her good, Georgia thought, for Johanna's skin had grown so translucent that it showed a cobbled blue texture underneath.

Mendaline groused. "Fine way to deliver a baby," she laid Johanna back gently once she'd drunk a little. "No birthing stool, no fire. Goats."

"Mendaline," Georgia pushed a goat away as it nosed into the beer. It bumped into another goat, and both animals bleated full throated and indignant. "Sister, I must show you this."

Georgia withdrew the relic from beneath her skirts. The red glow shone out, deepening the furrows across Mendaline's nose and forehead.

Sister Mendaline gave a small gasp. "So," she made the sign of the cross over the glowing stone. "So, the day has come." She laid her hand across Johanna's belly very gently. "Poor little one. What a burden."

"Yes, you see, Johanna must be delivered. Mendaline, this chance cannot pass. Tell me, what can I do?"

Mendaline looked up at Saint Isela's altar. "Prayer, Sister. Pray for us."

Georgia tucked the relic away, yet even with the light gone, the furrows along Mendaline's forehead stayed heavy across her brow. She shifted, placing both her hands over Johanna's belly. She turned to Alice. "Bring two slips of paper from my satchel, each one marked with crosses and the names of the four apostles. Lay one between her breasts, and burn the other. Smolder it with hawk's dung, and bring the embers to me. We will waft it over her." She turned back to Johanna. "After that," she crossed herself, *"Ave Maria gratia plena*, we can only wait."

CHAPTER 7:
Promises

IF PRAYER WAS ALL THAT COULD BE done, then that was what she must do. Georgia crossed herself. Next to her was the stone altar of Isela. Carved with birds and mountains and hyssop flowers, it anchored that corner of the church. She drew a cross on the stone and kissed the center of it.

"Lord, have mercy on us," she began a litany. *"Blessed Mary, pray for us; Saint Walburga, pray for us; Saint Bugga, pray for us—"* She included Saint Devota, Saint Godberga, Saint Catherine who had converted soldiers, Saint Lucy the fireproof. As she prayed, she envisioned each of the relics at the priory and imagined kissing each reliquary in turn. The breastbone of Saint Thomas the Apostle, the powdered skin of Saint Bridget, a chin hair from the martyr Wilgefortis, and a fingernail paring from Saint Jerome's corpse.

But of all the relics at the priory, Saint Isela's relic was the most precious. Inside the palm-sized bead of glass was smeared the blood of the saint herself, smeared as she lay dying, and imbued with the promise of her rebirth.

The glass bead had been set into polished bronze centuries ago, with the bronze ornately curled and inlaid with garnets and yellow enamel like a burst of sun fire. In the design, it was as if chaos released honeyed glass and all the hope of the world crowned. At the top, a slim silver chain threaded through the curls and loops of the bronze work, allowing the relic to be worn around the neck or at the belt, or suspended from a reliquary or candelabra.

"Saint Isela, pray for us." Georgia placed her hand over the relic, and as she did so, a hollow opened in her chest like warm rain poured into leaded

glass. She steadied herself against the heat, which, as it seeped inside her gut, turned to nausea. Her skin rioted, her eyes watered, and the mystery tumbled within her. A pulse came up through the relic itself, and cascading warmth spread into the core of her body.

Remember, a voice cried out. Was it her own? The word seemed to echo all around her. *Remember.*

Taking the relic from her belt, Georgia placed the chain around her neck, so that it hung down over the bodice of her kyrtle. Let the light shine out, she thought. This voice, this overwhelming passion, was yet another sign of destiny. Clasping the orb tightly to her breast, she recited the prayer of awakening:

Isela, we await you! By the mountain, we await you!
Behold the birth-promise! Arise the flock!
Arise the fountain! For the Chooser comes.

It was the promise of the Chooser's coming. For the Chooser would be the first one born—the one to choose if the time was right. If it was, Isela would follow. Georgia placed her hand over her heart. How many years had she waited? If she wept for all of them, she would drown in tears. *Isela. Isela—*

Please, Georgia thought. *Let this be the child.*

She looked down at Johanna. Her breathing was short; her face was pinched with pain, and she was pale from prolonged suffering.

Georgia spat on her thumb and drew the sign of the cross on Johanna's forehead. Georgia squeezed her eyes closed and imagined the child born and suckling at Johanna's breast. All her energy must be given to this. All the promises made from the beginning must be kept.

Yet at any moment, Romsfeld would return; Georgia had no doubt of that. In whatever time they had, something must be done.

And yet she was so tired. The image of Johanna and her newborn child faded, and instead all Georgia could see was death. In her mind's eye, the church blazed with fire. Such would be the price if she failed. *Mater Dei!*

When Johanna cried out again, Mendaline answered her with a soothing "tut-tutting." Agnes answered, too, with a loud, keening wail.

Georgia clamped her hands over her ears to block the noises out. This could not be the way the story ended. There had been too many years of waiting. Too much suffering. Too many tyrants.

Yet even through her clasped hands, Georgia could hear Agnes scream again, the treble vibration of a knife drawn through rock.

Georgia fell against the carved hyssop of the altar, put her head into her hands, and sobbed.

☙

Someone prodded her and prodded again. Mendaline cleared her throat. "Hmm—what's this, tears?"

"Let me suffer," Georgia said. "It is what I know."

"A martyr, then?" Mendaline's voice softened a little. "I remember a certain prioress when I was young. The year we starved, remember? So many came to our gates with bowls and empty bellies. And what did she tell me? She said, 'One day, all be well.'"

Georgia looked up, her cheeks and palms soaking wet. She wiped her hands on her overskirt. "If the church is set alight, I will never be free."

Mendaline shrugged. "Perhaps."

As Johanna tried to roll, Mendaline wedged her knee behind the young woman's lower back and stroked her hair to soothe her.

Georgia blinked; her eyes stung. "I do not know how it will turn out."

"No?" Mendaline looked around the sanctuary at the people clustered into groups. Taking a rag from a nearby bowl, she squeezed a few drops of water into Johanna's mouth. "Come on, then, Georgia. Stop crying and think. You're no ox for brains." She looked down at Johanna. "Mark me, all is not lost. She suffers greatly. I'll grant it. But she is stronger than she seems. *In nomine Patris et Filii et Spiritus Sancti.* Whatever this day brings, so be it."

Georgia wiped her face, the scratchy wool of her overskirt warming her cold cheeks. She nodded, "So be it."

"So be it," Mendaline said again, more forcefully this time.

Johanna lay still now, the spasm having passed. She took short breaths in succession. Johanna might be strong, yet even a lay woman would know the square shape of her belly was the fault of her labor. The babe was reluctant; it lay crosswise in the womb. Such a thing buried mother and child both.

Mendaline worked, and Johanna's breathing slowed, though she lay shivering. Georgia took the relic between her palms. How warm it was!

Mendaline spread yet another layer of oil over Johanna's belly as Georgia studied its squarish shape. Gently, she touched the relic to where the young woman's stomach bulged out, a stubborn lump that bruised the skin between Johanna's hip and ribs.

"Come you, angel," Georgia whispered, "through heavenly pity, I will guard you. I will always be with you."

The relic cast a red-orange glow across Johanna's skin. She shifted under it, and her stomach convulsed; the movement sent the relic slipping over her oiled skin, and Georgia snatched it back up.

Mendaline dropped the oil and the towel, and barked a short, rapt, "Balthazar!" Johanna endured another spasm as Mendaline pressed her palms against Johanna's belly and pushed. Her whole belly rolled.

Mendaline swept bowls and jugs aside with a wide swipe of her hands.

The embers of the hawks dung, now ash, scattered across the floor. "Alice! Get her to her hands and knees. Raise her shoulders first. We will try again. Turn!"

Alice hoisted as Mendaline slid a palm along Johanna's back, murmuring encouragement. "Hold up, wife," she said. "Be strong, wife."

Agnes began to shriek again, this time in sharp bursts. Mendaline grunted.

Georgia slid back to give Mendaline room to work.

Alice succeeded in raising Johanna, bruising her arms in turning her. Mendaline assaulted her belly with a ferocious shove, and then shoved again. On the third try, a gush of blood and dark fluid spurted across Johanna's thigh. Georgia crossed herself, but Mendaline smiled.

"Saint Margaret, what a day!" Mendaline ran her hands over Johanna's stomach. From a square, it was now oval in shape. The passage between her thighs bulged, and the liquid ceased to leak. "Matthew, Mark, Luke, and John! Peter, Paul, and James! Praise Isela! If there's fluid enough, all will be well."

Georgia fought her way to usefulness. *All would be well.* There would be a baby after all. If the child was the Chooser, she must perform the baptism. For she was the Bearer, the relic keeper, the one who knew the ages and held open the way.

Yet it seemed impossible. Unbelievable.

Agnes's shrieks reverberated across the church. Sister Thomasine barred the window to Agnes's cell, scolding her to absolutely no effect. Agnes's screams were broken only by grunts as she flung herself from wall to wall.

Sister Thomasine clucked at her. "Go on, then. Give yourself a great stoning."

Mendaline bubbled with energy. She cleared a wider space and barked orders. "Cloth!" "Toweling!" "A basin!" "Clean water!" "A fresh apron!"

Mendaline's surety seemed to buoy everyone. Georgia thought again of the rhyme of the promise. *When the Chooser comes.* If this babe was the one, it would be a girl, and she would bear the mark. There would be no mistaking it.

☙

Georgia hurried toward the sacristy to get what would be needed for baptism.

A black shape hovered near the sacristy door, as if unsure to enter the church. Sister Catherine's monk, unmistakable in a silk cassock and furred almuse. The thick hood of his cloak, trimmed in white fur, was thrown behind him, and his cheeks were raw.

Georgia grasped the letter, still tucked under her belt; she had again forgotten it. Whatever Romsfeld had said about the wishes of the new Lord SeVerde, the letter could confirm or deny it. She needed to know what it said.

"Sister Georgia," Sister Joan appeared, flustered, out of breath. "We kept the raiders from the byre, but they took the poultry cote. I think they killed every goose and hen and would have burned it. The archers gave them a turn but left them to the brewhouse like you said."

Georgia controlled her compulsion to hurry. She felt sticky with blood and grime and sweat, her eyes salt-burned from sobbing. "Encourage them to drink the barrel of first-pressed wine, if you can. It is stronger." She ignored Joan's look of horror—first-pressed wine was expensive. "When they are drunk, send in the men and bind and hold them."

"Yes, Sister." Joan turned and hurried out.

Georgia took the letter from her belt, her fingertips stuttering over the red wax seal. She tried to remember the monk's name—Benet—Brother Benet.

Sister Catherine hovered nearby, squinted, and edged away.

Brother Benet bowed quickly, set his balance squarely, and lifted his chin. "I can shoot. And I can fight."

Georgia sized him up, his thin beaked nose and melancholic complexion. This man was more scribe than warrior.

"I pray we have fighters enough, Brother."

In her rush she was abrupt. She handed Benet the letter. It seemed smaller now, and Johanna's blood had spattered it. "It is a writ, in Latin. I need to know what is demanded of us, and by whose authority."

Benet accepted the envelope. "*Glorious patri.*"

Georgia nodded, "*Mater Dei,*" and left him to it.

She took a bowl from the sacristy, a length of woolen cloth, and a pouch of coarse sea salt, that she placed into her bodice. All the rest she took back to Mendaline and Johanna behind the screens.

There, Georgia filled the bowl with water and plunged the relic into it. The baptism must be right, the water made pure by the relic itself. She said the blessing, just the fraction she could remember, "*per invocationem sancti tui nominis,*" repeating it thrice. *Let the devil tremble and be sent away.* Then, placing the chain again around her neck, she slipped the relic back into the bib of her kyrtle. She knelt behind Mendaline. All was ready.

Another spasm swept over Johanna, and it seemed it could not be long now. Alice wiped the blood from the young woman's thighs as she bore down. Mendaline massaged a glob of duck fat into the place where Johanna swelled from the birth, pressing a cool towel to help support her as the baby crowned.

Agnes screamed again. Then came the sound of a violent smack against stones and an abrupt silence.

Mendaline noted the quiet. "And that is also good." She smiled at Johanna, a feast of a smile, like the promise of capon and custard. "Come on, wife. We've got a baby coming. Push, push."

Johanna's breath caught as another contraction seized her up. It passed over her, and she pushed. The babe appeared, almost to the shoulder, and then receded.

Mendaline rinsed the towel and plied it again. "Good. Another just as that one. Yet this time bear down a breath longer. Just a breath ... hold! Hold!"

Georgia focused. She must be ready. The baby must be baptized. Too many stories had been told of the fumbling midwife who sent a child's soul to hell due to a botched or belated baptism. And this child might be ordinary, after all—a boy. Or a girl without the mark. After so hard a labor, there might be little time to save the baby's life.

"Good! Again! Hold ..."

The stillness grew in the waiting. The folk sat in silence, each no doubt waiting as Georgia did, for the cries of the mother to cease and the cries of the babe to begin.

But as Johanna's grunts gained strength and her breath deepened, a clattering, rolling noise undercut the suspended quiet of the church. The rolling sound broke in with the drafts and spread across sanctuary. It was the sound of horses once more on the path and the clattering of swords and helms.

A cry went up from the archers. "Master Romsfeld has returned. The sheriff rides with him!"

CHAPTER 8:
Miracles

Georgia did not move from her place near Johanna.

An archer pulled aside a leather window covering, and light flooded in. Romsfeld's reinforcements had arrived, perhaps twenty men, some with torches, in addition to Romsfeld's men-at-arms. The sheriff also had two men, armed and mounted. The archer let the leather fall back over the window, and the sanctuary dimmed.

Romsfeld's voice came through the oak front doors. "Hear me! This priory, its grounds, and all within must surrender the witch Georgia and the prioress, Dame Marjorie. Surrender now, and no one else shall be harmed."

She had lost before. She had been waylaid by thieves and rogues and pulled naked through towns on the end of a rope while people jeered her and pelted her with stones, offal, and excrement. Those memories, like so many others, pushed back under a veil she dared not lift. She had never known the terror of Saint Agatha, whose torturer had cut off her breasts and rolled her in shards and fire, but Georgia had her own horrors.

She held those memories at the edge of her remembrance. But they touched her now. They came on the deep mocking voice of Romsfeld as he shouted to his men.

Anger rose into Georgia's gut. How dare he! How dare he raise his voice, here, now, at the precipice of all things beginning. How dare he call her witch!

Johanna bore down hard and released a quiet, breathy scream. Agnes, awake again, echoed her.

Mendaline crooned, "hold … hold …" as the baby crowned again. With another glob of duck fat, Mendaline slid her hands along the baby's cheeks, and when the child receded again, Mendaline's hands receded, too. It was the shoulder she reached for. For the baby must turn a little to be born, and sometimes, if the shoulders were wide and the mother small, or the opening too dry or too swollen, the turning was not an easy thing.

Outside, Romsfeld called again. "Bring me the whore Georgia and the Dame Prioress, and no harm will come to any other."

Georgia stretched her fingers wide and then clenched her hands tightly into fists. Her joints ached. She should open the door, stand in the light of the afternoon, and put Romsfeld back into the hay field he was conceived in. Yet if she stepped out of sanctuary, she would be taken.

Sister Elizabeth moved in behind the screens; her eyes lowered. She curtseyed quickly to Georgia and then knelt beside her. Her gaze flicked toward the large sanctuary doors. "Domina, may I take your place?"

Georgia laughed. Imagine, if someone could take her place! A young, fresh girl such as this who did not know the rushed journey to death, or the slower one back to life. A girl who did not ache for a morning's sleep to end with everything as it should be. Georgia shook her head.

"Please, Domina," Elizabeth's voice hinted of urgency. "Sister Thomasine said we will burn. And if the promise is true—"

"If it is true," Georgia said, "I will be needed here for the child. I must perform the baptism."

Mendaline placed oily fingers across Georgia's arm. "Get up, Sister. You must settle this thing." Mendaline finished her point with a hard shove. "I'll not work to birth this child, only to see mother and infant burnt. Go."

Johanna bore down again, raising her head and wheezing. From her cell, Agnes's breath left her with a rattled, echoing gasp.

Georgia stood, but with reluctance. Once again, she found herself thrust back into the world. A world with no end, it seemed, to suffering.

As she stepped out from behind the screens, Brother Benet cleared his throat. "Sister?"

Georgia turned toward him, the soles of her feet tingling. She sweated under her cap. Behind her she could hear Mendaline's voice, "hold … hold …"

Outside, Romsfeld's tinny wailing assaulted her as he called again. "I will not wait. You will submit to me!"

Benet persisted, "Sister Georgia?" He held out the letter, but Georgia did not take it. She wiped her grimy hands together, wafting up a mix of sweet myrrh and childbirth. But it did not matter that she refused to take the letter, for he pointed to the words, ran a finger along the lines, and indicated the seal and signature.

"I have read it, Sister. It is written most plainly. The writ declares as invalid any land given to the prioress now, or at any time. It maintains the property structure of old, that the priory, its land, and holdings belong within the lord's properties."

"No, no." Georgia tucked her hair back into her cap, smearing oil across her forehead as she did so. "We are in proximity only. We are a peculiar. This is an old argument!"

"I know this new lord, Sister. Bishop SeVerde is a formidable man, and rising at court." Benet peered over his shoulder as if expecting to see the lord come charging in. "He holds lands in Suffolk and Darby as well as this new title. You must surrender. Perhaps there is a chance later to appeal your part. But for now, it is all in order."

Romsfeld did indeed, then, have the power to seize them, the land, the prioress, all of it.

Johanna released a short, sharp scream followed by a loud sob from Agnes. A gasp from Mendaline preceded a cry of delight from Alice.

"Ah! Ah! Brightly done, wife!" Pride and relief were unmistakable in Mendaline's voice. "Such a thing you did!"

Elizabeth squealed and clapped her hands. "A girl! A girl, praise Isela, a girl!"

But no baby's cry followed her declaration. Soft suctioning sounds followed. Mendaline was likely sucking the film of birth from the baby's nose and mouth, clearing the passages so the child could draw its first breath. For the space of an *Ave Maria*, then another, Georgia, the sisters—the folk in the church—all were silent, listening only for that first cry.

Oh, let it cry! Georgia felt her own fear and joy together, and the result seemed to force time backward. She could not even breathe so that her fingers and toes began to tingle and throb. The suction sounds continued. Johanna mewed, a sound of depletion, exhaustion.

The church stayed silent.

Then, a piteous wail—a croaking protestation worthy of Agnes herself. A wail that proved the child not only lived, but had the strength to complain as well. The church breathed at last, with even the lambs and goats bleating.

Elizabeth laughed. "Oh! She's perfect!"

As the child cried, Georgia would have cheered! But from outside, Romsfeld knew nothing. The tone of his voice told only of his distaste for being ignored, and he roared his indignation. "You will surrender the whore Georgia to me, or see the coals of this church!"

Saint Lucy, let Romsfeld be satisfied! The babe was born! She must perform the baptism. She pushed between the screens, one hand steadying the relic at her breast, the other grasping the pouch of salt she had stored under her kyrtle. The baby lay under a blanket. Mendaline placed the afterbirth into a basin, a final proof the deed was done.

"A girl," Mendaline said.

Johanna reached for her baby as Alice piled up fresh straw. Mendaline helped the new mother support the infant, for Johanna's arms shook with prolonged effort and exhaustion. But though she was weak, the new mother poked a finger into the blanket to see her daughter, to smooth her cheeks, and wipe away some of the blood and residue of birth.

Romsfeld's great petulance grated against everything. "I offer no further warnings!"

Georgia snatched at the bowl of water to begin the baptism, but Mendaline stopped her.

"Dame Marjorie comes," Mendaline said.

The prioress swept in through the sacristy and across the nave, calling to Georgia from across the church. "I've had enough of this. Come, Sister. We will speak plainly. They will know my lord husband's will in this matter."

"No, Dame, you will be seized!" Georgia stifled her urgency. The baby lay unbaptized in Johanna's arms. Romsfeld threatened at the door. And now Dame Marjorie readied to throw herself on the mercies of Romsfeld and the sheriff.

In the crux of it, Georgia's voice wavered. She put her hand to her throat and felt ashamed.

From her cell, Agnes wept inconsolably, though Sister Thomasine, likely bolstered by the happy outcome of the birth, reached in through the cell opening to shake her. "Oh, for pity's sake, Agnes! I'll have the end of all this shrieking."

Johanna relaxed against the straw, succumbing to her exhaustion. Georgia leaned in and scooped the baby up.

The babe stirred in the blankets, her little face bruised blue and purple. A tiny thumb poked up under her chin as she opened her mouth and rooted against the rough folds of the wool against to her cheek.

Georgia unwrapped the blanket enough to draw out the baby's tiny fist. A mottled circle blazed from the miniature palm: the mark of Isela. The same mark Georgia herself bore.

This child was the Chooser.

Georgia fought to bring the words of baptism to her lips. Long ago prophesied, the day had well and truly come. No word was worthy of it. No uttered charm or prayer could speak the truth of what joy it was that lay swaddled in her arms.

But Romsfeld would not wait. "Burn it."

A trilling of catcalls and taunts rose from the men outside the church, and a corresponding cry of fear went up in the sanctuary. The bowmen drew back their bows.

Georgia clasped the baby to her breast and raised a hand to hold the archers. "Stop! Stop! Open the doors!"

All faces turned to her—Benet and Sister Catherine, Sister Elizabeth, all. Georgia stepped forward as the baby pushed against the blanket with a tiny foot. She threw out her voice in defiance. "Sisters, an anthem! Let us have a song of celebration!"

After a stirring of confusion, Sister Thomasine dictated what anthem they would sing, and Sister Maud drew a recorder and started to play. Maud chose a different anthem than Sister Thomasine had decreed, and at first, both songs went at once.

Sister Thomasine attempted a futile redirection, but Maud completely ignored her. When the other sisters settled on Maud's tune, Thomasine coughed disapprovingly, but then added her vibrant soprano to the song. Benet also joined in, pulling a small finger flute from his belt.

Georgia held the baby close against her. "Open the door."

As the archers removed the barricading benches, Georgia walked a bloody trail to the church doors, the limestone pavers cold through the wet-stiffened leather of her shoes. Sunlight streamed into the church, drawing the breeze with it and the smell of lingering smoke along with the fresh scent of oat straw and moist fallen leaves. A few ravens collected by the door but took flight as the anthem, unleashed, pushed out into the afternoon.

Georgia walked, her hair spiking from her headdress and her skirts heavy and trailing blood. Yet she held the baby solidly against her, its cries lifting into the song.

Romsfeld's horde stilled their hooting as she stepped outside. Wishing for some of Maud's ability to frighten cowards, little boys, and horses, Georgia walked fully out of the church and placed herself at the center of the path.

"Go!" She commanded. "You have a writ, but you have not God's authority. Go, before you lose your souls in your assault."

Romsfeld lost his balance in the saddle, scrabbled for the saddle bar, and almost fell. "Arrest her!" he bellowed.

Georgia lifted the baby in her arms, holding her high in the air. "You cannot touch me. Behold what has come to us this day. Behold the babe! Behold the truth and the miracle that Saint Isela herself has brought to us."

Romsfeld circled his horse around the other men, edging them forward. "Whore! Witch! Surrender yourself ... Arrest her!"

As the sun warmed her, realization seeped in of the truth of what she said—that indeed, in her hands she did hold the babe, the Chooser, and soon the fulfillment of the promise. Nothing could be done to her in the face of this. No fire could touch them. They had divine protection. They had stepped into the cycle of resurgence.

She shouted again with all her voice, her eyes streaming. "Behold, the child!"

Romsfeld brought his horse next to one of the outlaws who stood gaping. The man's torch sputtered, turned to ash, and sprinkled harmlessly onto the dirt. Romsfeld kicked him in the back of the head. "I said burn it!"

Georgia took a few more steps forward, well out now along the center part of the path. The time for baptism had come, but she did not have the bowl or the water she had so carefully purified with the relic. Yet it could not be helped; she would have to make do.

"Child," she said, "I name you Lo. And I baptize you—" The ground moved under Georgia's feet. The soldiers fell forward, and the church and priory swayed—plank, mortar, and stone. Georgia held tighter to the baby as all around, from the trees and rooftops, the birds burst out, squawking, into sudden flight. She plowed on, "—in the name of the Father and of the Son—" Still the ground shook. She raised her voice as the horses reared up; their riders clutched at the reins for fear of being tossed to the ground. "—and the Holy Ghost. Amen."

A loud crack sounded beneath her, followed by a deep and resonant gurgle. Water saturated the center of the path. From under Georgia's feet, the water surged and then erupted into a gushing fountain. The cold, clear water poured up under her skirts and over her head, reaching higher than the roof of the church, splashing and washing the walls and doors. The water washed away the smoke and grime and blood from Georgia's hands, arms, and gown; swept away her headdress; and loosened the untidy rolls of her hair where it tucked over her ears.

The rising torrent lifted the relic from her neck and sent the stone spinning in the sunlight. The bronze work churned in the water, and the light caught the honey color of the glass, reflecting it into creamy golden droplets and showering the glowing water over the child in a perfect and miraculous baptism.

The water pooled in a well around Georgia's legs and sopped outward, inching, full and bright, toward where the men stood now transfixed by the cascading fountain. It spurted and sprayed, washing over a torch that sputtered, then went out. The man who had held it threw it down and jumped away.

He was the first man to break the line. But all was motion after. The raiders stood in awe and fright, or stooped to scoop the water up, as if disbelieving what they saw.

The villagers spilled from the church calling on the saints Wilgefortis, Winifred, Julitta, and others known to bring about miraculous water. "A miracle," they called to each other and reached out to touch it, cupping it into their hands and drinking.

A few of the raiders retreated down the hill as if they now feared the depth of their trespass. The sheriff inclined his head to Georgia and backed his horse away.

All around the battleground, torches lay extinguished and abandoned. The sheriff dismounted to drink from the pool, and those who did not kneel or drink fled.

The water flowed toward Romsfeld, and his mount shied, tossing its head wildly.

Romsfeld drew on the bit so savagely that the palfrey's mouth foamed blood. "This is not the end of it," he vowed. He kicked and turned the horse, almost trampling a man who had yet to budge from staring at the spectacle. Unbalanced and flailing, he cantered away and down the hill.

Georgia stood in the wet as the torrent of the fountain swirled and then calmed, bubbling up from where she stood, gushing over the dust and pebbles and small tufted grasses on the path, ultimately forming a shallow pool of rippling blue.

She watched Romsfeld go. Good riddance. Yes, she would have to deal with the writ and the new lord—this Philip SeVerde. Yet the Chooser was born, and that meant so much more. They must see it through. Or this chance, this hope for resurgence, could be lost.

The pit of her stomach ached. The blessing today had been great, yet the good stood in contrast to the smoking ruins of the valley below. Sister Agnes was right. In the crux of change, the enemy would seek their own opportunity.

Still, for now the victory was theirs. And the blessings bestowed on them as evident as the miracle that brought the baptism. The baby stirred in her arms, and Georgia crooned a song of deliverance. She rocked the child gently, for regardless of what lay ahead, this babe, Lo, was a most precious and amazing gift.

Georgia withdrew a pinch of salt from the pouch in her kyrtle and placed a granule in the child's mouth. The salt completed the baptism. The little soul made a puckering face, opened her eyes, and looked out at the world.

BOOK TWO

CHAPTER 9:
Barking Abbey, Near London, 1529

Philip SeVerde strode across the abbey grounds toward Markham House. The latest rain had saturated the stones of the path so that the crevices floated with bits of black mold and muddy lichen. As Philip walked, he plunged his staff into the cracks of the flagstones to ward away the filth. He found the resounding thwack enormously satisfying. It was power, after all, that proved salvation. Power and fortitude. Philip thwacked the staff again. A man of power was chosen by God.

Philip weighed the staff in his hand. He could crush a man's skull with this crook. It was made of polished hickory with the hooked crosier at the top set with spiking golden thorns. Inside the topmost spike was a thorn from the very crown Christ himself had worn on the cross. He struck out with it, bringing the base down again—*thwack*—sending a wave of mud into the grass and flinging up the black mold. The strike marred the hem of his crimson robes with wet.

Behind him, two menservants hurried to keep up. They carried his white chest between them. It contained his books, his robes, his jewelry, and all his correspondence of late. Some of the letters were infuriating.

One missive was from the king's whore, Anne Boleyn. He remembered their interview. She was a bulging goat-eyed woman wholly unsuited to

BOOK TWO

CHAPTER 9:
Barking Abbey, Near London, 1529

PHILIP SEVERDE STRODE ACROSS THE ABBEY GROUNDS toward Markham House. The latest rain had saturated the stones of the path so that the crevices floated with bits of black mold and muddy lichen. As Philip walked, he plunged his staff into the cracks of the flagstones to ward away the filth. He found the resounding thwack enormously satisfying. It was power, after all, that proved salvation. Power and fortitude. Philip thwacked the staff again. A man of power was chosen by God.

Philip weighed the staff in his hand. He could crush a man's skull with this crook. It was made of polished hickory with the hooked crosier at the top set with spiking golden thorns. Inside the topmost spike was a thorn from the very crown Christ himself had worn on the cross. He struck out with it, bringing the base down again—*thwack*—sending a wave of mud into the grass and flinging up the black mold. The strike marred the hem of his crimson robes with wet.

Behind him, two menservants hurried to keep up. They carried his white chest between them. It contained his books, his robes, his jewelry, and all his correspondence of late. Some of the letters were infuriating.

One missive was from the king's whore, Anne Boleyn. He remembered their interview. She was a bulging goat-eyed woman wholly unsuited to be queen. She had sat there, clutching at her Bible as if it entitled her to something. It was a mistake to teach a woman to read.

Yet Henry VIII must have his divorce, and he, Philip, was just the man to find a way for it. He had employed the perfect new secretary, Thomas Cranmer, to assist with this. Though a bit slow and pondering, Cranmer showed a distinct political acumen. Philip was sure he could be improved.

Markham House was just ahead. At last. Markham was one of many manors of Barking Abbey, and it was home. How long since the last time he had been here, he wondered. Four months perhaps? For when he was not with Henry at court, he was in Flanders, or Paris, or Rome pleading the king's cause. It was Cranmer's job to plead to Rome for Henry's divorce now, and report back. And Philip was glad to be home. Barking Abbey was a joy to return to, even if it was a nunnery. In grandeur it was as magnificent as Cambridge.

Philip ducked under the arch and through the main entry only to come to a full stop outside the door. He did not wait for the servants, who had now lagged an unacceptable distance behind. Instead, he thumped the lintel with the staff, the golden thorn at the top adding another dent to the darkened oak. Where was the chamberlain? He had business to attend to! Except, he realized, that king and crown and court would have to wait. For first, he must deal with his mother.

A chamberlain opened the door and immediately scraped his forehead to the floor in his eagerness to bow. Much better, Philip thought. If only his mother would treat him with the same respect. Still, he vowed, if it took his last breath—or hers—he would see that she confessed the evils she had done.

He pushed through the door, threw off his felted mantle, and strode directly through the hall to his mother's rooms. He entered without knocking. Sins could not be hidden behind closed doors, but must be exposed and burnt clean. The room was a shock to his senses, however, for his mother's chambers were spewing smoke and clammy hot.

Philip marched across the room and cranked open a leaded window. "What maid has stocked the fire with wet logs?" he said, glaring at a splintery chambermaid and the snarling, undecided fire.

His mother sat in a cushioned window seat, her embroidery over her lap. "So, Philip, you are home." She did not look up. "You shall have to endure the smoke, as there is no dry wood to be had. With all this rain, I scarcely imagine Noah had an easier time of it." She pulled a borage blue thread from her embroidery, a fleur-de-lis on white linen. She had signed the corner, as always, "Lady Ellen," her given name, and not with the family crest.

Philip threw himself onto a large upholstered bench. "Must you have a fire, madam? It is June, and warm."

Ellen pressed the needle into the linen and then looked up. She seemed wary, or maybe guilty, Philip thought. It was difficult to tell.

"The stone walls chill me." She clapped her hands together sharply. "Wine! My son is fatigued."

The chambermaid curtsied and disappeared.

"If I am fatigued, madam, then it is only with your stubbornness." Philip smoothed the Italian silk embroidery along the sleeve of his chasuble. His mother's needle was fine plied for altar cloths, but he did not allow her to embroider his own shirts. "I have spoken with your confessor, Friar Brindle. He is unsuitable to remain with you, and I have dismissed him." He had taken care of that little point of duty upon his arrival at Barking. "By now, he has left the abbey."

His mother paused threading the needle to stare at him. "Left the abbey? Of his own choosing?"

"Madam, we spoke of this before—"

"*You* spoke of this before."

"I must impress on you the importance of confession. The friar was not a suitable confessor."

"Why not? Brindle was a priest of Barking, and I want him returned."

"Lady, what need do you have of a priest? Your son is home, now, madam, and he is London's bishop, a powerful man! Surely absolution from a bishop is as tenfold above that of a friar scribe. A hundredfold!"

"My son is a fool to speak as if he were bishop somewhere else when he is right here next to me." She looked up again. "And did I give you leave to sit in my presence? No, I did not."

Philip made no move to get up. "Pray pardon me, madam. Yet let us keep to the matter at hand, for there are many sins of which I know you wish to be absolved."

"If there were, they would be of no concern to you."

"Your obedience before God must be absolute, madam. There is no alternate course."

"Obey God, Philip, or obey you? They may be the same in your mind, but they are not the same to me."

She put her embroidery aside and stood, shaking her gown so that it spread out over her shoes, the rich crimson color rippling as claret funneled into a cup. The color seemed unnecessarily costly, Philip thought. He made a note to check the household accounts.

She began to pace by the fire. "Sending you to the church was a mistake.

I should have sent Almund. He was much more suited and look at him now, struggling—"

"My brother is a fool. Yet, he at least decided his own fate. While I, on the other hand, was of too tender an age to make a choice."

"You were breeched."

"I was only just weaned."

"You were a thoughtful boy. You liked the monks." She turned at the hearth, her dress whirling a cloud of ashes to mix with the smoke from the fire.

"And you, Mother, had better things to do than care for me after father died." She stopped whirling to stare at him, but he looked away. "I hear, madam, that you have been entertaining yourself in London. Holding bawdy reveries at great tables."

"Oh, saints preserve me, Philip. I have a few friends. Why should that pain you so terribly?"

"And, while I was trustingly in Rome, sacrificing myself, pleading for the king's great matter, those same raucous and unseemly persons gathered, here, at Barking Abbey, with vulgar clamor and debauchery."

"I had guests. Of course I did. What should I do here all day long?" She picked up her embroidery and threw it down again. "Should I embroider altar cloths? I am not a nun."

"No, madam, you are a woman, and woman is weak and—"

"Enough, Philip. I am too old for debauchery. I only want company—" A liveried pantler entered with a decanter and two goblets on a silver tray. "Oh, saints be praised, wine." The goblets sparkled white with polish, and the crest of the London Bishopric gleamed from them.

The pantler set the tray carefully onto a raised table. Philip dismissed him with a wave.

"Madam, I insist on acting as your confessor."

Lady Ellen poured wine for herself, filling her cup to the brim. "According to you I am headed straight to hell."

Philip rose and strode to the small table, grasping it so that the second goblet fell onto its side. "Then confess to me so you may be absolved."

"Merciful Mary! What terrible sin have I committed? I bore one child a year for seven years and one child for every two years following. I bore three dead, and five died after. Of the five that lived past breeching, two more were lost to fever."

Philip picked up the fallen goblet and shook it at her. "Your submission, madam. You must confess your sin."

She took a step back, then another. She drank a large mouthful of wine. "I confessed myself to Friar Brindle. He was satisfied."

"But I am not satisfied. Confess yourself to *me*."

"I will not."

Philip poured wine from the decanter and sat down again. He twisted his head, trying to free the knot in his neck. Why did she have no pity for him? No pity for what a child he was when she discarded him, how she left him to the rod, to the monks, the cold edges of the schoolroom. "If you do not confess, I will deny you leave from this place. Nor will I allow you to invite carousers and idle musicians to your bed."

"To my bed!"

"I am your bishop. It was you who gave me to the church—"

"You cannot abuse me like this, Philip, not even me. I am a Tudor."

"My dear madam. You cannot claim a man's name who only busied your mother with a poke. You are no Tudor. You are the illegitimate daughter of a pretty whore."

"How dare you!"

A knock interrupted them, and a manservant entered and bowed. "My lord, His Grace the archbishop of Canterbury awaits you."

"Very well." Philip stood, took up his goblet, and drank all, snapping up the sweet, grainy herbs at the bottom. He watched his mother over the lip of the cup as she worked her fingers along the rosary at her waist.

It was gratifying, at least, that he had managed to make his point. He put the goblet down. He lifted his crook, and as she turned her back to him, made the sign of the cross behind her. "I will not let this matter rest, madam. At issue is more than your salvation, but my salvation, too."

She turned again; her eyes, bright as the light from the open window, cut through a layer of smoke. "You cannot save your soul, Philip, by harrying me."

"We shall see." Philip let the door swing closed behind him.

༄

The door latched with a hard click, and he jabbed his crook into the floor. He remembered when he was small, how he had clung to her. But it had not availed him.

But now he must think of what lay ahead. William Warham, the archbishop of Canterbury, waited for him in his private office. Waited. For *him*.

Warham would be wanting a quiet conference, a chance to rummage through the catastrophe at Blackfriars. It was a catastrophe not only for the king but for Thomas Wolsey and also for the church in England. And now, all Henry's favorites would fall. It was the perfect opportunity.

Philip paused at the door for the space of two paternosters. He was no rushing apprentice; he was the rising man of power in the English church. The trick would be in the manner of crowing, for Warham held the title of Canterbury yet.

Warham stayed seated on a plush, embroidered bench as Philip entered the room. It seemed that Warham looked even older and more haggard than he had just a few weeks before. Even seated, he leaned heavily on his jeweled staff, his gloved hands sliding down over the embedded stones. This, thought Philip, would be easy.

"I fear for England," Philip began smoothly.

Warham nodded.

"I fear the king will overturn God for a divorce borne from lust."

Warham sighed. "Dear Queen Catherine, a woman who is beloved by all of England—"

"And lucky the whore Anne, who is not."

Philip left his crook against the wall and picked up a stool; it was heavier than it looked. And cold. He placed it next to the hearth. He knelt and kissed the archbishop's signet ring and seated himself next to Warham.

"Your Grace, the time has come for us to act."

Warham sighed. "I am not up for it."

Philip clenched his teeth so that the muscles of his jaw ticked. No, Warham, you are not, Philip thought. You will fall as well. "I am ready, Your Grace. I can turn the king for the church, for Rome—even now. Let him have his whore as queen. We will use it. I will make him pay the price. I can build a stronger church!"

"Anne will not last."

"No. Once Henry beds her she will be as all the rest. A man who eats, after all, is sated. Then we will find him a more suited bride."

Warham nodded. "We have to get her to his bed so the business can be done."

"I can do it. But I have needs."

"Needs!" Warham said. "Money you mean."

"You know the cost of endeavors such as these. Heaven's streets are paved with gold, as so must be the way to grace. Carefully paved, mind you. That, or Henry will divide us from Rome for his divorce. No, we must grant it—for a price! Think, Warham. Who will rule after Henry? Do you wish to bow to the brat that may spring from Anne?"

Warham shook his head. "Send to my secretaries then. Let us just finish this thing and be done."

"There is one more thing."

"Enough."

"It is only a favor. Of a personal nature."

"Speak."

"There is a wild nunnery on my lands, in Yorkshire. They are almost as unbridled as the Scots! This group is lax and vain. They withhold rents and tithes, and spurn my authority. I have heard they have appealed to you, and asked you to authenticate a supposed miracle. Do you know of it?"

"That nunnery in Yorkshire? Yes, yes. It is most miraculous, most miraculous. An amazing work of God. I thought to see the fountain myself, and say a blessing."

"It is not so simple, Your Grace. For that is my priory."

Warham looked up. "It belongs to you? I thought it was a peculiar, with its own right—"

"It is a delicate matter. Of some embarrassment. I would be distressed should their lies prove also an embarrassment to you, Your Grace. For there is no miracle. These women live in vicious disobedience. They seek, with this lie, only to prevent me from my entitlements."

"Yet there was a full church to witness it. And the sheriff, too. In times like these, miracles are good for the church. They give the people something marvelous to remind them of God's work."

"The only thing that is marvelous about that priory, Your Grace, is the fleece of their herds that by right belong to me! They have a flock of hundreds, and yet they refuse me any due at all. They hide behind that miracle, Your Grace. A trifling bit of wet is not a miracle."

"How can I declare the water ordinary when all of northern England claims the fountain heals the sick and saves the dying?"

"You must deny them. These nuns are under my care and authority. Their laxity imperils my soul."

"God will not damn you for one wild nunnery, Philip. There are many wild nunneries in the north—"

"But this priory is mine!" Philip clasped his hand into a fist, the bands of his rings resisting him. He rose from the stool and sorted through the papers on his desk, withdrawing a letter and waving it. "My land, Your Grace, mine, granted to me by the king himself. Shall I be ridiculed for this? Shall I be made to suffer? This miracle is nothing more than a plot to keep me from my property." He threw down the letter, came back to the stool, and held his voice steady. "The king is swayed by English Bibles. If we are to win at court, we cannot be seen to give in to superstition and folk fancies. These simple townsfolk see miracles in the waste of pigs and birds. The nunnery is mine. The food they eat belongs to me. The linen on their backs is mine. They must be made to bend!"

"Wolsey has already ruled on this matter."

"Wolsey will soon be gone." Warham was a fool, Philip thought. He lowered his voice to make it smooth and cautious. "Who will pick up the cross for the church after Wolsey? Will you? Will Cramden or Santoa? What of Fisher?" Philip laughed outright. John Fisher had taken Queen Catherine's side all too publicly at Blackfriars. Fisher was finished. "Think, Your Grace, Henry will turn to *me*." Philip held the silence between them.

Warham lowered his head. "Is there not enough trouble with the north without molesting a favorite nunnery? You can rob them of their land without my help, surely."

Philip paused, swallowing. "No, it seems I cannot." Something crawled under his cap. Philip poked a finger under the brim to find it.

Warham hoisted himself up from the bench, leaning heavily on his staff. "Very well, I will declare that there is no miracle." Warham shrugged. He gestured to his man who stepped out of the shadows to help him. "Yet check yourself, Philip. For I am not dead, yet. And neither is Wolsey."

Philip watched him go. His palms sweated, yet he felt power in them. He, SeVerde, was well and truly one of the most powerful men in England. He stood, straight and tall, feeling the weight of his robes across his shoulders. Then, with a twitch, he snatched off his cap and groped for the flea that plagued him.

CHAPTER 10:
Saint Agnes

Georgia ran through another line of tallies, marking the ledger carefully with what supplies remained. It seemed more and more pilgrims came to see the miraculous fountain, and with the pilgrims came the need for food, bedding, and, in the winter, warm clothing. Bread and beer were the most important. They'd exhausted their supply of bread corn months ago and now were buying at market prices. Georgia ordered more fields turned to farmland, but even so, Mendaline guarded the barley sacks to ensure she had plenty on hand for the sick. Luckily, there was still beer in plenty. Sister Thomasine had seen to that, for she refused to work without her measure of it.

Georgia picked up a pouch of coins and weighed it in her hand. Now that she was priaress, money and supplies were her responsibility. The miracle gave them status, and this translated into enough clout to keep SeVerde at bay. But he harangued them constantly and often sent Romsfeld to demand his "due." Though they held out against him, they had been forced to accept a priest at the priory.

Dominus Ufroad was that priest. Nothing had seemed more shocking to the bishops than to hear that Mendaline and Georgia, two *women*, had acted as confessor among the sisters, while nothing seemed more shocking to Georgia than that a man should do it. Men, she had observed, knew little to nothing of women, and certainly not monks and priests. Though Ufroad seemed well intended, still, Georgia kept the relic always hidden under her skirts.

༃

The door banged open, and Sister Thomasine strode in, stopped short, and released a wriggling girl to the floor. The child jumped up and ducked behind her. The quick motion made the girl seem like a sudden damselfly with yellow veil wings fluttering over a blue gown. And now only her bare toes poked out from behind Thomasine's skirts.

"Go on with you, Lo!" Sister Thomasine reached behind her to pull the girl forward. "Make a curtsey for Dame Georgia."

Lo came forward a little. At almost five years old, she was small for her age. Her handfuls of Thomasine's skirts and petticoats served to hide her almost entirely, for her head reached only to Thomasine's belt. Yet the child ate enough. Sister Thomasine spoiled her with sweetmeats and cakes.

Georgia beckoned, but Lo stayed where she was. Why was the girl so hesitant? She seemed happy enough at the priory. She'd lived here since her mother had died of milk fever, and her father had died on the day the raiders had come. No orphan had been so indulged. Lo wanted for nothing, with each sister a mother to the girl in her own way. Lo loved even Maud and Agnes.

And yet, Georgia thought, the child always seemed to answer her own summonses with reluctance. Today she had resorted to bribery.

Georgia closed her ledger and held out an orange. "Look what came from the market today, Lo." The skin had hardened over the winter, but the fruit was heavy and promised to be sweet inside. It had cost her two groats, but it was worth it. She wanted the girl to like her.

Sister Thomasine clucked her tongue disapprovingly. "You're going to reward her with that when it took me a full Mass to find the little wretch? Idle, she was, and hiding in the duck house. I tidied her for you, though I don't expect thanking—"

"Yes, Sister. Thank you." Georgia addressed Lo. "It is difficult for you when all the pilgrims come to see the miracle, is it not?"

Thomasine snorted. "Saint Blase! That fountain better work a miracle or two, for the blessing of the throats seems to have been as useless this year as an extra tail on any beast. There hasn't been so much hacking and coughing in any part of England since the last plague—" Thomasine gasped for breath and crossed herself. "When the good Son turned the demons into swine, they at least had the decency to run straight off a cliff—"

"Peace, Sister." Georgia rose from her seat, keeping the orange in front of her and watching Lo. "Sister Mendaline will heal the pilgrims who come to us, and Sister Beatrice, though she is new to us, has aptitude and will learn quickly to assist her. That will ease the burden." She smiled at Lo, a smile she hoped would make her seem utterly harmless. Motherly, even.

Sister Thomasine took another full breath and continued on. "Perhaps that is so, but if you ask me that great pack of pilgrims won't shove off until they have nibbled away the garden and harvest both. I had to send to Bilsdale for extra bread every day since Saint Anne's. There's no keeping it. Dame Marjorie—God rest her soul—she would have laid in more cider, and kept a few more pigs—"

Georgia interrupted, "Dame Marjorie had the benefit of running a busy earl's household before she came to Saint Isela's. Now she has passed on. I am prioress."

Sister Thomasine gave a quick curtsey. "Yes, Dame. I meant no … it's just that the bread is out again, and I will be the one to find more of it—"

"They come for the water. It is a good work to feed them." Georgia thought of how Lo hid from the pilgrims and their outstretched hands. "They want to touch you, do they not? It is a trial for you."

Lo thrust her hands deep inside her apron pocket.

"Go on now, Lo," Sister Thomasine swatted Lo forward with a great swipe of her hand. "You are a great big girl! Curtsey for Dame Georgia. She'll think you haven't been taught proper." Lo stepped forward, and Sister Thomasine nodded in approval. "Now then, I'm off. I have a kitchen to manage." Thomasine bobbed a "by your leave" and let the door bang shut behind her.

Lo fiddled with the points on her sleeves and stood with one foot over the top of the other. "The lambs are all growed up," she said finally.

Georgia laughed remembering the spring lambs. Every day Lo had taken them into her lap, soothing their bleatings and allowing them to suck her fingers. When they had grown enough to go into the pasture, she had trailed after them, worried for each of them and some accidental trouble.

"You like oranges?" Georgia asked, though she knew the answer.

Lo nodded and curtsied.

Georgia drew the girl to the small altar near the hearth and knelt on a pillow. "There, then. This one is just for you." She let the orange tumble from her fingers into the child's apron. The orange landed inside the pocket with a plop, and a sharp, alarmed peeping followed. Lo cupped her hands over it and squeezed her eyes tightly shut.

The peeping continued.

"What have you got in there?" Georgia scooted the girl's fingers aside and drew out a sleepy ball of fluff. A duckling.

The pressure between Georgia's brows eased somewhat. Here was just a normal girl, a child to love lambs and colts and babies of all kinds. Why did this always seem to be so difficult? Surely it did not need to be.

As she smoothed the down on the duckling's head, she gave another smile; this one felt more genuine, even indulgent. "The lambs have grown, but I see there are ducklings," she said.

Lo's gaze stayed on the duckling until Georgia returned it to her pocket. It peeped again before nestling down next to the orange and back to sleep.

Lo cupped her hands over it again. "They follow the mother duck."

"Yes. As I follow Saint Isela." Georgia opened and upturned her hand so that the mark on her palm stretched out and up. She rubbed her finger over the circle of it. "I want to finish the story of the mark, Lo. But first you must kneel by me."

Lo sank into the prayer cushion. She was pale and looked so small. Too small. It would be better to have her grow quickly and strong, Georgia thought. For there was no way to know what life would ask of her. Not all lifetimes were kind.

"I will finish the story, but it is sacred, even more than a prayer. You must be careful if you speak of it after I have told you. If it is spoken without prayer, it will diminish."

Lo pouted as if to form a question.

"Diminish means to get smaller, Lo," Georgia said. "You wouldn't want to get smaller, would you?"

"Oh, no," Lo declared, her manner suddenly stout. "Sister Thomasine says I'm taller than a goose. Before, I was only taller than chickens."

"Exactly. The story doesn't want to get smaller either."

"Oh," Lo seemed to think about this as the duckling peeped again. "It wants to be as tall as a goose, too." She brightened and opened her hand to stare at her own mark. It rose like a raspberry circle from her palm.

Georgia held her hand out next to Lo's. "You remember what this mark is?"

"The mark of Isela."

"Correct. And do you remember our lessons about Saint Isela?"

Lo clasped her hands together, reciting. "Saint Isela is the beautiful lady who was born when women wore their hair down around their ankles and ran in the wind." She looked up shyly then back to her recital. "Saint Isela was so beautiful, all the men from all the world wanted to marry her. The men built castles to make her their queen. But she couldn't be a queen in a castle, so she ran away. The men fought each other like the king of England. They said they would take her whether she would or will. They tried to snatch her up. And they pulled out her hair."

"Yes, they said if she would not be a queen, then she must be a slave. What did Isela do then, Lo?"

"She died because she couldn't be a slave." She opened and closed her fist. "And she made my mark."

"And mine too."

Again the girl smiled. For a few heartbeats, Georgia felt the pleasure of a shared connection.

"Now I will tell you the rest. Saint Isela fled from the men who chased her and the banners they carried and the weapons they made. She ran all the way to the highest mountain, a mountain that stood higher than all the castles in the world.

"The mountain spewed light and earth up into the heavens. The sky sent fire back down onto the earth, felling all the men who tried to catch her. But it also felled all the villages on the mountain. This was a great sorrow because it was in these villages that the first people were born and lived."

Georgia blinked at the memory; then, licking her lips, she pressed forward again.

"As she ran, blisters rose on Isela's feet and burst open. Blood flowed behind her as brilliant as the fire. And because the world's kings did not relent, soon, all was destroyed, even Isela. But when Isela's blood poured out and joined the golden fire, the two together made a perfect red gold stone.

"There was only one person from those first villages left alive. A girl, older than you. The girl snatched up the golden stone. How it burned! But she wanted to remember."

Georgia shuddered but kept on.

"That girl lived. She could hear Isela speaking when she prayed. In her dreams, Isela spoke to her and said, 'You must bear it, for one of us must. And you are strong.'"

Lo reached out and touched the mark on Georgia's palm. "She got burnt on her hand?"

"Yes. And that's what made the mark." Georgia traced her scar with her fingertip, following where Lo had touched her. "And there were only two who were marked thus. The Bearer, who is me, and the Chooser, who is you."

Lo opened her own palm and stared at it, blinking once or twice. "What if I don't want to be the Chooser?"

Georgia shrugged. "It's just a thing that is."

Lo blinked again. "Will it hurt?"

"Maybe."

"Will the mountain set fire?"

"I hope not." Georgia clasped her hand together with Lo's. "But I will always be there, Lo, to protect you, to do whatever I can that needs to be done."

"You will stay with me?"

"Yes. Always. Will you pray with me?"

The girl stroked the duckling through her pocket and nodded.

Georgia laughed, "Do you like to pray?"

Lo wrinkled her nose. "Dominus Ufroad doesn't like ducks. Saint Christina the Astonishing would run away." She threw her arms out to her sides. "But I like to pray with Sister Agnes. She screams—" Lo demonstrated with a high pitch, "high."

"In fact, I think prayer with Sister Agnes is a good idea. You shall do so. But, there is something else for today."

Georgia unwound the silver chain from beneath her overskirt and drew Saint Isela's relic out. The lights danced from the candles and reflected from the scrollwork onto the walls.

Lo gave the relic a look of terror and thrust her hands into her pocket. The duckling peeped in alarm.

"Lo?" The girl's reaction surprised her, and Georgia felt a small knot at the back of her neck. "Child, are you afraid?"

Lo shook her head. Her buttercup veil fluttered, the amber lights of the relic dancing beneath it.

"I understand. It has a power that can be hard to bear. Have you dreamed?"

Lo nodded and then whispered, her round face dimpled with guilt and shadow. "In my dream, it—it goes away."

A shiver launched the full length of Georgia's back and buried itself into the knot at the base of her skull. "It goes—*away*?"

∽

A splintering knock on the door made them both jump. Without waiting for leave, Sister Elizabeth burst through the door, flinging it wide where it bounced resoundingly against the chest from Candlemas that held the blessed candles. They had more holy candles than they would need for all the thunderstorms in Christendom. That much, at least, Dominus Ufroad had been good for.

Elizabeth ushered herself in; her face flushed red. "A letter—Dame Georgia." She remembered, finally, to curtsey. "Sister Thomasine said to fetch it to you with all haste. It's a letter from Canterbury, Dame. Canterbury! It will surely be the final proof needed for the miracle, will it not? Thomasine said it is surely so. Sister Thomasine said we will all now be safe."

"From Canterbury?" Georgia tucked the relic away and examined the letter. She must send a runner for Benet; he would read it. In this matter, at least, Catherine's monk, Brother Benet, had proved a valiant ally. Benet not only read their letters but also composed missives to the bishops on their behalf. He had also been teaching those who were willing to read. "Good to balance sin," Mendaline had called their dependence on him. They needed Benet's flair with words and skill in diplomacy. He insisted, for example, that they send out costly gifts to secure the favor of the men of rank, the bishops and otherwise, that they petitioned. "Sister Elizabeth, tell me. Does Catherine see her monk tonight?"

Elizabeth's eyes flicked to Lo. "Dame—he—he is here."

"La! Then fetch him, Sister. Quickly."

Elizabeth flushed. "He is—they are ... pray you, Dame ... Sister Thomasine said—"

Georgia held up a hand for silence. "I can well imagine what Sister Thomasine said."

She turned the letter over in her hands. It felt light. With authentication from Canterbury, they could continue to defend themselves from SeVerde. The miracle was power. Georgia slid her finger under the red wax seal and opened it. The script uncurled hard-point lines with thick curved ascenders rising over set letters, the ornate hand of a well-paid scribe. Why, she wondered, were letters always composed in Latin? And in tiny, incomprehensible lettering? Though, on further investigation, the elaborate curls seemed familiar. Georgia almost cried out loud as she realized the letter was written not in Latin, but in English. She could read it.

She scanned the words, leaping past the salutation, and dug into the first line of text. "*It has come to us that our beloved daughters in Christ—*"

The church bells rang for evening prayers. The sound cascaded in a great ring through the priory.

Impatience vexed her. A call to vespers, and a full service. Though today was the feast day of no one in particular, and despite having endured his company for the feasts of Saint Mary Magdalene and Saint James the Apostle, Dominus Ufroad had stayed on. Yesterday, he expounded for hours about Saint John of Egypt, a saint who spent years of his life tending to a dead stick as if it were alive—and it was not even Saint John of Egypt's day!

Perhaps, Georgia thought, if this John had consulted a woman of any sense, she would have shown him how to nurture something living, a cutting or a shoot, and help it to grow.

Georgia motioned for Elizabeth to go ahead to the church and take Lo with her. As the bells pealed into echoes, she turned back to the letter. She picked out phrases, discarding the decorative and searching for the substance, "*tithes, rents, lands, houses, meadows, pastures, rights,*" "*in perpetuity,*" "*to make clearly known,*" "*improper authorization,*" and the worst phrase of all, "*no miracle has taken place.*"

She read the last sentences over and over again, but there was no mistake. The archbishop of Canterbury, the highest arbiter of religious law in England, had declared the miracle invalid and the water merely ordinary.

Georgia put the letter down. She doubled over as if she had been struck. Their miracle had protected them. Now things would be more difficult. God must not look away. He must not!

She picked the letter up, picked off the red wax seal, and threw it down, crushing it with her heel. If SeVerde thought to defeat them, he would find it a sore trial. If she had to fight him tooth and claw, she would do just that.

CHAPTER 11:
Barking Abbey, Markham Manor, England, 1533

Philip swung his crook furiously right then left, and then turning, fumed the full length of the room. He sweated profusely; the muggy late summer heat combined with an anger that seemed to burn over his skin. But it wasn't *he* who should feel the fire of the stake, but that panderer, that betrayer, his backstabbing secretary Thomas Cranmer.

Philip charged across the room again, this time to the library alcove where a monk copyist worked in the carrel over a set of letters to be sent. Philip's new secretary, Dominus Fenne, stood next to him, heating sealing wax.

"Cranmer is an ass!" Philip swung the crook, smashing the crosier into the breastbeam over the fireplace.

"His elevation was unexpected, Your Grace."

"Unexpected? Christ's blood!" How had he missed the intrigue? Cranmer! Plodder, nodder, panderer—and now the archbishop of Canterbury! "By his wounds! He's married. Married! *Twice*!" Philip turned on his heel and marched to the fire and back again. Marriage marked the ignoramus and the country priest. Ambitious churchmen did not marry. The archbishop of Canterbury did not marry!

The usurper! The nerves pinched inside his knuckles. "That title should be mine!"

But it was not he, the deserving man, but Thomas Cranmer who was now the supreme clergyman in England. All for the price of King Henry's illegal divorce and a quiet wedding to Anne Boleyn. Leave it to a Cranmer who was secretly married to have no moral qualm about secretly marrying anyone else!

"And worse, Queen Anne is with child." Philip squeezed the word "queen" out from between his teeth as if it were a strand of mucus.

"I heard the celebration bells, Your Grace."

Philip resumed his pacing. "Did they have to proclaim it from every church tower in England?"

"They say a boy is assured."

"They do, do they?" Philip charged back along the length of the room. "Let us hope it is not." If it is a boy, thought Philip, Cranmer will seem justified. If it is a boy, then he, Philip, would never ever have a hope of rising to his rightful place.

Philip lowered his forehead to the four-paneled window on the far wall. The breeze from an open panel felt cooling, at least on his neck. Philip leaned against it. He needed to clear his thinking.

"By the devil!" Philip jumped back as a swarm of insects dove through the window and circled him. "Fenne!" he said, stamping. Pulling off his cap, he swatted at the insects as they crawled along the buttons of his cassock. A sting seared his wrist. "S'wounds!" He flung his arm out, crushing the insects against the wall.

Fenne shut the window and swatted at the remainder of the bees with open hands. His sleeves flapping, he caught the edge of the table, overturning a goblet that then clattered into the rushes on the floor.

"Enough! Enough!" The mess at his wrist stained the white lace there. Philip dabbed at it with his sash, turned, and found himself face to face with John Fisher, bishop of Rochester.

John Fisher, the clergyman with the highest moral reputation in England, peered at the lace of Philip's glove and at the rising welt. Damn him.

"The bees are everywhere," Fisher said, making the sign of the cross and retreating. "An apprentice keeper, it seems, was careless with the hives."

Philip shook his arm as the cold fire of the sting burned between the sinews to the elbow. John Fisher, the man who in his uprightness and morality had stood with good Queen Catherine to please Rome. What had it earned him? Nothing. Not even a place in heaven was assured.

His calm was irritating.

Philip turned away from him, lifting the hem of his robes to pass over the spilled wine, his cassock cut shorter in the new way, away from the excesses of fallen men like Wolsey. That concession, too, had earned nothing. "No doubt you have come to crow at my disgrace," Philip said. The sting at his wrist sharpened its throbbing.

"Disgrace? You have not been named to Canterbury. This is true. But think, you have been made archbishop of York," Fisher said. "A powerful post."

"Mock me, then."

Fisher pressed his hands together at the fingertips. "I have not come to mock you. Only a madman would rage at the honor of being named archbishop of York—though I confess I feared that madman might be you." Fisher paused and then continued. "I thought you would need a councilor today. That is all."

"So you come to comfort me? My thanks to discarded Queen Catherine's great champion. You could not be more dangerous if you charged me with a lance."

"I speak no treason. Henry and Catherine's marriage is legal and proper before God."

"King Henry and Pope Clement ignore you."

"The pope, I fear, does not know how great the danger is to the church in England."

"You might write to him again." Philip gave a sharp laugh. "You are more likely to feel Henry's ax than Clement's gratitude. It is treason now to hold any allegiance above the king. Even an allegiance to the pope."

"I am not afraid for my life. I have my assurance in God to guide me."

Philip noted the plainness of him, the simple raiment, the black, modest shoes, and—Philip knew—a hair shirt beneath the linen one. An English Saint Francis.

"Only power can save your soul, John. Power is the test of God," Philip said. He hammered on the oak door along the longest wall. A thick serving woman curtseyed as she opened it and backed quickly away to allow Philip to enter. The room inside was dark, but with the door swung wide, Philip had command of both rooms at once.

"Make no doubt of it. It is total catastrophe," Philip said.

"Ah," Fisher said, "but Cranmer did what you would not."

"All hail to Queen Anne." Philip felt sick.

"Cranmer gave the king what he wanted. Would you have done the same?"

"I would have found some legal remedy."

"The king waited years for legal remedies. There were none. Catherine is deposed. Her daughter, Princess Mary, a bastard now. Anne's child will be heir to the throne."

"Enough, I cannot stomach it." Philip passed his crook from one hand to another before wheeling through the wide door and into the adjoining room. He halted abruptly over a large, canopied bed. There, under several layers of coverlets, his mother sat embroidering. She wore a simple tunic over a delicate lawn shift.

"And did you know about this, madam? That Queen Anne is to inflict a royal bastard on us all."

"I heard the bells." She pulled thread through her embroidery.

Philip called to Fisher in the other room. "My mother claims she has not been out." Philip moved by her bedside and knelt beside it. "You have not been out, have you mother? You are not well. And you have not confessed."

"I suppose I will just have to live a little longer."

He rose. She was stubborn, but so was he. He had brought her a gift at Michaelmas. Though the bulk of it, he saw, was hidden under a velvet drape.

In two steps, he was around the bed and snatched the drape away to reveal an enormous, looming statue. The stone gargoyle bulged into the room, its mouth open. The foaming rictus featured a split tongue curled around dagger-sized teeth. It had two bulging eyes, one fixed looking up, the other looking straight ahead. The corner of its mouth raised into a smirk. Philip had ordered it placed so that its forward-looking eye trained directly on the bed.

"I intend this to remind you of the peril that you face, madam. The beasts of hell will nibble at your flesh, and the gluttons will devour you."

"Philip, please. I have just eaten."

He turned on the chambermaid. "If I find the statue under drape again, I will have you flogged."

His mother was taken with a fit of coughing.

"Madam, please," he said, changing his tone to one of concern. "Why do you persist in this disobedience? Am I not a worthy son?"

"Philip," she sounded tired, her voice raw. "You have prohibited me from inviting anyone for company."

"Only to keep you from engaging in any sinful act, even by accident."

She returned to her embroidery, cutting a new silk with her teeth. "If you wish me saved, restore Thomas Brindle as my confessor."

"Did you hear that, Fisher? Not since the Jews left Egypt has there been such a plague of Thomases. Thomas Brindle, Thomas Boleyn, Thomas Cranmer, and yet another, Thomas Cromwell. Cromwell stayed with Wolsey after Blackfriars. Yet he is made chancellor of the exchequer!"

The sting on his wrist worsened. Philip stormed back into his rooms and dunked a small cloth into a half-drunk goblet of wine. He pressed it to his aching wrist. "Fenne, have Barking's abbess brought up immediately." He drank the remaining wine, shaking the empty cup at Fisher. "And I must beseech you, John, leave my house. You do me no good here. I must regain the favor I have lost. You must not be seen here again."

"You will not save yourself by siding with the Boleyns."

"The Boleyns? God rot them."

"Your conscience must decide your fate."

"And your virtue will decide yours. The king has claimed the whole supremacy of England, and he has not been struck down. Where is your God now? Go back to your skull and baby's milk, sirrah. To your straw mat. God is not watching you."

"As you wish, then. May the Lord keep you, Philip."

The chamberlain opened the door, and as Fisher stepped out, Fenne returned with the abbess.

"Dame Dorothy, abbess of Barking, Your Grace," Fenne announced her then returned to the papers at the desk.

The abbess curtseyed at the threshold. "Your Grace."

Philip took her arm and pulled her into the next room and right up to the canopied bed. His mother looked strong enough to smirk. "My mother is not well."

"You can be assured of the prayers of the abbey, Your Grace."

"Yes, yes. But she is ill and yet will not confess her sins. Dame Dorothy, do I not act as your confessor?"

The abbess colored a little. "Yes, Your Grace."

"Do not be ashamed for your sin, Dame. A woman cannot contain the flesh as a man is able. Yet am I not diligent in determining your faults? And merciful in granting absolution and assigning penance?"

"Yes, Your Grace is very generous."

"And yet you are so poor a sinner."

"Yes."

"So very poor a sinner."

"Yes, I am a sinner, Your Grace."

Philip kept hold of the abbess's elbow and shook it. "You see, madam. Here is a woman who does not find my service disgusting."

His mother nodded to the abbess. "Please forgive my son, Dame Dorothy. He is most solicitous of my welfare."

"Mother, I am not finished. On another matter, I will have a final word. Dame, my lady mother does not believe Friar Brindle corrupt and unfit to hold office in Barking."

Dame Dorothy looked at the gargoyle then quickly away again. "We thank you, Your Grace, for taking care of our troubles for us, even when we ourselves are not aware of them."

"You are welcome. You see, Mother? Thank you, Dame. You have done well. No doubt you should return to prayer."

The abbess curtseyed. "Yes. And I wish also to offer my congratulations to you, my lord archbishop, on your appointment. I hope you will take Barking Abbey's sincere good wishes with you when you go to York."

His mother laughed. A small laugh, mocking and defiant. Philip felt the fury drive back up. He jumped at her, digging a knee into the feather mattress and pinning her under the blankets.

"You are a menace and a sinful woman. Your sins will go unshriven, and you will take your mocking down with you to hell."

She held still under the tirade, but once he let up, she coughed for a long while. Philip strode out of her chamber and ordered the door closed behind him. Her coughs filtered through the old timbers and into the greater hall.

Philip marched to the smaller privy chamber on the far side but, having gotten there, changed his mind and turned back. He went instead to the alcove and, pushing Fenne aside, rifled through the letters on the desk.

"Where is it? That incompetent steward cannot manage a single nun. What is her name?"

Fenne pulled a letter from the stack. "Dame Georgia, Your Grace."

"Dame Georgia." Philip threw the letter into the fireplace where the trash had accumulated awaiting the first fires of autumn. He imagined the linen paper would burn quickly, the letters blackening, the edges contorting.

"No rent and no reform." He turned to Fenne. "Warham is gone. Wolsey is gone. And I am archbishop only of York." A pain lanced through his eye and down into the back of his neck. He twisted to try to release it. "I will not let what little I have go to the wretched Thomases between them. The king plans to empty England's monasteries and keep the money for himself. But this priory belongs to me. I'll have every ha'penny of it, by God I will.

"I am made archbishop of York, am I? Well, then, I have rights in Yorkshire now. If the wretches will not pay rent, I'll have every single one of them carted away."

Philip threw a new sheet of paper at the monk working at the carrel. "Well, get to it! Inform the abbot of *LeRouge*; he'll be in charge of it. *LeRouge* is in my diocese now. He'll do as I require." He turned away to the privy chamber again. He deserved a little solace.

"And Fenne! Some salve for this pestilence at my wrist. It aches."

CHAPTER 12:
Pilgrims

So far, Georgia had managed to evade Dominus Ufroad's requests that she confess herself to him. She still allowed Mendaline to serve as her confessor, but did not dare speak of it.

But it was Lent, and once a year during Lent even the plowman and the cowherd were expected to confess. To refuse would be to cause trouble she did not need, for while the letter invalidating the miracle had not been the catastrophe she had feared, it had made them vulnerable. Now she had to make concessions. They were forbidden, for example, to go to the markets, to conduct their services, or even to laugh out loud.

Certainly there was no risk of laughing today; instead her skin pricked with irritation. Here she was, forced to kneel next to Dominus Ufroad and say confession. She lowered her head into her hands and whispered the opening word.

"*Benedicite.*"

She waited for him to begin, but he did not. Fine, she thought. Let him gloat, then. She spoke the word again, louder this time. "*Benedicite.*"

Ufroad closed his book. "You are too late."

Too late? Outside the sun was low but still bright. "I have come an hour before vespers. At your summons."

"Dame, I have failed in every way to win your obedience. You reject my counsel, and you are contemptuous of my lessons."

Georgia felt her irritation rise. She endured enough from him without a lecture in addition. "In truth I do not think Saint John of Egypt such an example as you do—"

"Saint John set an example of self-surrender, Dame. You do not find this quality lacking in yourself?"

Self-surrender, how dare he, Georgia thought. Her whole life revolved around surrender. Georgia closed her throat to a retort and forced contrition. She need only endure his presumption for a few *Ave Marias* and a *Credo*.

"I have erred, Dominus," she said. "Yet I am repentant."

"It is too late." Reaching down, he brought a leather bag to his lap and placed the book inside. "Had you but listened, or followed the lessons, perhaps you would have found me worthy of your confidence. I sincerely sought to earn it. But now, what's done is done. My term has ended."

"You mean, you will not hear my confession?"

A village boy darted into the sanctuary and out again. "An abbot! An abbot! An abbot on a donkey!" The boy darted through the pilgrims gathered at the well, men and women, children and the elderly, all the while shouting. The pilgrims stilled their gossip, stoppered their bottles, and, jostling, rose to see better down the path.

"An abbot? Dominus, is this your news?"

Dominus Ulfroad opened his hands as if he had nothing. Shouldering his pack, he stood for a moment and stared at her. "You think me a great fool, I know. Yet perhaps I am not such a fool as you believed."

"But—"

"Dame Georgia!" Sister Elizabeth ran into the church. "Dame Georgia, an abbot comes through Attewater. He sent a runner." Her eyes shone. "Perhaps he has come to see the miracle?"

Georgia rose from kneeling too quickly so that she tread on her underdress. "We must prepare," she said. Many important persons came to the priory for the miraculous water, yet somehow, as she watched Ulfroad pack up and walk away, she did not believe this abbot came for the healing water. "Elizabeth, lock the dorter and the chapter house. If it is water he seeks, he may have it. But I fear it more likely he has come to rob us."

Elizabeth showed surprise, her mouth open. "But why would he—"

She could hear the abbot's party now. Bells rang on trotting horses, and horns blared as Georgia ran out into the courtyard. All around her pilgrims bustled, their faces glowing with excitement. They released a collective "ah" as the abbot crested the path.

Four bald and bareheaded monks accompanied him, two in front and two behind. The abbot rode a donkey, popeyed under him and invisible except for glimpses of hoof, nose, and tail. A large man, the abbot flapped in a milksop cassock puffed at the sleeves and lined with purple silk. As he swayed, he was flailed by ropes of jewelry.

Behind the monks rode the steward Horley Romsfeld with two men-at-arms attending him.

Georgia shook out her black overshirt so that it hung creaseless over her blue underdress, the blue showing now only at the hem. She ran her fingers along the rim of her cap, the embroidery rough on her fingertips. She wanted to be sure it was modest and low across her forehead.

The abbot stopped at the gate, and there was a sudden cessation of riding bells.

"My lord abbot," Georgia dropped into a deep curtsey. Good riddance to Ufroad and the lessons he claimed she could not learn, she thought. She ignored Romsfeld's smirk. "Reverend Father, Your Grace, you have honored us. Pray, allow us to tend your beasts."

The priory grooms assisted the abbot to dismount. He landed heavily and out of breath, offering his hand for Georgia to kiss. She did so, picking out the largest ring.

Romsfeld dismounted also, but caught his foot on a strand of bells, which jangled fiercely as he hopped to free himself. He waved the grooms away.

The abbot swatted a cloud of black flies that settled around his head. "Dame, I am the abbot of *LeRouge*. You must know that I am here at the request of His Grace, Lord Philip SeVerde, the archbishop of York, and your most stern and loving father."

Georgia caught her breath. Had SeVerde been made archbishop of York? An archbishop had tremendous power, too much power. She spun an *Ave Maria* in her head and rose slowly from her curtsey. "My lord abbot, you are our welcome guest, but—"

"Cease!" The abbot pressed his gloved hands together. "There are to be no childish attempts at negotiation. As you cannot know what is best for you, you will find me patient to the last. Still, I have been well warned of the trouble here, and I am well read and well prepared to deal in the affairs of women. It is our illustrious Saint Chrysostom himself who tells us women must show their submission through silence. And so it must be. You, all of you, will submit to the rule."

"We follow our own rule, here, Reverend Father. We are not Benedictine nuns, but a community of lay sisters. We are unprofessed."

"Not professed!"

"We follow the teachings of Saint Isela. These are our own lands. We manage them—"

"How can you manage them if you do not pay rents?"

"We do not pay them because we do not owe them, Reverend Father."

"Nonsense. No more of this. You are to learn the rule. You shall do it, and I shall go home. We must have this understanding immediately between us."

He waved his arm, and the pilgrims drew back along the path. He squinted, scanning the men and women, some in country aprons with their feet bare, most clad in green and blue and russet.

"Where is the dorter?"

Georgia hesitated.

The abbot turned slowly, sizing up the buildings behind the gate. "Ah, that must be the dorter, is it not?" He strode toward it, and his entourage followed, all the bells ringing again.

"Open it," he said.

Georgia gave the knob a hard shake. "It is locked."

The abbot motioned for one of the monks to try the door. Georgia blocked him. "Brother, we are sisters to you. Why do you bring this plague of rules?"

Romsfeld strode up quickly, pushing past the monk and kicking the door hard, striking it near her outstretched arm. The door swung open.

"It is not locked after all," Romsfeld said.

Georgia wedged herself across the door frame. "Yet you cannot go in."

The abbot sighed. "Dame, this is not silence or submission."

Romsfeld crossed his arms against his chest. He was dressed exceptionally well, in more colors than one might find in a dyer's shop. A long plumed feather rose from his cap as if he were a Frenchman.

Georgia adjusted her leverage and glared at him. "Do you plan a game of jousting or do you come in jest? Or are you a maypole, all in ribbons?"

Romsfeld pushed his face into hers. "For your taunts, you will be forced prostrate at the altar."

The abbot pushed Romsfeld away. "Tut, tut. There is hysteria enough to be found in nunneries, without you frightening them. I cannot stomach it." He turned to Georgia. "Dame, you have nothing to fear. We seek only to assist you. But we must deal first with the matter of your possessions. Where are your sisters?"

"Across the courtyard, Your Grace." Georgia pointed behind him, and when he turned, she closed the door and locked it.

The sisters were clustered together with the pilgrims, the two groups together watching the spectacle of the monks and the bells.

The abbot swatted again at the black flies. "These are all the sisters?"

Georgia curtseyed. "Yes, Your Grace."

The abbot rubbed his hands together as if he expected some great prize. Georgia wondered if SeVerde had bribed him with tales of the riches to be had from them.

"Praise heaven," the abbot called out, "for the time has come for your reform. Do not be nervous or hysterical. You will not be helped by wailing. First, you must surrender all possessions—" He stopped midsentence and eyed the dorter. "Dame? Did you close the door?"

"Yes, my lord." Georgia curtseyed, making a show of searching her belt and purse. "Yet I seem to have misplaced the key—"

The abbot snapped his fingers at a squat monk who stepped forward. "Brother, you will see to this. Pry the door open if you have to. And remember, however desirable, all women are as poisonous animals. As Eve tempted Adam, so may your trial here be."

The abbot turned to Georgia. "Now, Prioress, take me to your ledgers. I will need to see all receipts, rental lists, and income. All records and tallies. And you will surrender the priory seal to me."

Just a week before, the Italian wool buyers had come through Yorkshire. Georgia had gotten a considerable advance in coin from them, for they had ordered most of their wool. If the abbot knew of it, and if SeVerde knew, they would take all of it.

Luckily, there was more than one set of ledgers in the priory. There were the trade receipts, but there were also the tallies of the kitchen expenses.

Georgia curtsied. "To the kitchens, then, my lord abbot."

She led the way. Sister Thomasine followed her, and Romsfeld skulked behind them.

The kitchen lay just down the path across from the lower end of the dorter and stretched further past the refectory and almost to the brewery. Inside it, two corner ovens wrinkled the air with heat. At a worktable, a basket of fresh loaves poked up from under a drape of linen.

The abbot plucked a loaf from the basket and, tearing it open, stuffed handfuls of the soft center into his mouth.

"The ledgers, my lord?" Romsfeld prompted. He opened a corner chest. Inside, myriad utensils clanged together, bronze, iron, and tin.

The abbot shoved another chunk of bread into his mouth, speaking as he chewed. "Our good Saint Benedict exhorted his fellows to eat, good sir," he waved a hand at Romsfeld in dismissal. "You can go now. Count the sheep."

Romsfeld bowed but hovered near the storeroom. He took a handful of honey cakes and crammed one whole into his mouth, the sticky grains beading on his moustache.

The abbot rested his gaze back on Georgia, speaking around a mouthful of bread. "Tell me, nun. Where is your kitchener?"

Sister Thomasine drew herself up, but Georgia leapt in front of her. "Sister

Thomasine, my lord abbot, is our kitchener. Yet, she is but a half-wit, Your Grace. I am sorry to say it."

The abbot stalled his chewing in midbite.

Georgia twitched as Sister Thomasine poked her hard in the back. Thomasine then gave a lurching curtsey and laughed like a lunatic. She took up a loaf of bread and wiped her nose with it.

The abbot recoiled and threw the rest of his loaf down onto the table. Romsfeld spat his mouthful of cake to the floor. He turned and marched out.

Georgia gathered the kitchen ledgers and laid them out. As the abbot flipped pages, he spat breadcrumbs over each page. He wagged his fingers along serpentine columns. "What are these, here?"

Georgia leaned over the books. Over the years, the sisters had developed their own script. She knew it well, but feigned confusion. "Those are feast days, my lord abbot."

"Feast days? What then are these together?"

"Notations."

"Yes, I can see they are notations. But notations of what, pray?"

Georgia pretended to misunderstand. "Saints." She cocked her head to the side and spoke slowly. "Those whose feast days they are."

The abbot spat more copiously. "What, then, are these? Surely not saints. And these, are these not tallies of some kind?"

"In truth, my lord, I am not sure," Georgia crossed herself, for she lied. It was necessary, however, even though it was a sin.

The abbot began to huff and sigh loudly. "This is what comes from allowing women and fools to keep tallies—"

Georgia threw a quick look to Sister Thomasine, urging restraint. Then, as if speaking to the desperately stupid, she interrupted the abbot's rant. "Sister Thomasine is our kitchener, my lord. Did I not mention that she is but a half-wit? You do not believe, my lord abbot, that she is capable of keeping tallies?"

Sister Thomasine picked up a half-worked mortar and ground the pestle with a vengeance. The sea smell of eel and sweet marjoram wafted up. Georgia gave her a look of pleading and continued. "Nor I do not keep the accounts, my lord. That duty is performed by our treasurer."

The abbot looked annoyed. "A treasurer. Pray, why did you not say before? Bring her at once."

"She is Sister Joan, my lord."

"Do I care her name? Bid her come and explain it."

"She is mute, my lord." Georgia made the sign of the cross again.

"Mute."

"Yet you said earlier, my lord abbot, that women should be silent."

"Silent, not mute! And not a treasurer!"

"Surely one does not need to speak to write columns."

The abbot slammed the book closed, and, for good measure, picked it up and slammed it again, sending the smell of ancient grease out in all directions. "How am I to remedy your incompetence?"

"Begging your pardon, but we are prosperous. We provide charity to those who seek us and in addition—"

A shrill scream interrupted, echoing from the courtyard. It was a scream of hurt and fear, and it resounded over the priory. Another scream followed.

"My lord," Georgia curtseyed, turned, and ran to the courtyard. The abbot and Sister Thomasine followed.

Outside the dorter, the squat monk held a red streaked rag to his nose. As Georgia pushed through the crowd, Sister Elizabeth ran to her and grabbed her arm. Her lower lip swollen.

The abbot shoved through the crowd of sisters and pilgrims and examined the monk. He questioned the squat monk and waved his arms in exhortation. "Brothers! Be strong against temptation! These women are but misbegotten men. Saint Thomas has said it! Their beauty is phlegm, and blood, and bile, and rheum, and the fluid of digested food! So says the Father Saint John!" The abbot paused and belched before continuing. "We have been called here to serve as brothers in brotherhood. Guard yourselves. We must deal with this sin."

Mendaline arrived with a cup for Elizabeth to drink. She gave Georgia a look of warning.

Georgia asked in a hard whisper. "He touched her?"

The abbot pointed to Elizabeth. "She has drawn blood from a brother."

Georgia pushed Elizabeth back behind her. "He laid hands on her," she said. "She has the right to defense."

"In this convent of error?" The abbot swung himself around so that the bleeding monk had to duck to avoid being hit by ropes of jewelry. As he stamped, his chains knotted together, and his face grew as red as a pig's bladder.

"Prioress, you shall heed my authority. The offender shall be punished."

Georgia backed up, pushing Elizabeth farther into the crowd. "You'll lay no hand on her."

Romsfeld shoved past the abbot. He bore down on Georgia as if intent to flay a target. She could feel the edge to him and threw out her arms, sinking to a crouch. She grabbed a handful of dirt, prepared to throw it at him, to curse him, to frighten him away.

But he drew his sword and held it at her throat.

"Curse me, and I will carve you from my misery," he said.

Georgia swallowed; the muscles of her cheek twitched.

"Sheath your sword, you bloody fool," the abbot stamped all the more. "Will you frighten them? These women have but the minds of children! They need a firm hand, not a sword."

Romsfeld sneered, and Georgia willed the muscles in her cheek to be still. Romsfeld sheathed his sword and withdrew.

The abbot waved toward Elizabeth. "Now, now. I'll have that one, that one there is the trouble."

Two of the monks advanced. Elizabeth threw down the cup and ducked backward through the throng of pilgrims who made room for her to pass.

Romsfeld bellowed as she ran off. He turned and instead grabbed Sister Catherine, shaking her by her veil. "Then we will start the punishments with this, whom all the village knows for a whore."

Catherine did not wait for the other monks to advance. She twisted hard and elbowed Romsfeld in the gut. He doubled over but did not release her.

Sister Joan jumped in and pummeled him with her fists. "You are the devil's own monster!"

The abbot looked up at her in surprise. "The mute speaks."

"And the half-wit can cook." Sister Thomasine waved the pestle in the air, pulverized eel stuck to the bulb of it. "I am making cockscomb and testicle pie for dinner, lord abbot."

"Nonsense, woman. It is a lean day."

"You are mistaken, Reverend Father," Georgia felt her surety return. "It is a meat day."

Sister Thomasine entered the fight, and the pestle flew in all directions. The men retaliated, grabbing flailing nuns at random. Sister Beatrice ran into the infirmary and bolted the door behind her. A monk grabbed Maud around the waist, and she kicked him in the groin. He dropped to his knees with a pitiful moan.

Catherine broke free from Romsfeld and ran with Mendaline to the infirmary, pounding on the door and screaming for Sister Beatrice to open it. Beatrice peeped through the grate, but seeing men approaching, let out a cry of alarm and promptly sealed the hole again. The door stayed locked.

And then, as the men regrouped, covered in eel and swelling bruises, the villagers, pilgrims, and priory servants took up the nuns' part in fight. With a rising cheer, the multitude pelted the abbot and his monks with rocks and lumps of clay and whatever else, including chunks of dog and goat and horse manure.

Maud loosed the donkey and the horses from the barn, sending them terrified into the fray. They cantered off in all directions.

"Catch the horses, you fools!" Romsfeld yelled to his men-at-arms, but they were in full flight, the sisters and pilgrims chasing them around the priory. The intruders made for the path in retreat. Though he was by far the largest, it was the abbot who fled the fastest. He held his cap to his head as he fled and clasped his cassock at the knee. "A den of wickedness! A house of snakes and dragons!"

The pilgrims called taunts and abuses after them. Georgia stood at the center, her sisters beside her. A great cheer went up as the men retreated.

Romsfeld was the last to go. Though he was covered in dirt and his particolored hose hung torn in several places, he looked remarkably happy, too happy. He ducked a chunk of excrement, but his smile only widened.

"Such disobedience, tut, tut," he said. "You have sealed your fate."

CHAPTER 13:
Barking Abbey, England, 1536

PHILIP TAPPED HIS FINGER AGAINST THE HEARTH stone and watched this latest letter burn. Curse that abbot! It had taken a little over a year to get the man to visit the priory in the first place, and it had cost him a considerable number of plump pheasants and hounds, as well as several barrels of wine in the doing. And now, the abbot flatly refused to speak of what happened or ever speak of the matter again. Even the splendid hawk he sent with his last missive did not loosen the abbot's tongue. Soon, Philip vowed, he would go to *LeRouge* himself and shake that abbot to the ground.

If he could have afforded to leave Henry's side for an instant, he would have gone already. But that had been impossible. Henry VIII lusted after the wealth of the monasteries, and Cromwell was breathing down the necks of every ecclesiastic in England. Always Cromwell wanted to know about money. Philip hadn't even had the chance to spend more than a few weeks at a time in the archbishop's manor at York. It was too important to stay at Henry's side and guard what he could of what belonged to the church—to him.

But now things had come too far. He could not control Cromwell, and he could not hope to count on *LeRouge*. He must go to York himself, and he must get there before Cromwell's men arrived with their chests and money counters.

Philip twisted his knuckles together, entwining his rings. The injustice of it ached. The wretched nun had even shamed him in the Privy Council. Cranmer had pounced on him, accused him of allowing heresy, of denying the viciousness of the old church, of resisting the new doctrine. It was all the worse coming from Cranmer, that traitorous secretary. Cranmer knew how obstinate these women were. He himself had had no luck in reasoning with them.

Yet there was no time for that argument now. Money and power were at stake. Cromwell's reeves crawled with greedy fingers from monastery to monastery. These king's officers would soon be in York. Their goal was to claim all riches for the king. Philip must move quickly. Otherwise, his property would be part of Cromwell's ceaseless inventories, and every fleece, every stalk of grain would be lost to the royal treasury.

He must leave for Yorkshire tonight. The horses were even now saddled and the men ready to ride.

A manservant entered through the heavy door, bowing low at the waist. "The abbess, Dame Dorothy of Barking, wishes to speak with you, Your Grace."

Philip adjusted his purple sash of ecclesiastic office over his black velvet doublet and riding slops. A robe was too cumbersome for riding; tonight he needed speed.

Dame Dorothy curtsied. "Your Grace is set to leave?"

Philip grunted in the affirmative, straightening the weave of his hose. "Yes. For my lands in Yorkshire."

"I have heard a wild tale."

Philip stomped his foot into a riding boot. "Dame, there is much wildness in the world you cannot know, you who are wholly cradled by the cloister." Cranmer's face hung in his mind, the bright, inquisitive eyes of a clean-shaven rat. "I have no time for stories tonight. For you cannot understand my haste, Dame, or the treachery of men."

Her blinking irritated him. He stomped down into the second boot, shoving away the groom who tried to assist him.

"The Lady Ellen ails, Your Grace." She clasped her hands together. "We have begun a vigil."

"That is a kindness, but unnecessary. My lady mother will live to plague me another five years, so I am assured. I have had it from the doctor himself that the stars lie heavily in her favor."

"Five years?" She seemed surprised. "But she cannot rise from her bed."

"She sleeps." Philip tried to ignore her fidgeting. Rosaries were well and good, but not if the beads were ceaselessly ground together.

"I fear she is dying, Your Grace."

"Listen to me, Dame! I ride to my lands, tonight. The parliament has dissolved the monasteries, and all will go to the Crown. I must enforce my claim. I must ride tonight."

Dame Dorothy clattered the rosary as if to break it. "The Act of Suppression has been agreed? The monasteries will be destroyed? What of Barking Abbey?"

"Calm yourself." Philip clapped at the manservant to bring wine. Curse what women tried to understand—knowledge only alarmed them. "Only the smaller priories will be closed. Barking is a large abbey. It will not be harmed."

"For how long?" She spoke over her cup and then drank. The wine stained her upper lip a dark cherry red, and the heat of the drink fattened it. It was a look unbecoming for an abbess; he removed the cup and had it taken away.

"Submission and obeisance are your sureties." Philip grimaced. Rumors circulated unchecked. Pamphleteers inflamed the lawless as they printed broadsheets by the hundreds. No doubt she had come across some scandal in print that had alarmed her.

"But where are they to go?"

"Who?" He tied his silk purse and a silver knife to his belt.

"The nuns, Your Grace."

"They will be sent to larger abbeys, or else home."

"Home." She echoed it. "Barking is my home."

Her lip grew offensively fuller. Attractive nuns should be kept strictly within the cloister to tempt no one with their devices. "Dame, I have no time to give assurances. Those who have erred must pay the penalty for their laxity."

Dominus Fenne came quickly into the room. "Pray pardon, Your Grace," he bowed. "The doctor implores you to come. At your earliest—at once."

The abbess curtseyed. "I must go, Your Grace. I fear the worst."

Philip snatched up his riding cape and gloves from the chair where the manservant had laid them. He imagined Cromwell at the priory, his priory, this instant, herding away the sheep that by rights belonged to him. His steward Romsfeld had counted five hundred head at least. A fortune.

"Whatever it is, I trust you to deal with it, Fenne. Do I not pay you well? Must I always sacrifice everything for others? Of all the things I give and give, can I expect nothing for myself? Nothing!"

Dominus Fenne inclined his head. "It is your lady mother—"

"Yes. And?"

"She is dying, my lord. She asks for you."

He scowled. This was likely yet another trick of Cromwell's, he thought. Yet—she asked for him, did she? Could he refuse? He threw his cape and riding gloves to the floor. "Very well, Fenne. Lead on."

Philip followed down the corridor, and Fenne swept the door open and announced him. "His Grace, Archbishop SeVerde."

The sickroom stank. His mother lay in the bed, which had been moved closer to the hearth. As she coughed, she spat out glistening ropes of blood and phlegm. Sister Anne, a nun of Barking, dipped a yellowed cloth in slime-topped water and bathed the Lady Ellen's face and arms.

The doctor bled her from the neck. A sluggish line of blood oozed into the bowl, dark and oily compared to the bright blood over her chin. When the bowl filled to half, the doctor stopped the wound.

He gestured to Philip to come and lifted the bedclothes. She lay naked on the sheet, the mattress soaked and spotted, her feet black against the linen with blackening threads spread upward along her legs. Her hands, as well, had darkened blue, with the nails darker.

The doctor spoke through a cloth held over his nose and mouth. "Her condition is greatly worsened. Too many humors lie heavily on her—the phlegm wants heat, and she tended over much toward the sanguine. But too much heat has caused putrefaction of the lungs. I could not predict it." He replaced the coverings and drew a piece of paper from his bag, on it a jumble of astrological notations.

"The marks predict death, Your Grace."

The stone gargoyle, too, seemed to predict death. The statue extended a snarl from the center of the room under the canopy and toward the center of the bed. In the firelight, it seemed to flick its tongue.

Philip found he had to clear his throat before he could speak. "She asked for me?"

"Yes."

Lady Ellen coughed again, a slight, wheezing rattle in her throat.

Philip felt a panic. It had never been his intent for her to die without confession. Yet it was brutally inconvenient of her to turn so quickly for the worst even as the horses waited in the courtyard.

He watched the gargoyle, and the cold of death frightened him. And the torments of hell.

She stirred. He knelt beside her, "I am here, madam."

"Philip," the sound moved slowly over her lips. She seemed surprised. "You have stayed by the bed."

He willed his voice to stern chastisement, but the result sounded more like pleading. "Now is the time for obedience. Your soul rests on the very cusp of peril."

"You are a good son," she smiled. "You had yellow hair as a boy. Do you remember? Your father's hair was fair, but alas, your hair reddened. You look like a Tudor, now."

She resumed her coughing. Philip waved the sister aside and took the cloth himself to clean her chin and mouth. Her teeth had darkened and her eyes yellowed.

"Madam, upon my soul I cannot bear it. That you should damn yourself out of pure willfulness. You will damn me, also, in this."

"My son. In truth, I do not wish to pass from this world unconfessed."

At last. It was as if a terrible weight flew from him. "I will hear you."

"*Benedicite*," she began. She recalled things remembered and regretted, confessed her weaknesses, and spilled her disappointments. She had lusted; she had not honored lean days as she should; she had made merry during Corpus Cristi; she had secretly wished her husband dead and dreamed of poisoning him; she had wished to play the lute in the market place; and on three different occasions, she had spied on younger men, taking one of them to bed. Also, she had held anger in her heart toward her husband. For all that, she felt remorse and wished forgiveness.

She exhaled, and silence again settled in the sickroom, a silence broken only by the murmured prayers of the nuns in vigil near the bed.

Philip waited as the nuns crooned *Ave Marias* in unison, and then a *Paternoster*, and more *Aves*. He squeezed her hand, afraid she had slipped away before she had finished. He poked her ribs gently, and she coughed, a terrible grinding cough after which she closed her eyes.

Philip prompted her. "You must confess all."

She furrowed her brow, rolling her eyes under translucent lids but not opening them. "I cannot remember other sins. Please forgive me for what I cannot remember."

Philip gripped her hand tighter. It felt cold and inhuman. "But you must remember. You cannot speak only to stop before confessing those things which most condemn you."

She swallowed carefully. "I am tired. Perhaps you could remind me."

Philip threw her hand away from his. She jolted at the force of it, the wound at her neck resuming its ooze, and blood smeared across the embroidered bedclothes. The doctor laid a swath of linen across it and swaddled the cloth around her neck.

His mouth tasted dry as smoke. "Mother, you must speak of your own guilt. Absolution is for the repentant." He stood up. Distance, hate, love, the stink of the sickroom—it pushed balance out from under him.

Dominus Fenne touched his elbow. "The lady confessed, Your Grace. She is repentant."

"She is not."

"She must be absolved. It will be too late."

"She did not confess the matter most pressing!" Philip shivered as cold ate through him. A clamor built up from his gut, from under his ribs. He could not sustain control of it. He roared as he had once seen a wounded bear roar, with a pack of hounds at its throat. "She did not confess what she has done to *me*. I, who have succored her to the last. I, who have suffered at her hand."

A woman's voice wavered up from the bed, a woman's voice thin and hissing. A venomous asp.

"Philip, my son. You have suffered, and for that I am sorry. But you must understand, I was not free to choose what I would do. Mothers do not hold their sons, but must give them up to nurses and then to men. And I was young. I let them tell me what I was."

Philip tried to breathe through a shadow that seemed to suffocate him. Fenne hovered just beside him, an annoyance. The abbess and nuns watched; their prayer ceased. They were waiting perhaps.

Philip stepped back.

She pitched in her bed. A spasm bent her backward, holding the muscles of her face in a rigid grimace. In the candlelight, the gargoyle's shadow danced over her. When the spasm lifted, the shadow was gone.

For a moment there was a radiance, such as he remembered of her, in her youth, when he had longed for her. Then life released her. Her breath seeped out from her body, and a final bloody vomit drained from her nostrils as her eyes rolled back. Her hands twitched, then lay still.

Philip's stomach sickened. His body burst into heat with sweat following. He had not absolved her. She would never be absolved. She had died denying him.

Fenne pushed next to him. Hastily, the priest drew the cross from around his neck, spoke words of absolution, and began the last rites. The nuns pleaded to Saint Mary to speak for the lady before God, that he might spare her soul some of the torments of purgatory.

Philip fled backward from the room. His anger drove him back. He closed his ears to the chants of the nuns and the low murmur of the priest. The woman's soul was damned. And he, too, was cursed by her sin, unspoken and unpurged.

Philip bolted through the door and swept out into the hall. He would ride; he would ride. He would salvage what was left.

༄

He retrieved his riding gloves and cape and strode quickly outside along the outer corridor. A young man rounded the corner ahead, and there, on the precipice of his escape, Philip had to pull up short to prevent colliding with him.

"Make way, you fool!" Philip bellowed. The offense laid insult to his torments, and Philip drew a hand to strike him but held. The young man wore royal livery. This messenger, he realized, was a retainer of the king, and a nobleman's son.

The young man bowed. "His Majesty sends word on a matter most urgent." He extended a scroll pressed red with the king's seal.

It was a summons, and Philip opened the letter where he stood. The request was clear enough. The king had called him to his service. Yet again, the priory would have to wait.

He would ride today, yes, but not for Yorkshire. Rebellion flared in the north. Without haste or delay, Philip was to lead a southern army north to Hull, there to join with Lord Norfolk whose army was already on the march. In Hull, they were to quell a cotters' rebellion, a so-called Pilgrimage of Grace, an army of rabble—cotters, smiths and apprentices, petty merchants, tanners, goatherds, and all other wretches who could take a pitchfork to war. The rabble marched under none other than the abbot of *LeRouge*, the abbot who would not budge, the abbot who had fed on Philip's pheasant. The abbot who had refused to reform a tiny, sullen nunnery.

There was a single advantage. In this at least he could trump Cranmer. He would prove his loyalty. He could bring force to bear and carve a new order. He could cleanse the soul of England of rabble and rebellion. That insolent nun would answer to him with her flesh, for now he led an army for the king.

CHAPTER 14:
Saint Gertrude

Georgia defied the late autumn heat and fluffed her skirts underneath the table. Saint Bega's day was not usually so warm, and she had been wearing light wool and an extra skirt for two days—and suffering for it.

Neither was she hungry, and she picked at her food. Sister Thomasine sent her glances of disapproval, for it was a good meal, bread and onions soaked in wine, with even a bit of salted eel. But Georgia could not swallow any of it.

When Thomasine wasn't glaring, she gossiped with the rest. Dame Marjorie, the former prioress, had strictly forbade idle talk, but Georgia wished them to develop sisterhood in their own way. With so much of the day spent in the gardens, or prayer, or tending the sick and managing the influx of pilgrims, Georgia found the chatter during the single meal of the day, even lively chatter, important to their mutual affection.

Thomasine glanced at her again, and Georgia forced a bite of onion to please her. She felt her throat tighten against swallowing it and chewed longer than she should. Thomasine did not seem gratified at her effort.

Mendaline leaned over the table, her knife suspended and a slice of eel dripping in her fingers. "What is it?" She poked the eel in her mouth and chewed to one side, a raised eyebrow in Georgia's direction. "Such trouble over onions."

Georgia scooped at the sopped barley bread, this time sucking it. Saturated in a wine broth, it puckered her tongue and tasted pleasantly of salt. But still she could not swallow. Noting that Thomasine now ignored her, she spat the mouthful into her hand and tossed it to one of the roving terriers.

Mendaline acted as though her worst suspicions were confirmed. "You're spitting it out now? That's trouble, then. Talk."

"I am well, Sister. I need to pray in the church tonight. That is all. When the heat is less." Prayer would perhaps reveal something of what to do, although many of her questions seemed to go unanswered lately.

"You in prayer? Forgive me if I don't keel over in shock. No, I'm thinking there is more to it than that. You're as pale as Sister Agnes."

Georgia shook her head. "Carters came through Bilsdale today."

"Oh. We've never seen *that* before." Mendaline stabbed an onion. "Try again."

"Carters from Thicket." Thicket was a nunnery to the north. It had been dissolved by order of the king. The image of the carts piled high with barrels and sacks bothered her. The goods were for the king, of course. In the cart behind came the former sisters of the house. All now homeless. Georgia had spoken with Thicket's prioress as they passed through. The dame told her of the suppression, that the king's reeve had come to tally their belongings and take them away. In a week their money, books, ledgers, even the bells in the church were gone, everything. Some of the sisters were being carted to a large convent in the south; others were simply sent away.

Mendaline waved her knife between them. "You think we're next?"

"The folk of the village will protect us. We are loved here."

"Oh, and north in Thicket the villagers hated those nuns."

"No." Of course that had nothing to do with it. Poor as it was, Thicket had been the center of hospice and alms and education for miles around them.

"You'll think of something," Mendaline stabbed her knife into the salt. "But stop spitting out your food like you were Joan the Meatless. Eat."

"But, Mendaline, I cannot decide what we must do. We cannot escape into the hills. Or perhaps we can. Lo is twelve. She is of age to awaken. And yet she seems to linger in childhood. Yesterday I caught her cradling a piglet. Sister Thomasine had given her a sop to feed it."

"A sop? For a piglet? Just one? That sop would be gone in the time it takes a monk to sin." Mendaline chuckled, spilling the salt she'd collected on the tip of her knife. It scattered in crystals over the tablecloth. "Listen to me. You cannot protect that child from her own fortune. If she is the Chooser, as you say, we cannot ask small questions."

From near the sideboard, Lo and her companion giggled. Pocket was a yeoman's daughter and a year younger than Lo. She had come to Isela's two years previously. Both girls were orphans, and the two had proved immediate companions. No doubt they conspired to steal honey cakes.

Mendaline dipped her knife into the salt again. "You coddle that child. Tell her all the stories you like, but she was put here on this earth to live this life, and I think she has to do it. I knew a mangy old cat once, half blind, a big bald square pink bit of skin stuck straight out the back—" she paused, poking her knife accusingly. "You remind me of that cat. You are pink and all banged up. But you've still got all your teeth." She shoved a chunk of bread across the table. "For Saint Agatha's sake, eat something."

Georgia blinked. Fear rose up again, shadows, regrets. Georgia closed down on it, sealing it in darkness as if stopping a bottle with a cork. "The world is a terrible place, Mendaline." She grasped a slice of eel as if determined she would eat it, but then slid it back into the broth. "I have decided. We will take what we can and flee to the hills. We cannot wait for them to drag us off." She glanced at Lo. "Or worse, separate us. Lo will need me, Mendaline."

Mendaline shrugged, pinched a chunk of wine-sopped bread, popped it in her mouth, and sluiced it between her teeth.

Georgia rose. It was time to lead a prayer to Saint Bega and conclude the meal. She would break the news of their troubles to the sisters in the chapter house where they would go next for their daily meeting. If they wanted to keep as sisters together, they would have to flee.

The prayer concluded, and the sisters filed out of the refectory and clustered along the walk, laughing and teasing one another. Pocket squealed at some fancy and ran ahead into the courtyard and then stopped short. The priory dogs began to bark, and a few ran pell-mell to the courtyard gate.

"Georgia." Mendaline pressed a clammy hand over Georgia's wrist as they entered the courtyard. "Riders at the gate."

A stable groom hurried past.

Georgia turned. These would be pilgrims only; she chided herself for her worry. Though pilgrims came fewer now, some still came for the water. She nodded to the groom who swung the gate open. She stepped up to prepare her greeting but stopped. At the entry stood an officer of the king.

Behind him, ever a sparrow hawk, rode Romsfeld. He dismounted, his knuckles white on the palfrey's mane. Behind him were rows of carters: two large carts hitched to nags and men with handcarts as well. At the very last were two carts lined with straw. For the sisters, no doubt.

"Dame Georgia?" Mendaline whispered, though the sound was more like a hiss.

The reeve stepped forward, efficient in his movements save a twirling mustache and a hand that seemed to swat unbidden at flying insects. He handed the reins of his horse to Romsfeld. Romsfeld's face transformed into a snit of indignation as he shoved the reins at the waiting groom.

Carts! *Mater Dei*. Georgia hurried to the reeve, curtseying deeply. "Good sir, welcome to Saint Isela's Priory." She began to spin wild fancies in her mind. Perhaps he simply needed shelter for the night? Or perhaps this was only a visitation? He would inspect the priory and be on his way. She had heard of those.

The reeve gave a curt bow. "I am here on the business of our Great and Noble Lord, Henry VIII, King of England and of France, and Supreme Head of the English Church." He rocked back on his heels and looked beyond her to where the sisters clustered in the courtyard, their lively gossip now quiet. Quiet, but for a high, bristling wail from Sister Agnes.

The reeve looked up and around with a hint of worry at the sound, but then waved a roll of paper. "I am authorized to read this proclamation from His Majesty the King to the inhabitants of this priory. Pray, conduct me to the chapter house so I may do so."

"Of course," Georgia needed time to think. Something must be done. "Yet, sir, perhaps you have come far and are tired. Perhaps you would first take some refreshment."

"No." He strode past her into the courtyard.

Georgia followed, passing him to lead the way to the chapter house and ushering the sisters inside. Romsfeld planted himself directly outside the door and counted each one of them as they went in, as if to be sure no sister turned aside. As Lo passed, his gaze lingered on her. Color came to his cheeks, and when he did not look away, Lo fidgeted. Georgia stepped between them.

Inside, the sisters sat on the benches against the wall. The reeve took a place on the dais, unfurled the declaration, and gave a long and tedious speech. He would take inventory, he said. All items of value were the property of the Crown and would be carted away. The servants were to be dismissed. The sisters were to be taken south to *LeRouge* Monastery, and from there divided.

When he finished, he extended his hand, palm up. "Prioress, you will surrender the priory seal immediately."

Georgia strained to think. The documents and letters the reeve presented carried the authentication of the king and Thomas Cromwell, Lord Treasurer of England, but he had only waved them at her. He had not given her the chance to look at anything, or even to understand if there was anything that could be done.

"The seal, Dame. Now." The reeve stared at her.

The priory seal was a palm-sized ceramic and bronze ornament that, when pressed into wax, left an authentic imprint unique to their priory. The seal allowed them to transact legal business and trade and so proved their authority and asserted their independence. Without it, neither she nor any of the priory could transact any business, nor make any trade, nor send any official correspondence.

She went slowly to the chest and withdrew it. "Good sir, you must understand. This priory and this land do not belong to the church or to the Crown. It belongs to us. I cannot surrender it."

From behind her, Romsfeld snatched it from her palm, tossed it up, caught it again, and laughed. "Well, that was easily done!"

He gave it to the reeve who took the seal and placed it on the stones of the hearth.

"Good reeve!" Georgia called out as with a cold finality; the reeve raised the fire iron and struck it down, smashing the seal to pieces.

"I now claim the land, chattels, and all properties of this priory, in the name of the king."

He gave a cursory nod, and, beckoning to the man-at-arms in the doorway, kicked the pieces backward into the hearth. "With respect to the known viciousness of the sisters at this priory, they are to be removed immediately."

Georgia swallowed against her panic, working to keep her voice steady and polite. "Forgive me, but you cannot mean that we travel today."

The nuns from Thicket had said the destruction had taken a week. Saint Isela's was larger and far more prosperous. It would take longer to suppress, and in a day or two, they might yet make an escape. Or Lo might yet awaken at the last.

The reeve twirled his hand at the wrist in an idiotic gesture of command. "It is to be done by the order of His Grace the King of England. You may only take what is allowed under the rule."

"Which is nothing, sir," Georgia protested. "Our clothes alone."

"Yes."

Romsfeld stepped in front of her, his eyes glittering. "Do you resist, Dame?"

Georgia opened her mouth and closed it again. Surely there was some way she could counter the reeve's instructions, some weakness to exploit. The reeve seemed self-important, to be sure, and arrogant, but he did not seem corrupt. Yet perhaps he would be gullible.

What she really needed was a day, an hour!

Georgia clapped her hands sharply. "Sisters! We must retire to the dorter to gather what is necessary to travel." The sisters whispered, but even Sister Thomasine and Maud hushed at Romsfeld's glare and the reeve's vigorous, imbecilic hand waving.

Maud particularly seemed afraid. Though she had been accepted as a lay sister, she was by trade a servant. For her faithful service, the earl had paid for her to live her last years at the priory. Maud had no official standing as a nun. She would be turned out; she would be a beggar.

Georgia dragged behind as the sisters filed out, curtseying to the reeve's waving hand. If he was gullible, perhaps she could win his sympathy. Perhaps even convince him to let them stay an extra day, for it was already late afternoon. They could gather what they needed, then, and escape in the night. They would take only what really mattered: the Psalter, the relic, bread.

"My lord reeve, accept my sincere gratitude. His Grace the archbishop has often told us that our submission will bring us closer to God, and so you have done us a great service here. If there is any return service I can render you, I will do so gladly. I know all the accounts and inventories. In just a few days, I could offer you great speed and assist you in your most important duty."

From his place by the fire, Romsfeld laughed out loud. He picked up a shard of the seal and threw it at her.

Georgia pretended a long-suffering submission, directing a sigh at the reeve. "Perhaps we sisters are not quite so vicious as you have heard, good sir. You see how we are treated. We are abused when all we wish to do is fall on our knees to pray. We beseech your authority. You, who are an important man, a trusted officer of the king! I beg you, defend us from the wickedness of those who wish us harm and those who would disparage our reputation."

The reeve lifted his chin and redirected his waving hand at Romsfeld. "Steward, do not molest this good nun. See to the barns and the gathering of the stock."

Romsfeld scowled at Georgia, pushing past her as he stepped out to the courtyard. She made more of the push than there was, pretending to be thrown sideways. The reeve moved quickly to steady her.

Georgia leaned on him, feigning weakness and dependence. Yes, perhaps this tact would work. She stumbled slightly.

"I hope, sir," she said, "you don't think ill of us. I spend all my days in fasting, sir. To cleanse my sin."

"Yes, yes," he patted her hand.

She gave him a look she hoped would signify a humble, grateful obedience, and with a feigned limp, headed out to the dorter.

Yet outside, men already worked to fill the waiting carts, packing the priory plate in straw-filled barrels and ushering lingering pilgrims down the path. The guesthouse was empty save a few. The sisters could not hope that pilgrims would rise to their defense again.

Georgia felt a pang for Sister Agnes. Would the reeve force Sister Agnes from her cell? *"Ave Maria gratia plena ..."* she prayed for strength, for some memory that could help her know what next to do. What of Lo and the promise? How could she defend it if they were hauled away in carts? And what of the relic?

The relic! After Dominus Ufroad and the abbot had fled, Georgia had restored the relic to the altar in the church. She must get to it before the carters brought their barrels into the church to fill.

"*O Jesu!*" Georgia caught up with Mendaline and took her by the arm. "I must get the relic, then I will return to the dorter. I have found a way."

Mendaline raised an eyebrow. "I'll not climb into the rafters, if that's what you're thinking."

☙

The church was dark. Georgia could hear a servant in the sacristy, packing. Two bowls clanged together, and as they rang Georgia knew them to be silver.

As she stood in the church, a chill rummaged her skin, and a vision overtook her. The world around her changed. The church lay in ruins with the walls gone and scattered across the fields. The floor, paved with large, flat grit stones, was a tumult of holes and mounds overgrown with weeds. All around her was the sound of Agnes weeping. Not as she usually wept with punctuated screams, but with a ghostly echo that pricked Georgia under the whites of her eyes.

The vision faded. She stopped abruptly to avoid colliding with a church bench, reoriented herself to the familiar, the smell of beeswax candles at the altar, rosemary swept in on the wind, and sweet woodruff strewn over the church floor.

All had returned to normalcy; she could feel the flat of the floor stones underneath her feet. Normalcy for an instant, but then the candlelight went out. In the darkness, Georgia knew she was not alone in the church. Someone stood by Isela's altar, illuminated by a last amber beam of light. This someone lifted Isela's relic from its place and held it up. A man. A thief. Romsfeld.

CHAPTER 15:
Saint Genevieve

Romsfeld extinguished the candle and lifted the relic from the candelabra. As he did, the last of the flame light played across the orb's surface, shining outward from the glass. He revolved the glass slowly, entranced by the swirling glow.

Georgia crept along the wall, moving from bench to bench. The thought to kill him dominated her wholly, for with his touch he defiled the relic. Yet he had a sword on his hip and a dagger at his belt. She was unarmed.

She crept along the altar rail, reached the far corner, and coiled to lunge.

But Romsfeld turned coolly, readying his dagger as he faced her.

He raised the relic. "Come for this?" he asked. He tucked it down into his purse and seemed pleased with himself.

Georgia shifted her weight. "That relic belongs to Saint Isela."

Romsfeld laughed. "Not any more."

"I am sure the reeve will not take kindly to your having stolen it."

Romsfeld sneered. "He is an imbecile."

She took another small step forward, watching the dagger. He was careless with it, she noticed, his grip too light. "Return the relic to me, and I will go quietly. I will leave the priory. I will leave Yorkshire."

"You will leave anyway." He snapped his fingers, turning his head as if to call someone to assist him.

Georgia sprung, launching herself bodily. Ramming her elbow into his wrist, she managed to knock the dagger away. With her other hand, she spun him at the shoulder and clasped her hand over his mouth to stifle him.

He spat in disgust, grabbed her wrist, and threw her sideways and then down. She fell face first against the altar, landing so hard that she felt as if the stone had penetrated through her jaw and into her temple. The candelabra fell over and rolled off the altar stone, knocking several candles to the floor.

Georgia flipped over and jumped back up. "The relic, steward, give it to me. Or you will not live this day out."

Romsfeld struck her, shoving her backward and down again, this time onto her knees. She bit her tongue at the blow, and her eyes watered. It was harder now to see him in the darkness.

"Take your broom and fly where you will." He spat at her and turned away.

Georgia blinked to clear her vision. She must have the relic. Lo must awaken and learn her part in the fulfillment, whatever that part was.

Georgia snatched the candelabra from the floor. Raising it in a furious upsweep, she brought it down on the back of Romsfeld's head.

The "thlack" sound was sickening, like an iron striking wet wolf hide. Romsfeld staggered under the blow. Georgia grabbed him before he fell and struggled to steady him. She tried to reach his purse and the relic with it, but he crumpled in her hold. His muscles alternately spasmed and lay flaccid. He tried to push his feet against the floor but could not stand.

The main doors of the church opened, and light streamed in. The reeve strode into the sanctuary, peering at them through the shadows.

Behind him, two of the priory servants cowered, looking in.

"What is this, here? I heard there was—" he stopped in midsentence, his hand flapping.

"Good sir," Georgia gabbled, grasping somewhere, anywhere, for a thought or memory that could offer her something, anything to explain herself. She might just drop Romsfeld to the floor and confess to striking him, except that she still could not reach Romsfeld's purse. She realized she must look as insane and vicious as all the stories Romsfeld had thought to tell.

She tried to steady herself and compose her words. She twisted her shoulders, but still Romsfeld's bulging purse was out of reach. Then Romsfeld made a bubbling noise. A spasm brought his face violently forward, and he spewed a great arc of vomit.

"*Mater Dei!*" Georgia almost dropped him.

The reeve took a large step backward. "What is it? Is it sickness?"

Sickness, praise Isela! "Yes, good reeve, Saint Mary! Good Saint Anne! Sickness! If I had not ventured into the church to pray and seen it, who knows how this contagion might have spread?"

The reeve stuttered, his waving hand now pointed toward the servants behind him. "Go, you fools! Assist this woman!"

"Stop!" Georgia almost buckled as she shifted Romsfeld back. "It is the plague."

"Plague?" The reeve peered at Romsfeld with round eyes. "You exaggerate. Plague?"

"Tell me, when he rode today along the path, did he sway atop his horse and almost fall?" Romsfeld's poor horsemanship was legend in the village. Small boys would climb on the backs of unhappy goats, and then fall off with cries of "I'm the master steward!" But the reeve would not know that—she hoped.

The reeve took another step back, though smaller. "Well, yes he did—"

"Ah!" Georgia wailed. "It is as I feared!"

The reeve covered his mouth with a wad of linen, but otherwise seemed watchful. "He seemed only slightly drunk."

"Yes, Saint Arnold! The drunken plague. It is how it begins. He will ooze next."

"Ooze?"

Romsfeld made an unintelligible sound, arched backward, and vomited again. The vomit spewed up and over his clothing, hair, face, and clotted in his beard. He breathed in and choked, making bubbling, rasping noises.

The reeve jumped and retreated quickly, pausing only after he was outside the church doors.

Georgia took that as a good sign and continued. "Those afflicted always die, good sir. First the vomit, then the boils and fever. They die shrieking. It is said the fires of purgatory bring relief."

Georgia paused to gain her breath. She was strong, but Romsfeld was heavy and crushed against her, flattening her chest. Nor was she that inclined to breathe deeply, for he was so covered in pestilential slime that when she did, she gagged. And still, she could not reach his purse.

"I beg you, sir, send for Sister Mendaline. I must take him at once to the infirmary."

The reeve wafted his free hand; a servant bowed quickly and left.

Georgia focused on just holding Romsfeld up. If she could turn him, just a little! But he was able to move just enough to make everything impossible. He raised his head and tried to speak. The words garbled together and sounded as if his stomach and the devil bubbled up. He seemed to direct the words directly to the reeve. It spooked him, and the reeve fled. As he ran, he called out in a thin voice. "Plague ... plague in the church!"

Mendaline came in through the sacristy door, and Georgia almost buckled with relief. "Sister," Georgia said, "pray help me with this thief."

"Saint Genevieve, what's this? They say plague?"

Georgia shot her a meaningful look and spoke loudly. "We must sacrifice ourselves, Sister, to this plague."

Mendaline grimaced at the vomit and lowered her voice. "Have you poisoned him? This is your plan?"

Georgia whispered back, "I had to hit him with the candlestick. He put the relic in his purse. He would have stolen it."

Mendaline wrapped her arms around Romsfeld's chest. As soon as Mendaline had taken enough of his weight, Georgia tried to grab again for his purse, except that just then the reeve stepped back near the door of the church. She snatched her hand away, pretending to pick vomit from his belt.

The reeve, however, put his hand on the hilt of his sword. "What it this? I was warned of witchcraft—"

Georgia rolled her head backward and moaned as sorrowfully as she could. "Woe, sir. You are wise. It is true." She elbowed Mendaline, who gave her a look, and then she, too, moaned with contrition. "How could I not see it?" Georgia continued. "That we should have witchcraft practiced against us, now, so cruelly. God has sickened us in repayment for our sins. All the worse, your death will be on our heads as well. When the sheriff comes to board us up with all of us entombed inside. All who remain here will share this fate. We will all die screaming the same agonies, our faces covered in heated, bursting boils! We will eat of each other's flesh. And you who are blameless will suffer as well. You who have done nothing but your duty. You who would have advanced in the king's service to be given titles and lands, a rich wife."

The reeve twitched nervously from foot to foot. A small crowd of carters gathered behind him. A particularly bent bondsman stepped next to him, and he flinched and stepped further away. He eyed the crowd with suspicion and put the wad of linen again over his face.

Georgia and Mendaline dragged Romsfeld through the sacristy and toward the infirmary. As they gained the courtyard, the other sisters came out of the dorter and into the general uproar. Maud, in her surprise at seeing Romsfeld helpless and covered in vomit, skidded to a stop and crashed into the church wall. She rebounded and swayed untidily on her feet, her one eye unfocused and wandering.

The reeve watched her from near the gate, his expression of horror deepening. "The drunken plague!"

Maud tried to steady herself, but her look became increasingly more deranged.

The reeve retreated, tripping over the bricks of the fountain behind him. "My horse! My horse!"

Georgia called to the groom, "Bring the horses to the gate!" She continued to simper and grovel until the groom appeared and the reeve clamored up into the saddle.

"I will return on Saint Matthew's day," he called out as he turned his horse. And with a final parting shot declared, "This priory is dissolved by order the king!" He spurred the palfrey down the hill. The hired carters fled on foot, and Georgia shooed the priory servants along behind them. Only the sisters stayed, watching as the mules and carts clattered off.

Georgia knelt until they disappeared. Her blood felt hot and cold, alive with purpose. The reeve had fled. It was another sign of favor.

Mendaline and Beatrice moved Romsfeld to the infirmary. Georgia joined them. She was covered in stink. She would need a change of clothes and a lavender bath to clear it. Her clothes must be burned. The stench would never lift from them.

In the infirmary, Romsfeld lay on a truckle mattress, and Mendaline poked him. In response, he gurgled a little and blinked.

Mendaline frowned. "If he dies from this brain affliction, we'll most likely hang. If he lives, he will tell his tale. What then?"

Georgia cut the purse from Romsfeld's belt and pulled the relic out. "By that time, we will be headed north. We have escaped, Sister. And we still have this." She let the relic spin. Then, throwing a handful of hyssop into a basin of spring water, she splashed it down to wash it clean.

CHAPTER 16:
Penance

But though Georgia and the sisters planned to flee north, they could not, for the countryside erupted into violence. Commoners and tradesmen joined together with northern lords and abbots and took up arms against the king and the suppression of the monasteries. They called their rebellion the Pilgrimage of Grace, demanded relief from tithes and taxes, and demanded also the restoration of the monasteries and the Roman Church. The roads filled with rebels and soldiers, and robbers took advantage of the unrest. Travel was unthinkable.

Yet Georgia hoped that the rebellion would perhaps turn the tide in their favor, for mobs had risen up against the reeves in the north, and several were hanged. The reeve who had come to Isela's Priory fled south.

The sisters kept Romsfeld imprisoned. At first they drugged him to keep him manageable; for when he was sober, he raged. But Mendaline soon refused to continue administering the drink. Releasing him was out of the question, so to contain him they locked him in the cell below the kitchen. The room allowed a little light through a slit window, open only to the width of a few fingers. Georgia insisted they continue to claim that he was mad from fever. Only the lie was a sin, she said. Likely God was glad they locked him up.

Just a few priory servants remained. The migrant workers and smiths had fled for fear of plague. The bondsmen and villagers had joined the rebellion and marched south and west. The rebellion also disrupted the flow of goods into the north. The drovers did not come, and the untended geese were almost wild. Without the bondsmen and smokers, they missed the great salting. For Sister Thomasine had refused to butcher anything with legs.

So they ate fish. Even on meat days they ate fish. And while they were used to eating fish for lean days, they had not had eel or beaver tail or anything fresh caught for weeks. Instead, they soaked and ate salted cod. The rock-hard fish was stored in barrels, and they had them in plenty. Sister Thomasine drew them out one at a time, abusing the fish to satisfy her frustrations, before tossing them into fresh water to soften them and draw off the salt.

Georgia came into the kitchen as Sister Thomasine hammered at a particularly large piece. She used the blunt side of a plow mell for the work, swinging the stone down with desperate purpose. Sister Elizabeth watched her, all the while complaining about their fare and reminiscing of roasted mutton in ale.

"I will not argue over sheep!" Sister Thomasine struck with the last word and made an impressive dent in the center of the fish.

"I will butcher a ewe myself, then," Elizabeth said. "The stink of cod sours my stomach."

Georgia drew a misshapen loaf of bread from the basket as Thomasine readied another blow. "Sisters, we must not forget who we are and what we must do."

Thomasine guffawed and struck the fish again. "I'd ring the bell, but they took it down to melt it."

Elizabeth dodged a flying shard of cod and watched as it embedded in the straw-plastered wall behind her. Her nose wrinkled.

"They say the rebellion goes well—"

Georgia nodded. There had been riders the day before, rebels bringing news and begging for supplies. They took a dozen geese, and Thomasine had grumbled as they rolled away the last cask of third-pressed wine.

"The rebels took York. Surely we will win."

"'Tis warm in here," Maud's nose was ringed in red as she stepped in, bringing a burst of daylight and a cold draft with her. She drew up a stool and picked up a chunk of cod that had separated from the mass. She licked it. "Gaw, I miss my teeth." She puckered and feigned a spit. "You don't know what you've lost before it spits itself into your cup."

Sister Beatrice sat by the fire grinding herbs. Catherine was not in the kitchen, and Georgia frowned to think where she might be. With so many of the servants gone, she and the monk Benet had grown bolder.

"Sisters," Georgia said. "We need only wait a little time. We only wait for Lo's awakening. When it comes, we will know what to do."

"Are you sure of this?" Elizabeth's question was somber. "Are you sure a dream will come to her?"

"It is the way of it." Georgia infused her voice with conviction, though she herself had begun to doubt. "The memories stir early, then the awakening comes at twelve."

Elizabeth stared at her. "Lo is newly thirteen."

Georgia controlled the noise that crested at her throat. Thirteen. How had it come to be that Lo was now thirteen?

Thomasine and Elizabeth exchanged a look.

"All will be well," Georgia said. Yet she fidgeted, replacing the loaf into the basket. Mayhap it was different for the Bearer than the Chooser? Lo was a puzzle. The girl was clearly in the flush of puberty. Always that she could remember, Georgia had awakened at twelve. Lifetime after lifetime, it was always the same. She was the Bearer. She must hold the way open. Isela must return! The dreams were difficult, but she endured them. She became a woman even while she was still a girl.

And yet Elizabeth was right. Lo's twelfth year had passed them by, and she had not made the transition.

"What if she doesn't—awaken?" Beatrice sounded timid.

Georgia looked from sister to sister, and though Beatrice was still young at twenty-six, Georgia saw age in all of them. The years that brought Lo her girlhood had made Elizabeth a woman. She was now almost thirty. Sister Thomasine was in her fifties now, and Sister Mendaline the same. The years spoke of Georgia's ancient trouble, of time simply lost.

"Dame Georgia," Beatrice brushed crumbs from her apron and addressed her timidly, but as if to speak for the group. "We should try again, somewhere new."

Georgia ran the flat of her hand over the well-oiled oak block in the center of the kitchen. The block had taken more knocks than it should; the corner was crushed, a large rent tore the middle, and splinters rose up from the top. All the sides of the block were worn smooth, even around the many gouges. Where the water soaked it, it warped into untidy rivulets. So much abuse, and yet it stood. It would have to stand a while longer.

"We have the relic. Lo will awaken." Georgia hoped she sounded absolutely assured, for she meant to assert her authority. "But we will gather for penance tonight, after compline. If there is some sin that hangs over us, let us purge it, and move on."

Maud spoke as she sucked a sliver of slimy cod. "Why should I have penance? I've done nothing."

Sister Beatrice looked down and away; she would not meet Georgia's gaze. "And what of Romsfeld?" she asked.

Sister Thomasine swung the stone again. Usually they all pretended Romsfeld did not exist.

"He is contagious," Georgia spun the lie. "He is mad and drooling."

Thomasine flared her nostrils. "Is it a sin to wish him dead, Sister? A corpse at least is silent."

It was true; they would all be safer if Romsfeld were dead. "We must not fail, Sisters." Georgia said. "We will *all* do penance tonight."

Georgia turned and went out. She chastened herself. She remembered only snatches of what had been foretold, stories, dream images that broke into her mind as if from the heavy film of sleep. Hers was not an ordinary life. She lived the cycle of rebirth, tied to the fate of Isela. She lived lifetime after lifetime, in what must now span well over a thousand years. It was a cycle of lore passed memory to memory and then fading. So many stories were simply lost.

A giggle echoed between the kitchen and the stables, followed by a man's low laugh. Catherine and Benet! Georgia clenched her fists in frustration. "She will have twice the penance!"

The laugh came again, and Georgia recognized not Catherine's reedy, affected giggle, but a lighter girlish sound. Lo! Georgia relaxed. But the male voice that followed sent a prickle of foreboding under her scalp. The male voice was Romsfeld's.

Georgia moved forward slightly and could see her. Lo crouched close to the wall and peered through the small window to the cellar where Romsfeld was imprisoned. She giggled again, and Romsfeld pushed his hand out to her. Lo recoiled from the hand but dropped a late blooming clover flower into his upturned palm. Next she dropped a dandelion.

"Lo!" Georgia cut between them. Lo struggled to rise quickly. Georgia snatched her away, glaring down into the cellar.

A square of sunlight showed Romsfeld gloating. He flashed a happy smile. "Your beautiful daughter has agreed to help cheer me with a few blossoms." An insult. Lo was not her daughter, though some persisted in believing it.

Romsfeld dragged a purple clover along his cheek, opened his mouth, and flicked his tongue across it before clamping it between his teeth.

Georgia kicked dirt at him and shoved Lo away, marching her across the yard. Her mind raced. She turned Lo against the wall and slapped her.

"Fool." Her voice erupted thick, accusing, unbelieving. "Do you not see him lurking there? He does not want flowers." Georgia snatched the remaining few dandelions from the girl's grasp and threw them into the dirt. "What did he say to you?"

Lo kept her eyes down. She spoke in a whisper. "Mendaline says, 'Love thine enemy.' I was—"

Georgia shook her. "How often have you spoken with him?"

"I—I—I'm sorry."

"Not as sorry as you will be. Where's Pocket? You'll both be doing penance in the church tonight."

"Pocket is—in the pasture—with Roger."

"Roger … the shepherd boy? And you did not tell me? And you did not say? What is she doing there—wait! Do not tell me."

Lo remained silent. If she was anything, she was obedient this girl. She was hard to know, but obedient. She would submit uncomplaining to her penance.

"Fifty *Ave Marias* on your knees before the altar. You will creep to the cross from where you stand, and you will miss dinner this day. Go. Now."

"Yes, Dame Georgia."

Lo dropped onto all fours and crawled toward the church, creeping on her knees to the altar. Georgia watched her go. She had been too lenient. Far too lenient.

She charged back to the kitchen and flung open the door with a rage that brought in the cold wind and upset the balance of the hearth coals so that they flared too hot and the ale boiled over.

"Sister Thomasine, I want this place purged. There will be no more men and no more sin at this priory."

☙

Georgia fasted and prayed, but still Lo's awakening did not come. News of the world outside Attewater, when it came, told of victory for the rebellion. The rebels marched to Cumberland near Hull and prepared to meet the king's army for battle. Riders, carters, and the injured took the news with them from town to town.

When two riders came on a late afternoon, the sisters rushed out to greet them. They expected news, but though they were men of Yorkshire, they were the archbishop's men and wore the badges of SeVerde. And they brought with them a riderless horse.

Georgia braced for demands. Perhaps the archbishop expected her to feed his army now, with goods that were not his.

But the men seemed wary and careful. They did not dismount, but instead kept their distance. The taller of the two spoke. "We are messengers from His Grace the archbishop. He requests his steward, Horley Romsfeld, join him immediately at Hull."

Georgia took the measure of them. They carried weapons yet did not look dangerous. In fact, they looked afraid.

"The steward is taken with plague," Georgia had told the lie so often that she could spin it without thinking. "Even now he drools in his bed, half-mad with fever."

The men paled, exchanging glances as if their fears had been confirmed. But they did not withdraw. The shorter man spoke with a tremor of unease. "We had hoped he had recovered—"

The taller man interrupted. "Plague or not, we are under orders to bring him to Hull."

Georgia shook her head. "He cannot ride. Surely the archbishop cannot mean for you to take him under these circumstances—"

"We cannot return without him, Dame. Be he well, fevered, or dead, we have orders to bring him just the same."

"Perhaps I can send a servant in his stead. Someone to assure the archbishop of the severity of the steward's condition."

The tall man spoke again. "The archbishop believes the steward suffers only from cowardice and refuses to fight. That is why we must bring him. If he is ill, he will be cared for in the tents."

Georgia looked to Mendaline. Perhaps the time had come for the charade to end in any case. Romsfeld was the last man at the priory. His illness might be a lie, but his bellowing and whining was like a contagion just the same. Without his contamination, maybe Lo would finally awaken.

Georgia smiled with all the benevolence she could muster. "Sister Mendaline?" They would have to drug Romsfeld if they were to get him off without trouble. "Sister, will you prepare the steward's medicine? He must have a cup before he leaves."

"More than a cup, I'll warrant. Not even a barrel will be enough." Mendaline turned and marched for the infirmary, grumbling.

The men sweated and seemed nervous. It seemed cruel to frighten them, for they were men of Yorkshire and it was not wholly their fault that they were in the service of SeVerde.

"Do not be alarmed," Georgia said. "Romsfeld has long passed the point of contagion. And," she added cheerily, "I imagine a brisk ride in the country air might cure him of the madness altogether."

Sister Thomasine snorted at this remark. The medicine would sedate a person from prime to vespers. But after that, Romsfeld would come to his senses quite unaided by the brisk country air.

It took four of them—Georgia, Elizabeth, and Mendaline, with Thomasine clasping herself around Romsfeld like a vice—before he would swallow the drink. Yet the herbs were quick to work, and when the women brought him into the courtyard, he stumbled and drooled. He smiled at the horses and cooed, "My fine cocks!"

The men faltered, but, straightening their jerkins, lifted him into the saddle and tied him there. With a courteous bow, they took the path at a brisk trot, Romsfeld's head bouncing sickeningly against the horse's mane.

"If he doesn't throw it up, we'll have until evening before the gates of hell open." Mendaline peered into the bottom of the empty goblet. "Maybe we should have told them to give him more of it at sunset."

Georgia let her prayer beads roll over her palm. "By sunset he'll be well gone, as far as Nidton perhaps, and the two with him in haste to go."

"He's off to war." Elizabeth sounded almost cheery. "If there's to be a great battle, perhaps he will be killed."

"Perhaps." Mendaline brought the furrows of her face into a deep frown. "Though I don't like it. I'll wish no man dead, regardless."

Georgia almost laughed. In spite of the danger, she felt relief. Romsfeld had been like a canker hanging over them.

"Be well, Mendaline! It is for the best. By Saint Christina, the priory is purged of men. Now the awakening will come."

CHAPTER 17:
A Porta Inferi: From the Gates of Hell

GEORGIA STOOD AT THE CHURCH WALL AND pushed a warm milk sop through the narrow window into Agnes's cell. "Agnes. It is not safe for us to stay at the priory any longer. The rebellion is lost, with the king the victor. His soldiers roam the countryside and hang any rebel they catch. The reeve will soon return. We must away."

Agnes drew the sop into her cell. She hummed to herself.

Georgia raised her voice, refusing to fear the words of doom spoken out loud. Too many village lads had died. "The king's army hanged five abbots since the rout at Cumberland. They've sacked the monasteries at Nunburnholme, Sawley, and Bridlington. All at *Jervaulx* are accused with Abbot Selbarre tried for treason. It is Philip SeVerde who leads the inquisition. And *LeRouge* has fallen."

Agnes croaked through the wall, "That abbot was a great fool."

"Yes, but in this case I am sorry for him."

Agnes sucked the milk. "Are you afraid?"

The weight of worry pressed down on her shoulders, and Georgia shrugged to loosen it. Yes, she was afraid. "We must leave tomorrow."

Agnes shoved the bowl back through the opening. Not a morsel remained. "More honey in the next."

Georgia peeked through the stone window into the cell. Agnes sat in a near corner, her arms around her scabby knees and her skirts in shreds.

"Harm will come to you if you stay," Georgia said.

Agnes raised a bony finger. "Watch your own neck."

"I won't leave the priory without you."

"No. We will die here." Agnes's hands twitched, red and raw and bloodied, cragged with age and swelled with cold. She sighed, long and low.

Georgia withdrew. Agnes was right; if they stayed, it was to die, for surely the steward and the archbishop would come for them. But let them come; they would find the priory empty. All was packed, and she and all the sisters would leave in the morning for the hills. They would remove Agnes by force if necessary.

But now Georgia needed to sleep and gather strength. For despite lawlessness and a bitter cold January, they must walk to Scotland.

The dorter was not much warmer than the night even with the three fireplaces crackling. Georgia undid her belt, the scented pomander knocking against the slats of her bed, and then unclipped her prayer beads and worried them in her fingers. She laid her sleeves on the table by her bed and unclasped her veil and wimple, but left the tight linen cap in place. Untying the bib of her black wool kyrtle, she slipped from it, and from the blue underdress, before finally shedding half a dozen underskirts of the same hue.

She contemplated the pile of clothes that had been her habit for so long. She would wear them again, she comforted herself, but not on the morrow, or on the next.

Sleep was short, for Beatrice woke her for midnight prayers. She dressed quickly in coarse wool russet. She was glad that, although the homespun itched, the simple country dress was warm. She slipped her feet into new leather shoes. They all had new shoes; they would need them.

Georgia was the first into the church and found Lo fast asleep on a blanket at Isela's altar. It touched her for Lo to try so hard, even at the last. Perhaps this last night's vigil at the altar would bring Lo's awakening. She shook Lo slightly on the shoulder, and Lo opened her eyes. Hope and questions passed between them, but the girl looked away. Georgia drew back. They would leave without the awakening. They would hope for better in Scotland.

They prayed from matins to prime, from the midnight service to the office before dawn, purging worries and saying good-byes. They prayed for a safe journey and for those laid to rest in the cemetery: Lady Marjorie, Sister Joan, and recently, Maud as well.

Of the living, Sister Catherine alone would not go with them. After a long absence, Benet had risked Georgia's anger and the ban on men to come with news. He popped his head into the kitchen window and frightened them all, unrecognizable in a jaunty doublet, a cap covering his fading tonsure.

It was Sister Thomasine who broke the spell. "Oh hell," she had said, "let the gentleman in." She had clasped him in an enthusiastic embrace. "I've missed your sinning," she said.

Benet told them that Archbishop SeVerde had ransacked *LeRouge* Abbey and built a gallows in the courtyard. He then hung the abbot for all to see, letting him swing and choke fifteen minutes before he died. A few other monks had hanged as well, and the rest were allowed to flee.

Benet declared to them his plan to start a new life, and he asked Catherine to marry him. Georgia gave them both her blessing, for it seemed only right that Catherine should be happy. Benet and Catherine left soon after with the gift of a mule and one of the carts the reeve had left behind.

And now that Saint Agatha's day had begun, only two tasks remained, to gather up the relic and coax Agnes into a cart.

Fog hovered close to the ground, and Georgia stumbled outside the church, feeling her way over the rough patches she could not see. When she reached the outer wall of Agnes's cell, she ran her hands over the base, seeking the stone that had once come loose. She planned to pry it open, but as she knelt to look for it, she found the stone already pushed away and the cell open.

"Agnes?" Georgia peered in, but the morning was dark and the fog low. "Sister?" She reached into the cell and pulled at a mound of rags. The cloth slid out and left the cell empty.

Georgia stood up to gaze over the cabbage fields. The spinach stood in leafy bunches, prickling the foggy shadows. She thought she saw movement farther out, though the shape did not move in a human way.

"Agnes?" The shape hopped and then opened a wing. A crow. It speared the cold ground and clicked its beak.

"Agnes!" she called again. A mist grew, and arms reached from it. Horror prickled her scalp as the arms seemed to reach for her. A ghost. Her own ghost.

The clicks of the crow grew louder, and its dull wing beats pounded to a rhythm. The ghost faded, and Georgia wiped her eyes and cheeks.

Still the crow pounded. Or so it seemed. It flapped and hopped and pounded and flew away. Yet the pounding grew louder, and she could feel it under her feet. A cold shiver stabbed her between her shoulders. There were horses on the gallop, moving quickly, ten, maybe more.

She stood, listening. The rumble drew closer, breaking into separate drums and moving fast. An onslaught.

Georgia plunged through the fog. She must get to Lo. Lo had gone to the dorter, to dress, to pack.

The relic was still in the church.

She almost fell. The relic must be saved. Georgia flung a foot in each direction and went down near a gravestone. She could not save them both. Yet she must. She must.

She chose the dorter first.

The fog would hide her. Near the ground, the fog was thicker. She could see only two feet around her, no more, yet she knew the priory better than anyone else.

The fog thinned. Horses charged through the gate, shattering the timbers with their hooves.

Georgia ducked down again. Someone cried out, Beatrice perhaps. A horse screamed. Romsfeld's voice rose, fell, and sank everywhere. "Find the girl, and kill the witch."

Georgia tucked behind the gravestone. The dorter lay ahead, but she must cross the courtyard to get to it. The riders sped off in different directions, but Romsfeld stayed in the center on his horse. When Mendaline came into the courtyard, he drew his sword and struck her with the flat of it. She fell and lay without moving.

Beatrice screamed and ran. Romsfeld spurred his horse and kicked her in the back. She flew into the jagged remains of the entry gate, striking it with a mortal force. She rolled into a ball and curled up next to the fence.

He turned his horse and spurred away.

Another scream split the darkness. It was Pocket, her scream high and girlish, a scream of terror. A shout followed, a woman's cry—Thomasine. "Dare to try it! I'll thrash you like a barrel full of cod."

Georgia rose and sidled along the wall of the chapter house. She stayed low to the ground. As she got closer, she could just see Pocket crouched against the wall, her veil and one of her sleeves missing. She held her arms over her head. Thomasine stood in front of her with an ax.

Further into the darkness, a man snickered.

There were men round the stables, as well, where Elizabeth readied the pack mules.

A man howled, and Thomasine shrieked a victory.

Georgia plunged into the dorter, locking the door behind her.

Lo stood stricken in the center of the room. She stood absolutely still, a lit candle half burned and dripping in her hand. Georgia blew out the flame. "Come, child. You must escape."

A man in the courtyard shouted. Romsfeld yelled again. "The girl …

Search the grounds!" There was a charge at the door of the dorter, and the timber splintered.

Georgia grabbed Lo and ran down to the cellar. There was a chute on the far side; they could climb out. Once outside, the dark and fog would hide them.

More splintering was followed by the sound of men's boots overhead. Georgia pulled Lo with her, opening the hatch and pushing Lo through.

But Romsfeld waited for them. Without a word, he grabbed Lo by her belt and hauled her out.

Georgia fought her way through the hatch. As she gained ground, Romsfeld had already taken Lo onto his horse. Georgia latched her arms around Lo's knees, trying to pull her away. She bit Romsfeld's leg, hard above the boot, feeling her teeth puncture his flesh one after another. She felt the muscle give.

He hit her on the side of her head, but the force of the blow tore his flesh away in her teeth. He howled, grabbed her hair, and forced her head backward, spitting in her face. Raising his hand, he brought the force of it down on the bridge of her nose.

Pain overwhelmed her and forced her back, but she did not lose her grip. She would not let go of Lo. She would not! Lo slipped from the horse. The two of them tumbled to the ground together.

Romsfeld bellowed as the horse stomped. He pulled on the bit. Georgia stood, hauling Lo to her feet.

"Run," she said. It was the only thing that could be done. "Run!"

Lo fled through the fog, around the refectory and was gone.

Romsfeld drew his sword and struck, opening Georgia's side from her armpit to her hip. Through cloth and flesh and bone the sword tore through her. She cried out, and her legs gave way, leaving her sprawled face down in the grass.

Romsfeld left her there. He turned and pursued Lo.

Blood soaked Georgia's dress. Yet Lo would run. Lo could hide in the fog. Lo would be saved.

Georgia forced herself onto her knees, clamping her arm tightly at her side, folding the homespun around her to try to close the ghastly wound and stem the bleeding. She bound her shredded skirts around her middle and pushed up onto her feet. She turned toward the church.

Blood gushed and pooled in swampy clots, but she made progress. Thomasine screamed again, a string of curses. From the stables, she could hear the rise of cruel voices. Elizabeth cried out and began to sob. Her voice pleading.

Georgia forced another foot forward as Elizabeth began to scream. She sunk to her knees. All Georgia's soul pitched into blackness, Elizabeth! How, in the end, could all that was so beautiful be so cruelly used by men? And here, in this sacred place.

She dragged herself into the church, her tears cold over her face. She did not have strength for weeping, and yet she could not stop. The world had fallen.

She reached the altar and grasped the relic in her palm. She did not know where to hide it, but it must be hidden. Dark spots sucked at her vision, and still she cried.

From somewhere, Thomasine screamed a challenge, a scream that went silent at the center. All silent.

Georgia defied everything. She refused all. With the strength of rage, she pried at a stone on the floor of the church and found it gave just a little. She used her knee to wedge the stone up and split her side open with the effort. The stone's edge slit all the flesh along her shin as the stone came free.

With her fingernails, she scraped at the soft dirt underneath the stone, clawing up chunks of black earth. Into the hole she laid the relic down. Her eyes stung as she shoved the relic into the soil, packing the earth over it, and finally, with her foot, shoving the stone as best she could, dragging the weight of her body over it to tamp it down.

Her blood washed away the joins and masked the move, and for that she was grateful. She had managed it. The relic was safe, and Lo had escaped. At least, in all the other horror, she had done that much. And she would not surrender. She leant on a choir bench and tried to stand.

Romsfeld was still horsed when he rode in. Dawn grayed behind him as the horse cantered into the church. His triumph mocked her, for astride his horse was Lo. Her face bled, and her clothing was covered in mud, but it was Lo. Romsfeld gripped her with arms across her chest.

Lo seemed so small, like the child she was. As they rode into the church, she cried out, but he tightened his grip, and she was quiet.

Georgia slid along the bench to the ground. Romsfeld seemed to savor his triumph, for he swung his sword round and out, a wide arc, sweeping the blade through the air to feel the weight of it before he struck, finding his balance on the horse. With a triumphant sneer, he brought the blade down on Georgia's neck. It was a clean strike, and deadly. She collapsed forward, her body twitching as Lo screamed.

BOOK THREE

CHAPTER 18:
Schism

She struggled to right herself. She threw a hand against the bench across from her, upturning her toes and pushing them against the flat timber. Her balance remained unsteady. The savaged muscles of her right side ached, hip and breast, and ripped her body into spasms.

The pain forced her awake, into a morning cold and wet. When the carriage lurched again, she managed this time to brace herself. The pain stilled a little, subsiding into heat and quivering. Yet even so, Lo refused to fully open her eyes or choose between the living and the dead. She sought only the half-gray of sleep.

The carriage tilted hard left, and a horse whinnied. Ahead of her, a man cursed. "Hyah, hyah. Bloody mare."

A hoof or a wheel kicked a stone from the slicked muck into the carriage. She closed herself away from the tangy smell of mud, the creaking leather of the carriage, and the man who watched her.

The carriage shuddered to a stop, and everything seemed to grind together. The door swung open and flung in the wet. Rough leather, a man's glove, gripped her hand, and he told her she was wanted out. She ignored him. He pried her fingers from the rail and yanked her sideways. She landed on the cobbled street, and pain flared again. She kept her eyes down.

"Don't be a fool," Romsfeld whispered tersely, kindly.

She closed her eyes tight, wishing she could sear them shut. He was a monster. Yet he had been kind to her. She would stand up, then, and she would walk. But she would look away.

Romsfeld guided her to the door where the gaoler waited, a bulky man with unshaven whiskers clustered over his sagging jowls. Romsfeld growled at him, his hand on the hilt of his dagger.

"She will remain unspoiled," Romsfeld said.

The gaoler chortled.

Romsfeld drew. In an instant, the point of the dagger was between the gaoler's legs.

The gaoler stepped back. "She looks like nothin'," he said, his jowls working. "We got the others in any case."

The gaoler took her down a narrow stair and through a rotting doorway. It did not matter where. The earth, the mud, the mist, all of it so far away. She was a circling bird, high above and lost in the heavens.

Yet it was hard to stay removed from all the rot. A stink rose from the cellar of human waste, both sweet and foul with a disconcerting warmth. The gaoler opened a final door and shoved her inside. She fell into slimy straw.

Above her there were voices. Soft, tender fingers came next, fingers that searched gently and coaxed her. Lo opened her eyes, but focus came slowly. At first everything was fright edged with shadow. She blinked to see iron and stone and straw and then, Sister Mendaline.

Mendaline, who had nursed her through every childhood ailment. Mendaline, who had soothed her when her woman's courses would not come. Mendaline knelt over her now; the furrows of the older woman's face puffed into a ram's mask of swelling.

Lo wanted to speak, but instead she held out her arms and buried her face in Mendaline's dirty veils and torn wimple. The healer stank of mildew and sweat, but Lo detected the familiar as well, the smell of smoke and lilac, the sharp sap of birch and milkweed. Lo burrowed in them and wept.

Sister Beatrice and Pocket joined the cluster. They were soon all tightly knit and sobbing together.

"Alive." Mendaline dabbed her eyes, her cheek knotted with the ugly bruise. "They told us nothing of you."

Pocket touched Lo's arms and face, again and again, as if to see that she was real.

Sister Beatrice broke in with questions. "Were you hidden? Did you run? Have you news of Sister Agnes?"

Lo shook her head no. She wiped her nose with the back of her hand.

"Bless Mary!" Mendaline smiled. A few of her teeth were missing where the bruise swelled at its worst.

Pocket smoothed her hands over Lo's clothes, clean and unstained save for a few splatters of fresh mud. "You're so clean! Where were you?"

How could she tell them where she had been? She did not wholly know. A house, not a prison, that she knew. Yet she felt ashamed to think of it. There had been kindness there. And warm bread.

Mendaline pursed her mouth, and the bruise on her face contorted to a nest of yellow and green caterpillars. "Come then. Let's have a look at you."

Mendaline poked her, and she flinched. "Here? Does it hurt here? Tell me."

"My side." Lo managed to speak, but words felt sickening in her mouth.

Mendaline undid Lo's sleeves and overskirt with a systematic efficiency. She raised Lo's shift a little to reveal a nasty, seeping bruise that covered her ribs and breast and crept along the side of her belly.

"What in mercy?" Mendaline pushed at the greenish edges of the swelling.

"A—a kick—" Pain at the bottom of her soul threatened to jump into her gut. She remembered screaming. She flinched again.

"More than a kick," Mendaline dabbed at the clear fluid that seeped from it with a corner of Lo's shift.

Lo winced. "He was—horsed."

Mendaline pushed the shift back down over the bruise. "Only the kick?" Her gaze was direct and hard.

Lo did not want to talk of other hurts.

Mendaline's voice grew quiet, soothing. "Did he force you down? After the kick. Did he—did a man—?"

Lo closed her eyes again. The memories came back, pieces of them, floating. He was breathing over her, for days it seemed. She tensed her thighs, but there was no hurt there. He had not touched her in that way. Still, she felt ashamed.

Pocket squeezed her hand, and she opened her eyes again. Lo wished she were home. She laid her head in Pocket's lap, her nose stuffed so that she could hardly breathe.

Mendaline caressed her. "Whatever he has done, it is no shame to you."

"He did this." Lo held out her hand, opening her fingers and upturning her slender palm. The proud circular mark of her birth was now a weal of shredded, burned skin. Slash marks crusted across the full width of her palm and left a pattern of oozing scabs and ripe blisters.

Pocket gave a high-pitched cry, and Mendaline stared as if disbelieving. "The mark—Isela preserve us! Who did this?"

Lo felt the shame again. "Master Romsfeld."

Mendaline twitched. "Romsfeld." She crossed herself then made the cross over Lo's palm. "So that's it. And he didn't touch you? You are sure? Saint Agatha. *Mater Dei*."

The cell filtered with a small amount of natural light that came in through a shaft window near the ceiling. The light dimmed slightly, and a woman crouched outside the window on the street. She called down to them, "Sisters!"

Sister Beatrice went quickly to the window.

It was Alice, the gossip who had attended Lo's birth. Lo knew her well, for she often came for water from the fountain. Alice loved to tell the pilgrims the story of the siege, of the wife Johanna, and of the baby born that day. Lo closed her hand in shame.

Mendaline stood up, stretching carefully as if she, too, had some inner injury. "Good wife, I am glad to see you."

Alice pulled cloth bundles and leather bladders from a large basket, passing them in one at a time. "I brought medicine and a few eggs boiled. All the folk around have gathered things for you. Blankets. There's bread and this, too," she handed Beatrice a bundle wrapped in oily cloth. "Pork-blood sausage. For strength."

"Meat!"

"And oil and bandages, as well," Alice continued. "How does Sister Elizabeth?"

"She's took with fever."

In the far corner, Elizabeth lay curled under a ragged blanket. Her eyes were open and glittering.

"I'm sorry to hear it," Alice said. She looked around the street again. "Goodwife Proby said she saw Lo in Bilsdale this morning."

"Oh, yes—" Beatrice began, but Alice interrupted.

"She was in a carriage. Master Romsfeld helped her out as nice as you please. Letty said they were right friendly to each other. Seems strange that girl would run off with the likes of him. Some say they planned it all."

Lo cringed against the straw, her stomach so tight she almost vomited. Pocket looked at her with surprise.

"That's none of it," Mendaline retorted. "He's a right bastard. Silence that hen, that tongue of hers. Lo planned nothing of the kind. She is with us."

Alice peered into the darkness. "In the jail?"

Mendaline nodded. "I've had a look at her. He beat her, but she's not took like Elizabeth."

Alice reached back into her basket and handed down another leather bladder, careful not to catch it on the chipped edges of stone sill. "Some water for you. From the fountain at the priory. I sent my Osie up to fetch it in the night."

"Alice, what a steadfast woman you are. God bless you."

Alice shifted and peered more determinedly into the cell.

Lo tried to sink into the shadows.

"The water's for Elizabeth," Alice said. "Though Lo may need it, too. She's been days with Master Romsfeld they say."

Lo wished Pocket would not look at her so.

Alice moved in closer to the bars, and her voice changed to worry. "They arrested my boy, my Osbert this morning."

"Sweet Mary," Mendaline shook her head.

"They took Ralph and Angie Williamson, too, from their beds. And Hugh at Pig's Alehouse. They say they'll all hang." Alice covered her mouth, stifling a sob.

"Don't be grieved, goodwife," Mendaline reached up to touch Alice's hand. "We will pray for them."

"Bless you, Sister." Alice pulled back from the window. "If you hear any word—"

"I'll remember it to tell you," Mendaline said.

Alice nodded. "Good day, then." Taking the basket up, she hurried away along the street.

Mendaline brought the medicine to Elizabeth. Beatrice pulled aside bandages and rubbed Elizabeth's skin with the new oil. Lo could see that her thighs were purpled with bruises and streaked with blood; her belly also was bruised and gashed, as were her knees and ankles. When they tended her, they whispered as they would to a frightened child.

After they finished, Beatrice stayed with Elizabeth, cooing sweetly to her.

Mendaline brought the new medicines and bandages to Lo. She glanced over her shoulder at where Elizabeth lay, her eyes still open. "She'll be easier when the fever breaks," Mendaline said.

"Elizabeth said it was demons," Pocket whispered, her eyes shining in the shadows.

"Demons and men," Mendaline rubbed oil onto a clean cloth, "though what draws the two together I cannot say." Mendaline lifted Lo's shift to tend the bruise. "And you should know, child, Sister Thomasine is dead."

"She stood over me." Pocket sat, rubbing her hands over her skirt. "They chased me down. But she killed two of them—with the ax. A third one died yesterday, Alice said."

Pocket took an egg from the basket and peeled it. Lo watched her eat, thinking of Thomasine and of the fog. She heard a scream again. She shut her mind against it.

Mendaline poured oil on her hands and rubbed the bruise on her leg and up along her side. The oil felt light and smelled of oranges, rosemary, and mint. Mendaline's gaze lingered on Lo's face. "And child, Dame Georgia is also dead."

"Romsfeld killed her." Pocket whispered. "He cut off her—"

"Enough." Mendaline stopped abruptly.

Lo closed her eyes, but she knew Mendaline watched her. What should she do? What should she say?

"Did you know, child?"

The shadows surged, and Lo strove to stomp on them, to shove them away from any part of her they could hurt. Her side throbbed. She wanted to tell them she had nothing to do with it, to say she had run, that Dame Georgia had told her to run. But they would think she lied. They would blame her.

"Master Romsfeld—took—took—took me on his horse—" she choked, retched, tried again. How could she say what she had seen? She was not even sure herself. Everything had moved so quickly. Romsfeld had caught her. He had sought her out. He cared for her in his own house and fed her broth. He had been kind to her.

Silence grew; it felt so heavy. But heavier still were the words to tell. They refused to come.

"You cannot help what others do." Mendaline sounded tired. She smoothed Lo's shift and retied her kyrtle.

Pocket gabbled, chewing her egg. "They won't hang us, though. Alice thinks so, but Mendaline says not."

"Enough of hangings." Mendaline wiped her hands and turned her attention to Lo's palm. She poured a few drops of well water onto a clean cloth and applied it. Lo flinched; the touch burned. She flinched again and shoved the cloth away.

The scream in the darkness sounded again. Close. Terrifying.

Mendaline grasped her arms and pulled her up, clasping her into a forceful embrace. "Stop." Mendaline's voice forced pragmatism through the panic. "You are a daughter of Isela, Lo. Never you mind the rest. Lift your head up, child. The strength is in you. He cannot carve it away."

"Georgia is dead." Lo whispered it. "And I, and I, I—"

Pocket slid an arm around her. From across the room, Elizabeth drew a wheezing breath and cried out. Lo shuddered.

Mendaline took Lo's hand gently and caressed it. "Let me tend it," she said. Lo watched Mendaline work. She had perfect hands, square yet soft, with nose-pink fingertips and cream-white nails. They smelled of hyssop and were always warm. They seemed to know the truth inside, how to reach what ached, and how to soothe it.

Lo swallowed. "I am Isela's daughter," she said. A scream lingered in the darkness, but faintly.

"That's my girl," Mendaline held her palm and set to cleaning it. Lo held her hand as steadily as she could.

CHAPTER 19:
Jervaulx Abbey, England, 1537

A HUNTING DOG NEEDED ONLY FEEDING TO be loyal. Men were more complex. Yet whatever else could be said about the treasonous monks of *Jervaulx*, they knew the value of a good hound.

Philip surveyed the row of kennels that ended under the arched gate of the monastery and included some of the finest dogs he had ever seen. He would be able to purchase quite a few favors with them, more than a few. They only needed feeding.

He pointed through the iron grating at one pack of hungry greyhounds. "Give them meat, then send them, every one, to the king with my humble obedience." He pointed again, into a different kennel. "Send that mastiff pair to Norfolk, and the pups with them. A gift in honor of our victory, that we might rout the remaining rebels and return quickly to London."

A dirty soldier approached, dragging a mutt on a leather strap. The animal growled; the hair bristled along its back so that it looked like a wild pig, and ugly. Yet all around the kennels, hounds threw themselves to the bars and bayed.

The mutt was a bitch, in heat, though it looked to be rabid.

"You found that here?"

"No, Your Grace, this one's from the village. I thought to bring a little sport?" The man's eyes shone. Hope, lust, all the worst of men could be found in them. Yet there were certainly enough dogs to waste. There was not enough food for them and the soldiers both. A bit of sport might also quell complaints about the tight purse of the king, for he had refused to pay the soldiers more than eight pence a day.

Philip agreed. "But save out those that are the finest, and the greyhounds and Norfolk's mastiffs must not be touched. For the rest, fight them if you will. The winners will be fed." He surveyed the pack as they threw themselves forward on the bars. "I choose the boarhound as my wager. I'll put gold against any man's choice to beat him."

A general cheer was followed by the slapping of leather belts unbuckled for leashes.

Philip left them to settle it. For now, the idiot steward had arrived—an idiot who bobbled as he dismounted and then strode forward over the lawn, limping, leaving gouges in the painstakingly rolled grass. Not a bad fighter, this man, in hand-to-hand, a scrapper but well practiced. But he wore too many colors at once.

Philip stood straight, his head tilted back so he could seem to look down, for the idiot was taller. "You have returned the girl?" Philip asked.

Romsfeld made a curt bow, barely inclining his head. "Yes, Your Grace."

"You were to arrest the women only."

"That nun could not be trusted. She tried to kill me." Clearly, Romsfeld was the kind of cheater who felt entitled to his victory. And he whined. "She nearly chewed my leg off."

"You disobeyed my orders."

"They are witches, Your Grace. You gave me leave to deal with them."

"They were for you to arrest and for me to deal with, you idiot. Look at the carnage you have done, two killed, one raped. And this girl, what is it they call her, Lo? Raped also."

"No."

It was an answer made too quickly, and Philip doubted him. "Those nuns were in my charge, steward," he said. "This thing you did, do you not think it reflects ill on me? Where is the cause of justice? They may be whores, but their penalty is as *I* choose it. They may be sentenced to be whipped, or hanged, but never can they be seized and raped and carried off. What are we now, as Danes to England to ravage Saxon nunneries? You have defiled England!"

"The girl is not a nun, Your Grace. And not that witch—"

Philip noted that Romsfeld's face twitched. "Steward, these women are attached to *my* priory and are *my* property. So I thought I had made clear to you. Their books, their jewels, their bodies to be chastened, or their souls to be saved—all belong to me."

An enraged animal howl rose up, the distinct note of a dog bloodied, from the side yard of the monastery.

"The sport begins," Philip said. "I have an angel on the devil's own boarhound. Perhaps you care to wager against me?"

Romsfeld scratched himself before answering. "A bearbaiting?"

"A heated bitch only, but the dogs are hungry."

They rounded the kennels and strode across to the outer yard, a yard now crammed with men and dogs. Many of the hounds bled, their noses slashed to craze them. Their hunger also showed plainly enough, their bellies high.

The mongrel female, caged in the center ring, snarled and snapped. Two soldiers dragged the boarhound and tied it.

"What will you wager?"

Romsfeld opened his purse. "An angel, as you say."

"So be it."

They watched the boarhound as it scrabbled for the female, gouging the dirt as it sought purchase. But the leather tie held the dog inches out of reach. It yowled and whined.

Philip continued his questioning. "This girl you have stolen. It is said she works miracles."

"She does not."

"We'll see what the lord inquisitor has to say about it. He arrived in the night. If the girl can't work miracles, let her prove she cannot."

"She is nothing."

"Yet she bears a mark?"

"A lie."

"The inquisitor will determine what is a lie." Philip dropped a coin into a soldier's dirty palm. Three bloodhounds were brought to face the boarhound. The dog uncurled its tail and lunged at them.

The soldiers let the bloodhounds loose, and the boarhound suffered an early injury, a lucky bite that tore the belly. Yet he did not retreat, killing the first of his attackers with a snapping bite that wrenched the neck.

"See how he does it." Philip tapped his finger against his crook, a tap for each snap of the animal's jaw. "Not strength alone. That dog knows where to bite to wound and where to kill. He would not risk his pack with petty vengeance."

"Your Grace doubts me after the battle at Hull?"

"Against cotters? There was never any danger to you, sirrah, except that you might fall from your horse."

Romsfeld scowled. "I did as you asked."

Philip rounded on him. "Do you really so miss the point?" Another hound squealed, a sharp yip of pain. "This girl is a problem to me. That saint of theirs is best forgotten. After four days alone with her, you say this girl is yet a virgin?"

"She is, Your Grace."

Philip widened his nostrils for a full catch of air. "If she is a virgin, it is to her credit. Yet whether she is orthodox or not, my problem is the same. A virgin will draw believers. A whore will not. It is probably best I should have her burned."

He waited to see if Romsfeld would speak, but he remained silent. Perhaps the man could learn after all, for men like Romsfeld were jealous and greedy and so adept at graft as to prevent others from profiting by the same means. Such a man was useful. The wealth of Isela's priory, for example, or even of *Jeraulx*, need not be told in its entirety to the king. In this sort of bargaining, the girl was yet another coin to be spent in the purchase of loyalty. A valuable one.

Philip continued. "If I stay my hand, she will make claims against me."

"Give her to me. I will see she makes no claim."

"Give her to you? For your pleasure?"

"I can control her."

"Yet you have made me seem the whoremonger. How dare you ride onto my property with your breeches undone. What father can I be to them if I allow the daughters in my own priory to be raped? The very act stains me."

"These were no nuns—"

"So you say. Yet if the girl claims to hear the voice of God, what then? If she is a virgin, they will believe it."

"I swear to you, I have not touched her."

Philip returned his attention to the fight. The boarhound caught the second challenger and killed him in frenzy. With the first two dead, the third refused to face him. It rolled over on its back, its legs shaking. The fight was won, the third dog's belly and neck exposed. He whined and licked his snout, rolling his head toward the shouting men.

But the boarhound did not relent. He jumped forward, biting deep into the dog's belly and slashing a wound that spilled wet, writhing intestine and green bile. The boarhound picked the dog up by the throat, worried it, and threw it out into the crowd, among the crowing winners of the bet. It landed, twitching, at Philip's feet.

SeVerde scowled and stepped aside. Such carnage was necessary, perhaps, but it was better not to have it touch you.

A sandy-haired soldier strode up and, kneeling, gave a handful of small coins into Philip's palm. "Your winnings, Your Grace."

Philip weighed the coins before tossing them back out among the men.

Another cheer went up as the soldiery dug through the muck for them. Philip turned his attention back to Romsfeld.

"I need a man who knows what there is to be gained now that the monasteries have fallen. There were two hundred hounds in that kennel behind me, and other prizes, as well. A man loyal to me would be rewarded. Mayhap he would even be allowed to choose a favorite bitch."

Romsfeld twitched. He licked his lips.

Money changed hands again among the soldiers, the clanking of coins heard even above the yowling dogs and shouting men.

"I must burn her otherwise, if her only value to me is dead. I still might." Except, Philip thought with irritation, to kill her would provoke the sunken-skulled fools who clung to miracles and wonders. The last thing he wanted was for them to erect a shrine to this girl, a shrine to heresy, and on his property.

"What is your decision, steward? Shall I have your sworn obedience?"

Romsfeld clenched his jaw, and a muscle ticked under his beard. "I am your servant, Your Grace. I swear my loyalty to you. I ask for nothing. A warm bed."

The soldiers who had hauled the boarhound away replaced him with a gigantic mastiff, yellow with a black face and jowls. The beast lunged against the leather strap that held him. It stretched to the risk of breaking.

Philip called to a soldier below. "Chain that beast. I'll not have it get loose."

The man was soon occupied in looping chain. A braver second tried to wind it around the raging dog, but screamed when the mastiff latched its teeth into his calf. The dog refused to be dragged off, and in the end, the first man jabbed his fingers into the dog's rectum to make it let go.

Philip continued his point. "You say you are loyal, but you are not. You did not do as I asked. Have you given me a virgin martyr for her trial? If I burn her, then, I am condemned. So I think the only solution left to me is that I must see her married off. Her husband, however, must be common, and filthy would be best. A swineherd."

"The swineherd of Attewater is a fat ignoramus with a beard of marbled snot," Romsfeld said.

"So much the better. She will marry him, then. No divine providence in that."

"You would do this—you would give her to a filthy bondsman as a wife, to be used by him? And you would chastise me for rape?"

"Rape? In a marriage consecrated by God? It matters not if he beats her bloody. It is a legal marriage and the thing is done. My ends are met."

"Your Grace, this girl is not like any other. She is pretty, and gentle, and raised high."

"She is a cotter's daughter, is she not? Marriage to the swineherd is all the better then, for she must learn her place."

"I beg you. Give her to me."

"I give rewards to loyal servants only."

Three fresh hounds were brought; they squealed and writhed as a soldier slashed their noses. The mastiff panted, its tongue bright red and lolling.

Philip stood. He was tired of this now. He signaled to his guard that they should follow him back to the monastery. There were still accounts to see to. "I am tired of these games, steward. There is work to be done. Will you give your loyalty to me, or will you grab only what you want for yourself? For if we choose only for our own desires, we leave half of what could be ours behind us." Philip turned to face him. "I want an answer, steward. Do I have your loyalty? Will you choose a bitch, or not?"

A dog howled with lust. Romsfeld bowed. "I will choose one, thank you, Your Grace."

"Good." Philip tapped his crook into the muck. "Now go. You will await me in the treasury."

"Yes, Your Grace." Romsfeld bowed and retreated.

Philip scratched his chin. A man who nursed a grudge could be useful, provided his hand was turned away. He would await the verdict of the inquisitor. Was she indeed a virgin? If she was, it might be difficult. But if she was not, he owed her nothing.

The caged bitch howled. The few dogs left to fight pulled their leashes taut.

Philip was tired of the game. "You there!" He called to the nearest soldier. "Enough sport for today. Let go the leashes and release her from the cage. Let the rest use her and be done."

CHAPTER 20:
Inquisition

THE INCONSTANT RAIN CONTINUED, LEAKING MUD, SEWAGE, and the swirling gossip of Bilsdale into the prison. The gossip about her had subsided, but only a little, though Lo's stomach tightened to think what they said. In addition to the gossip, there was the groaning of wet boards as men hammered them together. The hammering had stopped yesterday. There was now a gallows on Market Street.

She hoped they would hang her. Then it would not be her fault that everything went wrong.

Alice arrived at the window with bread. Her son was to be tried for treason with the rest; he would be tried today.

"That's not all," she pushed her mouth through the bars as if frightened of the sounds she made. "The king's inquisitor has come from York."

Pocket pursed her lips. "What's an inquisitor?"

Clasping her hands to her throat, Sister Beatrice rolled her eyes as if she were taken with madness. "A demon. They burn you with rods to find out what you're thinking."

Pocket covered her face. "I'll tell nothing."

"How does Elizabeth?" Alice asked.

"Her fever's broken." Mendaline had coaxed the lingering bruises from Elizabeth's calves and ankles.

"Bless Mary, then. Maybe that's a sign that bodes well."

Lo was nestled in the straw beside Elizabeth. She had wrapped her prayer beads across her torn palm and kept them there. It was comforting to hold them. She placed her arm over the rise of Elizabeth's hip, so she could give some of that comfort to Elizabeth as well.

The rust-rotten door of the prison grated open. The gaoler strode inside, and two of the king's soldiers. The gaoler pointed a night crawler finger at Mendaline.

"Her," the night crawler wiggled. The men grabbed her, one at each arm. As she passed through the door, the gaoler winked at her. "The inquisitor wants to see you."

The cell darkened. Lo looked to the window to see an energetic crowd pushing one against another in an effort to get a look inside the cell.

Mendaline was marched away, but more of soldiers entered the prison. "Come on then, the rest of you," the gaoler said. The women obeyed, even Elizabeth, who rose stiffly and limped through the doors.

Lo followed last, working her beads as Georgia had taught her. She would be brave. She was a daughter of Isela.

But as she passed the gaoler, he thumped her on the chest. "Not you," he grinned. He backed her up into the middle of the cell. She was alone.

The soldiers filed away up the narrow stair, but two townswomen came down, with the town doctor following. Lo thought what comments Mendaline might make to see the doctor there. Mendaline disliked him and called him a mule for brains. For his part, he claimed that Mendaline used witchcraft.

The doctor followed the townswomen into the cell, holding his fingers spread apart, then closed, then spreading them again.

The women shut the gaoler firmly outside the door, but a soldier remained inside. At the doctor's beckoning, the soldier grasped Lo and held her arms behind her. She went rigid, from her shoulders to her toes. She did not want any of them to touch her.

A chorus of "ahs" erupted from outside the window cell. Whatever the doctor or the townswomen would do, a crowd had gathered around the window to watch.

The doctor crowed and spoke over loudly. "I'm here on business of His Grace the archbishop and his lordship the inquisitor."

He nodded, and the soldier hauled Lo backward into the blankets, impelling her to sit. She rolled a prayer in her mind, as Dame Georgia had taught her to do. *Ave Maria gratia plena. Dominus tecum. Benedicta tu in mulieribus—*

The doctor spoke again, his voice filled with self-importance. "Lo, daughter of John and Johanna of Attewater, the inquisitor has ordered me to determine if you are a whore or a witch. You may spare yourself an examination by confessing yourself one or the other."

Lo looked from the doctor to the women behind him.

One of the women smiled at her; she looked nervously at the soldier and then the crowd. "We need only to know if you are a virgin, child."

"Tell me," the doctor said. "Have you lain with men?"

Lo felt her face grow hot with shame.

The doctor clacked his rings together. "You understand I must examine you if you do not speak the truth."

He watched her with an accusing scrutiny, and she knew she was supposed to answer him. Yet her lungs felt clammy, and she did not know what response to make.

The doctor nodded to the soldier, and Lo felt the man's fingers pinch into the soft flesh inside the joints of her elbows. She let out a small shriek, and the crowd at the window responded, a few with whistles but most with what sounded like sympathy.

The doctor outstretched his fingers and waved them at her. She could see the lumps and calluses, a dark spot colored one nail. "Tell me, girl. Have you lain without your shift?"

He was going to touch her. She began to kick. She tried to scrabble backward, but the soldier held her firmly in place. What did he think, that she was a whore?

She cried out, "No! No!" She shook her head and drew her knees back tight against her body. "I—I am Lo. I am Lo!"

The lantern flickered. Lo thought of the raid on the priory—her injured ribs hurt, and her palm throbbed terribly. Romsfeld had hung over her, stroking her hair and her cheek. She remembered his breath, a gust of blood. She did not remember if she had worn her shift on the pallet by the fire.

The doctor clacked his rings again. "It would be easier for you to confess."

The soldier pushed her shoulders down into the straw. She looked up at him as he pushed her down, and she could see in his eyes he felt pity for her. And also there was kindness. Why, then, would he do this? She shrunk down on top of a pile of shredded blankets. The smell of urine wafted up, stinging her eyes and throat. She began to shake. She shuddered as the doctor poked at her ankles.

"Doctor," the older woman laid a hand on the doctor's shoulder, and he retreated from his position. The older woman knelt next to her in his place. She touched Lo lightly.

The second woman knelt beside the first and raised the lantern. There was what sounded like a crush at the window, and the bars squealed. Everything was suddenly so cold. Lo could not control her shivering.

"Pray, some coverings," the woman with the lantern said.

The doctor picked up a dirty blanket, and the older of the two women laid it over Lo. She did not feel warmer under it, but was grateful that it shielded her.

She squeezed her eyes shut. She could feel the woman's fingers at her knees and felt the shame of her nakedness as the younger woman held the lantern high.

"Be calm, child." The older woman placed a warm palm on her leg, a steady, reassuring pressure. "We will be quick."

Yet Lo could not bring herself to open her knees. The shaking felt uncontrollable. She clenched her teeth to stop them from clattering.

The doctor's accusatory voice boomed from behind her. "Do you seek to hide the truth, girl?"

The older woman spoke. "Pray you, doctor, you only frighten her." She positioned herself closer, her voice now smooth and reassuring. "It will take but an *Ave*. Then the inquisitor will be satisfied."

Lo unclenched her jaw. She was a daughter of Isela. Dame Georgia had said there may be many trials and had shared with her some of the trials she herself had faced. Yet Lo shivered all the more. Some of those stories terrified her.

Heat, then cold, then nausea coursed through her as the women forced her knees apart, gently, but with a firm pressure. Though they could not see, there were "ahs" of gratification from the window. The woman with the lantern brought the light under the blanket.

"She is a virgin."

The doctor thrust the women aside. Lo stiffened as he wedged his hands at her knees, but she could not protect herself. He pushed his hand down, squinting and groping.

"For shame!" The second woman scolded.

The doctor barked back at her, "S'blood! Shine that light where it will do some good."

His fingers hurt her. Lo tried to pull away. "No!" she said.

A call came from the window, "Have a care!"

The doctor sputtered, "Is it my fault if she shirks? What can I see in the dark?" He poked her, dragging a fingernail along her skin, then grunted, and withdrew. The older woman glared at him as Lo curled up. Sorrow and then rage filled her. For an instant, she thought of uncoiling her body to kick the doctor as hard as she could. But she did not. She was afraid.

"She is intact." The doctor wiped his hands across the front of his doublet. He sounded disappointed. "I will inform the inquisitor." He stood over Lo, his face red, his brow heavy. "It is to your credit, girl, that you are not a whore." He turned to address the folk at the window. "Yet you men be warned, a woman's lusts are never satisfied! A wife will suck a husband's bones dry as chaff if he gives in to her demands."

Ribald laughter echoed from the street. "My bone can satisfy your wife!" Amid the laughter another voice chided, "Shh, now. She's a virgin proper." A tongue clicked. "Poor thing. First a saint. And now this. Lo the forsaken."

Lo the forsaken. The name pressed into her shaking muscles. No. It was a lie. She was a miracle. She was the Chooser. Let them lie if they wished and say what they liked. But one day she would rise up. One day there would be another miracle.

The door clanged open, and the soldier released her. She curled up as the gaoler came back inside the cell, smirking. He had probably watched everything.

But she was not allowed to stay on the straw and cry herself to sleep. The doctor nodded to the soldier. "Bring her."

The soldier hauled her up, and Lo willed the shaking to stop. She was not forsaken. She was not. Dame Georgia would never allow it.

༄

Lo stumbled into the street accompanied by an escort of armed men. They marched with her past the gallows, the new wood creaking and engorged with rain. Beneath it a woman knelt. It was Alice, her eyes huge as if swollen from frost. Her son Osbert, Ralph and Angie Williamson, and another Lo did not know swung from a high beam, their heads tipped sideways and their faces grotesquely purple.

Lo looked down at her feet and did not look up again until they reached the guildhall.

One of the soldiers led her inside. The timber and stone hall was filled with smoke and guildsmen. A few hired men and soldiers stood around their masters or at the doors. Two men urinated into a fire that did little to mitigate a cold that white-misted the breath of any but the men nearest to it. All save those who looked poorest wore thick hooded robes or close fitting caps.

At the end of the hall, the lord's table was laid with a crimson tablecloth embroidered with the emblem of the archbishop. Several men stood behind the table or sat at the bench. Lo recognized the king's reeve among them. A monk she did not know sat with his head down, scribbling.

At the center of the table was a man slashed with shadows. Gray stretched his cheekbones and his chin, and they seemed to gape. Though he wore an archbishop's rich purple vestments, the shadows made him seem a starveling. He held a staff topped with a spiked crosier. As he stroked it, a multitude of jeweled rings thunked against the golden spikes. Lo guessed the starveling to be Archbishop SeVerde, but she hoped he was not.

The final man at the table wore a furred robe and mantle, the mantle clasped with an ornamental crest that indicated him to be of noble blood. He held a small marmoset in the crook of his arm. The animal chirped as the man rubbed it behind its ears.

Romsfeld was in the hall as well, but Lo averted her eyes as he paced along the wall. If possible, Romsfeld seemed even hungrier than the archbishop, though clumsier, ruddier, and restless. She tried to make herself tiny and insignificant. Perhaps she could disappear from their notice.

Mendaline stood at the center of the hall, two wagon's lengths from the table. She stood with her arms outstretched from her sides, clad only in her shift. Though she held her arms out straight, her shoulders sagged as if her body ached.

The man with the marmoset asked her a question. "Do you understand the nature of your crimes?"

Mendaline bobbed awkwardly. "I crave forgiveness for my sins, my lord."

"And yet you cast spells and sorceries?"

Mendaline shifted her feet. "My lord, I do confess I wrongly gave the steward a draft to make him sleep." A titter went up among the guildsmen. Romsfeld stopped pacing and put his hand to his sword as if daring any man to insult him.

"So, you do not deny that you have done this."

Archbishop SeVerde indicated to the monk next to him, who scribbled onto a flat of paper.

"I do not. It was a sin. Yet it was not witchcraft."

Keeping his quill in his hand, the monk stood from the table and called out across the hall.

"The physician will come forth!"

The doctor leapt forward with his fingers splayed as he bowed. Lo edged to where she hoped he could not see her. As she sidled away, she saw Beatrice under guard across the hall. Beatrice signaled her with a quick hand gesture, a gesture that asked if all was well. All was not well. How could it be? But Lo signaled back. "All's well," her fingers said.

The doctor cleared his throat. He gave a leather satchel over to the archbishop with another spectacular bow.

The archbishop resumed the questioning. "Does the prisoner deny that this bag belongs to her?"

"No," Mendaline said. "It is mine."

"Good physician," the archbishop addressed the doctor, "have you examined the contents of the satchel known to belong to the witch Mendaline?"

"Yes, Your Grace."

"And your determination?"

"Within were cord and herbs. The tools of witchcraft."

The guildsmen in the hall whispered together.

Mendaline shifted again. "I am a sinner, Your Grace. Yet not a witch."

The inquisitor allowed the marmoset to crawl under his chin as he strode around the table. He stopped inches from Mendaline. "There are numerous marks on the accused, Your Grace, that could indicate the succubus, the sucking demons, who do drink the blood of witches." He lifted Mendaline's arm at the wrist, raising it over her head. He pulled the sleeve of her shift down to her armpit. "Especially this mark, which looks like freshly drawn blood."

"She is a witch then?"

"In truth, I have seen worse marks on a witch." The inquisitor released Mendaline's arm but grabbed her head and tilted it up and sideways. "There is a mark here, also. Along the jaw. A nipple."

The men in the hall pressed close to see it. Lo felt confused as to how a nipple could be found on Mendaline's neck. She wondered if she had any strange nipples on her own body and if they would accuse her of witchcraft. She cringed, afraid the doctor would expose her here in the hall.

The inquisitor withdrew as the archbishop clanked his crook loudly against the table and indicated quiet.

"The accused will hear our judgment."

A man pushed forward from a cluster of townsmen at the far corner of the hall; he stood shaking. "Your Grace, I am Arnulf, Your Grace."

The archbishop gave the man an appraising glance, his gaze moving over the man's dress and badge.

"You are a fuller?"

"Yes, my lord."

"Very well, fuller. You may speak."

The man bowed and held himself down overlong. "Pray, forgive me, Your Grace. I wish to speak for the sister, Mendaline. She had saved my family, my lord. It was a bad birth, and yet now I have a son."

"It was the grace of God alone that saved your son, fuller."

"Yes, my lord. But there are none here to speak ill of the sister Mendaline, *except* the doctor."

Mendaline picked up her robe and pulled it over her shoulders. Lo could see the gratitude in her eyes. Her shoulders straightened as she turned to face the council. "Please," she said. "I am a good midwife. I have strength in my hands that I might heal suffering, a touch given by God, Your Grace. It is not witchcraft."

The mumblings grew louder in the hall. The archbishop seemed to study the faces of the men in turn. He pressed his hands against the table. "I am your lord. I will have you know I judge in fairness. You, fuller, will you pledge against your life for this woman?"

The man nodded. A few other men stepped forward, and more, until a dozen men stood out from the others.

"These men stand with you?"

The fuller nodded.

"Frankpledge?" The archbishop sneered. "A brotherhood, how quaint." He gestured for the men to come forward. "And it is your oath that she is not a witch? On penalty of your own deaths you will swear to this?"

The fuller nodded again. Lo noticed that even in the cold of the hall, he sweated.

The archbishop indicated to the monk. "Very well. Record their names, for they shall all swear, on pain of death, to bear the consequences of her good conduct."

The archbishop indicated to the master-at-arms, and he took hold of Mendaline.

"The woman Mendaline," the archbishop said, "an example must be made of you so that others may be reminded of the wages of sin. You are found guilty by this court. You are expelled from the religious life, and you are hereby sentenced to die by fire."

Murmurs echoed up and down the hall. Lo heard Beatrice burst into sobs.

The archbishop raised a hand for silence and continued. "The court declares this woman guilty, but hereby stays the sentence. Mendaline of the priory at Attewater, your life has been won by the strength of frankpledge. Though you may live, yet you will never again practice sorcery. You will be taken to the block, and by the flat of a sword, the bones of your hands shall be crushed." The archbishop banged his staff against the floor. "Master-at-arms, see that the sentence is immediately carried out."

CHAPTER 21:
Heresy

The master-at-arms marched Mendaline through the guild hall and out the doors. As she passed, Lo felt the hollow of uselessness, and a voice within her declared her a fraud and ordinary. All Isela's sisters, especially Mendaline, had risked their lives to protect her. She had failed, somehow, to be what they expected. She felt ashamed. She wanted to reassure Mendaline that she would somehow prove her virtue. But the guildhall doors were already closed.

The attention of the court shifted. Lo flinched as the archbishop regarded her, the angled shadows slashing a fascinated resentment across his features, as if she were a pretty bit of discarded silk.

Two soldiers nudged her forward. Romsfeld paced with them along the wall, and although Lo wore a woolen partlet that covered her from her feet to her neck, she shielded her bosom with her hands, unsure of how to defend herself.

Once she was before the council, Romsfeld stayed behind them, at the edges of the hall, circling. She shut him from her mind as she curtseyed deeply for the archbishop, sinking to her knees as she dipped down, and staying there. She would prove herself a good and pure daughter. If she did, she would be protected. It was how it worked. The innocent earned love and protection from those around them.

The archbishop spoke, his voice harsh. "You are the one they call Forsaken, are you not?"

Lo flinched. The word again. Forsaken. No, she thought, they were wrong. "No, my lord."

"Then you deny yourself?"

"Please, my lord," Lo tested her voice, bringing it louder, seeking a true note. "I am Lo of Isela. That is all I know."

"Witless girl. The name Forsaken is on the tongues of all the men of Yorkshire. Do you deny it?"

Lo was unsure what he meant. She answered the question simply. "I am Lo."

"And your father?"

"John of Attewater, Your Grace."

"And your mother?"

"Johanna of the same."

"Common villagers. And yet you wear a silken veil."

Silk was forbidden to any but the noble classes, though the nonnoble wore it, regardless, if they could afford it. Sister Catherine had worn silk in all different colors. She said there was no shame in a woman looking pretty, even a nun.

"It is what I was given to wear, Your Grace. But it is linen, not silk."

"Yet a fine linen. Not rat cloth, as should be worn by such as you. You were raised, were you not, by the witch Georgia?"

Lo kept her gaze humbly down and noticed there were small stones in the dirt. And a footprint, perhaps Mendaline's. "Georgia was as a mother to me, Your Grace. The sisters raised me so that I might be ready when—" Lo broke off, ready for what, she was not sure. The hollowness flared again in her gut.

The inquisitor cawed at her, and she looked up quickly. Had she made a mistake? Perhaps, for he stared at her, his eyes like a beady crow.

"Ready for what, child?"

"In truth I do not know, for nothing yet has happened."

The archbishop gaped at her. "Nothing happened? The witch prioress is dead, the king has summoned you to account for your sins and treacheries, and you call this nothing?"

A few of the men in the hall chuckled. Did they laugh at her? Lo opened her mouth but then closed it. She thought of Romsfeld, that he had caressed her cheek and her lips with the tips of his fingers. She looked down again at the stones.

The archbishop resumed questioning. "Do you claim to work miracles?"

She had seen a bear once, a bear chained at the neck that Mendaline had cured. It was the first bear Lo had ever seen. When the man who owned him beat him, the bear pulled against the chains and tried to flee. That man had rabbits, too. But when he clubbed the rabbits, they attacked him, fighting and scratching him for his cruelty. But the bear, though he could have killed the man, only sought to end his suffering.

"Well?"

"They say that the water is a miracle," Lo said. "The water came to baptize me when—"

"Enough." The archbishop pounded his crook against the table. "You speak in ignorance. This flood of water was nothing. No miracle, no wonder, and no baptism."

"Then—then I have not been baptized, my lord."

The archbishop sucked a quick breath, and the crowd stilled in a collective hush.

Lo's throat hurt as if filled with dry sticks. She looked up but quickly down again. She could not see the stones.

The inquisitor's marmoset scurried over his shoulder. "You are not baptized?"

The hush turned to uproar.

The archbishop pounded his staff on the floor, and the uproar quieted. "This is what comes of sorcery. Do you understand, girl, the depth of this error?"

Lo shook her head.

"Do you know the story of Adam and Eve, child?"

Lo nodded.

"So you know that Eve's sin caused all suffering. And that man is forever punished for Eve's treachery?"

This surprised her. Lo looked up, eager to explain what she knew. This, at least, she could set right. "No, my lord," she said. "Eve was a valiant woman, strong and true. She did what she must, knowing that ache would follow, to give men and women the knowledge they would need to seek God and live the promise of their lives. Because of Eve, we may love in the full flesh of our humanity as part of the whole of God's creation—"

"Silence!"

Lo obeyed midsentence, but silence did not follow in the rest of the hall. A cascading fervor rippled through the room. Everyone talked at once. The archbishop bashed his crook against the floor and then the table to no avail. The inquisitor hurried to the monk, checking over his shoulder, rereading, it seemed, every word he had recorded. Even Romsfeld stopped his pacing, his glowering given over to a look of surprise.

Pressure grew under Lo's ribs. Fear swirled around her, pressing even against her skin. Perhaps, she thought, perhaps things could never be put right. Was that a fault of hers? Perhaps it was.

It took twenty *Ave Marias* to restore order. Lo worked her fingers along her beads, trying to calm the pressure inside her with the string of prayers. When the men did quiet, it seemed they pressed in around her more severely than before. She heard the name again, Forsaken, and she knew that they named her.

The archbishop spoke quietly. "Your heresy is clear." He indicated the other nuns who were guarded near the far corner—Elizabeth, Beatrice, and Pocket. The guards drove them forward. They kept their eyes and faces lowered, kneeling behind Lo as the archbishop addressed them.

"Do you also herald Eve as having done a great deed in her sin? The glad servant of Satan?"

Beatrice spoke. "If you please, my lord. Lo has—she is mistaken. One story confused, perhaps, with another. For she is but young. Eve was weak, Your Grace, and so tempted by the serpent. Paradise was assured, but for her sin. We beg your forgiveness."

Again there was murmuring. Lo closed her eyes. When Georgia told the story, it seemed true. For the Golden Legend said that prosperity endangered the soul. The prosperous lacked adversity to shape and temper them. To learn compassion and humility, they must be set free from their gentle world. Was that not what Eve had done?

Romsfeld spoke next; his voice was one of low victory. "You see, my lord, the girl has been but poorly instructed, the victim of devilry. She can be reformed."

"Indeed not," the inquisitor shook his head, "she is an abomination." Lo did not look up. The marmoset chirped and chattered as the inquisitor continued. "Do you hear voices, girl?"

Lo shook her head.

"In your dreams, like the heretic Joan of Arc, do you claim revelation?"

"No." Lo whispered it. No indeed, she had no dreams at all. No dreams, no awakening, and no revelation. Dame Georgia said one day she would. But now, Dame Georgia was dead.

The room was cold; Lo drew into herself. "I am just a girl," she said. "Dame Georgia was wrong about me."

Again a cacophony of voices reverberated through the hall as each man spoke at once. Sounds of betrayal and disbelief mixed with stout defense. She could hear behind her, Beatrice and Elizabeth and Pocket as well, their women's voices distinct among the swell of men. Yet she closed her ears to them. She did not want to hear the name Forsaken from their lips.

Romsfeld pressed near to the archbishop, his voice distinct against the others in the hall. "Give her to me, Your Grace. I will see this thing ended, as we spoke before."

The archbishop gazed long at Romsfeld as if taking the measure of him and then demanded silence in the hall. He called the doctor forward. "You say this girl is an intact virgin?"

The word "virgin" seemed to echo, and the men in the hall settled down again to listen to the proceedings.

The doctor nodded. "She is, Your Grace."

"She is a virgin." The archbishop spoke with the inquisitor, and now the hall pressed with silence. A dog yelped and another scratched through the rushes near the fire.

"Lo of Attewater, your virginity alone has saved you. It is the court's determination that you have not sinned, but have been sinned against." The archbishop grasped his crook near the base and swept it wide over the table. Men ducked to miss it, and one was stuck across the chest. The archbishop's voice was thick with an indignant rage. "Women of Isela, you are the worst, most vicious of nuns. And on my land. Such sin as yours must be purged. I will make no martyrs of you, but will instead condemn you as what you are, rebellious and despicable. Know that I despise you. Know that as I despise you, so does God.

"I bring an end to all of this. You will grovel before God and in the public square give testament to your sin. You will profess to the true and rightful faith, or you will die under the lash of your reformers. You will be taken to Bishopsgate Abbey, and in the good and true nunnery there, you will submit, or you will die."

The archbishop thumped the crook down beside him. "Lo of Isela, you have nothing, no relations to speak for you and no dowry to profess as a nun. You are an orphan and a burden to the parish. I should expel you from my lands.

"Yet I know mercy, by God's grace. As your lord, I will see you returned to your proper place. You will work as a bondswoman on my land and there repay your life's debt to me. Let it not be said that I am not true and noble and generous in this matter.

"I remand you to the custody of my steward who will supervise your reeducation. You are a lowly village girl, ordinary and without value. See that you give each day a full day's work. This is the judgment of this court."

The monk scribbled madly on the paper. The men in the room spoke together, hushed and animated. Lo finished the bead strand and started her prayers again. She did not understand.

Soldiers took Beatrice and Elizabeth and Pocket away; she did not dare watch them. Two of Romsfeld's men stepped up to claim her. As they pulled her up, she reached forward and grabbed a handful of dust from the footprint in front of her and flung it away. May she never return to this place, she thought.

Romsfeld strode toward her and waved his men aside. He gripped her with an eager, rough touch, grasping her waist, holding her tightly. He pushed her forward and pressed himself behind her. The archbishop and inquisitor turned away, and the village men, guildsmen, and soldiers dispersed. Lo stumbled. Romsfeld tightened his grip. He sweated—the smell of men and dogs and horses. She closed her eyes. All her life she had been cared for, nurtured, and protected. But now she was alone. Only Romsfeld remained. She was indeed forsaken.

CHAPTER 22:
Saint Winifred

Jane woke, a cold draft overriding her dream. She tilted her head back and watched the family cow push its bony forehead against the house shutters, grinding them against the timber of the window sill. It was a shuddering note the cow played too often in the mornings, creaking and sawing, pumping the cool morning air into a house stifled with sleep, goats, and hearth smoke. It was spring, so the crisp of wild onions wafted in as well. The cow rolled its eyes white and bellowed.

Jane's stomach rumbled. She stretched her bare toes into the fibers of the pallet.

Her mother shoved the cow away to cease the creaking. The old cow responded with a heartier bellow. "Stop that noise, for Mary's sake," the woman scolded. "Jane, take the beast out."

The girl jumped up, and her head spun at the smell of onions, the stifling smoke, and her sudden movement all at once. Dizziness tossed up a fragment of her dream, a dream of a mountain and a bead of glass. And fire.

"Be quick now," came her mother's voice. "She'll trample the peas."

Jane steadied her feet and hopped across to the front of the house. Two goats and one of the dogs competed with the cow to be first through the open door as the flavors of the wet spring wafted in. Her mother gave the cow a slap though the animal did not need to be hurried—she was hungry.

"Put some meat on tha' bones," Jane's mother scolded. "I'll want milk today."

As the cow rushed by, Jane scratched at the tangles in her hair. She wiped her nose against the back of her hand and wiped the back of her hand against her skirt. "There was a lady in my dream," she said.

Her mother brushed the coals from the hearth. "Did she promise you a shilling?"

"No."

"Then I would'na worry much. Go on, now, after that cow a'fore she eats the tansy and her milk goes sour."

"Ma?"

"What child?"

"There's something I can't remember."

Her mother regarded her, and she laughed. Her mother often looked at her that way, as if she was used to the unexpected. "Perhaps you forgot to do as you'ere bid?"

"No." Jane turned, but stopped again just outside the door.

"Ma?"

"I ha'n't run off."

"Do I have a true name?"

"You're named after your godmother like any normal child."

"Ma?"

"I still ha'n't run off."

"How old am I?"

"Older'n Moses." Her mother threw a handful of crushed dried peas into a bubbling pot.

"Am I four years old?"

"Aye, you might be."

"Ma?"

"Enough!" The woman kicked another stone nearer the fire. "That great cow's g'na eat the garden t' nubs. To your work."

The cow lowed at the gate; the goats darted forward but then retreated from her stamping hooves. They made a ruckus.

"They'll not eat the garden," she said.

"You mind they don't."

Jane went out into the morning and closed the door behind her. She ran to the garden gate, lifted the latch, and followed the animals to a wider yard. She scratched the cow's scrawny neck as the beast strained over the wall to reach the green stretched tops of the onions. They had grown to within reach overnight.

Jane's uneasiness dropped away as the morning cooled her palms and the soles of her feet. She scratched the thickened skin of her knees and leaned across the stone wall, opening her hand so that it reflected the pink of an early sunrise. There against the pink of her palm, a strange round mark, like a rough-skinned fruit, poked out. She traced the strange mark with a fingertip. Her mother said it was a birthmark.

The cow snorted at her. "Get on!" Jane called to her. "There's grass by the Saxon wall."

She studied the mark again, opening and closing her palm to see how it stretched and then popped out. She thought of her dream and the name she heard there. She tested it, forming the word silently on her tongue, a little afraid of what it might sound like or what it might claim from her.

As she made her mouth round with the unspoken vowel, a voice from her dream whispered it beside her. Her true name. The word spilled into the cool morning air, as if lifted out of the very stones around her—*Georgia*.

The cow shook her head and bellowed. The girl bolted back into the house.

BOOK FOUR

CHAPTER 23:
Revelation

THE ONLY THING WORSE THAN SPINNING, Jane thought, was being made to work while others made merry. Tomorrow was Saint George's Day, and it promised to be more the warmth of June than April. Today was the perfect day for early merrymaking. But from spinning—Jane dropped a fiber-swollen bobbin into the basket by her feet—from spinning, there was never a holiday.

Today was the worst yet, for on this day her mother had put her outside to spin in front of everyone. Her mother said it would be good for her to spin outside in the sun, but in setting up the wheel, she had piled copious clumps of straw on the stool for Jane to sit on. She had then adjusted Jane's skirts so that the straw stuck out from under her at every angle.

Only women who had their courses sat on straw when they spun. Now every gossip with a son to marry off would know her courses had begun.

"Ho! Good morrow!"

A young man sprawled over the low stone wall that separated the garden from the lane, and posed for her. He wore a gray-white goat hide over his head with two white-fleshed sticks poking out like fresh-carved ears. And he was handsome, even half covered in goatskin.

Jane frowned hard to discourage him, for the heat her body seemed to drain away to cold panic. Would he notice the straw? She pretended to be very interested in twisting thread. The heat rose up again to think of him looking at her. She would ignore him. Blessed Mary, let him go on his way.

He only growled at her, and then growled louder when she continued to ignore him. Then, leaping over the low wall, he strode into the yard.

Jane ducked her head down. "Adam, go away!" It would be doubly bad if he saw her blush. If he knew, he would tease her—or worse, treat her differently, or be awkward. Her stomach turned over into cramping. She pretended to fidget while smoothing her skirt over the worst of the protruding straw.

Adam stopped to pose, pulling the goat skin away from his face. He leaned backward as if he would break in half and looked mischievous and full of glee.

She squinted determinedly at the spiny flax. "Shouldn't you be turning furrows?" she asked.

Adam put the goat hide over his head and pawed the ground as if to charge. "Ahr ..."

"Do you mean to be a dragon? If so you are a poor one." She hoped her taunt was contemptuous, but then she had to laugh. Her stomach twisted up slightly, not a cramp, but the funny twist she sometimes got when Adam was near. He smelled of salt. And there was always chaff or dung or straw sticking in his hair. Mary! She did not want to think of straw!

"So, you think *me* the dragon?" Adam gave an indignant cry and twirled the goatskin aside, twisting it around the middle and pinching his voice into a high-piped twitter. "Alas it is not so. For in this mystery play, I shall be the maiden." He struck an exaggerated girlish pose, then leapt straight at her, plunked himself down, and leaned against the stool to rest.

Her cheeks pricked hot. The clutch of straw under her seemed huge and yellow. A bonfire in the middle of the night had more subtlety.

"Come on," he lolled his head back and laughed at her. "Serious Jane, there'll be a dragon tomorrow, with a flaming torch. Can you imagine it?" He shifted to his knees. "If you'll come tomorrow, I promise to kiss you."

His eyes crinkled at the corners, and the strange feeling in her stomach pushed up again. Adam had not kissed her, and she had not wanted him to. Not that he couldn't kiss her, of course. He had kissed other girls. The thought made her skin prickle again.

"I promised to spin." Her voice sounded squeaky.

He made a sober face and poked the bobbin as it spun. The thread caught and broke.

"Mother Mary!" She made her thumb and forefinger into a cross and kissed it to ward away bad luck. "The fates will come because the thread is cut and all because of your foolery!"

He threw the goatskin on the ground and made a fun of chastising it. "Fie on this skin. It was the goat, not I, milady, who broke the thread. This goat with the devil in it." A more serious look changed the color of his eyes from autumn green to almost brown. "In truth, Jane, I'd have you come tomorrow." His gaze became mischievous again. "But perhaps as you're so cross, I'll have to kiss you now instead."

He looked like he might well kiss her. She twitched, and at her movement, her skirt slid back from where it had covered the straw. A great hatch of it poked out from under her, enough to strew an entire byre.

Adam stopped in midbreath and stared, reddening. He drew back, shifting from foot to foot. Then, swiping the goatskin up from the ground, he grinned again.

He resumed the maiden's voice. "You sit and spin then, milady," he disappeared under the goatskin then said in his own voice, "until tomorrow."

He bowed and was gone, leaping over the low wall and calling ahead for all to make way for Saint George's dragon.

Her heart pounded as he went. *Saint Anne, mother of Mary*! How could her mother have done this to her?

Jane unwound a small amount from the ruined start of the bobbin. Scratching a smooth section in the dirt, she dropped the thread from as high as she could. The twisted flax floated down and piled over itself in the dirt. She studied it for signs of what would come—a husband, children, or maybe fortune? Instead she saw a mountain with fire spewing from the top.

Adam was right; she *was* cross. Most girls could see ten or twenty children in such a casting, and no fewer husbands. But she saw mountains, this one exactly like the mountain from her dreams. As a portent of the future, it was frightening.

She stood up, pushing the straw onto the ground and bunching it to hide the glossy redness at the center. She did not want to hurry into womanhood. She shivered slightly. Was she to find love and a husband on that mountain? She imagined a hairy hermit with a beehive beard and shook the image from her mind. Whose future was it, anyway, but hers? Could she not decide for herself what she would do? Fie on the mountains! The image of a bearded hermit in her mind gave way to one of a boy with a goatskin. She giggled. Yes. Perhaps she would let Adam kiss her tomorrow.

She poked her toe into the dirt, grinding the bit of thread until it looked more like a duck than a mountain. She would go to the church, and she would pray to Saint Catherine who cared for spinners and maids. She would ask for a simple life.

༄

The church was small and square, with straw wattle walls daubed with pond clay. An altar remained at the north end, though she had heard that King Edward had forbidden altars. The priest took down the rood last summer. He sold the silver chalice and tray. Roods and silver were idolatry and to say the Latin Mass traitorous, so the king said. But the copper chalice remained and stood at the center of the altar with the lamps lit. They were set next to the new carvings of Saint Mary and Joseph. The village had purchased the carvings with the money from the sale of silver.

Jane took her prayer book from her apron pocket and turned the pages until she settled on the woodcut of the passion. She should begin her meditation with this, for the book had been her godmother's, and she had told her that every seven Hail Marys recited while gazing on the passion would mean a year less her soul must spend in purgatory. Purgatory was heresy, too, according to the king. Though the priest said that King Edward would discover the fires of purgatory for himself one day. Jane closed the book and closed her eyes. The priest said yes, and King Edward said no. Which was true?

Jane opened her eyes again. Perhaps what was most important was just to feel the pity of the passion for its own sake. Because, as there was hardship and shame in the world, there must be pity as well. She turned the page, and this one showed the baby Jesus in Mary's lap. This page was particularly worn. She stroked her fingers over the edges and along the lines of the words. She wished she could read them, especially the ones that were blurred and bubbled into little circles.

She stared at the picture more intently now. The baby Jesus looked so peaceful in his mother's lap, and Mary's gaze was one of adoration. She began a Hail Mary, "Hail Mary full of grace, the Lord is with thee ..." but the words thickened. They resisted her; they were so big.

Something swelled up from within her, like a giant standing up and stretching out. Tendrils of longing passed through her heart and erupted from the center of her body. They gnawed out from between the blades of her shoulders and through the soles of her feet. As the giant inside her stretched, it took her breath and shook her. And she remembered. *There is something left to do.* Her eyes stung and watered over. *Something. Something left undone.*

She buried her face in her hands. The giant expanded until it filled the whole church. Everything around her seemed suddenly changed, as if she'd entered a dream. And then a river rushed in. The cold water swept her out of herself. She tumbled over pebbles and seemed to travel over a great distance, across fields and hills, past villages, forests, orchards, and grand manors.

The vision set her on her feet among the ruins of a place. There were old stones, a round, thick pile of them. It seemed as if the stones themselves remembered something she did not. There was something in the earth beneath her feet. She reached down to touch it.

Something happened here.

A woman in a green dress stood beside her, smiling. The wind tossed her gown, and her hair fell free around her shoulders. Jane was used to this woman in her dreams. Was she an angel? She spoke in the wind.

"Remember who you are."

"I am a daughter of Isela." Jane remembered it. But she darkened her mind and tried to pull back. This was what frightened her. The darkness of this dream.

The woman spoke again. "You are the Bearer. You bear the mark."

"I am tired." This time the giant seemed to speak. Yet it was so. At the words, Jane felt consumed, wrung out, exhausted. She wanted to lie down and rest. But the stones poked up all around her. There was no place to sleep.

"You are my daughter. You must put an end to suffering."

"I have failed." And as she said it, she remembered this, too, was so. This was the darkness that made her look away. She had failed. A throb came from the core of her, from deep within her, from the bottoms of her feet. She *had* failed. Utterly. It was all gone. All hope. All life. Everything.

The woman spoke, "And yet you live. Never doubt your strength. You are of the lamb and the lily. You are of the one true heart."

"Stop!" Jane cried out. She steered her vision back, back to her own village, to the altar and the copper chalice, to the saints Mary and Joseph, to the light of an early spring. But the vision followed. It stayed on, the giant groaning. The images deepened around her. She smelled winter fires and felt a chill, the cold of February. She shuddered.

The texture of her skin changed. Her hands grew wet and sticky and covered in earth. She had returned to some earlier time, some earlier moment. The stones around her reassembled into walls. An altar rose up next to her. Her head pounded, and her whole body ached. She felt unendurable pain and pushed with all her might on a paving stone to flatten it.

A woman screamed. Jane struggled to stand as a horseman thundered into the church. He rode without a helmet, and against the saddle bar he had a girl, her face and gown smeared with muck and grass.

Jane braced to run. But as she tensed the pain struck her down. She grasped her side and found it gaping, the cloth and skin sliced through and clotted with blood.

He bore down on her, the forelegs of the horse pounding into the floor of the church. The walls shaking. He swung the sword and readied it to strike. He was so close; his eyes glowered with hatred, and his lips snarled back over his teeth.

She threw her hands up and screamed for release. Yet neither the vision nor the swordsman relented. He would kill her if he could. He intended it to be so.

If he succeeded, everything would be lost. There would be no one to stop the onslaught—none to withstand the terror of men who twisted the world over onto itself. This rider was a monster sprung from the world that made him. She was the daughter who bore the burden of knowing that truth. She must bring the future.

Jane drew herself up within the giant inside. She planted her feet on the flat cold of the stone floor. As he readied to hew her with the blade, she struck out with her hand. She seized him at the wrist and clamped her fingers on the hilt of his sword.

He countered, curving the sword to come up under her, to slash her through her belly.

She twisted to evade the blow, though agony ripped through her. She bit down against the pain and struck again, buckling his arm, bending it behind him, and flipping him from the horse. The sword clattered to the ground. The man landed hard and rolled. The girl on the saddle bar fell after him, striking her head on the stones.

He kicked, but Jane snatched up the sword. She struck him hard with the hilt on the side of the head. He writhed and then lay still. His breath rattled the cold air.

Her side ached, an unimaginable pain. She wrapped her skirts around her wound and knelt, pulling the girl into her lap, stroking the muck and grass from her dress.

A voice spoke, the wind again. The woman or the vision or the angel was within the church. A warmth surrounded her. *Fear not.*

Jane choked. "I remember." She blinked and felt tears fall. An orb of light appeared in front of her, spinning slowly, an amber glass surrounded by a bronze flame.

"And this?"

"It is the relic. I must find it. I must bear it."

"Yes."

She felt the cold of the paving stones beneath her. She was inside the giant now. "It is buried under the church stone."

"You are one of the true heart."

Yes. She nodded. "I am Georgia."

The girl, the man, the sword, and the horse all melted away, and she was alone. Her body felt small again, and cold.

She had survived. She blinked at the dim inside of the wattle church. She was a girl again. Jane. Her clothes were as they had been before, though her arm ached from the jarring blow she had given out. She was Jane still. Yet, she was not Jane. She would never be Jane again.

She had awakened. She felt her girlhood stretch. She was twelve years old, soon thirteen. She was as old as Moses. Her path was to the mountains, the mists, and the grit of ages. She would leave the rest behind.

She thought of the grassy hilltop and of the stones she had seen there. It was a priory. She wondered at it. She had never seen a priory. She had never met a nun.

"I am Georgia." She wiped the tears away. She was strong. She was the Bearer. And she must move quickly. Twelve years were already gone.

CHAPTER 24:
Hallows

Jane became Georgia on the drover lanes through the wilderness. She had seen mountains after all. And dogs loose on the moors. Carters on the road had aided her, fed her, and chased her. Her feet had cracked on the first day. She learned to avoid the villages, that bread was dear, and kindness dearer. All the while she followed the hum of the relic as it resonated in her belly and breast. She was Georgia now.

And she was so close. And yet Georgia was lost, cold, and wet through to her bones. She followed a thin slip of memory, like the ghost pealing of church bells. But the storm left her numb. Her thighs trembled, pushed to the limit during her cross-country pilgrimage back to this place, scattered and hurried, and now lost on a hilltop in the pitch dark while the rain soaked her through. Yet this must be right, the grassy crest, the wide river, and smaller stream bed.

She had expected to find people here. A church, something. But it was as if she had stumbled across a tomb. The rain poured, and she could see almost nothing. Yet she must find the relic, the orb of the vision. It was hidden here, somewhere.

She brushed against a woody shrub. The scent of rue lifted through the storm. Rue! She stopped to touch the new spring growth and woody stem. It was an older plant, two feet tall and dense. There had been a garden here.

She searched with her fingers, plucking up the surrounding leaves to place them, the bright crisp of mint, the flat leaf of wild-seeded borage. There had been sweet woodruff in this garden, too. Once. She herself had planted it.

The thought felt icy, impossible. As if she crawled away from her own death. She moved forward. The sense of dread deepened rather than receded, and her nape prickled. She looked quickly behind her, her heart quickening. Though it was dark and the hillside empty, she felt as if someone watched her from the darkness.

She shook her head to clear it. She must focus on her task. The rue, the mint, they had been planted in the courtyard garden, just outside the dorter walls. The memory righted itself. That meant the kitchen and buttery were to her right, the guestrooms and lavatory left, and behind her the brewhouse and refectory. She had used sweet woodruff in wine and to strew the floor of the church. The church, then, was straight north, not thirty paces.

She crawled over the ground, sliding her hands through the smooth wet and clumps of lichen. She found a foundation stone next to a spire of thistle, and next to that stone, another.

She touched every stone and clump of grass, all the time headed as close to north as she could figure it. The borage had reseeded everywhere, and the mint had run wild. She could smell the spiny sweet of strawberry.

She almost missed the opposite wall, but a shard of limestone pierced her knee. She pulled up and knocked against another stone, a cornerstone. Or so it seemed.

In front of her, a barrow shape loomed against the black of the storm, an enormous, haphazard mound. The sense of a tomb returned to her. And of eyes in the dark. The hair on the back of her neck spiked against the coarse linen of her shift.

Something was wrong. She ran her hands over the thick mud and stones of the barrow and over the base of smooth curving bricks, some now crushed. She worked to place the familiar sense of it.

When she remembered, she jumped back as if jolted. This hulk was once the miraculous fountain. Underneath the carcass of stones and mud and debris was the source of the miraculous water. She threw herself over the mound and wept, feeling every bit the child she was. Too much was lost. It was impossible. No girl could do what was asked of her.

Her muscles cramped again. The wind picked up, and she could smell sweet woodruff as if it edged between the raindrops or wafted from the shadows. The smell oriented her, for if this was the fountain, then she knelt now at the entrance of the church.

She turned west through the weeds and into what had once been the sanctuary. As she groped, she found a paver stone still embedded in what had been the church floor. Flattened and smoothed on top, it was of local grit stone, rough and porous. If there was one stone, there would be others.

She rose. The rain still pounded, and the moon sunk on the horizon casting eerie light sidewise between the drops. She had at least two hours until dawn. Two hours would be enough.

As she moved deeper into the ruins of the church, a cool finger stole down her soaking back, and fright bumps trawled under her skin. She heard the sound of clattering, as if disturbed pebbles cascaded over one another, or of unnatural voices. Or dwarf echo. Her eyes watered, and she crouched down shivering.

No sound but the rain followed. Chastising herself for girlish frights, she pressed on through the ruined church, searching for the remains of the altar or back wall. Instead she stumbled onto a circle of tumbled bricks.

Within the circle, the earth was almost bare of grass or weeds. The water pooled in muddy patches and showed a pattern of wear as if some steady persistence paced back and forth across it.

She stepped into the circle, and a cold spike shattered her between her shoulder blades. Everything seemed suddenly to stop. All except the rain. The blackness was as pitch. She could barely see two paces in any direction.

A figure, yellowed in shadow, emerged from the dark. A woman shorter than she, with beetleish eyes and a face pitted and hollow. It outstretched its arms and, palms flat, shoved her hard in the center of her chest. Georgia fell, sprawling backward out of the cell.

She scrambled to protect herself, but the woman, or whatever it had been, was gone. Yet her chest hurt, and she could not catch her breath. She clenched her teeth to keep them from clattering. What had it been? A madwoman? Or perhaps another trick of memory?

Yet she must find the relic. The orb was like a hunger in her core. She must find it. The hour was already late.

She could feel the dread thing linger, so she swung wide of the circle and found a line of foundation stones. The main altar was a few paces back with Isela's altar to the left and the relic somewhere beneath her feet.

She remembered the day she had buried it. She had been wounded, desperate. She had taken the relic toward the sacristy.

She paced it out, where the choir had been, the altar, the great timbers that plunged from floor to roof. She dug her toes into the soil and found her spot, there. Her skin prickled again, and she looked up quickly. But what could she see in such a night? With no moon and the rain pouring?

She willed the terror down. She must dig.

She pressed her fingers into the earth, but no floor stone was to be found there. She felt right and left, but still none. The stones in this part had been pulled up. She could feel the spongy depressions filled in now with curling vines and spear-leafed dandelion.

She flinched at the emptiness, for if the stones were pulled up, the relic would be discovered and already taken. Yet she could feel it, a small hum, a warm strand in the rain. No, the relic remained. The stone that guarded it had not been overturned.

She widened her reach and found a stone buried under a film of mud. It seemed too small. She searched for another, but found none. She returned to the stone; it must be the one.

Her skin prickled again. She turned around, grabbing up a sharp shaft of limestone and brandishing it to focus her courage. She could sense eyes, a madness in the dark, but no onslaught followed.

She returned to the stone. Forcing her hand steady, she took the small knife from her belt and sunk it along the edges of the stone, clearing out roots and scooping up the soft mud. She grasped the buried rim of the stone and heaved.

The mud and wet worked against her, sucking at the sides, fixing the stone in place. She shifted to gain more leverage, and the corner lifted. The mud gulped air as the stone turned on its side atop a gaping hole.

Whatever it was that lingered in this place, she did not know. But the dread around her deepened. It was behind her; she could feel it. She jammed her hand down underneath the stone and into the mud, thinking only to find the relic and run. She sought the bronze work or the smooth bead of glass. She found neither. She jabbed the blade of her knife into the ground and lifted out cupped handfuls of earth, but the relic was not there. She had chosen the wrong stone.

She sat and said a Hail Mary, two, while waiting for her heart to calm its beating. It was no good if she was deafened by her own fear. The dread eased a little. Good. She took a breath and resumed her search.

She crept a few paces more, feeling each lump and weed. There was another stone. With a prayer of hope, she crouched over it. But as she felt for the edges, the terror bit into her again. Two ghastly hands rose up flat from out of the darkness. The hands came at her with a fury.

The impact sent her sprawling. She fought to roll upright, fright-shivers cascading over her skin and her muscles spasming. She retched, gagging as she wiped at her eyes, searching the dark, her heart racing.

Just ahead, the shadow of the madwoman rose again. She was so close. The pits in her face yawned of an uneasy death. The wraith unleashed a defiant wail, a banshee wail that split horror through the night. Yet something about the cry of the ghost hung in memory.

Georgia fell to her knees, tucking her body in and bringing her hands over the back of her neck to protect herself. The eyes watched her. She could feel them. Perhaps it would kill her if it could.

She tried to remember what her mother had taught her about spirits. She stood up slowly, watching the faded yellowed patch that hung back in the darkness. She crossed herself and spat on the ground. Then spat again. It left her mouth dry.

"Let me pass," she said.

The ghost rose up, and icy fright pricked over her. She clenched her fists. She must remember who she was. She was no ordinary girl. She threw her head back. Into the night and the rain and the silence she called out, "Let—me—pass!"

A thin wail rose from the ground, and the ghost faded. The night was black again.

Georgia spat at third time. Her scalp prickled, but the ghost did not reappear. The rain stopped. To the east, the night faded ever so slightly. She was losing the night. She must dig.

She returned to searching, but the madwoman's blow had taken her from the stone she had found. She groped again in the darkness, through the mud and weeds. She ran her hands along a cluster of fallen stones and realized with a chill that these were the bricks of the circle, and that she had come again to the small cell. A nausea swept her. The woman appeared again, in the center of the patch. She hung there, wraithlike, the white-yellow glower of its eyes like rotted fleece in candlelight.

Georgia scrabbled backward but dared to look. The familiarity gnawed her. The form wavered between flax-fiber shadows and solid gore with pits and rags and bony fingers.

Memory fleshed out shapes and gave Georgia a name. Agnes. The word trembled as she spoke it, "Agnes."

The recollection buoyed her. Agnes had been a sister of this church. A seer. A screamer. Yet what part of Agnes was this thing that remained, she wondered, what part the angel, what the devil, and what a remnant of a maddened will?

"Agnes," she said it clearly.

The edges of the madwoman sharpened. It outstretched its arms as if to charge again.

Georgia panicked but did not run. She raised her arms to shield herself. "I am Georgia!"

No force attacked her. She lowered her hands and saw that the ghost now only hovered. It seemed to wait.

Despite the rain, Georgia's lips felt dry and tight. She rubbed them together as she spoke. "Agnes. Hear me. I am no enemy of yours. I am come for the relic."

The ghost swelled again. Swelled, and then faded.

"Wait." Georgia sweated with sudden heat. She did not know where to dig. This ghost, there was a chance, maybe, that she would know. "The relic. Agnes, I need your help."

A groan rolled like a death wain across the darkness, and a cavernous mouth formed words. "Cannot you smell your own blood?"

Her own blood? Again memory brought the vision of the man and the horse. The pair clattered through the church, and the rider raised his sword to strike her down. Blood spilled and soaked the floor, pouring over the stones and closing the chasm she had opened.

Georgia scrabbled again over the ground, scooping handfuls of earth. When she found it, she knew. It had a tinny, metallic smell, sour and soft. Blood. And the weeds grew thick.

The morning wind thinned the clouds and opened the sky for dawn. She needed to work quickly; she should already be away.

She scraped out taproots and feeder shoots with her bare hands. The weeds came up, fat thistles and spidery Queen Anne's Lace, a three-pronged dandelion root. Memory surged up as she dug—Elizabeth, Thomasine, Beatrice, Maud. The terrified, pale face of the girl on the horse. She clutched the hurt in her chest. How had it all come to this?

She grabbed at the stone, pushing so that her sinews stretched and popped inside her knees and shoulders. She groaned in frustration as the growing light pressed in on her.

And then she froze. For now, as the day dawned, she could see what lay beyond her on the hill. She stopped to gape. On the second rise, where the upper pasture had been, was an enormous manor. It stood three stories tall, perhaps taller. Barns and huts and fences were set all around, a wide configuration that swept up the low sloping rise. So close. She had not seen it in the dark, yet in the coming dawn, it seemed on top of her. She could hear dogs barking. Shouts.

She crouched down. She did not dare to be seen. She reached for her dark wrap but could not find it. She had left it somewhere in the night.

She shoved at the stone with all the strength and haste she had. It teetered as her grip slipped along its sides, smashing her finger and scraping along her wrist. More dogs barked. She could hear the scrabble of geese. Men's voices carried down the hill, low, annoyed rumbles, and on the wind the smell of sweat. But the stone was free. She poked her fingers into the compressed earth beneath. The smell of her own blood was all around her.

I am Georgia.

Under the stone her smallest finger met the relic, sliding along the smooth glass under the soil. The touch of it sent a thrill of wonder and joy and hope through her, and she almost lost herself to the ecstasy of the reunion. The very touch was like a song or prayer.

More dogs barked, and a bloodhound bayed. Men from the manor headed down the hill. She must flee. Grasping the relic, she crouched, ready to run. Three dogs ran in her direction, ears back, anticipating a chase. Behind them, two men followed. Georgia leapt up and ran as fast as she could. But the dogs gained; they would bring her down.

From behind her came an earsplitting wail. The dogs yelped and the men cursed. Georgia looked over her shoulder as Agnes rose in the dawn, a figure of solid gore. She bawled in the faces of those who pursued, and was gone.

The men cowered and cursed; the dogs cried, retreated, and slunk at their masters' feet.

"S'blood, I hate this place. Damn these dogs."

Georgia splashed through the stream and lay belly flat on the other side. She watched as her pursuers retreated up the hill, faster, it seemed, than they had come. She held the relic in her hands and pressed it against her. The warmth of prayer filled her with hope. She swooned into the river of it, allowing her body to spill joy, particle by particle, into the water.

And then she remembered Mendaline. And Lo.

CHAPTER 25:
Whores

Bilsdale was a bigger and busier town than Georgia could remember having been in before. The market was three streets wide, and many of the houses were new. Inside open doors and behind shop windows, the townswomen worked looms, some in bright colors, but most in the dun of homespun wool or flax.

Carters moved along the streets and sometimes gawked at them. They hawked goods from wagons piled high with barrels and sacks, calling to passersby and haggling with shopkeepers. Carpenters, coopers, leather workers, chandlers, and butchers crammed their industry into the brick and timber buildings that lined the streets like boots laced to the knee in contrasting textures of lime, tar, and weathered timber.

A small fenced yard contained ducks and two routing, smallish pigs, and Georgia skirted it, skirting also the throng of tradesmen and hobnailed workmen jostling around her. A carter offered her a penny for sex. When he leered and touched her bodice, she wished to drive him into the pen with the pigs.

She wished, too, that she had taken as much care to wash herself as she had taken with the relic, now tied safely under her skirts. The grit of the stream made a perfect scrub for the muddied bronze so that now it gleamed, yet her own homespun clothes were muddy and torn at the hem. She chastised herself for not having paid better concern to how she would look to tradesmen in a busy market.

She considered returning to the stream to wash, but then saw a woman who seemed familiar. The woman bobbed roundly in a brightly colored apron and the red, sweaty face of a vigorous gossip. Alice, the name came to her.

Georgia watched her, planning to speak to her when she was alone. Yet Alice went from one cluster of folk to another with no more than a step separating the end of one sentence and the beginning of another. Finally, as Alice turned in midsentence from a merchant's wife, a dyer, Georgia planted herself directly in front of her and curtsied.

"Pray pardon, mistress," she used a tone of careful politeness. If she looked dirty, she could at least seem mannerly. "I seek news of the woman Mendaline. She was a nun. There was a priory here—"

Alice's mouth snapped shut. "There are no nuns in Bilsdale." She nodded to the dyer, turned, and retreated into the market place.

No nuns. The dyer stared at her curiously. Georgia put her hand over the relic to boost her courage. It felt warm, even through the mud caked into her skirt. There must be nuns. She ran to follow Alice.

"Pray, you. Just the woman Mendaline, then."

"Shush, girl." Alice did not even turn to look at her.

Georgia felt like a skinny child. She ran to keep step as Alice took long strides along the market street.

"Please, mistress. She is a healer, a midwife. She was of a priory, Saint Isela's—"

The woman grabbed her by the arm and pushed her behind the nearest stall, pinching hard enough so that her arm stung. Alice's gaze darted back and forth along the street. She backed Georgia against eel barrels stacked one on top of the other.

"Make no trouble for me." Alice squared her shoulders to close the two of them off from the street.

"I only seek—"

"Are you on pilgrimage? It is forbidden. The fountain—" Alice looked over her shoulder again before lowering her voice to a whisper. "The fountain was destroyed and the prioress killed. You best be on your way unless you wish a whipping or a brand or worse."

Alice's words wound out like a lash, and Georgia leaned back against the barrels for fear she would fall. The top barrel tottered against the one below and grated an iron-edged whine through the centers of her teeth.

The prioress killed. She saw the sword again, and the horseman. In the vision, she had vanquished him. But twelve years ago the outcome had been different. He had killed her on that day. Coldly. Ruthlessly.

She slid down along the barrels and sat in the dust. It had been too easy to think of the dreams and visions as some forgotten story from long ago. But it was real. She had been that prioress, not in memory, but in flesh. She had died that day on that deserted hill. And the shame that followed, the ruined fountain, the ghost—it was her shame.

Alice stood over her, her hands on her hips now and her face streaked in sweat and also sorrow.

Georgia hugged her knees to her chest. "I am sorry, mistress, for the trouble."

Alice gave a short sob. "I lost my son to it," she said.

So much pain to mend! It was vanity for her to sorrow like this, as if all the tragedy had been her own. She had died that day—but she was not dead now. She would put things right. She raised herself and smoothed the dust from her skirt. The tear on her hem was ragged, and the fabric dragged on the ground.

"I will pray for him," Georgia said.

Alice sighed. "Look at you, like a dirty bundle of sticks. If it is a healer that you seek, follow the old streets to Fish Street at the end. The sisters live in Briker Row, at the end by the ale houses."

The sisters! No nuns, yet she had called them sisters. "Thank you," Georgia bobbed a quick curtsey. Perhaps she would find them after all. Maybe things were better than she thought.

She ran on the balls of her feet through the older section of Bilsdale where the buildings were of wattle and still roofed with thatch. The last house boasted a dried sprig of sage tied to the bellpull. The sprig denoted that a healer lived within—Mendaline.

Georgia pulled the bell so eagerly that the bell inside clacked instead of ringing. In her heart, she wanted to tear the door open. She would find Mendaline there. And Lo. She would find Lo. The last twelve years would melt away.

The door opened, and a girl, perhaps nine years old, stared frankly at her. Her teeth splayed at the front, but were white and the tip of her nose pink.

Georgia curtseyed quickly, peering in. The smell of herbs encouraged her—comfrey, tansy, ragweed, birthwort, and the bitter-sour arnica.

"Is Sister—is Mendaline within?"

The girl kept a neutral expression. "Strangers pay first."

"I have no money. Yet Sis—the healer Mendaline will know me."

The girl opened the door wider and called to the back. "Mistress? A girl. She's got no money."

"Let her come in." A reedy voice spilled easily from a back room. Georgia recognized it at once.

She forced a calm walk through the open hall. That she remembered, she had never been in a two-story house before, and noted the wooden stairs in the corner that turned up and out of sight.

The girl led Georgia through the house and into the back kitchen. She then returned to her work over a low table. "We're pressing pansies," the girl said.

The back door stood open with the windows unshuttered and light flowing in. An old woman sat near the fire in a workspace piled with jars, pouches, and baskets. The woman balanced a large clay jar on her lap, knocking spiny leaves into it from a large mortar.

So old she was! Too many years had passed by. Georgia felt like a young, stick-legged bird, and awkward. Yet this was Mendaline, her confidant and her confessor. She wanted to fling herself onto the hearth at her feet.

And then she saw Mendaline's hands.

Mendaline had perfect hands. But these hands were red and gnarled and contorted, the hands of a monster, not a healer. She used them as pinchers, steadying the jar between her wrists before setting it down. She grasped the pestle under an elongated thumb and over a flattened palm. As she ground the pestle down, she wedged the mortar against her side.

"It hurts her feelings if you stare," the girl plucked petals and discarded the stem.

Georgia looked away, into the fire, at the floor, anywhere else. She gave a quick curtsey. "Pray pardon."

Mendaline did not look up from her work, though her gaze flicked to Georgia's own hand. "That finger of yours will take a week to heal at least," she said, "and you'll lose the nail bed, mayhap. Your foot will take longer to heal, but it's no use to treat it if you're just planning on running off again." Mendaline glanced up then back to her work. "I'm out of paste, but I'll make some new." She glanced up at the girl who worked over the pansies. "There's chicken fat in the bowl, girl. Fetch it if you please and place it on the hearth to warm."

Georgia considered her finger. It throbbed, yet the injury seemed minor, and the hurt was now crusted over with blood and sand. Her foot was worse, for she saw that she had split the heel. Her feet were a plague, though this wound was the worst yet. Cold had some uses after all. It only hurt now that she had seen it, and it hurt worse near the fire.

The girl sighed to move, lifting the bowl from a low shelf and placing it at the hearth.

Georgia sat down in the ashes of the hearth. The hurt, the smells, the memories that rushed at her of herbs on the fire, of jars of petals, stems, seeds, pastes, reeds, and flowers dried, branches, bark, nut, and flower oils. She remembered Saint Isela's infirmary, the beds lined up, the bowls for bleedings, the linen bedding, the smell of the sick, and the pleas of the dying.

She remembered standing in the doorway watching as Mendaline worked; she remembered her own sicknesses, and Mendaline's touch against her forehead and the back of her neck. Mendaline checked for rash, fever, worms, ulcers, and sweat with her beautiful, sensitive hands.

Georgia knelt next to her, reaching across the mortar to take one of the healer's hands into her own, turning up a splayed palm. Scars twisted deeply into the flesh, the smallest finger gone, and the four fingers remaining thickly webbed. The heavy smell of hawthorn hung all around them.

"Pray, forgive me," Georgia said.

"Child, what have you done?"

Georgia raised her head. She remembered the furrows on Mendaline's face, furrows that now seemed to ring the older woman's forehead and cheeks like the petals of a flower. Yet perhaps the years were not as brutal as they seemed, for Mendaline's eyes were still intense and direct—and kind. That much, at least, was the same.

"'Tis me, Mendaline. 'Tis Georgia."

Mendaline sucked a long breath, holding on as if afraid to let the air escape. The pestle clanged to the floor.

Georgia sat quietly. She had done this countless times, and yet she did not know what to do. "I'm sorry," was all she managed. It was not enough—not nearly.

Mendaline released her breath slowly. "Sweet, sweet mother Mary," she said. "When I was a girl, a prioress I knew died of fever. She was an old woman, then, but I remember the girl of twelve who came later to the priory to be a nun, a girl who knew a prayer as she breathed it, and led me in my faith. She said she lived a hundred lives. I believed it then. But she is dead."

"I cannot die, Mendaline. I must not." Georgia thought of Lo.

Mendaline pursed her lips. "Your teeth are crooked."

Georgia almost laughed. "It is the soul only that is reborn, not the body. Yet I remember—though not always very well. And I remember that you, Sister Mendaline, you are my dearest friend."

"And you are too short."

"I will be taller."

"Taller will not matter."

"I have this." Georgia reached under her skirts and untied the relic. She brought it out, and the light of the fire caught in it, the amber glass swirling with orange and casting warmth into the room. The bronze gleamed.

Mendaline sat with her mouth open. "Oh, my prayers. Sweet Mary I dreamt it."

"I hid it under the church stone."

"They tore up the church."

"I saw the ruins of it. And," Georgia swallowed. The hair on the back of her neck stood straight up. "I saw Agnes there."

Mendaline nodded. "Hellish screams on that hill," she crossed herself. "God bless our Agnes! They couldn't build the manor there, so they hauled away the stones." Mendaline laughed at the thought. But then she pursed her lips again. "Look at you. You're just a girl."

Georgia looked down. "It is even how I seem to myself."

"And you look hungry." Mendaline turned to the girl who had assisted her. "E'beth?"

The girl had left off the pansies altogether and now stared at the relic, her eyes wide and shining.

Mendaline clucked her tongue. "E'beth!"

"Yes, mistress." The girl blinked but continued to stare.

"Bread and ale. Quick as a rabbit."

The girl blinked and jumped away. She returned in a flash with a jug of ale and a small loaf of bread.

"Beatrice's daughter," Mendaline said, indicating the girl. "Her name's E'beth, after Elizabeth who was her godmother."

"Beatrice? Sister Beatrice has a daughter?"

Mendaline nodded. "Beatrice runs an alehouse next door. She was always better with ale than healing."

"Is she married? And the others? Sister Elizabeth, Pocket, Sister Thomasine—" Georgia felt the distance and the familiarity of the names, but she could not match faces to all of them.

Mendaline held up a hand. "Sister Thomasine died. The morning you ... died. Sister Elizabeth—lived. We lost her to fever, though, a few years ago. The rest were hauled away, but drifted back here one by one. Except Catherine. She and that monk live in Hull, with three children and him a wool merchant. Oh, and Pocket is called Amy now." Mendaline paused. She stared quietly. For the length of a Hail Mary, there was silence. "I don't believe it still."

"Who did Beatrice marry?"

"My mother has no husband," E'beth said. "My mother's a whore." She shrugged as if it was what it was.

"She sells ale now," Mendaline said. "As for before, and as for Amy and Diota," Mendaline again made the sign of the cross, "well ... money had to be gotten somehow, and men pay pretty well to lay with a nun."

"Diota is a nun who's a whore, too," E'beth volunteered.

"Mind yourself, girl," Mendaline's tone sharpened.

E'beth bobbed a quick apology, but her gaze stayed on the relic.

"Diota was a nun of Bishopsgate. It's where they sent Amy and the rest, after you—died. The king turned all the nuns out of Bishopsgate the very next year, so Diota came along with Amy. They both make money in the way they can."

Georgia listened without comment. The story seemed old to her. "And where is Lo?"

"Lo? Well, in that matter we did what we could."

"In what matter? Where is she?"

With an awkward shift, Mendaline picked up the pestle, worrying a stray leaf into the lumpy paste. "It has not been so easy for us. The priory ruined, the stories lost. You—dead. We are watched." Mendaline raised her hands. Georgia flinched at them.

"I had to stop delivering babies," she said. Real regret showed on her face. "I help with cures. I help. But I cannot do the work."

Georgia studied the scars and wrong curves along the finger joints, the misshapen nails.

"Yet I was allowed to live." Mendaline scraped the pestle into the mortar. "I get by."

"I should have fought him."

"You did." Mendaline turned again to the girl. "E'beth, go and fetch your mother. And see if Amy or Diota are at the market. But hush. Say nothing of this." Mendaline flashed an intent stare back at Georgia. "You, my girl, will be hard to explain. Indeed, I hardly believe myself." She worried the leaf again, the paste rising up the sides of the mortar. "We were divided, wounded, shipped away. Amy's womb has threatened to quicken so many times, each time with a child given by some drunken lout with a shilling to spare. She's drunk kettles' worth of tansy to keep her courses." She stilled the pestle and raised her shoulder to wipe her eyes. "It's over, Georgia. I'm an old woman, now. Forgive me, Isela! I am tired."

Georgia ran her fingers over the smooth glass of the relic. Even touching it seemed to call her, with the ground opening and prayer rising up. "I will go alone if I must, Mendaline. But I know what it is to be tired, too, and hollowed out." She forced a smile. "But surely Lo will come. She must be young, five and twenty. Where is she?"

Mendaline poked the fire.

"Mendaline, pity's sake! What of Lo?"

"She is lost to us."

Georgia almost choked. "Dead?"

"She lives," Mendaline poked the fire with savagery, "but she belongs to Romsfeld now, mark no bones. He has destroyed her."

Romsfeld. The name came back with a face to match—the horseman—the sword. The enemy. Georgia clenched her fists and shook them. "This cannot be so."

Mendaline was quiet.

"Mendaline, deny it. It cannot be the truth."

"What could I do? You were dead."

"I am not dead!" Georgia screamed it. Romsfeld had been right; they were all whores after all. She imagined running him through with a rusty hook. She'd carve out his belly first.

"You had hopes for her, I know," Mendaline said. "But there is no promise anymore."

E'beth came into the kitchen through the back door and nestled herself where she could see the relic. Beatrice came in behind her, and Diota and Amy followed.

At the sight of the relic, Beatrice simply gawked. She made a cross into the air and began a litany. Behind her, Amy stopped so abruptly that Diota almost tumbled over her.

Amy reached out a hand as if too touch it. "I hardly remembered it," she said.

E'beth watched the light dance across the bronze work around the orb. "It's so pretty."

Georgia regarded them. A disheveled, dirty group, and herself the dirtiest. And Lo with Romsfeld. It was all wrong.

CHAPTER 26:
Saint Regina

Georgia marched out of Bilsdale with a will to rescue Lo. She imagined it, imagined Lo's relief, the gratefulness of her embrace as together they would flee, swept back into Isela's care and ready to restore things to be as they should be.

She led the way along the path with Mendaline lagging behind and E'beth gamboling in multiple directions at once. They took the worn path, yet this, too, seemed wrong to her. This path took the stony route over the steepest part of the hill. It circumvented the priory. Perhaps it was Agnes's restless spirit that had driven the path south.

They passed the outskirts of Attewater. The village seemed listless, the houses in need of repair and the livestock thin and few. Yet if the folk seemed poorer, the manor was larger and more opulent than the priory had ever been. Mendaline said that the archbishop had visited only twice since its building. It was Romsfeld who made full use of it, hosting second and third sons to dinners and on hunting parties.

Mendaline panted coming up the hill, but Georgia surged ahead. The landscape filled her with memories of Lo—as a baby, her first steps, how she would follow behind the last duckling until the mother duck accepted her as just another in the line.

"Slow down, girl," Mendaline said, red faced and out of breath. "You may be young again, but I am not."

"We must make haste."

Mendaline grimaced. "Twelve years gone and suddenly there's fire in the streets? Would you have me drop dead from tripping over one of these great stones?" She adjusted her satchel to ride higher on her hip.

Georgia backtracked, taking the satchel to lighten the older woman's burden.

Mendaline issued a warning. "Mind now. Master Romsfeld will be about."

They crested the second hill and approached a wide courtyard. Dogs scattered as Mendaline cried, "Shoo! Shoo!" but no one else took any mind of them save a gangly youth who chased away an irate goose determined to attack.

The whole place smelled strongly of a cloying oil that Georgia did not recognize. But everywhere, in every face, every corner, Georgia searched for Lo.

In the courtyard garden, a small woman in a yellow gown sat embroidering on a stone bench. Georgia had at first skipped over her—the gown garish with cuttes, the bodice cut too low, and a badge of livery sewn to the sleeve.

Yet while Georgia hesitated, E'beth did not. "There she is," the girl pointed. "If you bring her strawberries, she will like you."

Georgia paused. It could not be right. She was too old. And on her face, there were bruises.

The woman looked up from her embroidery and smiled. The sun and her smile together transformed the bruises on her face. It was indeed Lo, the girl grown into a woman. And despite the shadows, she was beautiful, the very soul of promise, a wonderment.

Georgia went faster to greet her. It did not matter the gown or the manor, for the relic would restore all. All would be well. She called out, "Lo!"

Lo smiled again. Georgia ran faster, but as she made it into the inner courtyard, a man stepped out from behind the courtyard gate and took Lo's hand. Georgia stopped. Lo had smiled for him. Romsfeld.

Lo upturned her face to him. He lifted her chin, his palm against her cheek as he ran a thumb over a bruise that darkened it. Then he kissed her.

Georgia felt turned to salt. She let the wasps fly across her face. Mendaline had warned her, but she could not believe it.

Mendaline trampled up past her and cleared her throat.

Lo waved to see her, but Romsfeld did not leave off a second kiss, lowering his mouth over hers and consuming it.

Mendaline barged between them before a third kiss and clucked over Lo's bruises. Lo sat dutifully as she examined them.

Romsfeld hovered over Mendaline. "Come to cast a few spells?"

"I made a poultice." Mendaline's answer was curt. She felt over her hip for the satchel. When she found nothing, she called to Georgia. "Come on, girl! My satchel."

Georgia wanted to defy her, that she could preside so casually over such as this, that she could stand by for twelve years while he beat her.

She scanned the grounds for a weapon, something to defend the girl she remembered. A garden tool, a stake.

"You, girl!" Mendaline called again. She turned to E'beth. "Child, run, fetch the liniment."

Georgia relinquished the satchel but still did not move.

Romsfeld released Lo's hand as Mendaline tended her. He pointed under the trees.

"And this?"

Mendaline shrugged. "My—a new apprentice. From Derbyshire. She's come for work."

"Work, eh?" Romsfeld called to her. "Well, come on over. Let me look at you."

Georgia's jaw clenched. She felt her face twist. She did not move.

Mendaline straightened up. She threw a warning look over her shoulder. "I mean work for me, Master Steward. I've taken her in."

"How old is she?" Romsfeld gazed steadily.

Lo followed Romsfeld's gaze. Alarm pricked her expression, and Georgia thought fear as well. Certainly the color rose under the bruises.

"Twelve." Mendaline returned to the examination.

"Healthy?"

"Well enough."

"Reluctant little thing. I'd say even spiteful." He winked at Mendaline, and Lo looked away. "Yet that can be amusing in its turn."

Mendaline applied a thick green paste below Lo's eye with a scarred, curled finger. Lo did not flinch.

"Call her over," Romsfeld said.

Mendaline stopped her work and cast another worried look at Georgia. "She's not much. Not worth your trouble."

Lo squinted over the ointment. "You've taken a new apprentice, then?" She dabbed at the paste with a corner of her sleeve. "That will be helpful for you."

"Will she not come?" Romsfeld seemed on the edge to fetch her himself. He called out to her. "I'll know your name, girl."

Georgia thought only to defy him. She strode out from under the tree with as much indignation as she could manage and looked directly at Lo. "My name is Georgia."

Romsfeld flinched; that, at least, was pleasing. But Lo paled, shock, fear perhaps.

Mendaline threw a cloth down into the satchel. "The girl forgets her place."

Romsfeld regained a little of his composure. "Georgia, is it? Now that's a foul name, eh? One would expect a shrew or a wretch." He pinched the back of Lo's neck. "What do you think of such a name, my love?"

Lo cast her gaze down. "I do not care to think of it, my lord."

"You'd not?"

"Forgive me, no."

Romsfeld released her and turned on Mendaline. "She does seem a wretch, though, does she not? Have you been feeding her? Let me see your teeth, girl."

Georgia bared them like a dog. She wished for a weapon. Anything but the horror of standing here and watching him touch Lo.

"So then, what can you do?" Romsfeld asked.

"Most anything I like."

"Pert, isn't she?" He stared at her breasts, her waist, and her ankles. The hem of her skirt was shredded and too short.

Georgia grimaced. How small and pointless she must seem to him. She tried to make eye contact with Lo, wishing to send a message that all would be well. But when Lo looked at her, the gates behind her eyes seemed closed and guarded.

Lo smoothed the embroidery on her lap. "We have servants enough, Horley."

He ignored her. "But I am in mind to be charitable. You need help in the courtyard garden, do you not?"

"I can manage, my love."

Georgia spoke up. "I don't need your work."

Romsfeld rocked back on his heels as if he thought the whole thing a great game. "Mendaline, am I paying you so well that you can afford to keep two apprentices? Surely not, for see how thin she is. Did you even wash her before you dragged her up the hill? And what of my lady, I'll not have her toiling in the mud when this-a-one is so well suited for it."

"I do not mind." Lo spoke timidly.

"But I mind. And this girl who seeks to best me with sharp daggers in her looks? Tell me, girl. Who are your parents?"

Georgia crossed her arms over her chest.

"Mendaline, will she not answer?"

"She is—she is," Mendaline sent Georgia a look of ferocity. "She is not right. No one can keep her. An orphan, sent to me for curing."

Romsfeld grinned again. He strode close to her, circling as if to find Georgia's madness. "But she can answer?"

"As I like." Georgia spat the words at him.

Romsfeld's expression changed in a flash, as a snake strikes or a toad extends its tongue and snatches it back. He grabbed her by the wrist, staring her full in the face and shaking her. "I am most offended."

Georgia refused to look down or away, though now she thought to fear him. She was not a woman anymore, nor a prioress. She had only a child's strength. She must be more careful. "I am pledged to serve Mendaline."

Romsfeld released her, and she stumbled. He smiled a wide, yellow-toothed victory. "And so you are now pledged to serve me. It is a small thing, but the lord Philip SeVerde is generous to all orphans. Lo can attest to this generosity, can you not, my love? And you," he glared victory and contempt, "you can be grateful as you will."

Lo looked stricken. Georgia felt rage welling up. She had handled the whole thing wrongly.

"If you are lazy you will be whipped." Romsfeld leaned back, laughing her, at all of them. "If you're caught stealing you'll hang. If you've been coddled, you will learn to work, and you will learn your place."

Georgia grappled for some sense. She tried dignity, adding a lie as well. "I regret I am not free to take up a bond in your household. I must care for my aunt, who ails. Mendaline will teach me healing. I cannot accept."

Romsfeld raised a hand as if to proclaim final judgment. "You cannot decide the matter. Mendaline has given you to me. And though you need feeding, you will forgo food this day for your impertinence."

Georgia could care a hair's width about supper. "In truth I would not work here. I am not given to you. Mendaline cannot give me so." Georgia stomped her foot. "And I won't. You, whom I despise."

Romsfeld slapped her with the back of his hand. The blow sent her to the ground. He called to one of the men in the courtyard.

"Tucker! Take this tiny scold to the barn and strip her to the waist. Take the lash to her. Beat her until she falls. Perhaps she may even wear a scold's cage over her head, with a metal prong to keep her tongue from wagging."

Georgia could not believe it. She had never been beaten. She could not imagine it. And a scold's cage—she had seen women humiliated in this way, dragged through town silenced and unable to eat or drink, with metal cages locked over their heads.

All had gone wrongly. She had come to mount a rescue, to flee. She looked for escape.

"If you run, girl, I will beat Mendaline in your place. Perhaps I will beat her anyway for bringing such a thoughtless girl to me. What say you, leech?"

Mendaline gave a quick curtsey. "Forgive me. I meant no offense."

Tucker stood from where he had been slouching. His hands were as thick as he was, and he gripped Georgia at the back of the neck, lifting her easily and shoving her toward the barn.

She would be beaten, and she could not escape, not and risk harm to Mendaline. She was a prisoner.

The muscles rippled along Romsfeld's jaw. He turned to Mendaline and growled. "I should have you run from Bilsdale. I should find a stool and have you cucked."

Mendaline curtsied low and held her head down.

Romsfeld stormed away. Lo took her embroidery and ran to follow him.

CHAPTER 27:
Saint Wilgefortis

Two seasons had passed by, and still she could not make it work. Georgia pounded her hand on a particularly stubborn stone, with no success. This was the miraculous fountain, yet it was clogged hopelessly with rocks. In her dreams, there was clear, fresh water underneath. But after three nights of hammering, her fingers raw and her wrists and ankles scraped, Georgia could not find anything but mud.

It would be easier if she could see. But the clouds had slid below the waning moon and turned the night a silken black. Perhaps even too dark for spirits, Georgia thought, for Agnes had not emerged to shriek at her. She crossed herself. Sweet Isela, let Agnes leave her be.

She looked quickly over her shoulder to soothe the fear crawling over her skin. She climbed up onto the rocks, seeking more leverage. Crawling over a tumbled, sharpened spine of stones, she sunk her toes and knees into slits filled with mud. A rock came free, but no water followed. She twisted at another, but in doing so, she split open the scabs across her back and had to stop to catch her breath.

This latest beating hurt still, though she endured it. Romsfeld's tooth-rotted housekeeper, who insisted she be called "madam," had caught her in the manor house watching Lo instead of tending to her duties. Madam had surprised her with a blow to her jaw and followed with several bruising swings of the rod. Georgia had fallen backward into the hearth and against a pair of iron dogs. The fire had not been lit, though the iron had scraped along her back.

Yet it was no worse than that, she thought. She stretched back, pushing her shoulder blades together so as to relieve the pressure on the wound. Madam could be as evil as she chose. Georgia would withstand it. This was not even a real beating, by the standards she was learning. Real beatings were administered in the barn and with the lash. Those were far harder to endure.

Georgia cursed the foolishness of having blurted "I am Georgia" that first day at the manor house. She had tried to fix her mistake, saying instead that she was called Jane, but Lo did not forget.

A whooshing sigh sounded in the dark, the sound of rain passing over weedy broadleaf. Was it the rain? Or was it Agnes come again? Her heart pounded, a deluge in her ears, neck, and into her throat. She set her jaw against it. Another lesson yet to learn, she must control her fright.

She forced a slow turn, expecting to find Agnes's ghost nose to nose behind her.

She saw nothing. A light rain only that swept across the old foundation stones of the ruined priory moving west.

Georgia returned her attention to the well, remembering how the pilgrims would sit at the edges and cup their hands for water. She felt along the base of the pile and along the lip of the fountain. Years ago, she had paid a mason to brick the outer edges of the well in the shape of a cross.

The touch sparked a memory of Lo splashing her hands in the water. Georgia laughed out loud. Lo's two bottom teeth had just erupted, white and proud, and the girl had wiggled on the bricks while Sister Thomasine tried to prevent her from crawling in and drowning herself.

In the end, it was Thomasine who slipped, splashing water high over the little girl's head. Lo had gasped in surprise at the cold splash of water but then jutted her jaw forward in glee, her two new teeth poking out from pink gums.

Another sound rattled from the dark and quenched the memory. Georgia was sure now of something behind her, and more than rain. There were footsteps, perhaps, but certainly the sound of breathing, gasping even.

She spun into a crouch, her back to the ruined fountain. Cursing her diminished hearing, she tried to calm her pounding heart. She needed all her senses. Twenty paces east, she judged, was a shadow darker than the rest, and moving. She forced calm, telling herself that whatever it was, she was fast and could outrun it.

The shadow lumbered. She sensed no otherworldly dread as she had when

Agnes pushed her in the dark. It moved awkwardly, definitely not a ghost. And she could smell it. A man.

The man hesitated but continued forward through the brush.

Georgia called out a warning. "I am more than what I seem. I can defend myself."

The man coughed. Georgia spoke louder. "A banshee defends these grounds. I will call her out." And in that instant, she felt that she could. The power frightened her.

"I mean no harm," the shadow spoke. A man's voice. One of those who worked the manor.

"I've done my work for the day. Leave me be," she said.

The man came closer. He had jutting shoulders and long, gangly arms. A boy, not a man, perhaps fifteen years old and wearing thick homespun hose that stretched to squealing down his long legs. A bondsman. Not so much as a cotter's son.

Georgia almost laughed. "Oh! You are only the goose boy."

His reply was bitter. "And you are only the chicken girl."

The chicken girl! Georgia stood to her full height, though she was short. She tended the courtyard garden. The chickens were not her concern except that they ate the insects, pecked around the good king henry and the salsify, and mizzled their droppings in the soil.

"I am called Jane," she curtseyed a mock introduction, "and you are called Manwell." The cloud passed over. The waning moon returned, illuminating the mist-patched earth as the rain stopped. "You should not creep up on people in the dark. I thought you were—" Prickles erupted on her skin as she stilled the name Agnes on her tongue. She finished lamely, "someone else."

He seemed no happier. "Who?"

"It is no matter of yours." Would he report that she was on the old grounds at night? "Unless you have a bargain with the whip master."

He shifted, placing one hand over the other as if working a callus. "Did you come to see the well?" He pointed to the ceramic jar next to her, open and wet from the rain, though still empty of the water she had hoped to collect.

She wondered if there would be a price for his silence. "For herbs," she lied. "You had no cause to follow me."

"Maybe I did." Manwell skirted around to the rocks behind her and brushed a stone that jutted from the top. He nodded toward her jar again. "Have you filled it?"

She stayed silent.

"My mother brought me here when I was a baby," he said. "It was a fountain, then." His tone seemed earnest. He circled the rocks slowly, allowing his fingers to slide over the stones. "My mother said the water here smelled of roses."

Roses! Mendaline had strewn the fountain with rosemary, hyssop, mint, and rose petals. She had forgotten. The memory almost made her weep.

"Not just roses," she blurted, "and from the center it gushed around the edges, here."

He cocked his head. "I don't remember it. I was ... How old are you?"

Georgia hesitated. She had spoken without thinking. "Please do not tell that I was here, tonight."

He deepened his voice and thrust out his chest. "I'll hold my silence like a sword."

Georgia almost laughed. She was fairly sure she could best him in a fight. For, if she was just a witless girl, he was just a sack of gangly bones. Yet his awkward courage had a sweetness. That he wished to please her, to recommend himself, left her with a queasy stomach.

Love. The woman inside her frowned. It was best to put that notion to rest, and quickly.

"I am not free," she said.

His disappointment showed. He looked around the night again, as if he thought she had some other lover in the darkness.

"The dairy wife says I smell like the geese," he sounded mournful.

"Yes, but she is old and smells of sour butter." Georgia felt the division in herself, that she was both a woman and a girl at once. The girl wanted to laugh. The woman spoke. "I have sworn fidelity to God. I am ... a nun."

This seemed to surprise him. Certainly it did not have the stilling effect she had hoped for, for he stepped closer. "There are nuns in Bilsdale. I know them. They are ... Well, they are—"

Georgia felt angry. The nuns he knew were whores. Submission had been finally and utterly forced on them. It was unjust. And it had not been of their choosing.

"I am not a—" she wanted to say "whore," but the girl that blushed inside her would not allow it. "A nun is a woman of faith. A believer in the Latin Mass." Though it was forbidden, she held to the saints, the floats, and to the mysteries. She carried her godmother's prayer book with the woodcut of the passion. When her heart sickened, it was this that held her up.

"But ... you cannot be a nun." Manwell sounded certain of this.

"In my heart I am so. I am sworn away from—" sex, men—she felt her heart race to say it. She decided she would not and pointed to the pile of rocks. "I am here for the water."

Manwell picked up a small stone. "My mother brought me here after it was all destroyed. She showed me this."

He hunched over in the dark and drew out a triangular shaped chunk of limestone. It twisted under his hand, and water bubbled up.

"Oh!" It was just as she had dreamt it for weeks. Joyfully, she pushed in next to him and wet her hands, splashing it over her face and her arms and drinking it. It tasted absolutely pure, perhaps still with the faint taste of hyssop. She wept outright, letting the water splash over her. It was so beautiful.

Manwell stood close, but was quiet. Georgia forgot him in her elation. Forgot him, until his arm brushed her side. He dabbled his fingers in the flow and looked shyly at her, his face just above hers. The corners of his eyes crinkled, an earnest good humor in them. He reminded her of Adam, the boy from home, the boy who was the goatskin dragon. He had said he would kiss her.

"Where is your jar?" Manwell asked.

"What?"

"Your jar, I will fill it for you."

"Oh, yes." She shook off the water and retrieved the ceramic. He filled it as she held the lid.

He stopped the flow by returning the triangle stone, twisting it again, although it seemed harder to replace than to release. He kicked his feet against the rocks to brace himself.

"It's very late. I'll let you sleep tomorrow, if you like." Manwell smiled shyly again. "The hut's big enough. I can watch for trouble."

"Are you saying I should sleep in the goose hut? With the geese?"

Manwell shrugged. "It's as good as a truckle bed. I saw you were tired yesterday. Is this where you come at night? If they catch you sleeping in the day they'll whip you. And I can keep the ganders in the field for the morning at least."

Georgia moved away from him. The euphoria of the water seeped away, and now she felt cold. The jar was heavy, and there was still much to do.

Manwell stepped up beside her. "I can carry that."

"No, I can manage it."

They walked together a few more steps.

"Where will you take it?"

A cave. A memory, and an ancient one. She had begun to be able to discern the differences between dreams and memories, both old and new. The older the memory, the deeper the hum that bubbled under it. "Thank you. But I am not in need."

"Is there—" Manwell shuffled his feet. "Is there someone else?"

She hurried; perhaps she could outpace this foolishness. A boy, especially a boy who reminded her of Adam, would only be a nuisance.

She changed her tact. "Manwell, if you plan to help me, perhaps you should return to the hut and sleep. That way you will not be tired in the morning."

He brightened, and the corners of his eyes crinkled up again. "So you will come to the hut?"

"I—" Georgia cringed. She needed him gone. And she would need to sleep. "Yes. I will."

༄

She found the cave, but the journey was longer and more difficult than she had anticipated. Partly because the jar was full and must be held steady, partly because despite the sliver moon, the night was dark.

The cave was of limestone, and the opening lay behind a curtain of sorcerer's weed and morning glory so that the entrance was completely hidden. Eventually, she had to put the water down to run her hands along the wall of stone, feeling over the pits and powdered chalk until the rock under the vines gave way to an open dark.

The floor inside was partly grit stone and worn smooth. A thin layer of chalky powder covered it, the detritus of sea creatures that were now cave creatures. Yet it was wholly, completely dark inside, even when she pulled back the curtain of vines to let the cloud-damped moon shine in a little.

Still, she would have to manage. She brought the jar inside, placed the water down, and knelt, bringing the relic out from under her skirt. The relic pitched her into prayer. A vision carried her to a bright, glossy meadow. She knelt there next to a jug of water. She spun the relic high, then dipping it, let the chain release its spin as the water churned.

"Tomorrow I will bring a light," her prayer-self said. "For tomorrow will be a new beginning."

༄

The next night Georgia brought a bowl, oil, flint, flax, and a box of candles. Her heart beat quickly at the memory of having stolen the candles. The blacksmith would likely not notice they were missing, but stealing, even so small a thing, was an offence that would hang you.

"Women don't hang," her mother had told her. "They plead the belly." A woman was spared the noose if she was pregnant or feeding a baby from her own milk. Women's prisons had no shortage of men willing to help condemned women win their lives.

Georgia struck a spark into the flax. It flared as if edged in a tiny frond of daffodil. She fed it oat straw, and the flame grabbed the wick. She lit the lamp first, then said a blessing, and dipped the candle into the flame. The candle must not burn away in an hour as most candles did, but burn all day. She could only return at night to change it.

In the candlelight, she could see that there were three rooms, the main cavern on entering, and two smaller rooms that pushed out like gills on either side. She chose the room to the left to set up an altar. In that room, the natural stone layers provided an ideal ledge. The remnants of a rough cross were carved into the limestone above the ledge. She deepened it. She would need to say a blessing here as well.

She turned next to the water. Standing in the center of the room, she lifted a cup of water high over her head. Turning to each direction—north, south, east, and west—she called out the names of the apostle saints: Saint Matthew, Saint Mark, Saint Luke, and Saint John. As she poured the water on the ground, she remembered snatches of the prophecy, words from her dreams that seemed to float even as they faded:

As my death,
so is my life,
so steps my footprint
trailing the blood
of the birth-promise.
So be it.

The water from the cup cascaded down onto the dirt, and from there began to bubble until it disappeared, leaving only a damp hollow in the stone floor. Georgia took another cup of water and, repeating the invocation, poured it in the hollow. The water bubbled again, and the hollow widened a little more. As she brought a third and then a fourth cup, the hollow widened to a basin, and finally, water sprung up from underneath. It filled the basin to the edges.

At first the surface of the pool was flat, the crystal top of still water. Then it rang, making a noise like a chime from a glass bell or a flute made of birds' bones. The water rang, then rippled in a widening circle to the edges, and chimed again.

From the ceiling of the cave, water dripped into the basin below. She wondered if she had missed this drip, and caught a drop on her finger. It smelled as the water of memory, of hyssop and roses. She sucked it and another drop fell.

She drew the relic to her heart. Perhaps now, with the miracle renewed, things would change. Though Lo still shunned her, perhaps, if she could bring Lo to see the water, she would know that her destiny remained.

Before she left, Georgia knelt at the cave mouth to say a prayer of protection. This place was now a home for the followers of Isela, like the homes she had made countless times before. And even in this very cave long ago. The prayer she chose was the one her mother had taught her:

"*Hail Mary full of grace the Lord is with you. You are blessed among women and blessed is the fruit of your womb, Jesus. So be it.*"

CHAPTER 28:
Saint Lucy

SOMETHING CALLED GEORGIA FROM SLEEP—A NOISE, SOME alarm rousing her, pulling her and the dream up into the waking mind. She rolled over slowly, over the sweet grass and alder leaves Manwell had piled into the hut the day before. She could taste a smokiness and feel the warm awkwardness of a caress around her shoulders.

Manwell. His eyes laughed at her. "There are many good things in the world," he said.

A shrill scream dragged her from the dream. Georgia shivered at the sudden loss of his touch and flung her hands out, seeking balance, trying to remember where she was.

She was alone in the goose hut. She had been sleeping since early morning after another night of prayer at the cave. Two large ganders looked down over humped beaks with a disapproving glare. She cringed; ganders bit. Hard. Manwell usually kept them out while she slept.

Manwell. The thought of him made her feel queasy. Had she just dreamed? Or had he been here with her?

Another scream pierced the hut, this one of pure, defiant helplessness. Georgia sat up in the straw, sending the ganders backward, honking. Lo! It was Lo who screamed. Romsfeld was beating her. Georgia had heard the sound enough to know it. Georgia jumped to her feet and over the bed, catching her balance on a low beam. A whole year gone to this. A whole year twisted with bruises and beatings and rage.

Mendaline urged patience—aching, nauseating patience. Mendaline said that Lo must learn to trust slowly, that she could not be rushed. But while Mendaline healed her bruises, she did not have to endure the screaming.

Lo shrieked again, a scream of fury and despair. Georgia stumbled toward the door, tripping over the low planks.

The screaming stopped. Now there were hoof beats, men calling to each other in the barn, the clink of metal, and Lo, shrill and angry from the courtyard, screaming for Romsfeld to never return.

Georgia wrenched the door open, squinting and blinded, into the midday sun. She ran directly into Manwell. He wrapped his long arms around her, thin as ever since that night months ago on the old grounds, but stronger now.

She tried to dodge under him, but he held her, drawing her back into the hut. "Hold. Hold," he said, as if she were overwrought, as if she were a child, or one of his goslings after a dog had chased it. She fought him.

"Be still." He turned his head to avoid a blow. "If you go out there, you'll only earn another beating."

It was true; she had intervened with Lo before, and it was trouble. Romsfeld had ordered her hung by her wrists and whipped bloody, a terrible revenge that kept her from the cave and from her prayers for a full month. Worse than the beating was how Lo had run from her.

Georgia struggled. "What do you care if a woman screams?"

Manwell looked hurt, but Georgia felt only the smallest pang of remorse.

"Tell me then," he said. "What should I do?"

"Kill him." Georgia fought again to get up, but only managed to smash her wrist against the wall. It hurt. A splinter was imbedded just above her wrist, and it bled.

Horses whinnied in the courtyard. Romsfeld called out to his men, and they galloped away, the dust from their hooves filtering into the hut and smelling of fungus, manure, and chalk.

Another scream from Lo, a plaintive call to a retreating foe, pushed through the afternoon. Her cry hit a somber tone, one of rage and grief and desolation.

Georgia remembered stone walls, the smell of beeswax candles, and a horrible shriek—Agnes.

Georgia clamped her hands to her temples. "Give me a memory I can use!" It was all wrong. She was now almost fourteen. Fourteen! And still, Lo would not talk to her. The water had restored nothing.

"You're bleeding." Manwell took her hand and examined it. She flinched. She usually kept the mark on her hand hidden.

"Be still," he said and held on firmly. "Don't make me call the geese to guard you."

She thought to snatch her hand back, to kick him and run. But now that Romsfeld was gone, whom was she fighting? She chose to sulk instead and relinquished her wrist to him.

He took her hand, slipping his thumb over the mark but otherwise ignoring it, paying more attention to the pits and splinters in her skin. How, she thought, did she end up dependent on a boy in a goose hut?

Yet with his help, she could go to the cave almost every night. There she could try to make up for the years lost and prepare for what was to come. Already word of the hermitage had spread. Women came to the cave, now, in secret, and pilgrims as well.

Mendaline and Amy and Beatrice came often. And little E'beth, who loved the relic and declared that she would be a nun. Georgia left the relic at the altar, now, as there was always someone there to guard it.

But she shared nothing of this with Manwell. He was male, if not yet a man. He would eventually tend oxen.

He squinted and picked out two of the larger slivers. She refused to flinch but chastised herself for her contrariness. She was not a child. Not in her soul. Saint Isela, help me to remember!

Shivers formed below her neck and ran down her spine. His hands felt warm with a light, filmy dust, and his arms were bare and streaked with sweat. His hair clumped and curled, and as he hung over her hand, it fell in tangles over his eyes.

He looked up and caught her studying him. He smiled, and small wrinkles formed at the bridge of his nose. Again she was reminded of the boy from home. If she had stayed there, would they be married? Would he have kissed her?

Manwell pinched out a larger splinter, but squinted over a twisted line embedded under her skin. With a quick look up at her, he brought her hand to his mouth and sucked gently to bring the splinter to the surface.

She should have yanked her hand away, but instead her body cascaded into a thousand shivers. Why did she dream of this boy? This morning she dreamt he had lain next to her on the hay. And now she wished the dream back again. She had not thought the wrist so vulnerable.

He stopped to check his work, and then sucked at the splinter again, this time more industriously. Clearly, this was medicinal. He pinched two dirty fingernails together. She felt a sharp pain. Manwell surveyed the bleeding with satisfaction.

A gander squawked; Georgia nearly jumped from her skin. A pair of geese herded goslings into the hut, and a deafening squawking burst out.

"Saint Martin! Quiet your geese!" Georgia pressed her hands over her ears.

He clucked at the geese until they settled and the flapping subsided. "I never knew someone to dislike geese, so."

"I do not dislike them." She sweated, and her skin itched.

"You do. You never let them into the garden while you're working."

"They bite."

"But you like the chickens."

"We've talked of this before."

Manwell scooted closer to her. He followed the fall of her headscarf, across her shoulders and along her neck.

"You like the hens and the capons, but not the cocks. You like the capons because they are fat and because they are not men."

"Chickens are not men."

"No." He leaned toward her, but she could not shift away as she was already against the hut wall.

She willed herself to stop sweating. "Philosophy from a gooseherd."

"And philosophy from a cotter's daughter is better?"

"I should think."

"Just so you know, geese are fabulous." He leaned away again, smiling and cheeky.

She found she was watching his grinning mouth. It curved up higher on one side than the next. She rubbed her hand against her arms. Wake up! What do you remember of these things? He's just a boy.

"In fact, geese are spectacular," he continued, "and it's not only the geese that love me, but ducks as well, and the doves in the cotes, and the larks and sparrows."

Georgia had to laugh. "And the fleas and the mites," she dared to pick a beetle from the roll of sleeve at his elbow. One of the geese nipped her on her calf. She screamed. "Call your dog off me!"

Manwell nestled in as if testing what closeness she would allow. His gaze went to her lips and hovered there before gliding to the ties at the neck of her shift. She lifted her hand to cover the opening at her throat. He flicked his eyes away, but didn't move back.

"There's only one way to keep the geese away," Manwell lowered his voice and whispered like a conspirator. "You have to be kind to the gooseherd."

"What sort of 'kind'?"

His gaze was intent. Behind the brown of his eyes she could sense—something. Wake up! She pinched her leg where the gander had bit her. Why couldn't she remember what to do?

He moved again. He shifted so close they almost touched along the length of their bodies, side by side in the straw. She felt confused. She was convinced he'd been practicing. If only she could hate him.

A goose honked. Manwell's gaze lingered over her face, her cheeks, her mouth.

Goosebumps started over the bones of her ankles and spread over her skin, crashing over her knees and elbows and the tips of her fingers tingled. He was seventeen. Too young for her.

He leaned in, an intended kiss, a slow movement that sent curls falling around his face.

Perhaps he misjudged the distance or changed his mind at the last, but whatever, he lost his balance and had to thrust his hand against the wall behind her to still his clumsiness. He blushed and retreated, but his eyes lost none of their intensity.

"So you call that a kiss then?" Her pride nudged her. She'd let him steal her breath. A boy.

"Almost."

Her mouth tingled. She remembered the caresses of the dream. He had been older then—no. She closed her eyes and searched for something else. Some other memory. Some other time. But all she could think of was him, his mouth, his warmth, the taste of his skin. She chided herself. She, who knew what men were. She did not want kisses.

ɞ

The door to the hut banged open, and Manwell rolled away from her. She jumped too quickly. The geese shrieked, and feathers flew in all directions. A young boy stood in the doorway, shadowed by the afternoon and out of breath.

"Manwell, you must go. You must go to town to fetch the doctor!"

Georgia was on her feet. "What has happened?"

"Mistress Lo ate the wolfsbane, the blood and everything. She's got the fit."

Manwell was already out the door. Georgia grabbed him by the back of his tunic; the thin cloth tore.

"Not the doctor—Manwell. Mendaline, get Mendaline."

Manwell nodded and ran out.

Georgia spun the boy around. "Where are the men?"

"They rode out with the master."

"All of them?"

The boy nodded. He stooped to scoop up goose feathers and then sneezed.

Georgia left him, running across the grounds, past the stables and across the courtyard. The door to the hall stood open, and she did not check her stride until she was well within and squinting in the diminished light.

She had never been farther than the hall and kitchens. She knew that Lo slept upstairs, but not exactly where. And Lo might not be there at all.

Madam the housekeeper called from an upstairs window. "For pity's sake, the feathers!"

Georgia took the stairs two at a time. The smoke of burning feathers was a known remedy for hysteria, for quelling the ill humors of women and the womb. Yet there was nothing hysterical about a woman's desperation after years of rape and bruises.

Georgia had waited too long. Patience, Mendaline had said. Patience! No longer. No longer. She must never again wait.

She reached the top of the stairs and shoved past the housekeeper and into the room. The older woman sweated like a slug in salt. "Insolent girl."

Georgia ignored her. Let Madam beat her if she dared. This time she would fight. Lo writhed on the bed, her knees drawn tightly to her stomach. If Lo died, all hope for the resurgence, all hope for women, for a better life, for a new way, all of it would be lost.

"Lo," she gathered her into her arms, crooning. "My daughter, my daughter—what have you done?"

CHAPTER 29:
Nonita

GEORGIA WRAPPED HER ARMS AROUND THE WOMAN who used to be the girl she knew. If Lo died, all the struggle, the heartache, the separation, all would be for nothing, a destiny erased.

Lo's mouth gaped wide open, and her breathing came in short pants. A dark fluid dribbled down her chin, and Georgia wiped it with the linen sheet. She ran her hands over Lo's arms and legs, checking temperature, breathing, pupils, and pulse. Lo's cheeks were soiled with fresh bruises. She looked far older than a daughter. A sister perhaps, a woman grown.

"Insolent girl!" The housekeeper glared at her, pulled the short stick from her belt, and smacked it against her thigh. Her skinny nose brushed quarter-inch hairs against her upper lip as her nostrils flared. "This is no place of yours."

Georgia turned on her. In the past year, she had endured the woman's brutality, had seen how she struck the child servants of the household, and seen how she had used Lo to gain advantage in the house, keeping her down so that Romsfeld could use her as he pleased. It sickened her, and Georgia would no longer abide it. She vaulted from the bed and struck the woman across the mouth.

"I'll say it was you who poisoned her," Georgia shrieked. "For by Saint Benedict it's true."

The housekeeper struck back, first with a sweaty fist and next with the stick, a one-two that missed Georgia on the first, but struck her in the chest with the second.

She choked, but not waiting to catch her breath, she rammed her head into the housekeeper's gut sending her backward against the wall.

The housekeeper regained her footing and reached out to grab her hair. Georgia twisted away at the sideboard, and in the scuffle Madam dropped the short stick. She grabbed a candlestick instead and aimed to throw it. "The devil take you!"

Lo moaned and twitched on the bed. Georgia looked over at her; her skin was white as an eel from the salt barrel.

Georgia turned again to the housekeeper. This business needed to be settled. She raised her hands in a wide arc over her head. "You will abide me. If she dies, I will tell the master you have done this. Out of jealousy. Out of spite. Poisoner. Defiler."

The housekeeper purpled except for her nose, which hooked yellow like a beak. "Ha! Such a thing you imagine yourself to be!" she said. "The master will never believe you!"

The young boy who had raised the alarm arrived with the goose feathers as Georgia launched directly at the housekeeper. Thin and girlish, Georgia nonetheless felt the fuel of a thousand years. She thought of how Agnes had attacked, with outstretched arms and her palms flat. Georgia did the same and, using the heel of her hands, hit the stocky woman square in the chest.

The housekeeper flung the candlestick but missed. It landed back against the wall and rolled under Georgia's feet. Georgia lashed out again, shoving the housekeeper backward toward the latrine. She pushed the housekeeper inside it and slammed the door. Then, with a quick swipe, she took up the candlestick and wedged the latch. The housekeeper screamed threats and beat at the door, but the joints held. Georgia spat at it to ward the devil away.

She turned next to the boy. He offered the feathers with an expression of disbelief, as if something impossible in his world had just happened. Georgia took the sack but threw the feathers down. Leave it to a small mind to imagine a suicide as female hysterics. The last thing they needed now was burnt feathers, unless it was to waft the smoke under the door of the latrine.

Yet at the boy's frightened look, she tried to calm herself. She needed his help.

"The master will be angry if she dies," Georgia said, her voice a higher pitch than she wished. "I need you to fetch medicine. I need almond milk, a measure of it, and equally, clean wood ash from the fire. Send the kitchen girl. And you must bring me a noggin of stonecrop. If there's none dried, there is some growing in the garden. You know it?"

The boy nodded.

"Good. Almond milk, ash, stonecrop," she repeated. "Haste."

The boy looked from the latrine to the feathers to the short stick near the foot of the bed where it had come to rest. He turned tail and ran down to the stairs.

Stonecrop and ash were the first step. The ash would calm any ill humors in the stomach, while the stonecrop would purge them, bringing the poisons up and out. Georgia returned to the bed and stroked Lo's forehead, crooning, glad to feel warmth in it. Lo twisted, grimacing.

"Mendaline's coming. And I am here. Georgia is here." Think, Georgia told herself. Think. What to do. What to do.

The boy returned with an older girl who almost dropped the jug of milk at the pounding of the latrine door. Georgia took the ash and milk and poured them together with the stonecrop, shaking them thoroughly.

She pointed to a washbasin on the sideboard. "Bring the bowl."

The girl stared at the vibrating door, but the boy complied. Georgia raised Lo's head up from the pillow and drizzled a little of the slurry into her mouth.

"You must take this. It will make you well."

Lo spasmed, bringing her knees up against her chest and almost upsetting the drink. When Georgia returned the cup to Lo's mouth, Lo jerked, her arm slack and out of control.

Georgia yelled at her. "You'll have to face Isela next. What will she think for you to fail her? Drink!"

Georgia waited until Lo tilted her head back for air and then dumped the mixture into her mouth. Lo sputtered and spat up but swallowed perhaps enough of it to do her good. She rolled into a tight curl, her face contorted, and her skin now flushed.

The boy and girl stared at them.

"The wolfsbane," Georgia addressed the girl. "What did the cook use in it?"

"Chicken blood, glass, and hemlock," the girl said. "There's some first growth by the stream. It's for the foxes—"

"How much did she eat?"

The girl shrugged. "There were three of them."

Georgia rolled her eyes. It would take a determined person to eat three egg-sized chunks of blood and ground glass.

"Bring me a spoon of mustard ground to a paste if there is some. Seeds and a mortar if not. Also a jug of old ale. Quickly."

The girl ran. The housekeeper pounded on the door, and the boy jumped. The candlestick shook with each thud.

"Mind it holds," Georgia said. The boy nodded.

Lo retched. Georgia caught several large greenish, claylike chunks in the bowl.

"Good. And again."

Lo complied but without the will to do it. A thin, milky green fluid tricked out.

"More to come. Hold strong now."

First the milk and then thick, stinking globs of curdled blood and black material spewed into the basin.

The girl returned with mustard and ale.

Lo's vomit changed in color from green to a yellow fluid. When her breathing shortened, Georgia drew Lo's head slightly back to keep her breath moving as freely as possible.

What was taking Mendaline?

Georgia smeared the mustard and ale into Lo's mouth, and Lo took it in when she swallowed. Her eyes shone, awake, and yet she seemed not to see what was around her. She looked as if she had accepted death. Georgia rolled her over onto her stomach and rubbed her back and legs.

Mendaline arrived with E'beth at her side, too out of breath at first to speak. Manwell swept upstairs with her; he seemed uncomfortable in the house but had breath in his lungs to spare. Georgia almost burst into tears at the sight of them.

"Ground glass and hemlock," she gabbled. "Wolfsbane."

Lo lay unmoving. The door to the latrine shuddered under renewed pounding. Manwell and the boy exchanged a look.

"I'm minding the candlestick," the boy said, his look intent.

Manwell nodded. "That's well-done of you."

"What did you give her for it?" Mendaline dropped her satchel, wheezing.

"Stonecrop and ash in almond milk. Mustard in ale."

Mendaline nodded. "You remembered something."

Georgia could not be excited by this small thing she remembered when there was a great ocean she had forgotten.

"She's cold." Lo had gone pale again.

Mendaline nodded. She opened her ugly hands, pressing the flattened mass of her left against the bruise on Lo's face.

"Wine. Manwell, red wine, hot. E'beth, get the spice oil and give it to Georgia."

The girl pulled a linen cloth and a small vial from the satchel and handed them to Georgia.

"Rub it into her," E'beth instructed.

Mendaline rolled Lo onto her side, but her hands were too clumsy to manage the stays of her bodice. E'beth worked them as Georgia rubbed the oil over Lo's skin; it smelled of nutmeg and white pepper. Lo curled and retched again.

Mendaline frowned. "How much did she eat?"

"Three lumps. Here." Georgia kicked the basin.

Mendaline wiped a trickle of blood mixed with the brownish yellow of the mustard from Lo's nose and smelled it. She bent to smell Lo's breath and wipe her tongue clean.

Georgia rubbed harder with the oil, down Lo's calf and ankle, over her heel.

Mendaline did not share her vigor. Instead she sighed and sat back. "*Anne, Margaret, Mary, Ursula, Christina, Marina, Isela, good cross, worthy cross, holy cross, let evil flee. Amen.*" She crossed herself and made a cross over Lo. But Lo made no movement. Mendaline closed her eyes for the space of a Hail Mary. Life seemed heavy on her. She turned to Manwell. "Fetch the priest from Saint Mark's."

"The priest?" Georgia stopped rubbing the oil. "Why the priest?"

Mendaline pressed the back of her hand into Lo's neck, feeling for her heart beat. "He is a good man, Georgia. We must make her as comfortable as we can. At least we know her suffering will be eased."

Georgia roiled with frustration. She shook the vial of oil at Mendaline, her fingers slipping over it. "What eased? In harming herself? How can you say such a thing? Why did you come, if only to give up? Will you sit by and let her die, as you stood by and let him beat her? Wait, you said. She must heal, you said. We will not call the priest. I forbid it. Isela needs no priests. I remember—"

"You remember stories." Mendaline gave her a warning look. "The sisters of Isela had many heresies."

"What of the mark?"

Mendaline was silent before speaking again. "Things have changed from what they were. There will be trouble."

"Mendaline, listen to me. This cannot be. She is the Chooser—the *Chooser*." The pounding from the latrine stopped, and Georgia cut her voice to a hard whisper. "She will bear a child. She will bring Isela back into the world—hope back into the world. The promise—*when the Chooser comes*—you must heal her."

"She has her own way to make. I have always said it."

"And if she dies? Is that her way? To die by her own hand?"

"Child, you can't know everything."

Georgia let loose a little shriek of rage and frustration. Know everything? She knew nothing! She was an idiot girl. Bony, gangly, flat chested. She remembered nothing! What she must do, where she must go, the stories of the promise and fulfillment, or the language of mysteries. She managed only glimpses from dreams and prayers. There was so much more to know.

"I know this," Georgia said. "Lo is the Chooser."

"There is something you do not know."

Georgia writhed. "You mock me. There is everything I do not know! But this one thing at least I remember. Lo is a harbinger—*the one who comes before*. It will be her duty to choose in what way the promise will be realized. When all is ready, she will have a child. She will know the time. She will make the choice. She must live to do it."

Mendaline caressed Lo's cheek. "How many lives will be lost until then? Twenty? Three and twenty?"

"Not any lives lost. Not one life. Not one life!" Georgia thought of her own lives lost, one after the other blurred together like leaves dotting the length of a sage branch, with always a new leaf growing at the end.

So many lives lost. So much time lost. The horseman pounded into her mind, his sword drawn. She felt her throat tighten. "We will not fetch the priest."

Mendaline sighed again, "E'beth, the red pouch."

Georgia took Lo's hands in her own. "Lo, listen to me. Can you remember what a happy girl you were? The stories I told you?"

Mendaline sandwiched a cup between her ruined hands while E'beth poured herbs. "A little more ... more ... right." She swirled the herbs and held the cup out to Georgia. "For you." The note of compulsion in Mendaline's voice was absolute.

"What's in it?"

"A little bitterness."

Georgia remembered Mendaline's bitterness, how she gave a bitter leaf to those who needed a distraction from their pains. How Mendaline said, "Let them think of something else."

Georgia threw the cup to the floor. "I already know bitterness."

Mendaline surveyed Lo again, listening to her breath. It slowed and then stopped. She rubbed her awkward hands together and placed them across Lo's shoulder blades. "There is one thing," she said. "But it will be called witchcraft—though it is not. We will burn for it if they find out."

"Sister, you must do what you know to do."

Mendaline rolled Lo over again, propping her up and circling her in an embrace. She drew measured breaths, drawing in through her nose and exhaling through an open mouth. When she spoke, it was a song, a bell resonating—a sound that could be felt in the center of her gut.

"*I slay the beast, I slaughter the beast, I kill the beast.*" Mendaline drew another slow breath. *"I slay the beast, I slaughter the beast, I kill the beast."* And another. *"I slay the beast, I slaughter the beast, I kill the beast."*

Georgia crossed herself. She added her voice to the invocation and heard E'beth in unison beside her. *I slay the beast, I slaughter the beast, I kill the beast.*

Lo gagged. Her legs twitched, and a spasm racked her.

"Lo," Mendaline rocked her, "breathe, breathe."

The spasm left her body, and she collapsed. She loosed a rattling cough, but yet drew a breath.

Mendaline still looked grim. "She breathes. But will she live? I cannot say. Perhaps if she can purge again. But I cannot heal her from what she has suffered. I can do no more for her."

Georgia bent over Lo, full with horror and sorrow. It was wrong, so wrong. This was not as it was meant to be. If only she could remember something, anything— "Water." Georgia sprang upright. "She must drink the water."

Mendaline stopped rocking. She seemed younger. "E'beth," she directed, "run to the cave. Take a cup. Bring—"

"No. It will be too late."

Georgia screamed, a loud, short burst that released some of the tension pinching the back of her skull. "We must take her there."

No one argued. The housekeeper resumed her pounding, but they paid no mind to her.

Georgia snatched up the blanket. Lo fell slack as Manwell lifted her from the bed, and Georgia covered her. Georgia caught his gaze and held it, trying to communicate the importance of what they did.

"I will lead you," she said.

CHAPTER 30:
Saint Bega

They reached the cave, and Georgia dropped blankets in a nestled corner.

"Place her here," Georgia said. "E'beth, fill a cup with water from the pool."

Manwell set Lo gently on top, and retreated to the shadows. Two pilgrim women moved from the altar as Georgia hurried for the relic, taking it down and placing it around her neck. It bulked out from her chest.

E'beth brought the cup, and Mendaline maneuvered Lo up and across her lap.

Steadying her hand, Georgia poured a few drops of water over the relic, letting the droplets drip back down into the cup. Then, as Mendaline held Lo's mouth open, Georgia dripped the water onto Lo's tongue. The water filled her mouth and trickled over her lips, her chin, and the blankets that tucked around her. Lo thrust out her jaw and seemed to suck.

Georgia took strength from the miracle of the water; her hands were wet with it, and her arms as well where the water dripped from the sides of the cup and over her wrists. When she spoke, her voice echoed through the cave, multiplying echo over echo, until a thousand women seemed to speak at once.

"Remember," the voices said, "you are a daughter of Isela."

Night came and then morning with little difference to Lo's illness. Georgia stayed at Lo's side, squeezing water onto her tongue and washing her body. She drew Lo's hand into her lap. She had seen the damage to Lo's palm, but only from a distance. Now, she studied the scars.

Lo's mark peeled from underneath and rose in nodules, as if harrowed or turned inside out. Georgia washed it gently; the shiny pink and jagged crimson lines were as if a path of roses had been obliterated.

Georgia wept to see it. The ruins of a life—two lives. Both of them, herself and Lo, at the mercies of those who would destroy them. She smoothed water over the scar and watched the water bead and slide away. She had not thought so pearly a pink could be so violently made.

Manwell returned to the manor and Mendaline to town, but the pilgrims remained. A young woman brought an infant into the cave to bless and bathe him. The baby's cries echoed over the limestone, but Lo did not wake.

Mendaline returned at dusk. "How does she?"

Georgia shrugged.

Mendaline pushed aside Lo's blanket and ran her hands over her.

"Has she moved?"

"No. But she swallowed more water this afternoon."

Mendaline nodded. She sat back on her heels and wrapped the blankets back around Lo, leaving Georgia to tuck the edges in.

"Romsfeld searches for her," Mendaline said. "He has threatened to burn all of Bilsdale to find her."

Georgia closed her prayer book in surprise.

"What?" Mendaline chided. "You thought he'd not notice that she was gone?"

"He does not care for her."

"Do you really think that?"

"She will never go back."

Mendaline clucked her tongue.

Georgia slipped the book into a pocket. "We will go to Scotland."

"Child, look at yourself. Have you slept? You must eat something. There are rumors in town of a girl who does not eat and yet lives. She is called the 'fasting girl of Isela.'"

"Dame Partlet—gossip."

Mendaline pinched Georgia's arm. "See how skinny you are. E'beth worries for you. We have brought bread. Eat."

Georgia shook her head. "I have ill humors of the stomach."

"No doubt it is hungry! Eat. This will be gentle enough." Mendaline took out a dish, and E'beth poured milk into it. With twisted fingers, Mendaline tore some of the bread to soak and gave the bowl to Georgia. "If you starve to death, it will not help Lo."

Georgia pinched a morsel of the bread and sucked on it, but she could not swallow. She spat it into her hand and threw it into a corner.

"Spitting," Mendaline sounded worried. "I remember this."

Georgia picked up a cloth soaked in spice oil and rubbed Lo's feet, easing away the dead skin. "Leave it. I will eat more soon."

Mendaline looked doubtful. "I think you won't." Her gaze flicked to Lo. "We cannot keep her here. The cave will be found out. Manwell is already in the stocks."

"Manwell?"

"He held his tongue through the lash. But the brute Romsfeld will search for her until she is found. She has been here two days already."

"She is not recovered."

"For Saint Clare's sake, Georgia, keep your mind. A swine-brained woman, you always were. You steal a man's mistress, and then you sit here like a skinny hen waiting for her to hatch."

"Even in my prayers, Isela teaches me."

"Isela tells you of things?"

"Stories."

"And you think Lo will have a child."

"Lo is the Chooser."

Mendaline eyed the sleeping, almost lifeless Lo. She whispered hard through her teeth. "You talk of dreams, but while you were gone we lived those years, Lo and I. Lo cannot bear a child."

Georgia closed her eyes. She did not want to remember her failure. She did not want to remember the price she paid.

Mendaline continued, "Romsfeld raped her. She was young and small. Always small, you remember. She tore worse than most after a rape. Fever set in. He let the doctor tend her first. That made a further mess. Romsfeld called me only when he worried she might die."

Mendaline grunted and scowled, the lines along her brows taking a fierce downward angles. "I don't know who did worse to her, Romsfeld with his prick or the doctor with his irons and prods. I did what I could, but the pus was running and her fever high. And I was helpless. They had crushed my hands. The wounds were fresh." Her voice wavered. "Sweet Mary!" She wiped her tears with the cloth of her headdress. "We cleaned her up, Alice and I—God bless dear Alice. We tended her with herbs and bindings, but her womb went putrid, and the waste flowed green." She cleared her throat. "She lived. By the grace of God she lived, but her womb healed hard as river stone.

She's never had her courses and never quickened. She's barren, Georgia. Lo can never bring a child into this world."

Georgia sat back and hugged her knees. There had been a sheep in the village where she was born that had suffered a putrid womb. It was said boys had tormented it. It cried and seeped and stank, and finally it was slaughtered.

Georgia balled her fists. She pressed her knuckles into her eyes, and for a while, the world went black. But the pressure in her head mounted, leaking yellow before bursting blood red. Yet she did not care if she went blind. She deserved far worse than that.

Someone touched her. A palm, a warm palm on her wrist.

"You must not blame yourself," Mendaline said. "What shame there is belongs to the one who did it. Not to you."

Georgia got up to refill the bowl but stumbled as she returned. Water spilled over her dress. She watched as her skirt darkened. Rat-colored, the skirt was.

"I pulled her from his horse." Georgia mumbled, feeling gritty from lack of sleep. Her eyes felt as hot as if they had boiled. "I bade her run—"

A light laugh echoed in the cave. In the pool, a naked infant kicked as his mother splashed water over him. Water to protect babies, to ward off illness, and to bring miracles. Lo had been baptized in it.

"This can be undone." Georgia drew a deep breath, as if to begin a chant, so that her lungs filled almost to her toes. "There are cures. Mare's blood—and urine. What is the recipe?"

"You think I have not tried so simple a cure as that?"

A low sob echoed along the floor. Mendaline and Georgia turned to see Lo stutter through a breath and roll over onto the dirt. She put her hand over her mouth, curled up in a brutal spasm, and vomited.

Georgia rushed to her, Mendaline soaked fresh linen, and Georgia wiped Lo's face and hands. Lo pushed the cloth away with outstretched fingers. She tread, kicking through the blankets.

Georgia tried to hold her still, but Mendaline pulled her back. "Let her roil. Let the blood flow."

Georgia held onto Lo's hands so she would not scratch herself. Once more Lo pulled her knees across her belly, coughed, and vomited. Lo kicked harder and then stilled, resuming her breathing, her fingers twitching. She rolled back into the blankets and fell quiet.

Mendaline threw her head back and shouted. "She lives!" She laughed, a throaty, wheezing laugh.

Georgia wrung the cloth in the water and shook it; her eyebrows knitted together at the stink.

"Have you no joy?" Mendaline poked her. "You are the most joyless, starveling child. Lift your arms and shake them, hurrah! For it is your miracle."

Georgia cleaned the vomit from the corner of the blanket. She gagged, and her eyes watered at the reek.

"You should sleep," Mendaline said. "Rest yourself. Though it stinks it is worthy of rejoicing, for now she will recover. Sleep."

"I will do as I like."

Mendaline raised a brow and then shrugged.

"As you will, then."

Georgia did sleep. She cleaned the mess then closed her eyes and curled into the blankets next to Lo. When she woke, it was morning, and Lo sat awake against the wall. She was quiet and staring, with her gaze fixed to the relic.

Georgia knew the look. A look of struggle as the body pulled memory from each cell, each fragment circling as birds to a flocking point.

"What did you dream?"

Lo put her hand to her mouth.

Georgia picked up the relic and let it spin. The small lights in the room illuminated gold streaks on the cave walls, and the pilgrims quieted to watch them, some kissing the walls where the light flickered.

Georgia stopped the spin. "Tell me, what did you see?"

Lo looked from the relic to Georgia. "How did you get this?"

"I am reborn. I am the Bearer."

"The relic," Lo whispered.

"And the burden," Georgia answered. "You are the Chooser. Do you remember?"

"I remember lies. And heresy."

"It is no heresy, and we are only women. And when Isela comes, she will show us the way of women. And we will live in kindness without men."

Mendaline brought a jug from the fire. She smelled now of horehound and marjoram. She tipped the jug into a cup and nudged Georgia with her elbow. "Not *without* men, surely, for they have their uses." She laughed loudly.

"Without them if we choose," Georgia glared at her. Mendaline seemed far too cheerful.

"What of Manwell?"

Georgia ignored her, frowning.

Lo touched the amber glass. "I remember the story of Saint Winifred. They cut off her head, but it was restored to her and she lived. She became an abbess."

"Yes!" Georgia cried. "And a fountain sprung up from where her head touched the ground. I had forgotten that story." She smiled and shot Mendaline a look of victory. "And we will also spring up from the ground. We will go to Scotland. We will leave as soon as you are well enough—tomorrow."

Lo withdrew her hand from the relic, and her face closed. The gold light on her skin faded to the green and blue of old bruises.

"The next day, then," Georgia said. "All who wish to travel can come with us."

"I will not go," Lo said. "He will despair without me."

Georgia opened her mouth and closed it again. "He beats you!"

Lo shrugged. She drew her arms across her breasts. "He is afraid. He needs me." She lowered her eyes. "And I—I am useless."

Georgia sat back on her heels. She dropped the relic into Lo's hands where they were cupped in her lap, the ornate scrollwork resting against her palm. In the center was an immense pool of glass.

"Tell me," Georgia said, "have you been to the old priory grounds and seen the well?"

Lo nodded.

"Then you have seen what they have done to it. They plugged it and covered it in filth. Yet it is not the fault of the fountain that this is so. The fountain is blameless. That part that is the well, the water and the swell of the soil, that part can only be as it is, perfect and pure. Regardless of what is done to it. It is as it was born to be.

"God made the water and the well. And Isela has brought it. Look how it flows here, its true nature only as it can be, sweet and pure and filled with goodness. The same is true for you."

Lo was quiet. Then she pushed the relic away. The blanket fell from her shoulders, and shivering, she pulled it up and wrapped it over her.

"You are young," Lo said. "I have seen you with the chickens, chasing them from the garden and scolding the dogs."

Mendaline laughed. "A true word. This girl who prays but kicks like any child."

Georgia smoothed her fingertips over the relic as she picked it up. "We can live again as sisters."

"You have no sword. How will you fight?"

"Isela will protect us."

Lo shook her head. She uncurled her legs from under her, and steadying herself against the cave wall, rose slowly. She returned the relic to Georgia. "I have little hope in that."

"You have every hope in that. Do you remember nothing of what I taught you?"

"I remember."

"What of the promise?"

"The promise." Lo's voice echoed, or maybe her words were just reflected by the hollow of the cave. Lo wavered a little, but held herself up, stretching her bare toes for balance. Drawing the blanket more tightly around her, she crossed her arms over it. "There is no promise now."

"But he will force you."

"It is easier to lie still."

Georgia flinched. Mendaline placed her arm around Georgia's waist. Kindly, it seemed, but the touch was unwanted. Georgia shrugged her away.

Mendaline clucked her tongue. "We must carry our burdens in our own way," she said.

Georgia kicked Mendaline's satchel, and the vials clanged together. "Do not talk of burdens as if they were nothing heavier than a bag of corks and pouches."

"Foolish girl," Mendaline grabbed the strap and slid the satchel away. "You are not the only one to know suffering."

Lo retreated to the cave mouth and drew aside the vines that darkened it. Swaying a little on her feet, she raised her arm to shield her eyes against the sunlight.

"Wait!" Georgia blinked at the brightness. Beside it, Lo was only a shadow. "If you return, so must I. And the monster will beat me. Likely, he will kill me."

Lo sighed. "You have this," she raised her arm and indicated the cave, the women crouched by the altar watching and listening, and E'beth curled up asleep in the corner, still asleep, despite the voices. "You can stay here."

"Lo," Georgia felt the pleading in her throat, "think before you go. Think what you return to. What of Isela? What of me?"

"You died."

Lo's gaze passed from Mendaline to Georgia and away. She stepped outside the cave, and the vines closed behind her.

CHAPTER 31:
Markham Manor, York, England, 1551

Philip surveyed the room, a privy chamber at the center of which sat an oak table, dark rubbed and laid with bowls of cherries and a fruit called pineapple that the king seemed to find entertaining, though Philip thought it pus yellow and covered in spines.

Thomas Cranmer, archbishop of Canterbury, stood by the table ladling posset into a glass goblet. The presupper posset, a curdled milk drink of sweetened ale served warm and loaded with spice, smelled to Philip of a fetid barn. Cranmer filled his goblet with it.

Philip gave a short bow. "Your Grace. I trust your wife is well?"

Cranmer nodded, swallowing deeply and with appreciative sucking noises. "Delightfully well, though I would think that would vex you, Philip."

The only other person in the room was John Dudley, the Duke of Northumberland. Dudley held reigning power over the Privy Council, the council that ran England until King Edward came of age.

Philip grimaced to see the two of them. He threw the box he carried onto the table, and it slid. "The king is not here?"

A broad smile swept Cranmer's hairy face. "No, our young Edward has other pressing matters."

The box stopped inches from where Dudley worked, and he raised his eyebrow questioningly.

"Dragees," Philip said. "Sweets for the king, though I had thought to deliver them myself."

"Most unhappy," Cranmer drank the posset in a final gulp.

Dudley poked at the box, pinching a sugar-spice candy between his thumb and index finger. "I am fond of dragees, but what I really like are those sugared almonds. What think you, Cranmer?"

"Ah." Cranmer helped himself to three of the sweets, popping them into his mouth one after the other and letting them melt on his tongue. "Mmm ... these are better. Why wait until after dinner? It is a fine way to start the stomach."

He slammed the box lid down as Dudley reached for another. "Though the rest will wait."

Cranmer nodded toward the roll of papers under Philip's arm. He carried documents tied in a blue ribbon, and with a private note in his own hand, penned for King Edward VI of England. Philip had not intended to surrender them to Cranmer.

Dudley's gaze stayed on his work. "Bring forward your petition," he said.

Cranmer took the papers and plunked them next to Dudley.

"King Edward is fifteen years old, is he not?" Philip said. "He is of age to deal with such matters himself."

"We are the council," Dudley untied the ribbon, his cloth-of-gold doublet gleaming under a furred mantle.

Cranmer took up the box of sweets, pinched another candy out from under the lid, then another, and chewed them by the fire. The hearth light glanced off the elaborate lace and Italian silks of Cranmer's jewel-lined doublet and cape. Despite the vulgarity of a full beard, Cranmer's supposed mourning for King Henry had not inspired him to shed ornament or wealth.

"It is no matter," Philip grumbled with resentment. They could not barricade him away from the boy forever, for Edward was a king and would make up his own mind. "Pardon me. My business can wait."

Cranmer cleared his throat. "But my business cannot." He brushed his hands together. "Tell me. How goes it in the north, Philip?"

"The north?"

"You bring us these," Cranmer poked at the papers as Dudley read them, "to protest the prayer book's distribution in the north, do you not?"

"Not to protest." Philip spoke carefully. He was a known dissenter to the religious changes and the new books. Before, when he had brought forward his concerns, Cranmer had agreed and sympathized—in private. But made no rectification.

"If not to protest, then what?" Cranmer asked. "Whom do you claim to speak for, if not for your own sake? Not for pious Edward, our king. Do you speak for the rabble, Philip? Or for unintelligible priests who wave their hands around and mumble in Latin?"

"Your prayer book is folly in the north, Cranmer."

"Why, because the north is filled with the heresies of saints?" Cranmer leaned in across the table, his voice hoarse and his face flushed. "If we do not push them, Philip, we cannot bring England forward. To God. To light."

"What God? By his wounds, Cranmer, with that great beard you look like Thor. Are we all now to be Germans? The last book caused rebellion enough, but the next one will be worse. Lord Dudley, have you army enough left to put down rebels intent on sacking York?"

"I have army enough to quell any threat against the king."

Cranmer unrolled one of the scrolls and glared. "You, Philip, are indulgent of popery. You resist the reforms. Even the most basic visitations have not been done in York. All Saints Church gleams with idolatry. This is your failure."

"York obeys the laws of the church," Philip said. "But if you release those books, York will be overrun with rebellion. Should I be made to suffer in purgatory for your vanity?"

"Purgatory?" Dudley echoed. "You are awash in superstition today, Archbishop."

Philip gripped the high back chair in front of him; it stunk of horsehair. "I cannot be blamed for this, that the priests hide Latin Bibles, that they sell the silver yet keep the copper for the Eucharist. You move too quickly and tread too close to heresy."

"And yet you understand that the books are even now being pressed?" Dudley said.

Cranmer spread his hands out as if he had not done it, as if he himself were helpless against it.

Philip wanted to shake him. The prayer books were Cranmer's pet project. The first book had caused uprisings all over England, and Dudley himself had put down the largest of them.

"The king has decreed that the new prayer books go out to all the churches in the north." Cranmer stared accusingly. "Will you delay progress? Coddle the Latin mumblers?"

"I served Henry, and I will yet serve Edward," Philip strode forward and snatched the papers back from Dudley, rolling them. "But I will not be idle as you scratch the faces from the saints and burn all that is sacred in England."

Dudley swooped forward, his breath clove-oiled from the dragees. "I can have you taken to the tower, Archbishop. You are on the gully of it now, as we speak, and may yet tumble in."

"Try to push me, Dudley. I will bounce back up."

"My lords," a manservant entered and bowed at the waist, careful to make no eye contact, "dinner is served."

⁂

The great hall was set with fine linen. Between each place was set a silver plate and goblet to be shared. The king's salt cellar rose tall on the table as a majestic dragon from the sea, tide foaming over the boat it threatened to swamp, the dragon's great tail lashing.

The courtiers came in, rich ladies on the arms of rich men, entering according to rank and precedence. They would take their places at the table with scrupulous attention to the order of power. Philip's own place would be near the king. But the members of the Privy Council, Dudley and Cranmer, would be between them.

The grand master of the household and a liveried hall porter stood in front of the king's table. The porter passed a unicorn horn over the final pouring of salt, checking for any trace of poison.

Edward stood at the sideboard while the fresh boat of water he was to use for washing was also tested for purity. Water was first sprinkled over a unicorn horn, and that being well, a little of the water was poured over the hands of a porter who waited there, his hands at the ready. When that porter remained sound, the king extended his own hands over the bowl, and the water was then poured over them.

Philip did not go to his place at the table but bowed before the king. He would take what opportunity he could manage, for if Dudley had sought to keep him away, he would not succeed.

"My Liege," Philip bowed low, sweeping his cap from his head. "I crave your ear on an important matter."

"You may speak." Edward was small for his age, but both thoughtful and intelligent. He had none of his father Henry's lustful qualities, but was studious and pious. Philip was glad to see the boy attentive.

"Majesty, as your humble servant, I must warn you of the trouble that will arise in the north from the prayer books that are even now being printed. The people, I fear, are not yet ready to receive them, and the trouble that will follow may be worse than the last."

The pantry porter kissed a clean linen towel and passed it to the pantler who also kissed it. It was then checked with the horn.

Philip kept his cap off as Edward regarded him. The boy's fingers dripped with water.

"Do you wish to bring England from sin?" Edward asked.

The cloth passed the test of the horn and was then given to the first chamberlain who gave it to the master of the household.

Philip bowed again. "My Liege, I have lived my life to purge sin, and led an army for your noble father to quell the Pilgrimage of Grace. I am an expert in this matter. These books will flare the passions of the north. In that way, they will lead toward sin not away from it. The books brush the cloth of heresy."

The master of the household gave the towel to Lord Dudley who himself laid it carefully over Edward's dripping hands.

"God will not fault us for our efforts," Edward allowed his hands to be patted dry, "even if blood is shed."

"Even the blood of innocents?" Philip pressed his point. "You are as wise as the most learned king, My Liege, yet if France crosses into Scotland and joins a rebellion, perhaps even goads it, we may lose the north entirely."

Dudley received the damp towel from the king and passed it to a butler who took it away. "You worry only for your own lands, Archbishop." Dudley sneered. "Perhaps those lands should be given to men better prepared to keep them."

The pantler scuttled away as Edward turned toward his seat at the table. Dudley sat Edward before sinking into his own chair and allowing the chamberlain to serve him wine. He plucked a sugared almond from a silver bowl and ate it.

Conversation was impossible as courtiers took their places and an army of ushers filled silver goblets with hippocras pouring from a fountain in the center of the dining hall.

Once the room quieted, Philip returned to the subject. "Pray you, My Liege. If you would but read my petition." Dudley and Cranmer exchanged glances.

Dudley whispered something, and Edward replied, "Yes, we have heard that." He tilted his head with curiosity. "Archbishop, we have heard that the north talks of miracles, of saints restored to life."

"You must understand, My Liege, that the northern folk are simple and attached to superstition."

"But we have heard of a fasting girl," Edward continued, "who does not eat and yet lives."

Philip considered his answer. His steward Romsfeld had told him of the rumors of such a girl, though he did not know exactly if she existed.

"Whatever you have heard, Majesty," Philip said, "I can assure you that no mere hungry girl is a threat to the church or to England."

The courtiers laughed and Philip with them.

A line of ushers and serving valets streamed into the hall, and a sigh of anticipation rose over the softer swish of aprons and linen cloths. The master of the household looked on sternly as loaves of bread and silver platters of *Blanc Brouet de Chappon,* a dish of chicken, eggs, and almonds that smelled of bacon and ginger and grains of paradise, were set on the table.

The chief cook, bald headed with rolled up sleeves to show no place for a treacherous knife, laid a platter before the king. This was the first dish of a multicourse feast, and the cook beamed with pride. There was a promise of elaborate *entremets* to come, a fire-breathing cockatrice, an entire palace made of sugar with duckling and oranges, and then the finest imported cheeses at the last, to set the stomach to a simmering digestion.

The pantler took up the unicorn horn and passed it over the king's dish. Next, he took up a sop of the ginger-egg sauce and made a show of eating it. No one paid any mind as the pantler chewed and swallowed. Yet when he bowed, the signal that he had suffered no harm, a collective "ah" went up. The king could now safely eat, and with him, everyone else.

Conversation dampened as courtiers speared egg-drenched slices of the chicken, dripping the juices over bread.

Philip did not eat; he had not finished his point.

Dudley chewed enthusiastically. "You think this fasting girl is of no concern of yours, Philip?"

Cranmer waved his hands as if in happy conversation. "What of Elizabeth Barton? The Holy Maid of Kent was she not called? Who aspired to visions and fueled an insurrection. She had come from your diocese, had she not?"

"Elizabeth of Kent was hung at Tyburn." Philip kept his tone calm. He watched Dudley and Cranmer carefully as they played the interest of the king between them.

"She was trouble enough for a serving girl." Cranmer poked the dish with his knife.

"That same girl," Dudley added, "charged a rebellion that cost Henry an annum to put down."

Edward raised his cup; he seemed genuinely curious. "We have heard this girl of the north, this fasting girl, lives and yet she does not eat."

Dudley shook his head. "A right nuisance."

Cranmer speared a chunk of chicken with his knife; egg yellowed the corners of his mouth. "You are in charge, Philip, yet you allow this abomination to continue?"

"I do not allow it." Philip came down hard on the words, as if emphasis could keep his power from slipping away.

"But you have done nothing to prevent it."

"Majesty," Philip spoke directly to Edward. Cranmer had chosen an argument too easily turned, and the boy had sense. Philip could reach him.

"These are precisely my concerns. To bring the prayer book into a climate such as we have in the north will only tempt the devil to prod the rabble to rise up. We have the Six Articles of Faith that I myself assisted your noble father in writing, articles to ensure the purity of England's very soul. All else is heresy by your own laws. The prayer book holds the line so thinly as to provoke open rebellion."

"The prayer books are approved by the council," Edward said.

"Then perhaps there should yet be more debate, My Liege, with you to lead it." Philip almost gloated. He had done it. Any boy would seek the power that was his, and Edward was a king.

Dudley raised his cup for more wine. "You forget, Philip, that it is your responsibility to keep the countryside in check. You are the archbishop of York. Yet you do not act. One wonders where your loyalties lie."

Philip bared his teeth. "Let me be clear. Elizabeth of Kent is long ago hanged. Right now, there is no evidence that this fasting girl exists. My lands are in perfect order."

Cranmer pulled a velvet sack from his girdle and withdrew a small glass vial. He held it high above his head. "Then what of this?" He slammed the vial on the table.

Courtiers jumped all along the tables, as if they feared the vial contained poison. His gaze on the king, Cranmer broke the wax seal and poured the contents of the vial directly onto the tile floor. A clear fluid. Water.

Even the musicians took notice. All in the room waited in silence for what terror might come next. When nothing happened, the musicians finished the last bars of their piece, and the courtiers burst into a riot of laughing.

Cranmer let the conversation bubble before interrupting. "A maidservant confessed to me. She claimed to be one of a dozen pilgrims at a well collecting water. The fasting girl there was very real, I assure you. You are lax, Philip. This girl exists, and the well with her. And the maidservant said one more thing. She said that this group of heretics is led by a nun they call Dame Georgia."

Georgia. Philip felt his gut tighten and the blood pound at the back of his neck. He had hoped never to hear that name again. "Impossible. She is a heretic. I saw her dead."

"Did you?" Dudley almost smiled. "Perhaps you have been duped, as a small child might be."

Edward rested his knife on the corner of his silver plate and sucked egg from his fingers.

"You actively work against us," Cranmer sloshed his wine. "You foment rebellion on the king's lands. You are a traitor to England."

Philip smoothed his hands over the linen tablecloth leaving an oily streak over white. Cranmer and Dudley had planned this, planned his humiliation, had used this excuse to shame him, to invalidate his argument and push the heresy of the prayer book.

The ushers came in again with replenished chargers and set the platters down. Philip had not even touched the food and realized in his defeat that he was hungry. He would lick his wounds. There would yet be time later to address the king. And he would take another tact. The boy king was already almost a man. Cranmer and Dudley could not maintain a hold on him for long.

"Majesty," Philip felt the gorge rise in his throat to be played for a fool before the entire court. "I am deeply grateful to have this brought to my attention. I will, of course, see to the matter of this girl myself. You can be assured, there will be no heresies on my land." He picked up his knife to eat.

Cranmer held his cup expectantly. "My dear Archbishop. You would leave such a troubling business unresolved?"

Philip looked from Cranmer to Dudley and to the king, at Edward's open expression and Dudley's arched brows.

Philip bowed his head. "Of course it cannot wait. I will tend to the matter at once. My lords have been most generous to hear me in this matter."

Philip rose and strode out the length of the hall and through the ornate doors. Cranmer rose to follow him, and even at a distance, Philip could feel Cranmer's breath against his neck. His secretary. Dominus Cranmer. Now so bold as to presume the power of a king. Curse him.

Cranmer stopped him in the archway. "The books will be introduced and the north must be readied. If you do not wish to lose your lands to the French, or your head to the tower, then there can be no more heresies. Choose your allegiance, Archbishop."

"I will see to it." Philip wanted to strike out, but instead clapped his cap onto his head and strode away. A fasting girl and a pretender, and on his land if Cranmer were to be believed. Romsfeld, it seemed, had kept the girl, Lo, overlong. He would see to the problem himself. He would ride tonight.

CHAPTER 32:
Virgins

Georgia felt warm, a homey warmth she had not felt in a long while. Not the sweaty intensity of a summer barn, but an internal, buzzing vigor, like the softness of a trembling touch or a handful of down when it is taken up and cupped in the palm.

The warmth drifted across her neck, down her arms, and along the smooth, lean curves of her body, from her thighs to the bottoms of her feet. The softness relaxed her throat, her brow where she held the muscles knit, and the back of her neck. The muscles of her lower belly grew heavy and soft, and the place between her legs tingled with a drowsy pleasure.

A damselfly perched above her on the blanket like an iridescent sunrise. It flickered and swept away. The whir of color made words: "Life is a gift. Receive it, and be joyful."

The dream faded. When she woke, it was already well into morning. Georgia fidgeted to tie her shift tighter at the neck. These dreams grew more frequent and were an embarrassment. She pressed cool fingers against the heat of her cheeks. There was work to do, and now she must say extra Hail Marys to purge herself of the pleasure of the dream.

First she had a visit to pay. She had secured a delicacy, an orange. A pilgrim brought it as a gift after prayers. One smell of the sweet reminded Georgia of the priory and a little girl there who had a taste for oranges.

After Lo left the cave, the consequences had fallen hard and sharp. Manwell spent two days in the stocks and the next two weeks recovering from chills and fever. Mendaline had been thrown into the gaol. It was only the influence of the powerful town guildsmen that brought her out, two of them with wives full bellied and soon to be delivered.

Georgia dared not be seen at all. She stayed in hiding. Though she was now isolated, the days in the cave were restful and offered a quiet satisfaction. Here, she could keep the hours openly, indulge in the sweeping joy of prayer, and plan their eventual escape.

Lo had also suffered with the rest. While her return ended Romsfeld's hunt for her, it did not sate his anger. He refrained from beating her but, to calm his bleating petulance, had demanded sex, its intimacy and reassurance. What happened next had passed from gossip to gossip into local lore—for she had refused him. Not just refused him, but fought him, leaving a scratch across his face that did not heal for his constant picking at it. Raging, he locked her in the buttery with the wine and ale, cheeses and barrels of salted butter. Later, expecting her to be contrite and eager for his approval, he brought her a basket of delicacies, sweetmeats, and spiced bread.

She refused him again, and he came away hurt as any unbreeched child, raging and swearing. He locked the door and left the housekeeper to watch over her and gloat. He swore that until Lo received him, he would never release her.

So far, he had not relented. But neither had she.

Georgia put the orange in the pocket of her kyrtle. Though it was dangerous, Georgia had taken to creeping every day onto the manor grounds. Lo was a prisoner, but not from Isela. Georgia had a lifetime to redeem. She would show Lo that she was loved.

She picked her way through mud and puddles. The standing water shimmered as the sunlight bounced from pool to pool, flirting with the damselflies that skipped stone over stone in pursuit of one another. At the thought of damselflies, Georgia felt a rush of dream-swept pleasure. She almost laughed. Then, admonishing her weakness, she cooled her warming cheeks with a splash of cold water from the pool. It was unseemly. Such thoughts led to trouble. Men brought unwanted challenges, she reminded herself sternly. She was a nun. Her mind must be as chaste as her body. Always.

This thought, however, made her blush again. For her body had begun to change. The bony angles had given way to softer curves, and her breasts swelled beneath her shift. She felt cross to think of it. The good bread Mendaline brought to the cave was to blame. And Beatrice, as well, for she brewed a sweet-rich beer spiced with clove and honey and grains of paradise.

Georgia emerged from the woods and stole low over the grassy hill, prepared to lie flat against the grass if a shepherd or plowman came into view.

She pulled her modest headdress down over her face. If any glimpsed her, let her seem as any other bondwife on the manor.

She must be careful, for besides her own safety, there was the danger that the cave would be discovered. New pilgrims came almost every day to dip into the water. Those who knew the name Georgia passed the name from lip to lip. Some on the manor knew her as "the fasting girl," and one maidservant who frequented the cave had brought her a rosary as a gift. She slid her fingers over it; it was the finest thing the girl Jane had ever owned, though Georgia remembered far more beautiful things.

Despite his trials, Manwell remained steadfast. He teased her for retreating to the cave and refusing to share his bed in the goose hut any longer. He laughed at her, as if they had been lovers! But he watched out for her, and she was grateful for it. Where she crossed at the stream, Manwell often waited for her, walking the geese and sometimes raising the signal not to come into the field too soon. Today she was late, and Manwell was already gone. The geese, too, had gone, leaving slimy white droppings along the fengrass.

She was vulnerable until she turned the first corner into the garden. There, a low wall formed a walkway next to the house, and if she crouched, she was hidden as she moved along it. The walkway opened to the medicinal garden and a copious planting of woody rue. If she pulled her knees up, she could hide behind it completely.

She sat there now, next to an arrow loop in the wall. On the other side of the wall was the buttery, and Lo. The window between them was covered in oiled linen from the inside. The opening was just wide enough for a defender to shoot an arrow, or for the slender hand of a girl to reach through.

Georgia touched the outline of the stones. These were her stones, stones taken from the priory, down to the very foundation, and used to build a manor for this lord. She slid her fingers over the closest one and wondered where this stone had been—perhaps in the dorter wall. Or the chapter house, or perhaps the church.

"Georgia," Lo whispered from inside.

"Good morrow!" Georgia scooped the orange from her pocket. "I brought you a gift." Shoving her thumb deep into the center of the shriveled fruit, Georgia prised it apart. She passed one half through the window and heard the exclamation of delight from within.

"An orange! Where ever did you find it?"

"A pilgrim," Georgia whispered. "It's not Michaelmas, but nuns the matter." Georgia laughed at her own joke. She pushed the second half of the orange after the first, and Lo took it up, but pushed it back out.

"We'll share it," Lo said. "You have this half."

Georgia poked it through the window again. "It is for you. Do you remember how I would sit and watch you eat them? With the juice sticky on your fingers?"

"And the bees," Lo laughed. "And the dogs sniffing at my face." Lo shoved the fruit out again. "But you must have it. I am not a child anymore to take it all. Besides, you must eat. You must get so fat they will not call you the fasting girl anymore."

I am getting too fat already, Georgia thought, but she said nothing. Laying her arm across her chest, she tried to squeeze her breasts flat. The orange, however, did smell wonderful. She nibbled where the seam of zest divided the pulp and the rind and realized she was hungry. She sucked the pulpy flesh and enjoyed the flowery smell, like an entire bouquet pressed into a fist. The sting of the bitter rind accented the satiny, sweet fibers of the inner fruit. She spat the creamy seeds into her hand. She would keep them. Perhaps she could coax them to grow.

"Mendaline brought me an orange, once." The rustling from the window indicated that Lo had settled close to talk. "I was sick and had only barley water to drink. The orange tasted as if I could circle the garden with my arms outstretched."

Georgia laughed. "I could have done with an orange the day I tried to make that monster stop beating you. Tucker enjoyed whipping me that day."

"You were so angry! I am sorry for that."

"It is not your fault, and in any case it is done," Georgia said. Then she considered. She had been angry, very angry. So angry she had wanted to beat them both, Lo and Romsfeld together, and afterward bury Tucker so deep in swine muck that he could never swim to the surface again. She laughed to think of Tucker covered in slime. Her anger faded. "I made promises I did not keep."

"I ran when you told me, too. I did run. But he came up ... I thought you would never come back."

"I thought I was invincible." A dry laugh made her cough. She should have known better. "I am mortal, after all. Your anger is just."

"I was angry! You abandoned me to him. If I wanted love, it had to be from him. And so ... I wanted him to love me," Lo said. "I wanted him to love me because—because perhaps he was the only one who ever would."

"He does love you—" Two bees flew from the woody stems buzzing. "For all that he is a monster and a bastard and a wretch."

"I wanted to love him, too. Then perhaps he wouldn't beat me. After you left, after Mendaline came and I got well ... I imagined perhaps I was to make a holy sacrifice, as Saint Pharaildis whose husband beat her. She made a well spring up, you know, that cured children. I thought—it is silly, but I thought if I loved him—even that he beat me—if I loved him, I could make a miracle somehow. And … I suppose I hoped that if I was good, God would cure me, and I would have a child. But I am barren."

Georgia shook her head. "Men are devils, Lo, no better than the rut."

"Do you believe that?"

"I do." Georgia spat the last of the seeds in her palm. They looked beautiful. Like pearls.

"I think not." The oiled paper in the window crinkled as Lo shifted. "When I was sick, Mendaline stayed by me. It was hard because her hands—one swelled huge and painful. But she comforted me. She told me that she had loved a man once."

"Mendaline?" Georgia left off waving at the bees in surprise.

Lo laughed. "You are young and flirt with Manwell. Are you so shocked?"

"Lo!" Georgia frowned. She did not flirt with Manwell.

"It is no use. Mendaline and I have both seen it. You will not admit you see him kindly? Him and all his geese." Lo giggled.

"Lo!"

"He is a man, Georgia. The same."

"Not a man yet," Georgia said. "I must perhaps fast to prove myself."

"No more fasting!"

"Tell me of Mendaline."

"She fell in love with an apprentice cart maker. She was sixteen, she said, and he wasn't much older. Yet she was a knight's daughter. They ran into the forest and laid together. She said it was wonderful."

"The forest?"

"No, the lovemaking. How old are you supposed to be? Yes, Mendaline said when you love someone, when you lay together—you feel—unlike any other thing. Like the blue of Mary's robe washing over you, as vivid as when it is painted on glass."

"Mendaline rutted with a cart maker?"

"Oh! It is not rutting between lovers. To imagine all as rutting because you hate men."

"I do not hate men," Georgia said. Though it felt like a lie. Did she hate them? She thought. All of them? Or just the ones who had hurt her? She used her spit to wipe her mouth. "Yet Mendaline was a nun. It is desecration."

"She was not yet a nun. But I have heard stories of nuns, also, laying with men. They say nuns bore bastards and lived evilly."

"It did happen, yes. But not as often as they claim. The reeves want to excuse what they did. But much of that talk is a lie."

"Perhaps, but people now believe it."

Georgia shrugged. Scotland would be better. "What happened to her lover?"

"I do not know. Mendaline only said that love was possible. That I should not judge it by what had happened to me, by how Romsfeld had hurt me. She said some day I might find someone and I—and I—could take pleasure. I think I hope for that still. When you laid beside me in the cave and the relic spun—I hoped—I was afraid." She paused. Georgia could hear her scrape her hand along the wall. "He will never touch me again. I will kill him first."

"There is hope. You are the Chooser. You will have a child—"

"Then it will be a miracle for I have never bled."

"But you are a daughter of Isela."

"I do not wish to be a nun, Georgia. I would choose my own lover, as Mendaline did. A gentle lover. With warm hands."

Georgia pressed against the window. "Lo, we must go to Scotland. Romsfeld will come to the end of his patience. In remaining here, we risk being found out. We are all prepared. We can leave tomorrow. We wait only on you." A bee crawled along her skirt. Georgia grabbed it between her thumb and forefinger, pulled out its stinger, and flicked it away. "More pilgrims come every day to the cave. Many in Bilsdale and Attewater know already of it."

"If I come, do you think—" Lo's voice crumbled, as if the words cracked open. "Do you think—that I will yet have a—baby? It would not need to be the one you think of, Georgia. No," her voice softened, "just any baby." The question was a whisper. "Do you think it is yet possible?"

"Yes."

Silence followed. Georgia could hear Lo crying softly and the rustle of fabric against stone. When she spoke again, her voice shook as if the pit of her belly ached. "I will go then."

Georgia almost cried out with joy. She was ready; all was ready. They only needed Lo, dear, sweet Lo, to gain her courage. Georgia had already planned it out. "There is one way. You must drug him. Mendaline has the pouch. I will get it from her tonight. Tell him you are ready to receive him. Wait until dark. Put the powder in his cup."

"He will kill me if he suspects."

"I will watch for you. You are the Chooser still, Lo. The promise protects you."

"The promise seems ... far away."

"You are Isela's daughter. You are like my own child."

Lo laughed. "We are a strange pair."

"Then you'll be ready?"

"Bring the pouch. If I do not die, then I will run." She cleared her throat.

"From now on, I will choose my own lover. And I will choose one with brown eyes."

"Tomorrow." Georgia closed her palm around the orange seeds. She would plant them in Scotland.

Georgia darted back along the walkway and, scanning the grounds, walked quickly to the stream and crossed it. She went only a few yards before Manwell jumped up from the grass.

"Good morrow!" He spun around her, taking her hand. Often he met her to walk her back to the cave, and sometimes he hung around after that, to watch her. It did not seem to worry him that others deferred to her, as if she was a prioress and not a skinny girl. He only laughed.

She scolded him. "What, no geese to frighten me today?"

"I have been apprenticed to the plow maker." He tightened his grip on her hand, a warm, secure touch. "Now I can marry you."

She stopped and stared at him. Did he really expect that one day it would be possible to marry her? Even despite what he knew of her?

"Manwell—"

"Hush if you are only to refuse me. I will not allow it on such a fine day. Tomorrow you may say what you like."

She thought of a tart answer to give him tomorrow. Yet tomorrow she would leave. He could not come with her.

She clasped his hand, this time holding onto his warmth. She felt a spongy sickness in her belly. For all he was a man, she would miss him.

He squeezed her hand in return. "Fie me! You are too serious today." He broke into a run but did not let go. The sickness chased her as she ran to keep up.

CHAPTER 33:
Ecstasies

Georgia gave the pouch to Lo the next morning.

"All, give it all," Georgia whispered. "He must drink half at least. He will be delirious for two days. It will taste bitter, so mix it well in aged beer, not ale, for it will aid the effect. This is what Mendaline has said. Can you do it?"

"Yes." Lo's voice sounded tight, but then she laughed. "I'll just unbung a barrel as I'm in the buttery. I feel strong today. Only promise you will lock Madam in the latrine again."

"I'll do better, but as soon as it is dark. We must wait for dark."

"And—" The tightness returned to Lo's voice, as if she were trying to speak through a single thread of sound. "Promise you won't leave me."

"I will wait for you."

"Promise."

"I promise. Glory be."

"Glory be."

Georgia did not dare to stay longer outside the wall, not today when so much was so near. She took her leave. There was still packing to be done. Beatrice had it well in hand, but Georgia would need to take the relic from the altar at the last and say a blessing.

They would begin under darkness and take the mountain track north as far as they could go before dropping down to the northern towns. They would travel as light as possible, Diota and Amy, E'beth and Beatrice, and the rest. In addition to the sisters, a number of the pilgrims also wished to go. Four women wished to join as nuns in Scotland. That is how it went, lifetime to lifetime, when things were good.

Mendaline, however, said she would not come. She claimed she was too old for adventure. Though it was only March, this year, 1552, would see her turn eight and sixty. Except for her hands, she was fit. Yet she felt loyal to Bilsdale. She was needed there.

Georgia came to the end of the sheltered walkway, tucked up her skirts, and dashed across the muddy chicken yard toward the stream. As she jumped across it, she saw Manwell, already waiting in the field.

She could see against the late morning sun why he had been apprenticed to the plowman, for his shoulders had broadened and his body had grown thick. He was now eighteen and had finally begun to fulfill the promise of his long bones. He would have the strength now to sustain the heat of the forge and wield a hammer on the long blade of the plow. He would handle the oxen. He looked like a man.

She was confused. He seemed more frightening to look so strong. But as she ran across the stream, the March wind passed a sensation between them from skin to skin over the open field. It was a wind filled with budding apple and cherry trees, a wind that started in the south and blew north to where the mapmakers did not know. To dragons, perhaps. In the cold of it was the truth of her flesh. That at the heart she was simply a girl.

Her step slowed, her toes sinking into the spongy soil. It was the same earth she had walked for many lifetimes. The same dampness, the same wet that insisted itself to drip from the branches and the leaves until it had no place else to go and petered out.

This was the land she loved, the nun's land, a woman's land—the land of Saint Isela, of Gotesind, of prayer and penitence and psalms. Though the priory was ruined, the grass stretched out beneath her, the gardens she had raised from seed, wintered over year by year. It was a gnawing loss that she could not stay.

She would miss it, and the village below. She would miss the work of it, the beating of the bounds, the children protesting as their parents knocked them against rocks and trees so that they would never forget the land that was theirs.

Always the women stayed, mothers, grandmothers, daughters, lovers, wives, while the men took to the towns, to whores, or took up soldiery, or crusade, or pilgrimage, or simply left, their labor sold, their fortunes rising or turned to naught. She shivered as the wind tossed the cold of budding apple across her skin. Perhaps, she thought, perhaps the sin had not been so much in keeping the women with the land, as in removing the men from the touch of it.

Manwell stretched out waiting. She studied the muscular outline of his back, and the homespun fabric of her kyrtle felt suddenly too rough against her skin.

She would miss this place, she decided, as she would miss the girl she could no longer be. And she would miss this boy who would grow to be a man she did not know.

She giggled, and the happiness she felt surged up into a laugh. Tomorrow would come. But today she would remind this boy that he was a son of this land, and that he need not pursue any other. Maybe this is what Mendaline had meant.

She came up behind him quietly. Slipping her hand into his. She brought his warm palm to her heart and pressed it between her breasts. He turned quickly. His eyebrows shot up in surprise.

"Let's away," she whispered.

Manwell stumbled as she led him up in the forest to an outcropping of rock. There was a natural basin just beyond the rock that would shelter them. She crouched down into it and drew Manwell along, finding his mouth with hers, tasting his sweat and effort at the plow. It was a first kiss, and as she watched the tight-bunched curls arrayed across his forehead, she wondered why she had been so reluctant to kiss him before.

"You taste of barley water," he whispered.

She scooted next to him and loosed the tie of her shift. Timidly, he stroked a finger where it opened at her neck and then placed his palm, shaking, on her chest. He left it there for a breath—two. Then, with a quick excitement, he plunged his hand under the loose fabric and over her breasts. He pulled the neckline downward so as to see her naked bosom, and she shivered, anticipating the cold wind on her nakedness. Her nipples itched, anticipating his touch. She remembered this from the dream, but he was far dirtier now than he had been then. He smelled of leather and fire and sweat.

Yet his mouth was warm. He reached under her skirts, and she wondered where all these memories had gone. Had she always been a virgin? She could not remember. She could only think that she was a girl, and here was the boy she—loved. Did she love him?

He did not leave off kissing her as he lifted her skirt, stroking her thighs and then her insides with a thumb and forefinger. She ran her hands over his arms and chest, feeling the strength in his shoulders as the tension mounted in her legs and belly. This was something you could not forget, she thought, yet it was nothing she remembered.

"Manwell."

He pulled himself over her, grinning. She had to laugh at his boyish arrogance, proud of her arousal, crediting himself, no doubt, for her sudden willingness. Yet she decided to allow it. And when he pressed into her, the world at her temples lit fire.

Afterward, she flicked her skirts down over her legs as he rolled across her. She curled into him, and they lay together in the shelter of the rocks.

"What sort of name is Georgia?" he asked.

She studied his face. She would leave tonight.

"It is an old name. But it is mine."

She felt older again, the girl retreating. She began to feel self-conscious to be so close to him, he, who seemed suddenly so young.

Georgia sighed. She did not want to think. She felt tired and satisfied. Yet her face felt hot, now, thinking of the heartbeats shared, of her eagerness and her vulnerability. She took refuge in the familiar, in their easy, teasing banter.

"Aren't you happy? You've been wanting to kiss me."

"More than kiss you."

"And so you did."

Manwell moaned slightly. "And marry you."

Georgia sat up on one arm. "I'm a nun, Manwell." She was feeling older again.

He grinned. "I guess it's true then, what they say about nuns."

Georgia thought of Mendaline with her own lover in the woods long ago and laughed.

"Perhaps I am not yet a nun."

Manwell lay back down and stroked her cheek and neck, pulling at the undone ties of her shift.

"You're leaving."

"No," Georgia lied, though she knew he would not believe it.

"Marry me."

"I can't."

"I love you."

"I am not free. I am a daughter of Isela."

"Daughter, daughter." His face retained his humor, but a fine line showed at the jaw where he clenched it. "Why all these daughters but no sons?"

"You wish to be a nun?"

"I wish to marry you."

"It is impossible. I will never marry. Men are violent, and horrible."

"Was I horrible, then?"

"You are not yet a man." Yet he did seem a man, and beautiful. She pushed the curls that fell forward over his face, and again she kissed him.

"Say the vow with me," he whispered; he stroked her breast.

"You wish betrothal, then?" She cocked her head, but his expression was serious. According to law, marriage vows were binding, whether said at the door of the church after banns or in the forest with only bears and squirrels to witness them.

He raised his hand, stroking his thumb along her lower lip. "You must marry me. Then if you go about your prayers and I stay a plowman, I will be happy."

"You're drunk."

"Not today."

"Very well, then." Georgia laughed at him. The law might think of vows among the rocks as binding, so be it then. Today, if it eased the sting of her leaving him, she would comply.

He pressed his brow together, thinking. "Do you know them?"

She laughed. "No. I can't remem—wait. I think we only need declare." She laughed again. "Manwell," she said, suddenly serious and at the same time overwhelmed with the urge to break out giggling. "I plight my troth with you. You are my husband."

He scratched his thumb across his nose. "I don't think those are the words."

Georgia shrugged.

"Well, then. Georgia, I plight my troth with you as well. And now, if you are now my wife, we will seal it with a kiss."

He leaned in and lingered over it and then drew back and watched her carefully, a guardsman. "If you won't stay, perhaps I'll have to come with you."

"You cannot."

But he would not listen. He moved on top of her, anxious, hungry. He put his hand to her breast and whispered through a kiss. "Will you ... again?"

"Yes." She returned the whisper. He moaned deeply as if his need rose through him and overwhelmed him. Taking her shift, he pulled it high over her head and threw it off. His warm hands searched over her body, for what she did not know, only that his touch was smooth and strong and warm. She opened to his intent, and they moved together. When they finished, they slept.

⁂

She woke, and when she moved, she laughed to herself that it was no good beginning a journey when you were so sore between the legs that movement was difficult. The sun hovered at the horizon. She stretched and woke Manwell.

"Wake up. There'll be hell to pay, I think, for all your shirking."

"You call it shirking, do you?" He rubbed his eyes. "Daylight still?"

Georgia laughed playfully, but already the day was left behind. She felt a sudden keenness for the night, for the progress finally into the next step, the journey. She was beginning to feel old again, older than old, ancient as the rocks.

From across the hill, horns blared. The ringing sliced through the trees and threw the sunset off balance. At first Georgia worried that a hunting party might discover them and rushed to straighten herself. But as the sound grew nearer, it became easier to distinguish. The metallic blast was that of a winded herald, and that would mean an important visitor to the manor.

Manwell jumped off the rocks and out of the cleft onto the new shoots and unfurling fronds that carpeted the woods. The horns blared again.

Manwell took her hand. "I must return. There will be work to do, and I will be whipped if I am idle."

Georgia teetered on the rock before jumping off. A whipping was the least of her worries. An important visitor to the manor could ruin all her plans. She ran through the woods. She would get to the vantage point and see who came along the road. If the light held. For night was falling fast.

She crested the upper hill just behind Manwell. Below was the winding convoy, a small party made up of a gleaming guard, helmed and mounted and moving quickly. The trumpeter ahead.

Manwell kissed her hurriedly on the cheek. "Farewell. I will come later to the cave. Wait for me." He ran like fury down the hill. Georgia chased after him.

"Stop," Georgia cried. "No." She grabbed his hand and pulled him to a stop, almost losing her balance and tumbling over her own feet. Then, realizing she was exposed on the hill above the manor, she flattened against the grass, down on her stomach. Manwell stood over her, out of breath.

"Pray you, what is this?"

"Down!"

Manwell obliged, crouching low beside her. "What?"

Georgia felt sick at the foreboding in her gut. She pressed her palm against her temple, willing some image that would shape her stirring memory. "He knows. He has heard."

Manwell laid lower to the ground. "Who?"

She remembered thick linen paper under her fingers. She remembered the marks on the pages, marks with the power to take all. Something was wrong. Something had come undone. She felt fear. Fear above all things.

"I must away. An old enemy has come."

CHAPTER 34:
Demons

Evening deepened. Below, on the manor grounds, lanterns bobbed a firefly frenzy from the doors and windows as servants rushed between the house and stables to ready for the visitors.

On the lane, shadows stirred the night with uncertainty as the archbishop rode straight through them. Philip SeVerde. With him came ten fighting men on rounceys, their swords clanking over the horses' hocks and echoing up the hill. The party traveled scant; not a single wagon trailed behind them, and each man had but a page each.

What Georgia remembered of this enemy made her head ache and her hands ball to fists. She remembered his arrogance, condescension, and threat. She wondered if she had ever seen his face, and then knew that she had not. Nor did she wish to see it tonight.

The train of men and horses rode hard, thundering along the final leg to the manor in neat ranks. As they entered the courtyard, all was motion. The stable grooms steadied frothing horses, smiths readied to repair saddle bindings and horseshoes, chamberlains slung dirty cloaks over their arms and loosed saddle bags, and boys fetched and carried whatever might be wanted.

The nearest man threw aside his riding cape to dismount. His armor glowed red with the torchlight, a full breastplate, pauldrons, and taces over his hips. His boots came fully up the leg to midthigh, folding just below a pair of crumpled slops with cuttes flattened by hours of hard riding. Like the rest, he wore a hanger at his side, and through that, the glittering knuckle bow of a Spanish sword. Georgia shuddered. The blade spoke murder, and the whisper passed right through her.

"I must get to Lo," Georgia said.

She rose bent legged and ran hunched over, hugging the dark outline of the meadow grass. Manwell grasped for her but missed.

"Wait. You must wait—"

Georgia lowered to a squat and, gathering her strength, felt the fatigue of the fight to come. She pushed Manwell away with a calm that surprised her.

"I am Georgia," she said. "I am the one they speak of. I am the fasting girl, the Bearer, the walker, the nun." Ages echoed within her as she spoke. She felt the giant again, stretching out, loosening the husk of youth around her. Had it been a thousand years? Or more? She drew her cloak tightly, a shield.

Manwell touched her shoulder. "I will defend you. Stay with me. Let me help you." He gripped her, turning her toward him. "I love you."

Love. Her heart beat twice as she faltered. But there was no time for love, only duty. And there was Lo. She pulled her shoulder free. "They will hurt her."

She headed straight down the hill. He followed after her, his tall, lanky form unsuited to a low downhill run over clumping grass. She heard him stumble and curse. He managed to catch her just before they crossed the stream onto the manor grounds.

"Hold." He tried to catch his breath. "I believe you. What you say. But you cannot run. Not from horses and riders. You cannot steal Lo away from men with swords!"

Georgia's heart beat at her temples, the rhythm of hoofbeats. "I promised I would not leave her. I promised."

"But if they find you—"

"I cannot leave Lo. Not this time. I cannot."

She jumped the stream. Mud splashed over her legs and feet as she slapped through puddles that followed, the noise lost to the louder calls of horses and men, the general bustle of leather against tin, and above it all, the eel-toothed whine of Romsfeld's miserable housekeeper as she tended to the hurried guests.

Georgia ran to the garden, along the walkway, to the window and to Lo. Manwell crouched next to her behind the woody rue as she pressed her face into the arrow loop in the stone wall. Two lines of cold indented into her skin as she pushed the oiled cloth back.

She called softly, her ear now turned to the opening. But there was no sound of Lo. She bit her tongue.

Folly. She had spent her day in folly, and it had led to this.

"Is she within?" Manwell asked.

"No, she is gone." She wanted hurl herself into something she could destroy.

"Gone?"

Manwell's odd-angled knees stuck out behind the bushes, and Georgia squeezed down next to him. Perhaps Lo had already drugged Romsfeld and was away. Yet, what if he had drunk the powder, but Lo had not yet made an escape?

The door of the buttery opened, and a lantern struck a line of gold along the length of the window. Voices filtered through as several moths flicked their bodies against the luminent oilcloth. A wine barrel creaked and was rolled away. From the hall, Romsfeld called for a brighter fire, more wine, and fresh boots.

He was not drugged, then.

The door closed, and the noise and light extinguished. The moths battered the oilcloth and then ceased.

Manwell stretched a long leg under the rue bush. "Perhaps she is already to the cave." He spoke with optimism, but such good fortune would be unlikely. Romsfeld would have known the archbishop was coming; a harbinger would have given him an hour of warning at least, though the party had been riding fast.

"I can go to the barn," Manwell shifted to a crouch. "Ask questions."

"I must think." Georgia put her hands to her temples and tried to lessen the chargers that pounded there. It was a puzzle.

Romsfeld's voice boomed again, this time out across the yard. "Fresh horses! I will ride the new palfrey. Prepare the white for His Excellency! And trim the bells. We ride silent as soon as appetites are met."

Ride silent. The clanging ornaments were to be taken off. This party of fighters intended an ambush or a raid.

"The cave," she said. Did they know of it? They must. Why would the archbishop have brought a raiding party otherwise? She threw her head backward against the stones, defying them to strike her down. Yet she could not risk herself. And she could not be in all places at once.

She turned to Manwell. "Pray, go find out what is known and warn Beatrice and the rest. I must find Lo, but I will follow as quickly as I can. If things do not go well for us, then the rest must begin to Scotland without me. And quickly."

Manwell nodded. He unbuckled the knife at his belt, a seven-inch blade used for just about every purpose, from hacking windows through walls to slaughtering geese. Today she had seen him use it to spear the small white slugs that clumped near the stream.

He handed it to her. She refused it.

"Take it." Manwell opened her palm. "I will find out what I can, then go to the cave. But you must return to me." He whispered, brushing his cheek against hers. "You are my wife." He grabbed her in a rough embrace and ducked away.

She held Manwell's knife at the hilt. The air still smelled of him. She had forgotten herself, and that had led them to foolishness. If she was a wife, then she was a fool thrice over, or more, and this time her punishment would be more than the price of her own blood: she would pay with Lo's.

She turned to the manor wall and fell headlong over a figure in the near dark. She croaked in surprise, a too-loud rasp that bounced back at her from the stones. The figure snatched at her and grabbed her firmly at the wrist. An old woman, the dairy wife who packed the tubs of butter in the spring. Her age belied her strength; her grip held fast.

The old woman shook her. "Child, I searched for you. Mistress Lo was put away to hide her. I tried to pry the boards when it grew dark. But Halkan came."

"The swineherd?" Squat and yellow haired, the swineherd fermented a sour barley beer for which he hoarded the hairy galls of tun-hoof that grew in the low hills. He was a slavering drunk.

"She's been with that brute all afternoon?"

"Nah. He's had work to do. Two suckings and a sow ordered up, and wood to chop. The master ordered the door boarded shut to keep her in and him out. But his drink's in there, so he's gone and pried the boards away. The fuss he made! I heard her scream. If he touches her, the master will kill him, certain."

The swineherd's shack stood in the cluster of farm buildings between the north woods and the dairy. An unbaked, six-foot hut with a lean-to shelter on one side where always two or three farrowing pigs were kept. She would have to walk through the manor grounds to get to it.

She did not wait to thank the woman, but hurried, holding to the shadows, her scalp tingling as every noise seemed to bring potential danger.

Romsfeld resumed his shouting, barking for a wagon and a hackney to pull it. The men streamed from the house wiping smears of ale from their beards with the backs of their hands. The courtyard bobbed with horses, lanterns, soldiers, grooms, and servants. Georgia slunk along the wall as the men remounted on fresh horses and a few of the pages with them. They ended up a horse too few, and Romsfeld shouted again.

Romsfeld mounted last, bobbling as he stuck his boot into the horse's shoulder and the mount shied. A groom held the palfrey's nose and clucked to soothe it. Once mounted, Romsfeld trotted to the front and led the line, a group of tired men with fresh horses and full bellies, their eyes war bright and intent on the road.

They cantered down the lane that led to Bilsdale, and the wagon rumbled after, unable to keep pace, its wheels spinning. The party came right past her, with Romsfeld at the center with the archbishop, a mere, sunken-cheeked shadow in a black wool cap. The shadow man looked neither left nor right as the party thundered away.

As soon as the men were gone, the courtyard bustled with servant folk tending fires and gossiping. Jugs of ale were passed from mouth to mouth. They collected around the fires, or returned to the barn, or squatted down to dice.

As quickly as she dared, Georgia slid through the darkest parts of the yard, passing the stable and the manor well before coming onto the wide path to the dairy. Here the light dimmed, coming only from the embers warming the smithery, and she moved openly. A pig squealed. She was close, only a few steps farther to the hut.

Then she saw Lo.

Lo crouched next to the smith's barrel and vomited. Then, swaying to stand, she leaned over the barrel and splashed her face with water.

Georgia ran to her, encircling her arms around Lo's waist. She stank of rose oil, bitter chalk, and vomit, and Georgia pulled back, recognizing the bitter chalk smell as from the powder Mendaline and given her.

"Lo, tell me of the pouch. Where is it?"

Lo shook unsteadily. She wore a clean dress of the sort Romsfeld always provided—the low bodice exposing her bosom, her shift heavily embroidered, and cuttes at the sleeve. Her headdress folded at the crown of her head in the French style and left her neck and nape bare. She looked not unlike the gentlemen's whores who came with burgesses through Bilsdale, except that she was beautiful.

"The pouch," Georgia said again. "The drug. Where is it?"

Lo gave the herbs over, and Georgia tossed it up to gauge its weight. "You didn't give it to him."

Lo swayed again, gave a hiccup, and wet her lips. "I had—a bath. But he brought the oil himself. He wanted—none to drink—only that I should love him." She made a face of disgust. "After was too late, for—the news of the lord arriving." Saliva accumulated in the corners of her mouth.

Georgia shook her. "Did you take any?"

Lo shook her head but, in the shaking, almost fell. It seemed she might throw up again. Georgia pushed her into the shadow.

"I won't be struck again." Lo covered her bosom with her hand and swiped at Georgia.

Georgia smelled her breath, a sour sickness. "On your life you didn't drink it?"

"Only beer."

Beer. "The swineherd's beer?"

Lo nodded.

"Lo!" Those who tried the swineherd's brew usually did so on a dare, and never again. It caused colors to run together, or so Manwell said. Manwell had seen white griffins and a unicorn.

Lo opened her mouth to speak but gagged. A dry retch, and it was good to see that Lo had already purged what she had drunk, for there was no time to wait for vomiting in the shadows.

"Where is the swineherd now?" The door to the hut was open, and the firelight glowed from inside.

Lo choked a sob; she brought her hands to her throat. "I'll not be struck again."

"Lo," Georgia held her steady, "where is the swineherd?"

"I am not what you think I am. I should die if I should wish to."

Georgia wedged her shoulder under Lo's armpit and wrapped her cloak over her. The cloak was rough, but warm, and without it the wind blew cold.

"Tell me of the swineherd. Will he follow us?"

"He fell against the hearth stone."

"Fell? Is he harmed?"

"He took the jug."

"Is he drunk?"

"I am barren. I will never have a child."

Georgia looked warily over to the hut. The door was open, and a small flame flickered inside. But there was no sound.

"What did you do?"

"I am Lo."

Georgia looked back and forth from the hut to the path. Whatever had happened, it was better they should get away. She prodded Lo hard in the ribs. Lo groaned, but she moved, and together they stumbled through the cold, moving around the outer buildings and into the dark.

They reached the coursing stream and slogged headlong through the water. The cold revived Lo, and her sporadic retching stopped. Her eyes cleared. She no longer leaned so heavily on Georgia's shoulder, though she limped still. By the time they entered the ravine near the cave, she was walking better, though painfully, throwing out her hand occasionally to prevent a fall.

Georgia hurried her along. The thought of the women at the cave, Beatrice and Amy and the rest, packed and waiting for them, spurred her on. She must not be the cause of delay. They must go quickly into the mountains. From there, all would be well.

As they came upon the cave path, Georgia plunged ahead. It was Lo who staid her. Lo pushed an arm in front of her, and Georgia stopped short. From underneath them, the ground rumbled with the stomp of hooves. Ahead a horse whinnied and men's shouts echoed over the night. A woman screamed. Another scream followed, a cry that ended abruptly.

Georgia stayed immobile. Already they were too close. Through the brush she could see horses, their tails swishing in circles, the swords formerly packed at their haunches now in the hands of men. The rosemary and vinca that had covered the mouth of the cave had been hacked away.

Horsemen. Soldiers. The archbishop sat tall on the white warhorse, with his hands clasped together over the reins. Another chunk of the vinca fell.

She had not tarried, but in the end it mattered not at all. They were too late.

CHAPTER 35:
Libra Nos a Malo;
Deliver Us from Evil.

They were too late. They were too late and too close. They would be seen. Georgia pushed sidewise into the bracken, dragging Lo with her. Her legs shook, and her feet blistered with cold. She swiped a branch from across her face, knocking it sideways. They crept down into the hawthorn and juniper, the branches so thick in the middle of it that sight was impossible.

The long ago memory of the raid on the priory bubbled up like a tightness across her chest. The rider and the sword screamed from deep inside, leaving her to shudder as thrashing hooves ripped at her insides. She choked and forced the memory away, away with the others like it that bubbled and popped, tramping down the veil that covered them. If the veil tore open, she feared she would be torn to madness from the onslaught.

For again Romsfeld had ridden in. Again the prisoners would be taken and tried, and this time, there were no nunneries to be banished to. This time they would burn, for King Edward's heretics died by fire. She could not leave them to such a fate.

Georgia curled her fingers around a stone and pushed away the branch that separated her from the fray.

"No." Lo grabbed her by the arm. She controlled a hiccup. "You will be killed."

not be the cause of delay. They must go quickly into the mountains. From there, all would be well.

As they came upon the cave path, Georgia plunged ahead. It was Lo who staid her. Lo pushed an arm in front of her, and Georgia stopped short. From underneath them, the ground rumbled with the stomp of hooves. Ahead a horse whinnied and men's shouts echoed over the night. A woman screamed. Another scream followed, a cry that ended abruptly.

Georgia stayed immobile. Already they were too close. Through the brush she could see horses, their tails swishing in circles, the swords formerly packed at their haunches now in the hands of men. The rosemary and vinca that had covered the mouth of the cave had been hacked away.

Horsemen. Soldiers. The archbishop sat tall on the white warhorse, with his hands clasped together over the reins. Another chunk of the vinca fell.

She had not tarried, but in the end it mattered not at all. They were too late.

CHAPTER 35:
Libra Nos a Malo;
Deliver Us from Evil.

They were too late. They were too late and too close. They would be seen. Georgia pushed sidewise into the bracken, dragging Lo with her. Her legs shook, and her feet blistered with cold. She swiped a branch from across her face, knocking it sideways. They crept down into the hawthorn and juniper, the branches so thick in the middle of it that sight was impossible.

The long ago memory of the raid on the priory bubbled up like a tightness across her chest. The rider and the sword screamed from deep inside, leaving her to shudder as thrashing hooves ripped at her insides. She choked and forced the memory away, away with the others like it that bubbled and popped, tramping down the veil that covered them. If the veil tore open, she feared she would be torn to madness from the onslaught.

For again Romsfeld had ridden in. Again the prisoners would be taken and tried, and this time, there were no nunneries to be banished to. This time they would burn, for King Edward's heretics died by fire. She could not leave them to such a fate.

Georgia curled her fingers around a stone and pushed away the branch that separated her from the fray.

"No." Lo grabbed her by the arm. She controlled a hiccup. "You will be killed."

The branch swung back and stung her, swiping across Georgia's brow and the bridge of her nose.

"Hush." Georgia pushed Lo further into the brush. "I must. You know I must. Wait for me." Georgia pushed her into a hollow under a cluster of hawthorn.

Lo grabbed her. "No! They will make me go back to him. I cannot go back."

"You will be safe, here. I will not let them take me." But Lo looked terrified. "If I do not come back this way, go to Gotesind's cave at the top of Nunshill," Georgia said. "Do you remember it?"

Lo nodded, and Georgia wondered at how she herself had known it was there. Yet she knew it, what it looked like, and that it bloomed virgin blue with chicory in summer. Some memories, at least, were useful. She focused on the soldiers ahead and pushed through the gorse and broom, keeping close to the ground.

Georgia crawled, her wet skirt catching on the twigs her knees snapped under them. Every snap lifted the hair on her neck, each seeming to echo the metallic crack of swordplay.

When she could see the cave, she paused to take stock. The leafy vine covering the cave mouth lay cut and strewn and trampled, with the entry gaping open like a dead man's jaw. The horses pawed up the soil and dug holes of turf, and all were riderless, save one.

The archbishop sat astride the muscled warhorse like a shade on a monster beast. He was lean with graying hair, his cape thrown back to reveal a heavy gold crucifix over a black doublet girded in a purple sash. Though richly dressed, his expression was that of a hungry beggar.

Of beggars there were two kinds. Some had known joy, so that when the baskets came with charity, it fed them and they were sated. The others were those who starved for more than bread. Those whose hunger crawled under their skin. Years of warm fires and safe beds would see them slink away, unsatisfied. This man was such a one as this. Though he was rich, his cheeks had the hollow of a starveling. His hunger claimed him. It was how he knew who he was.

A soldier ducked out of the cave holding in front of him a sword that shined as if coated in a dark oil. Georgia peered into the cave, but the torchlight did not shine brightly enough to see anything inside but dark robes piled onto the floor.

At the entrance things were more visible, through the cave mouth where it had been shorn open. From under the shorn vinca, a limb, clad in green brown homespun, poked from the pile. Torches lit the outline of a woman's body there. No living person could have lain in such a way.

Georgia clasped her arms together. Whoever it was lay unanointed and unshriven. She balled her rosary into her fist and whispered for Mary. "I implore you, font of mercy, holy lady, Mother of God …"

The whisper was almost silent, but the sob that followed quivered the leaves. The archbishop on the white horse turned in the saddle, searching with a needle gaze. He spun a finger in the air, an order to search.

Two men took up the order and hacked at the underbrush. The one who came near her hacked at the ferns and then away. He moved next to a clump of broom, but then swept wide with the sword, stepping through the juniper directly where she knelt. She scrambled to avoid him, but her skirt was under her knees. She rolled, found her feet, and fled.

The branches cracked as he came after her, swiping at her, tearing the scarf from her head. She turned to face him, bareheaded with her hair unrolled, ready to gouge out his eyes and blind him. He stopped with his sword poised to strike. He was not one of Romsfeld's men; she would have known him otherwise, and perhaps fooled him, or bargained. This man wore the insignia of the archbishop. He was from York, and judging by the scars on his face, he had survived foes worse than she.

He flicked his eyes over her headdress, kyrtle, and shoes. She was in dirty russet, her shoes only leather slippers and tied in bands of cloth to make them last. She was a peasant and nothing more; there would be no redress to him for hurting her. He threw his sword and helmet to the ground.

She hesitated. She could not remember where she had left Lo. She must not lead him to her if she fled. She spun instead, to be a moving target, and struck out with her fist.

He dodged her strike easily, taking hold of her skirt at the hip. One hand on each side, he flipped her, hurling her to the ground and flat on her stomach.

Georgia had seen throws such as this at the market between the fishmongers or in the meadows at sheering time, an ewe grabbed by the fleece and cast down onto the grass for the shearers to do their work. This man intended rape, and she was not his first victim. He kicked her legs apart and landed between them.

He straddled her skirt and knelt on it, pinning her, throwing the extra fabric up over her waist. Cold air hit the back of her thighs and her behind. He put his hands on her and forced her down while he shifted; his knees pushed between her own as he twisted her skirt in his hand to secure her down.

She could not gain the leverage she needed to throw him off. He placed a knee on the back of her thighs as he pulled at his jerkin.

She tried to scoot forward, caring only to get away from the bruising crush of his knees. The muscles of her thighs stretched and cramped as he ground down onto her. She thrashed as if a seizure shook her, desperation driving her, and pain. She searched for leverage, any leverage that would enable her to escape. She felt a smooth, hard metal, cold on her palm. A knife. Manwell's knife.

The rapist shifted again. The pressure on her thigh lessened, and she jerked her leg out, sliding her knee so she could pivot to the side. He teetered slightly, and her skirt came free on that side.

Her knee ground into the hard stones, but she did not care. She found the leverage she needed. A rising anger filled her. This was her battle, and she would win it. She knew this fight. She rose, twisted, and rammed the blade into his lower belly where his taces were now raised open and the slops pulled back.

The knife met bone and slid. He jerked from the blow and groaned, a constricted sound of betrayal and surprise. Georgia kept hold of the hilt and kicked ferociously. The knife slid higher into his gut. Her skirt tore from the bodice as he pulled back, but he still pinned her, one knee buried in the muscle of her thigh.

Yet she was no longer naked. That gave her courage. She raised the knife to strike again, wanting now to slide the blade between his ribs. He wore a breastplate, but with his armor raised below the waist, she could strike him lower. She swung the blade again, sliding the knife up into his gut, pointing the tip up under his ribs.

He collapsed backward. She pulled the last of her skirt out from under him and found it heavy, sticky, covered in blood, decaying leaves, and dirt.

The soldier looked up at her. The scars on his face elongated, and his eyes were hard with shock. As the leaves crushed beneath her, Georgia was terrified he would scream. She grabbed a handful of litter from the woods floor and stuffed it into his mouth.

Georgia leapt on top of him and ground the breastplate downward. Blood oozed from his nose, and he worked his jaw as if to spit the leaves out. She could not risk that he would yell. In one motion, she raised the knife and cut his throat.

His body seized, and she clambered off. He raised his hand to swipe at her, but his eyes glazed over, and he was dead. Georgia stared into his empty face, searching for curses. She found only sorrow there.

There was a rustle in the bushes. Georgia bolted as if another foe had come to slay her even in her victory. She whirled with the knife, ready to use it again, and again, and again if need be. But behind her was Lo.

Lo crawled to the dead soldier and touched his blood with a finger. "Did you—?"

"Turn away." Georgia scuttled backward to push Lo from the body. She placed herself between them, her hands sticky in the dirt, and the bulk of the dead man pressed against her back.

Lo blinked, rubbed her hand in the dead leaves, and looked away.

Georgia scooped last season's leaves over him and threw the helmet into the brush. He had deserved death. He had killed himself. She looked over her shoulder, but Lo did not retreat. Georgia pushed her with her feet.

"You must hide yourself."

"You think he will not find me?"

Georgia put the knife in her belt. "There, I have put it away." She turned to the dead soldier and made the sign of the cross over his body. "May you learn of pity. So be it," she said. She pushed Lo back into the hawthorn.

❧

Though she was shaken, Georgia was resolute. If she must, she would kill again.

She crawled through the thick broom and hid behind a pair of young linden trees. The muscles in her legs filled with blood-bruises as she crouched to watch the archbishop. He sat in the saddle as a gargoyle draining a stink into the street. She imagined clawing him from his horse.

Romsfeld appeared from the cave, grim and grinning, brushing his hands together as if well satisfied.

The archbishop did not seem to share his enthusiasm. "Where is the one they call Georgia?" he asked.

"Your Grace, if there is a one who claims the name, it is falsely done. I swear to it. I killed her myself. You saw her dead, my lord. The whole of Bilsdale can attest to it."

Two men at his side nodded in agreement.

"And what of the fasting girl? Is she, at least, to be found?"

Romsfeld shouted into the cave, and two men shuffled out carrying between them what looked like a bolt of wet cloth. They threw it down, and Romsfeld kicked it over with his foot. Georgia smacked her hand over her mouth to prevent a scream. It was no cloth, but a body. A girl who had come to the cave half-starved and they had fed her. She had planned to come to with them to Scotland.

"You are sure that is the one?"

Romsfeld stroked his beard. "No. In truth I do not know." He laughed, as if it were a brilliant joke. "But she is not from here, Your Grace, as the fasting girl is not, and she was killed at the well, and tried to fight."

"You there, man." The archbishop called to one of Romsfeld's men. "Tell me, do you know of this fasting girl?"

The soldier looked uncomfortably between masters. "Yes, milord, I have heard of her."

"And this?"

The soldier looked at Romsfeld uncertainly. "The girl is said to be a virgin, and beautiful."

The archbishop threw back his head. "I asked only if this be her."

Another of Romsfeld's men pushed forward, his face eager. "It is she. I know her for I have seen her in Bilsdale. I killed her with my own sword."

"Ah," the archbishop smiled, "my purse." He threw a pouch of coins to the man who caught it, grinning, bowing several times.

"God save you, my lord. God save you."

The archbishop gazed over the other men. "And there is another bounty for the man who knows which one is the one called Georgia."

"I have heard she is an old woman," a man said. "And by a miracle young again."

"It is said she wears robes of gold," one of Romsfeld's men ventured.

"I have heard she cannot die."

The archbishop glared at them. "And have you found such a one?"

Romsfeld postured. "Whoever she is, she is a pretender and must be dead, Your Grace. The job is done. There were none who escaped."

Georgia kept her hand over her mouth. His words echoed in her mind—*none who escaped.*

"Good." The archbishop threw another purse at a nearby soldier. "That is to share among you, for your service to me." He turned to Romsfeld. "But there is yet one more claim, steward. We spoke of this before, and my mind is the same. You must surrender the girl to me."

Romsfeld caught his balance against the cave wall. He spoke in harsh, low tones, watching over his shoulder at the other men. "Your Grace, she is nothing. She has had no part in this. She has been shut up in the house for … disobedience."

"You will surrender her to me, steward, to your peril."

"Pray you, Your Grace, I can speak for her."

"You are blind and a fool. She is a magnet for heresy. You should not have waited for so long to deal with … this." The archbishop poked an accusing finger at the cave and the bodies on the ground.

"Your Grace, I swear it. I have kept her as you said." Romsfeld shoved a hand down the top of his breastplate and drew out a silver chain. "Wait. I can ransom her, with this." He brought the relic of Isela into the torchlight. The orb floated amber against the cave mouth, shifting the green of the remaining eaves to blue and then to the color of new wheat.

"This is the relic of Saint Isela, Your Grace. It is said to be the source of miracles and make the old young again." The relic twisted on the chain and caught the light of the torches, sending bronze-yellow rays across the world. Romsfeld held it above his head as he would hold a brace of rabbits, as no more than a glistening trophy. He defiled it.

"I'll have that and the girl both," the archbishop said.

Romsfeld bared his teeth. "This glass is the center of everything. When we destroyed the priory we could not find it, though we searched."

"Destroy it, then. Smash it on the rock."

Romsfeld balked. Then, with a curt bow, he wound the chain around his palm to smash it against the rock wall of the cave. As the relic gained momentum, the light of the torches spun out in flurries, sparking as if a falling star would explode and destroy the night.

Georgia felt the light of the relic as if it came from inside her very soul. As Romsfeld raised it to smash upon the stone, it felt as if all her bones were near to breaking. A screeching tore out from under her skin. She could not bear it. It must not shatter on the rocks. She threw her head back to scream.

The archbishop raised a hand. "Wait."

Romsfeld let up, nicking the wall only slightly with the scrollwork as he drew back. The blow hit Georgia in the pit of her stomach, but she quieted. A near miss. Her shoulders ached.

Philip nudged his horse and extended his hand to take the orb. He watched the light swirl. "Perhaps there is value in this after all." Wrapping a white cloth around it, the archbishop stuffed the relic into a saddle pouch.

A trophy. Georgia shivered. Every muscle in her body hurt. It was as if the world rotted with the stink of men.

A page rebuckled the pouch, and the archbishop gazed sternly at Romsfeld. "When she was given to your charge, it was with the promise of reform. Her lusts sway you, but I am not swayed. You will bring her to me or you will surrender yourself in her place." He backed his horse. "Instruct your men to finish this business."

The archbishop turned the horse and headed back down the path; his escort followed him, cantering along the ravine. Georgia stayed frozen in the brush, her gaze following the man who had the relic. Light extinguished from between her ribs, between her teeth, under her nails, it was as if a river dried up. The ground grew hard and cold under her.

As the archbishop and his men rode off, the hackney and wagon rattled past them on the way up, only now catching up to the rest of the party. Romsfeld called the driver to bring the cart to the cave mouth.

"Bring them out."

The men retreated into the cave, and two of them returned carrying between them a sagging cloak. They threw it into the cart, and it rolled over. Another corpse. E'beth.

A death cart. The raid had never been to capture or bring a trial. It had been murder from the start. Georgia curled forward; the husk of youth clamped down over her skin, binding her, encasing her. The child inside her cried open mouthed.

More bodies piled into the cart. Georgia spilled prayers, over and over, rocking with grief, a witness to each life, to each death.

"So be it. So be it. So be it."

CHAPTER 36:
Officium Pro Defunctis: Office of the Dead

She stayed long enough to see the men drag the bodies out before leaving. Amy, Diota, Beatrice—everyone had waited for her. Georgia crammed her fists into her eyes until dark and light exploded simultaneously, pain overwhelming thought. Her mouth open, she breathed heavily, the cold against her teeth as the wind hollowed and dried her throat.

The cold won. She pulled her hands down from her face. She lifted her overskirt around her head and shoulders for warmth, for she had given Lo her cloak. Lo had collapsed into sleep as soon as they had reached shelter and had not moved since then.

They were now at Gotesind's Cave, a cave no more than a hollow carved in a crest of rock. It had been the only place Georgia could think of to go, for they needed shelter and safety, though this place might bring neither. For one thing, it was too shallow to offer true respite, for the crisp March wind whicked the painted-yolk daffodils to an icy froth.

Before they built the priory, the anchoress and martyr Gotesind had lived in this hollow. The markings on the wall were the marks of a stone she slid back and forth over the rocks in rhythm to her chanted prayers. After the founding of Isela's priory, the cave was used for meditation, though few remembered the anchorite or the hollow now.

Georgia looked down over the hills and across the valley. It was a sweeping view, although the manor itself could not be seen, obstructed by rounded hills and remaining woods. But she knew where it was, and she imagined the gloating there, the ghastly, croaking victory as the men overflowed tankards near the fire, congratulating each other as they passed the coins from the archbishop's purse into bloodied hands.

She imagined the archbishop taking the relic from the cloth wrapping and spitting to shine the glass. At the thought, she brought her fists to her eyes again, her mouth open to breathe over the nausea. He would defile it. He would kill and walk away rewarded. She could not abide it.

Georgia stood up and paced the threshold. It was daylight now, but come the evening she would go. She would sneak back to the manor, to the archbishop himself, and take the relic. And if she had a chance to kill him, she would do it. No, not simply kill him, but slit him neck down, across his gut as a common quisling rat, pour smoking oil into his eyes, and curse him, a true curse if she could learn one.

Lo fidgeted.

Georgia stopped pacing. "How now?" She crouched next to her, drawing Lo's skirts up over the knee so she could see the wound on her leg. She had wounded it in the scuffle with the swineherd, though Georgia had not seen the blood until the early light. She bandaged the wound with what was quick to find, alehoof, mugwort, and a ribbon of linen. It looked swollen.

"Does it hurt?"

Lo sucked her lips together. "My head aches more."

Georgia poked carefully at the wound. No redness, although a clearish liquid gathered at the edges.

"You need water. The spring is not far, and runs well." Georgia wondered what she could find in the woods to carry water.

Lo pulled the cloak tight around her shoulders. "I won't bear a child if it be a son," she said, "for boys must be given over to be raised as men."

"You will have a daughter," Georgia thought of the male faces at the cave, greedy enough to murder for a share of the archbishop's purse. "Isela will come."

"Soon I hope. For it has been too long waiting." The words echoed from the hollow and down the path. Lo ducked, and Georgia sprung to her feet, ready to fight, though to hide might be better.

The noise grew closer, shuffling or dragging. A bent figure swung up the last steps of the knoll and looked up. It was Mendaline. Mendaline perspired heavily, and her skin looked pale and wet. She pushed her shoulders back and rested a hand on a hip. "You look affrighted. Am I so ugly now that I frighten children?"

Georgia gave a yelp of gladness and ran to hug her hard around the waist. Mendaline returned the hug, reaching with an open hand to Lo.

"We thought you were dead." Lo crouched at her feet, hugging her around the knees.

"I knew *you* weren't," Mendaline pinched Lo's cheek, "they're chasing like hellhounds through Bilsdale looking for you." She sat heavily on a stone and looked around. "Where are the rest?"

Lo buried her face in Mendaline's cloak. "There's only us."

A muscle twitched in Mendaline's cheek. "No other? Amy? Beatrice? E'beth?" Georgia shook her head.

"What of … Manwell?" Georgia asked.

"They said he went down fighting in the wood. I do not know if he lives." Mendaline's voice broke. She looked haggard. Her eyes hollow.

Georgia knelt. She reached with her heart for the relic, to find its comfort, to open a pool of prayer, but the ground was cold and did not open.

"Then none survived," Georgia said. The words were hard, like a hasp run over splintered wood. "I watched them pull the bodies out. They took the relic. They destroyed everything. And Mendaline—I thought that you, too—"

Mendaline pushed her hands deep into her lap. When she spoke, her voice sounded distant. "… *the saints and angels will cry not louder for a scattered clan than we who keen for Saint Isela when the Chooser comes.*"

"The promise," Georgia whispered. "You remember it."

Mendaline nodded. "Some."

Lo lifted herself from the crook of her arm. "Isela will never come." She pointed her finger, trembling, accusingly, at Georgia. "Only soldiers come. We are all dead because of you."

Mendaline grasped Lo's hand and held it to her breast. "Georgia's just a girl," she said. Yet she cocked her head as if to ask the question.

Georgia opened her mouth but shut it. What could she say? Always there were soldiers.

Georgia looked down the hill and away. The wind drove her tears back under her eyelids. Of everyone, she wanted Lo to understand. "We are kindred," she said. "You are Isela's daughter, and so have you been as my own daughter."

Lo spoke slowly, each word emphasized. "My mother died." She picked up an acorn and threw it. The seed hit Georgia on the shoulder.

"There are women alive in this world yet." Mendaline sounded terse. She wiped at her face with the back of her sleeve. "We must remember them."

"I always remember them," Georgia said. "It is all I know." *A scattered clan.* Yet everything was supposed to be different. "When the Chooser comes—" she broke off.

"Chooser." Lo echoed, her voice hysterical, like a little girl on the edge of rage. "That is a lie."

Georgia raised her skirts high, so that her leg showed well above the knee. She took the knife from her belt and brought it down, hard, so that it punctured through into the muscle of her thigh. She winced at the pain, pulled the knife out, and wiped it on her skirt.

"There. Now we have the same wound." She cupped her hand to pool the welling blood and poured the blood into the dirt. She mixed it to a paste, adding a stream of spit. She smeared the paste over the indentations Gotesind had made into the rock. The blood brightened the carving into glossy rings and crosses, and it looked as if the cave had been swamped by the tide from a shallow red lake. "I am not released. I will fight."

Mendaline nodded. "Then it is decided." Her gaze fixed on the blood that oozed across Georgia's hand. "Let me see that knife."

Georgia passed her the hilt. "It is Manwell's."

Mendaline tucked it into her satchel. "I'll just keep it here out of harm's way, shall I?"

"It's mine."

"And so it is, still. You can have it again, anon. Unless you make such a fuss that I have to toss it out into the forest?" Mendaline cinched the satchel closed and sat on it. "Now. There's water and supplies down the hill. You'll need to fetch the bundle." Mendaline turned to Lo. "And what of you? Has your wound been tended?"

"I did what I could," Georgia said. "Though she is also sick from drinking the wretched beer."

Mendaline examined Lo's face, pulling the skin down on her cheeks, looking into her eyes where the lids peeled back. "You drank the powder I sent? Bah! Folk ask me, 'poison, Mendaline. Poison!' But I won't fix it, and this is why. I haven't seen a good clean poisoning in twenty years."

Lo pulled away. "I took none of the poison."

"She drank the swineherd's beer."

Mendaline made a face. "You'd have been better to drink the powder, then. Well, you look hearty. A good hot piss will help as much as anything. Haul the water up, Georgia, and we can see to it. Now what about your leg?" Mendaline dragged herself up from the stone and knelt heavily next to Lo, her knees creaking. She rubbed her finger into the clear liquid from the wound, smelled, and then tasted it.

"What did you treat it with?"

"Alehoof," Georgia said, "though I didn't have water to seethe it in. I then bruised mugwort to fill the wound."

Mendaline cocked an eyebrow. "Mugwort?"

"Yes, I found some on the overslope. There's more. I could gather some."

Mendaline's brows furrowed. "Don't be daft, girl. Mugwort's no good for this. What a memory you have for milk, to remember bits of cheese and forget the whey altogether. Mugwort's for to help a woman conceive, to heal the womb, though there's a charm to it to make it right. You think I didn't already work that charm again and again? But mugwort won't help this wound any more than it helped the other. It'll only make the skin weep. Find some hound's tongue, if you can manage it. Dig it up whole and bring it to me."

Georgia drew back. Had she really used an herb for woman's healing? She had.

"Go on, child." Mendaline pulled the blackened fibers of mugwort from the wound with a crooked, hooked finger. "I'll need your help to bind the wound. These mashed flaps of mine are no good."

"I am not a child," Georgia said, furious at herself for this mistake, for all her mistakes.

"No, I suppose not," Mendaline said. "Though I always liked a girl of twelve or twenty. Spirit and health and fight in her, before she knows the world she was born in. But you, all wet behind the ears and none of the innocence. As if you were born without hope."

"Of course there is hope," Georgia said. "It is just hard to win it. But for now we must avenge ourselves. The archbishop has the relic. I must get it back. Tonight."

"You plan to go all the way to York tonight?"

Georgia blinked. "To York? No, to the manor."

"The mighty archbishop rode for York this morning. He has demanded Romsfeld find Lo, and when she is found, bring her to York as well."

He was gone, and with him the relic. No wonder the ground had felt so cold to her. She put the flat of her palm against the cave wall and held it there.

"I am sorry to tell you. I saw him ride. I stayed the night with Goodwife Brade's daughter. She's had pains over the belly though the child is not ready. They hid me, then gave me bread and ale." She sighed. "I cannot go back. My home is gone."

Georgia let her hand fall. Her stomach rumbled. "You have bread?"

"You? Hungry? Such a thing! Yes, child, I have bread."

"Do not call me a child." Georgia struck the ground with her fist; her leg ached. "I am fifteen. I am taller than you are. And I will go to York. I am the Bearer."

Mendaline shifted from her knees, scooting her satchel around where she could reach the pouches inside it.

"Don't be a fool. Pray, gather some hound's tongue. There is a great patch down the rockside way. Beatrice makes sure it is well sown." Mendaline made the sign of the cross over her heart. "And God bless her, too, for her work was well-done."

"God bless her," Lo echoed.

Georgia gazed southeast over the hillcrest. "York is over the hills. We will need to travel across to hide us and meet the road lower, past the market track. It will take a handful of days to reach the next village. That loaf the goodwife sent will not last."

Lo gave a small noise. "What will we eat?"

Mendaline took a thin digging stick from her belt. "We will all make sticks to loose the soil. We will eat the mast."

"What, from the forest floor? Like the pigs?"

"Such a complaint! Pigs are fat enough."

Georgia's shoulder still smarted from the acorn Lo had thrown at her. "You wish to go back, if you hate me so? Go back to him, then, as you did before."

"No." Lo glared at her. She grabbed the stick from Mendaline. "I will eat according to what I like." She rolled away from them, pulling the hood of her black robe over her head.

"And I will fetch the bundle," Georgia said. "We must prepare. It will not be safe to stay here."

"And I will sleep." Mendaline stood slowly, wiping her face again with her sleeve. "For I cannot walk with my heart so heavy as this. There are only so many times you can crush something and it will live. I think this time is too much." She chose a spot behind a stone, covered her face with her hands and wept. After a while, she softly recited prayers in Latin. Many of the older people did, though it was forbidden. *Ave Maria, gratia plena* ... A sound of soothing, crooning.

Georgia set her jaw. If she bowed to sorrow, it would destroy her. She felt spite, a giant pike, within her, but threw it aside. She would not carry that weight again. As for revenge, that was like a sword, and she would have it. She would find the relic, and when she did, she would see the archbishop suffer for what he had done.

They must leave tonight.

CHAPTER 37:
Saint Etheldreda

They must escape to York without being discovered. There was no time to waste as there was no telling what the archbishop would do with the relic. All over England reformers carved idolatry from parish churches with chisels and knives. Shrines were robbed and spoiled; artworks and relics were smashed and burned, or stolen and hoarded away. Depictions of the saints were hacked away and torn from altars. Isela's orb could suffer the same fate.

Georgia fetched Mendaline's bundle and found that in addition to medicine, bread, and ale, there was also a heavy robe. The robe was woven in a full circle and hung heavy and long. Georgia steadied the black fabric between her teeth and cut a triangular shape at the hem. There would be enough material in the one robe to make shawls and hoods for Lo and Mendaline both. And they would need hoods at the very least, both to cover and warm them.

Georgia planned to take the rim way, behind the hills and down into the forests of Ryedale to the east. From there, they could pick up the carters' track at Arden, join a market-bound company, and ride among the carters' inventories. Georgia just needed to finish with the seams before the light faded.

Lo lay curled, but she was not restful. Her nostrils flared at every noise, and a cough deepened in her chest. At every breath she seemed to expect armed men to ride in and capture or kill them. She watched the forest and the path like a nervous hare, twitching at each noise.

Georgia did not need Lo to remind her of her failures, or that their position was precarious, no, desperate. And it had been all of her doing. Her lapse. Worst, she had let the relic be taken away. She should have gone after it at the first.

The black thread broke clean when she bit it through. It was a quick, loose stitch, with the needle run through the open ends of the robe, but it was done. The fabric would not hang well, but no matter. All the better if the edges frayed and grimed and dissuaded highwaymen.

Mendaline slept. Georgia laid a newly sewn half of the robe over her as a blanket, its side seams pursed and pocketed. She laid the second half over Lo.

Taking up her own russet wrap, Georgia shaped a hood for herself from the remaining cloth. She would look like a beggar, in patches, but that, at least, would deter robbers on the road. With the last of the daylight, Georgia headed out to forage for supplies. She dug up the roots of dandelion, thistle, and caraway—a favorite of Mendaline's. And as Lo had taken a cough into her chest, Georgia sought coltsfoot to give her strength. Georgia also gathered elfwort against stitch.

She returned at the swell of moonlight to find Mendaline retying Lo's bandage. The wound was healing well, though for her part, Lo looked sulky and nervous. She would not get up when Mendaline bid her. Georgia thought of coaxing, but Mendaline clamped one hand firmly on her hip and with the other knocked her staff into the earth by Lo's feet.

"Up or I'll haul you up."

Lo raised herself. Mendaline drew on her new shawl and tucked the hood around her headscarf. "Steady your feet," she ordered and pressed a twisted hand to Lo's cheek. "Shake off this melancholy or the bile of it will blotch your skin."

Lo looked at the ground as Mendaline took the second robe and arranged it over Lo's hips and shoulders. She then handed Lo a sturdy walking stick to use on the journey.

Mendaline looked toward Georgia's leg. "And what of your wound?"

"I retied the bandage already. It is well." Georgia wrapped herself in her own shawl and drew down the hood. It was warm at least. "We will wash a few of the roots at the stream when we cross it, and sup after. It will be a good break before the steep way beyond."

Yet nothing seemed to make a good anything on the path. The moon was fickle, diving in and out of thick cloud and obscuring the dark with shortened, then lengthened, shadows. The wind dragged a wet, sour smoke up from the valley, and owls swooped and hooted with high, shrill cries. Each cry unnerved Lo more than the last, and by the time they passed through the thickest parts of the wood, Georgia worried that Lo would lie down on the path and refuse to budge.

They rested at prime, sleeping past matins, and then kept walking until late evening the next day when they had made it down the other side of the high hills and were in the softer, rolling hills above Arden. There they found shelter behind a quartet of protruding stones and slept.

They set off again before dawn, passing south of Arden through the lightly wooded sheep pastures, always careful of the freshly turned fields so as not to invoke the ire of the villein who had set in a crop of lettuce and artichoke. They continued south when the alder woods thickened, veering toward the market road to York.

By midmorning they met the cart path, and from there they hugged the tree line parallel to the road, stumbling over roots and beneath the canopy rather than risk being sighted by any who might come along.

Yet the rough going tested their weariness. The old trouble with Georgia's feet returned; she could feel them blistering in the rough leather of her shoes, and the linen bands had begun to wear away. Mendaline huffed red faced, head down watching each step and balancing each stride, while Lo twitched between, flinching at twig snaps and looking over her shoulder as if pursued.

Finally, the road opened ahead of them, and sunlight streamed in along the track. Ahead were the contours of wide, cultivated demesne and the fields beyond. There would be houses near those fields, and a well with fresh water and bread.

"Rest ahead." Georgia felt bold where the sun seeped in along the road and stepped out onto where the damp surface eased her feet. They could risk the road now, she thought. They had come already far enough, and the road allowed a faster pace. Each step brought more of the sun. Georgia embraced the elongated rays that swept new-petal pollens in under the forest canopy, drawing the fragrant warmth under the folds of her wrap.

"Smell that?" she said, raising her arms and throwing her hood back from her face. "Sloe blossoms."

"Aiye!" Mendaline skirted to avoid Lo, ramming her staff into a wheel rut to steady herself. Lo did not apologize for her sudden halt but stood listening.

Georgia clapped her hand sharply. "Lo, we are far from Bilsdale now. Not even Mendaline with her satchel will be known. You cannot jump at phantoms."

Mendaline took Lo's arm. "Steady on, girl. There's meat ahead."

Lo stared behind them. "He will never stop searching for me," she said.

Georgia clapped sharply again. It echoed all along the road the way they had come, reverberating under the canopy. A noisy echo returned the same way, clopping back toward them from the shadows where the road turned and darkened out of sight. This sound was of horse hooves pounding along the road. Georgia stopped to listen, looking back, as two horsemen turned the corner through the trees.

The first rider swayed on a palfrey that flicked its head up, its ears full back, the bit frothy. It was Romsfeld. The second rider followed close behind the first, his mount releasing steamy clouds from what must have been a hard ride east. Both men wore the colors of the archbishop of York.

For a few pounding hoofbeats, Georgia grappled with her senses. Then Mendaline pushed her from behind, and she fled through sprouted raspberry and juniper, forcing her way through the cracking gorse. The worst of it prickled and tore, but Georgia threw herself to the floor among the thorns and turned to watch the men pass, Mendaline next to her.

Lo remained in the road. Georgia almost screamed to see her there, for she stood under the fronds of an engorged mistletoe in plain sight, dead center in the road, with her hood back and her arms thrown out to stop them. A death-grim figure, she moved straight along the center of the path, and she widened her footing. Her hands, raised up and white as ghost clay, took the few rays of sun directly through them.

Georgia tried to scramble back, but she was tangled in gorse and struggled to free herself. She kicked into the dirt but only churned up years worth of litter and mulch. The vines held fast.

Romsfeld's horse, frothing already up into its nostrils, spooked at the sight of Lo. It reared, stamped its hind legs, and churned the air inches from her face.

Lo didn't move, and it looked as if the flailing hooves, so close, had also gone right through her. The horse screamed and came down hard to the right. It then pitched back again, catapulting Romsfeld from the saddle, tossing him high into the air before he fell onto the road flat on his back. His head bounced with the crack of bone against a wheel-hardened rut. The wind left his lungs like steam emptying a vat.

Lo remained immobile and ghastly dark against the light behind. The palfrey screamed and pawed and spooked. The rider behind spurred his animal forward, yet there was no room. Romsfeld's raging palfrey descended. The horses clashed, slicing and gouging with flailing hooves and bared teeth.

Romsfeld's man tried to circumvent the thrashing stallion, but Lo, implacable as fate, her arms still raised and her head pulled back, did not give ground. The horse did not challenge her. It reared in terror and in pain, turned, and fled with its rider, out of control, plunging straight through the trees as if seeking a crow's path back to Bilsdale. Romsfeld's palfrey also fled, but back along the path the way it had come, screaming as it went, the long leather rein trailing behind and spurring it to the further terror of pursuit.

Lo lowered her arms. In the hole of quiet, she stood over Romsfeld as he lay splayed and breathless. A deep gurgle sounded in his throat. Perhaps he wished to speak, or perhaps plead with an avenger. His hand twitched.

Georgia found a niche for her feet and shoved into it, snapping vines though the thorns bit into her. She pushed through the gorse and branches. Yet she was too late. Lo lifted her staff high over her head and released a massive, plunging blow, driving the nubby base down into the center of Romsfeld's chest.

The forest absorbed a terrible crack as the sternum bone split. Romsfeld's arms and legs jerked and shuddered, and then he lay twitching. His neck arched, and his head lolled left.

Georgia stumbled onto the road, disbelieving, as Romsfeld snarled last, his tongue massed between bared teeth.

Mendaline scrambled up and past her, kneeling next to this man who had brought plague to them all. She pressed a thickened knuckle into his neck, and ran her hands along his thighs and arms to soothe the twitching.

"He is dead," Mendaline said.

Those words had never been so unnecessary to Georgia's mind. Romsfeld was a man hollowed out, expunged. It was as if he had never lived.

Mendaline made the sign of the cross over him and then crossed herself as well. She kissed her rosary and touched it to her forehead, and then began last rights, spilling the words over her tongue like a spindle. With a final nod, she folded Romsfeld's hands over his chest and closed his eyes.

Georgia watched his eyes even after the lids had closed. So much had happened all at once.

Lo stooped to cut Romsfeld's purse from his belt. "I'll have no man hurt me again, nor hunt me," Lo said simply. "I'll have my own life."

Georgia felt sick. Lo was the Chooser. Lo must be pure. She grabbed her by the arms and then released her. "Yet he is slain!"

Lo returned her gaze evenly. "You have killed. I have done the same, and been more justified in the doing. You took a man's life who only bared your legs." She tied the purse at her belt and then looked down at Romsfeld. "He took more. The hurt—*O Jesu*. It shreds you. I am what is left."

Mendaline's stern, crisp voice wedged between them. "If we're found out, we'll hang. All of us." She indicated for them to each grab a leg and pull Romsfeld in where the alder grove thickened. He was lighter than he looked, and they dragged him and then covered him with leaves. The wild dogs would find him, but perhaps not for a day or two.

Mendaline knelt over the body, chanting a rumbling Latin, a prayer that would likely work half as well as it should. For if ever there was a soul to linger in purgatory, this was one. Georgia touched the rosary at her belt and found she pitied him.

The shallow burial complete, they obscured the hoof gouges in the road and resumed their way. They must take another route now, and not the carter's way. Not yet. They would keep instead along the edge of the wood and then find a drover's track. They could perhaps risk a carter's train tomorrow.

They picked carefully along the edge of the wood, skirting fields and weaving through the mottled sunlight and shadows of walnut and oak trees. Lo no longer lagged behind and no longer spooked at every snapped twig or flushed sparrow. That, at least, was a relief.

After a little going, Lo stopped and drew her skirts high around her.

"Sister!" She gave a cry of surprise and stretched her leg in front of her. Along the white skin trailed a glossy line, a smear of blood. It ran all the way down between both legs, smeared between her knees, down her calf, and over one shoe. Lo peeled a dock leaf from where it stuck to her. Her face was transformed bright and pink and her eyes wide with disbelief.

"Blood."

This was the first since her return that Georgia could remember anything like happiness moving across Lo's face.

Mendaline stopped huffing and gaped, dumbfounded. "Glory be. The mugwort!" She slid her finger through the line where it smeared at the knee, rubbing the shining blood between her gnarled fingers.

Lo smiled. "It is my courses come. My courses! Georgia, I *will* have a child." She wiggled her feet in the grass, and then danced in a circle, her skirts whirling around her.

Georgia threw her head back and laughed as well; she looked again at the astonishment on Mendaline's face and laughed the more. Turning, she grabbed Lo and hugged her tightly.

"This has naught to do with mugwort," Georgia said. "This is a miracle. Praise Isela, a miracle!"

BOOK FIVE

CHAPTER 38:
All Saints

Lo bled for two days and then left off. Her flow resumed the morning they spent bouncing in the back of a wagon along the carter's road south of Arden. The women rested at the center, making the best of their body heat against the damp. Wet sacks, stocked with grape and honeysuckle cuttings, walnut, quince, and sour apple saplings bound tightly together, padded both sides of the wagon. Lo lay against Georgia. Though she still coughed, her condition was improving.

Georgia thought ahead to York and of the many tales surrounding it, of the lawless, wild apprentices and masterless drifters she had heard thronged the city, of plague and treachery. And rats. It was said that the rats of York grew so enormous that the cats had fled the city. It was also said that the pestilence of the Ouse River produced a stink surpassing even the Thames river in London.

Lo curled sidewise, and Georgia laid a hand across her forehead.

"I don't fever," Lo said, "but I have pain across the belly."

"I also ache during my courses." Georgia opened her palm and pressed her hand firmly against Lo's lower back. While she doubted the warmth of her palm would penetrate Lo's many layers of petticoats, the pressure would at least be soothing.

Mendaline opened an eye. "Pains?"

"Oh, sleep," a note of exasperation edged Lo's voice, "I live still." Another cough welled up from her chest.

"Hi yee!" The carter slapped each knock-kneed mare in turn from one cart to another. The men guarding the carts quickened their step, adjusted their jerkins, and brushed off their hose. Finally, they were in sight of the gate.

The wall of York, a crown of pink and yellow clays, curved like a clean-edged furrow at the horizon. A few sentinels paced the top, their black caps dulled in the overcast sky. The outer landscape teemed with the overflow of the city, squatter communities of huts and lean-tos, smoking fires, butchers, tanners, and even an elaborate smithing forge.

Georgia slid from the cart. It felt good to be on her feet again. Yesterday they had crossed the swollen Rye at the bridge at Nunnynton, paying a toll to the miller for the privilege. At Hovington they had discarded the black woolen slops they had made in Gotesind's cave and purchased three felted travelling robes such as the northern townsfolk wore. Georgia had chosen a peas-porridge tawny, a hue that reminded her of spring growth in mealy mud.

Mendaline tied her satchel and smoothed her own cloak, a watchet, bluish green, but dyed deeper than was Lo's. Lo followed Georgia out of the cart, and together they helped Mendaline climb from the wagon as she cursed the ruts, the jolting boards, and the chicken grime.

The carts waited at the gate, not so as to be checked, for there seemed little interest in that, but because the road into the city was impacted with carters, sellers, dogs, cooks, handcarts, barrels, and hungry apprentices. Dairymaids offered ready cheeses, curdled milk, and eggs boiled or raw to those who pressed through the gate. Bakers hawked barley, oat, or rye bread.

Any sort of necessity, it seemed, could be purchased right at the gate, including every sort of ale, by the barrel or just enough to fill a noggin. Tavern boys sang the praises of inns inside the city, and a few whores, their foreheads shaved so they would look more appealing, smiled and winked to the throng. Above them the magnificent spires of the Minister, York's famed Cathedral, poked the sky.

Georgia linked arms with Mendaline and Lo and marched through the crush and sweat and shouts at the pedestrian gate, and started down Saint Leonard's street. She felt almost happy to be in York. There were simply too many people, she thought, for anyone to remember who was who. She pushed straight through along Coppergate, through the coopers and carpenters and sawdust, and then into the wide market square where all manner of traders and goods and, it seemed, most of the barefoot inhabitants of York, collected.

They avoided Swinegate and its stench, and instead went to Petergate. From there Georgia slowed her pace and then stopped abruptly in the street. Several men behind her, two with great sacks over their shoulders, swore at having to jolt suddenly aside to avoid her. As they passed, the men splashed up puddles of filth, but Georgia paid no mind to them or to the others she jostled as she moved, just as abruptly, across the street and into a labyrinth of low wattle tenements.

The lanes smelled of decomposing, bubbling yeasts, the warm reek of human waste, and an underlying bile of lye over cooking fires. Had it been a hundred years? More?

"Do you see something?" Lo asked.

"I grew up here," Georgia said. As she spoke the words out loud, she realized it was so. Only the people had changed.

"In York?"

"Once."

The memory came in flashes. The clack of a loom. Stale urine hung in the air so thick it could be tasted on the tongue. A pack of barefoot girls shouting like barbarians in the filthy lanes, jumping where the swine had overturned a garden in the night. She looked out across the thatched roofs and plastered fronts pitted with lime, and then set off toward a small church. She ran her fingers over the timber frame that marked the threshold before she ducked inside.

Lo and Mendaline followed, Lo coughing as Mendaline collapsed into a bench. She lifted her rosary but was too out of breath to begin a prayer.

Georgia unwound memory from the niches along the whitewashed walls. There had once been colorful murals of the saints, here—Saint Francis, Mary suckling the holy infant at her breast, the trip to Bethlehem, the angel Gabriel, the archangel Michael—they were all gone. Gone, too, were the small statues and carved benches, the holy sepulchre, and a shelf of holy relics.

Only the earth felt the same. She tapped the ground, and a shiver spread along her back. She had awakened here, once. She had come into the church, and she had prayed. The vision, when it came, called her to Isela's service, humming through her body as pure cord, reminding her of who she was.

She turned her attention outward, her mind to that thread, that cord. She reached for the relic, searching the city block by block with the core of herself. She knelt, lowered her head, and the world slipped away. She forgot her breath and left her bones behind, knowing only the search, listening for that distinctive pull, waiting for the ground to open up.

She did not find an opening. Instead she felt a terrible fatigue. The cord snapped and rolled away.

"It's not here," she said.

"What's not here?" Lo whispered, though there was no one to hear them.

"The relic." Georgia wondered again at the walls. A few bands of ocher showed through under the whitewash. For the first time in a long while, Georgia wondered how her parents were, and her baby brother, breeched now, she thought.

"Where is it, then?" Lo whispered.

Georgia shrugged. "Not in the city." The weariness wrapped around her.

"What do we do?"

"We search for the one who stole it, for the one who slaughtered children for it. Someone will know where he is."

☙

They moved again through the bustle of the streets, taking rooms over the Cat & Ram, a wide, two-story wattle and daub building shot through with oak timbers. It smelled of the yeasty, bilious foam of the kitchen brewer and reminded Georgia of Beatrice.

Their room was small, but warm and also dry. The bed coverings added to the yeast the smell of mold, and when Mendaline struck down on the bed with her staff, the heavy blanket wafted up an impressive cloud of dust. Mendaline directed Lo to pick off a few dark fleas and, with a doubtful glance, offered a quick prayer.

"*Matthew, Mark, Luke, and John, bless the bed that I lie on.*" With that she climbed up, spread out, and snored resoundingly.

Georgia left Lo and Mendaline to sleep and walked along the Ouse River toward the fish market, glad that the breeze pushed the stink of the river south.

All Saints Church poked a sturdy figure between the small city lanes, the large stone bricks of pink and gray and the high-arched windows pinched at the top like arching echoes in glass. From the threshold, it smelled of chalk and tar and smoke, and inside it stunk. Numerous guildsmen washed in oily perfumes moved along the halls with nosegays and rolls of accounts. More numerous than guildsmen were the stonemasons and plasterers matted down with mortar dust and sweating over vats of steaming tar. They toiled over a huge renovation.

In this church, too, history seemed to have been scraped away. No paintings of saints or depictions of the virgin could she see, not even of the annunciation. Gone were the hens and dragons, the demons of hell, and the tonsured, writhing monks suffering the torments of purgatory. The high altar was now only a table dragged down from the dais and set plainly with a white cloth, but no chalice, candles, or cross. Elevated instead was a wooden lectern; a book lay open at its top.

Georgia stopped a painter's apprentice as he pushed past, cleaned brushes clutched to his chest.

"Boy," she said, forgetting that she was herself only a girl, "where are the holy relics kept?"

The boy glanced over his shoulder and answered in a lowered tone. "There's a timber from Saint Andrew's cross in the wall there. And a bone of Saint Helen." He pointed a wet brush at a small alcove under a heavy balcony. "Saint William's blood spilled on the far step, though they have his silver at the Minister. Or they did. Likely it's been taken off like the rest."

"Please, I seek a certain relic. It is of golden glass and scrolled in bronze with a silver chain. Is it here?"

"No." The boy shook his head. "Though a great pile burnt yesterday."

"Burnt!" Georgia stumbled over a stonemason who worked almost directly under her.

The boy shrugged. "His Grace the Duke of Northumberland ordered them all burnt." He pushed out his chest to utter such an important name. "Aye, they burn the splinters of the true cross, right enough. But if it's silver, like you say, they'll likely take it to Bishopsthorpe. Or sell it."

"Bishopsthorpe?"

"The archbishop's manor house. South from the bridge, a half day's walk."

The stonemason under her floundered, coughing. Georgia shifted again to avoid him. The boy edged aside. He nodded a terse good-bye and ducked away.

☙

The Ouse bridge swarmed with travelers and craftsmen. A chapel where carters paid a toll stood squarely at the mouth of it, but the whole was paved with flat stones and arched to allow the barges to drift underneath.

The Ouse drained slowly, too slowly, even with the added meltwater of spring, and as Georgia walked over it, she could smell the stink, not only of the oily fishmongers nearby, but also the heaping, twisted refuse that bobbed up and down. Half-split carcasses of unrecognizable beasts and slime-fleeced objects swirled near the shore or tucked under the girders of the bridge. She held her breath over the river and emerged at Skeltergate, a cesspit unto itself and swarming with squatters, shanties, and starving dogs who fought to eat human filth. In addition, the breeze blew south, so once she was over the river, she felt the full stink of it and of Fishergate on the north shore. She covered her mouth with her cloak.

She had not gone far, however, when the city receded, and the scenery brightened. Bishopsthorpe Lane was marked by a carved cross, and as Georgia passed the town of Middlethorp, a single bell rang out in cool tones, reverberating along her spine. She had not brought her prayer book, but she shivered with the call of the bell. Turning off the path, she knelt in a weedy field to pray.

The rush almost toppled her, for as she opened herself to prayer, the ground widened, and she felt the tugging, surging force of the relic. Her head swam in a warm current as she was caught in the force of the connection so suddenly returned. The relic was near. She was close. It tasted of honey mixed with wild rosemary and buttercup; her whole body seemed to turn to liquid—

And then something struck her with a bruising force. Something rough, something that smelled of donkey, chalk, and ash. The ground closed, hard, and she fell sideways into the weeds.

"Heave thee!" A woman screeched. "Fie! Hold her well, you great clout. A girl, only. Hold her now!"

"Peace, woman." A grunt.

Georgia blinked, and choked. A man squinted above her, his face puffed and red, his nose running. He breathed heavily through his mouth, over crumbling, black-spotted teeth.

Georgia screamed, flipped, and rolled lengthwise out of reach. She gained her feet, but a second man knocked her flat again.

"Ow. Hold, she'll up again! Fool!"

"Silence your tongue," the man with spotted teeth grimaced. "An end to it—I'll have the bloody end to that noise."

Georgia kicked as he lunged at her with a moulded sack. The second man put a foot on Georgia's back, pressing her into the weeds. The first man came at her with the sack again. She bit him, tasting salt and chalk, and open sores. He pulled up in a rage, flailing, and dragged the second man down with him. Georgia jumped up, and the second man grabbed at her, pulling her headscarf free. He bellowed as she ran.

The woman jumped into the fight. Georgia dodged but the woman shoved her, and Georgia spun, tripping over weeds and woody stems. She managed a look at the second man and recognized him. He was the wheezing stonemason from the church. Her surprise cost her a precious second, and she regained control of her spin too late.

Spotted teeth closed in. She aimed to uppercut his jaw with the heel of her hand, but missed, catching him instead under his nose. He staggered, cursed, and punched her hard in the gut. She doubled over, and he followed the first punch with a second that exploded over her right ear.

Her lungs flattened together as she fell. He kicked and pounded her, totally possessed with rage. Behind her, the woman screamed. Georgia drew her knees up and tried to clear her head. More blows came as the man cursed and cursed. She felt a rib crack and then another. He stomped on her arm, grabbed her hair, and shook her. She could not move her fingers. The world turned black at the corners.

"You'll kill her! You'll kill her!" The woman shrieked.

"Bloody hell, hold up," the stonemason said.

The man with spotted teeth struck the woman behind him. She screamed louder. The stonemason pushed them apart. Georgia lay still. She could hardly draw breath.

"What do you think you're up to?" the stonemason said. "He'll not pay us for a dead girl."

"Damn fool. Fie!"

"Shaddup, wife."

When spotted teeth returned, his look was grim. He mashed a dirty hand over Georgia's mouth.

"She's breathing all right." He shoved the sack over her head and another over her legs, and then bound the sacks together. Someone hauled her up. The air inside the bag was thick with mold. Dust and blood clotted her nose.

"To Bishopsthorpe, then?"

"The archbishop himself?" The woman balked. "With twenty shillings in the dock? Half-cocked fool, we'll not. You wish to be thrown in the gaol, and there to watch while my roof tiles pay your debt?"

The man shook Georgia roughly. "That's what we got her for, right?"

"Right."

"To the archbishop, then."

They changed direction. It hurt too much to breathe, so Georgia gasped instead, as shallowly as she could. She had been a fool to take the road alone. Now she would be sold to the archbishop, another prize for his collection. Her eyes stung, and the world turned to black.

CHAPTER 39:
Purgatory

She could not move. A gray world clotted her nostrils, forcing her attention to each breath and away from the stabbing, aching pain that penetrated her shock. Someone gripped her, like a spider grips a cocoon, thumping it, and the way she was slung darkened her senses, her head downward and pounding and filled with blood. A searing pressure built behind her eyes and at the center of her forehead.

Her captor shifted, jarring her upward, then down. She tumbled onto a floor of cold stone. Her hurts exploded but then eased slightly as the frigid stone seeped in, cooling her bruises. Shouts echoed; she recognized the men's voices and the shrill voice of the woman who had helped capture her. Someone stepped on her, the boot pinning her legs firmly through the sack. More shouts, then footsteps, and a conversation she could not understand.

And then the sack came off. The room was dim, and she could make out people and shapes. The boot belonged to a liveried guard, a livery that belonged to the archbishop of York. The guard crossed his arms over a raised knee, stilling her as if she were a sack of chickens at market.

An immense fire burned in a gigantic fireplace and lit a goodly length of an elaborate hall. Tables lined the walls under rippling windows through which shone a fading daylight. At many of the tables, men in black robes with shining tonsures sat with ink and paper, or colossal books. Almost all had turned from their work to stare, and some left their posts for a better look.

The high-arched hall seemed to have no beginning. Yet from a shadowy end, a tall man strode in. He clutched a weighty crook that curled at the top and glittered with what looked like thorns. She was bound and battered, but she knew him. This man was Philip SeVerde, the archbishop of York, powermonger, murderer, thief. Two armed men preceded him, and a shuffling, obsequious priest followed behind him.

Georgia blinked to gather her wits as he closed the distance between them. She searched for calm but found she was filled with hate. She was in the immense hall at Bishopsthorpe Manor, and this was the man on whom she had sworn vengeance. If he expected her to grovel or cry out, he would not find satisfaction. If she would cry out, it would be to God.

The guard shoved her with his foot. In spite of her resolve, she groaned. Biting down on the soft flesh inside her cheek, she prevented another groan from following the first.

"Still alive, Your Grace."

The woman's overly loud voice traveled like a scraping hog. "I told the men so, Your Grace. Alive and wiggling I said. She's worth a—"

"Peace, woman." The archbishop held a dangling gold crucifix against his belly. He poked Georgia with the end of his staff, digging the heel of it into her chest. Her eyes watered, but she controlled a welling cough.

The archbishop addressed the stonemason. "And this is what?"

"She was asking about a relic, Your Grace," the man answered. "One of golden glass. I remembered what you said—"

The archbishop held up his hand for silence. He returned to Georgia. "Is this true?"

Georgia pressed her tongue to the roof of her mouth. She was not sure she if could speak, and she wouldn't satisfy him with some other sound.

He snapped his fingers at the priest. The priest ducked out of the hall and returned with the relic on its silver chain.

The archbishop snatched it up, swinging it back and forth. "Is this what you wanted?" He let it twirl in front of her.

Yes. The whole world, yes. Sick as she was, the rolling orb called to her. She blinked hard to clear her eyes of crusted blood now softened by a weeping she could not allow.

The archbishop brought the relic closer until it dangled inches from her face. She could see the fire through it, as if the glass and the warmth were part of her. As it spun, it was easy to forget her aching flesh. Her right arm useless, she scooted her left arm from under her to reach out for it. She brushed the cool glass with her fingertips as it bobbed away and out of her reach. She splayed her fingers in the spot where it had been.

"Hold." The archbishop spoke to the guard. "I'll see her hand."

Georgia tried to withdraw at the assault, but the first guard was joined by a second, and they wrestled her left arm still, forcing her to extend it by applying a paralyzing pressure behind her elbow. The second guard wrenched her fingers open as the archbishop called for a torch. He stared at the flesh under her thumb with narrow eyes, releasing his breath in a malignant, triumphant hiss.

The priest behind him bent almost double staring at her palm. "S'blood! Look at this!"

Spotted teeth's woman gave a cluck of happiness as if she knew the value of their find had just increased.

The archbishop studied Georgia's face with curiosity. "Who is this? The girl's mark was destroyed." A faint, vindictive curl raised one side of his mouth as he addressed her. "Do you and your kind burn holes in each other's flesh?"

A few who had gathered snickered. The woman released a prolonged, toadying laugh.

"Bring a basin and towel." A servant complied as the archbishop passed his staff to the priest and pushed his sleeves back to the middle of his forearm. The guard increased the pressure on Georgia's legs as the archbishop knelt.

She recoiled from him, his breath a rancid heat of verjuice and sugared ale, his gums reddened and fat and raised up away from his teeth.

He grabbed her hair. She thought to spit on him, but he sloshed the towel in her face and wiped it. When he withdrew, the towel was covered in clotted blood.

The archbishop studied her again. "Do any here know this girl?" He raised an eyebrow to the guards, but they shook their heads. Georgia did not recognize any faces herself, except for the guard with his foot on her legs. She thought she remembered seeing him from the night of slaughter at the cave.

"Hmm. Where are the rest of you?"

She did not reply. Mendaline had the knife. Yet she had the digging stick at her belt. It was hard oak and sturdy. It might make weapon enough to strike at him.

The archbishop stood, took back his staff, and jabbed her cruelly in the gut. "Speak."

Georgia choked on a cry of pain, but the ensuing coughing brought more tears. When he jabbed her again, she groaned. He returned to dangling the relic.

"Tell me of the others? Where do they hide? Perhaps they have tired of the caves and are making nests in bushes?"

The relic spun so beautifully.

"Where is the girl, Lo? Does she live?"

Lo—where was Lo? Georgia tried to clear her head. The relic spun gold from light. She could taste honey on her tongue. Lo.

The orb swung back and forth. The priest made the sign of the cross, and the guards shifted nervously. Yet the archbishop's voice was steady.

"My steward is dead, girl. Killed. His man was a witness to murder. He claims to have seen—" When the archbishop stalled, the priest finished the sentence with a shudder.

"—a ghost."

The archbishop twitched and made a sign of warding.

Georgia hated him all the more for his weakness. Let all whom he had killed rise up as ghosts, she thought. But for now, she would not confess to murder.

She sucked air into the bottom of her abdomen, and words erupted like a croak. "Perhaps he fell from his horse," she said.

The archbishop laughed. "Very likely, for he was a fool. But did he also drag himself into the woods after he was dead? To be eaten by wild dogs? Or was that the work of angels?"

"Do angels not have their vengeance?" Georgia croaked again; the warm rays of the relic infused her skin.

The archbishop snatched up the relic and gave it to the priest behind him. "Enough. Speak your name."

The priest slipped the relic into a pouch at his waist. She could still feel it, but the sweet of honey left her mouth and the sour of blood replaced it.

The guard kicked her hard in the back. Her mouth gaped open, and she drooled across her cheek.

"Your name," the archbishop repeated, his tone harder.

Anger brewed in her, yet she must not be a fool. There was the promise, and there was Lo. He would kill them both. She must live. She swallowed what tasted like cowardice.

"I am called Jane."

"Jane." The archbishop turned to the priest behind him, surprise and satisfaction in his voice. "Jane! The fasting girl of Isela?"

Georgia cursed herself. Spotted teeth's woman gave a trill of delight.

The archbishop peered down, pleased and crowing. "The same girl who claims not to eat? Not to defecate? Yet who has not submitted to be examined by any authority?"

Georgia didn't answer, and the guard kicked her again. This time the pain sent strange lights into her eyes that stayed in her vision.

The archbishop addressed her captors—the stonemason, spotted teeth, and his wife. "You. What was she doing when you found her?"

The woman's voice sounded a victorious superiority, as if her words confirmed Georgia's guilt. "She was praying, Your Grace."

"Praying." He threw the word away. "But did she say anything? Do anything?"

The woman indicated her husband. "She clouted my William, please you, right vicious, she was."

The archbishop looked from one to another of the three. Georgia followed his gaze, from the blood over William's face to a purple splotch across the woman's cheek, to the stonemason, who favored his right foot, his neck and arms scratched and covered in dried blood, and a rip in his shirt revealed a deep gash.

"How many were there?" the archbishop asked.

"How many?"

"How many others?" He sounded impatient. "You captured this girl, but who were her companions? How many fought?"

The stonemason shuffled. "None others, Your Grace," he seemed embarrassed. "She was alone, outside Middlethorpe."

"Alone?" The archbishop looked at William's bloodied face once more and returned a hard gaze to Georgia.

She tried to get up, but the guard held her down with his foot and kicked her hard in the ribs. One of her lungs bubbled.

The archbishop leaned over her. "Tell me about Georgia."

"Georgia died." Despair caught at her. She felt tears and didn't care. It was true; it was a great regret. She was only Jane, a girl. The real Georgia was dead, a strong woman and now only a memory. The true Bearer who would never have let her enemy crow over her.

The archbishop seemed impatient. He strode to the fire and returned with a glowing iron.

"I won't ask again," the archbishop warned. "Where is Georgia?"

He would burn her. Her heart quickened. She tried her legs. Now that the guard was off them, she sensed they were not broken. Her right arm was useless, but testing her left, she found she could open and close her fingers and that there was strength in them. She thought again of the digging stick at her belt.

The guard held the poker over her, and she could feel the heat of it. When the archbishop nodded, he poked it toward her face.

She would have screamed defiance, but she needed all her breath to fight. With a high kick, she wrested her legs from the sack. Scissoring the guard's legs between her own, she brought him down and flipped herself over at the same time. He fell like a tree falling, and his head cracked against the stone floor. The poker came down and fell away.

Georgia tore the digging stick from her belt and, her left arm free, brought the point under his ribs, threatening to pierce his belly. One upward thrust would stop his heart.

There was complete silence in the hall save her own shallow gasping. The guard in her grip was still. She felt his muscles sag and tensed her own. Though the pain in her ribs had turned to heat, she would not give in. Only the slick foam on her tongue worried her.

"Damn it to hell!" The archbishop threw his staff at the priest who caught it, spearing his fingers on one of the thorns. Sweeping the hot poker from the floor, the archbishop rammed the heated end, now marbled in a black crust, deep into Georgia's right ear.

This time she did scream, a hoarse, foaming noise that seemed to dislocate her ribs. The agony of the burn split her head open even while she lived. From deep within her, memory bubbled. Memories she had refused to acknowledge erupted from the pockets in her flesh, from between her bones. They rolled and then swarmed over her—murder, the whip, a chase through pitch-black woods that ended in fire as the soul peeled away. A three-year-old girl, her face streaked with a dirty slime, tied to a stake while bristling dogs tore at her. A babe ripped from her mother's arms thrown down and killed. A crow's cage. Blood. An old man without skin. A girl backed into a cellar by a gang of bluecoats. She tried to beat back the onslaught, but the veil bunched up and blew away. Her head split open. The whole side of her face on fire as her flesh burned.

The archbishop tapped the poker on the stone floor, his voice thick with contempt. "Take her to All Saints Church and put her in the pen." The woman made a noise, and he answered her. "You'll be paid." Then, swinging the metal handle downward, he struck Georgia on the back of the head. Pain.

The roar of memory stilled at once.

CHAPTER 40:
Torments

IT WAS AS IF SHE WAS BURIED alive. What little air penetrated the dark stunk of animal sweat and chalk. Even with her mouth wide open, she couldn't breathe around whatever jabbed into her belly. A jolting bounced her head against something hard, her cheek abraded on the coarse hemp fibers of the sack. A worse stink leached through the sack, the stink of the Ouse River. There was no mistaking the rot of it even through the crusted blood and chalk that caked her nostrils.

But the stink told her where she was. Unless the direction of the wind had changed, they had not yet crossed the bridge. They would soon be at All Saints Church. She did not know what the "pen" was, but shuddered to think of it, likely a basement hole where heretics were tortured and shaved before they were burned.

A ghoul from memory came at her in an open-mouthed scream—she champed her teeth down against it and forced the memory back. She must not succumb to terror. She must escape. Yet she could not keep air in her lungs. She could only manage a shallow pant as one side of her chest felt heavy and wet.

She could hear carts grinding around her, and voices. The man with spotted teeth spoke, grousing. "I'll need twice the measure of ale after this. To march all the way to Bishopsthorpe and back, and a third measure for the pain in my nose."

"It's capons and pheasant after this," the woman crowed. She might have pushed him because his footsteps fumbled and he cursed. "And a new gown. No more empty purse."

"Fie, woman. I've seen no gold yet."

Georgia tested the space around her, pushing gingerly with her legs. Whatever was under her felt spongy, yet her head met with—timber, perhaps. She winced as the whole of her jolted again. Straw, she realized. She lay on straw and in a wagon. A prisoner's wagon.

She wanted to writhe but forced control. There would be guards. Prisoners were usually tied to the wagon so they could not escape. Her right arm was numb and limp. She tested her left, and she could not raise it. A rope tied her elbows securely at her waist.

The cart jolted again, a violent jerk that reminded her how desperately her body hurt. She wished for some of Mendaline's bitterness and clenched a fist to ward the pain away. Yet in the jolt, she had not felt a second rope. She was tied around the middle, but perhaps not to the wagon at all.

The wagon glided now, a smoother ride, and Georgia could hear the grinding of metal-rimmed wheels over stone. They must now be on the bridge itself and crossing over. *O Mother Mary*! She would rather die on the bridge in chains than be imprisoned and face torture and despair. She coiled her legs and found the boards beneath her. At the next jolt, she kicked as hard as she could.

She launched up from the straw and landed off balance, something solid and rough against her hip. She teetered and flipped backward. She landed on stone. She bore the worst of the fall on her seat, her tail bone jarred into her shoulders.

Spotted teeth shouted, "Bloody hell!"

Something grabbed at her, and she rolled. The sack over her head slid off, and she blinked to see spotted teeth holding the sack limp in his hands as both he and his wife stood bug-eyed in the moonlight.

Without the sack, Georgia took in a glorious breath. The blood-crusted cake over her nostrils loosened, and the mortar of her throat eased. She could see around her, the wagon and the men. The prison wagon rolled on. Two of the archbishop's men lagged behind. They quarreled, swapping insults and playing cards between them.

Spotted teeth's woman shrieked.

The guards looked up at the noise, and their faces transformed to shock. They threw the cards down and put their hands to their swords.

"S'blood!" The stonemason snatched the sack from his companion and plunked it back over Georgia's head.

The woman shrieked at her husband for his incompetence, and Georgia heard him clout her in return. The archbishop's men shouted for everyone to get out of the way.

The stonemason grabbed Georgia around the shoulders. She could not push him away as her arms were tied at the elbows. Instead she used the strength in her legs, launching straight up and thrusting her head under his jaw with enough force to throw him backward. He tried to hold her, to take her down with him, but he only grabbed a handful of the sack, and it came off again and left her standing.

The guards were closing in. She saw the bridge rail was to her right and threw herself over it. If she drowned, at least she would be free. And for a time, she would forget.

Shouts followed her as she plunged. Someone grabbed at her ankle, but it was too late. The Ouse sucked her in and swallowed.

She sank. She had no better breath than the one she fell with. The water stung her eyes and seeped through the lower sack still tied around her middle. A maggot-fed decay oozed wet between her teeth as the fabric sucked around her. Spinning and sinking, Georgia caught on something under the water. Or, it caught her, like a skeletal hand, an iron barb, or the rib of a sunken ship or ox. She kicked and twisted, but she could not get free. The barb penetrated past her belt and through her skirts and poked into her back.

She found a foothold and used it to brace against what held her. The fabric tore. She kicked again, and the fabric tore again but this time, the rope tore with it. She found she could move her arm a little, but her lungs were emptying. She kicked a final time. The barb held, but the tear widened. The rope loosened, and she found she could wiggle inside the fabric of her shift.

She could not escape upward, for her dress was held fast to the barb. Twisting, she wormed down and away, withdrawing her arms from the sleeves, her right arm clumsy and unfeeling. The barb held all, her kyrtle, underskirts, and shift. She had to leave it all behind, yet she was free.

Free, but blind, naked, and cold. Her lungs turned inside out in desperation for air. She kicked for the surface, but her breath could not wait. Even as she fought it, her muscles spasmed and forced a gasp. She sucked a gummy, watery film into her throat and lungs. She shuddered and gulped as she surged upward, swallowing water and filth and an elongated chunk of slime that coated her throat as it slid down her.

She crested the surface retching, her skin coated in slime. She collided with the bloated carcass of an ox and grasped a fistful of the animal's sludgy beard, clinging to it and vomiting. Water exited her stomach and lungs both. The rope of slime in her throat slid, long and mucousy, a putrid eel, back into the water. She retched and retched again, drifting down the river, her eyes stung by putrefaction until the fishmongers dragged her out.

Days ran together. Georgia kept her eyes shut, but sleep and prayer in turn refused her. Unwelcome memories rose like boils under her skin, and the flux proved that hell was real enough, the spasms doubling her over and drenching her in white-flecked excrement.

Mendaline prepared egg yolk and spirit concoctions and stirred jugs of wine. Georgia could smell cumin in the pastes that Lo fed to her, and chicken fat in the lanolin oil Lo smeared onto her burns and bruises. Yet despite their care, Georgia balled into a knot and exploded with heat. Images, caresses, and terrors intermingled with thorns and colors as a bouquet pressed too tightly in the fist. The second day dragged into the third without seams or edges; the fourth merged into the fifth with only candlelight in between.

The feeling in her arm returned on the sixth day. It was as if a blacksmith had wrought a white-hot hammer to pound it with. On the same day, her eyes frothed with ropy pus. Lo smeared paste into them, and the world disappeared under a fetid river of green slime.

Lo placed a rosary in Georgia's hand and squeezed her own over it. "We will pray the Marys and the paternosters together," she said.

She prayed, but she could not track with whom or when. Lo or Mendaline came and went, always returning from the market with some new herb or medicine to induce healing. Today Mendaline returned with a lumpy sack. The innkeeper hovered outside the door, covering his nose with a corner of his sleeve.

"Pigeons," he said. "I heard a sack of pigeons came in here?"

Pigeons were a known cure for plague. Mendaline clanked the fire prod noisily. "*Sweet Mary*, pigeons! There's no plague here. Nor would I split an animal alive to cure it."

Lo slid from the bed, leaving the rosary across Georgia's palm. She kept her voice low. "Be assured, goodman, it is pippins, not pigeons, in the sack. Apples alone." She untied the sack and withdrew an apple. The open sack smelled as if the apples inside had already begun to ferment. "For fever."

"Not plague?"

Mendaline threw the door open. "There's no contagion. Have a great, bloody look 'round if that'll decide you. The fire's there, see, and the sack, and there's the honey, and the bed with the girl on it. She's quite alive. I'll pinch her."

Mendaline did pinch her, hard, and Georgia moaned, rolling over on her side and leaving the rosary behind.

The innkeeper sounded mollified. "All the same, it'll be six crowns for the week."

"Six crowns!"

"The lord mayor will order me boarded up from the gossip alone. Should a man harm himself?" He waved an accusatory finger from the corridor. "I gave no lease for pestilence."

Lo latched the door behind him. "Six crowns. We have only a few shillings left—"

Mendaline returned to the fire and sat heavily on the low stool, leaning over a boiling pot. "We'll send a letter to Sister Catherine in Hull. For all her empty head, she may aid us. Lo, you will have to write it."

Mendaline fished a bubbling mass from out of the pot, bringing it as a swath of steaming linen to the bed. Green paste oozed from the weave. "We have been here overlong. It is too much risk. Someone will know us. So I have wrought a cure. It is a hard cure, but that can't be helped." She slid the blanket off and laid the roll over Georgia's belly and chest. The roll was hot, hotter than her own skin, which already boiled. "She needs turning."

Lo rolled Georgia as Mendaline unwrapped the linen over her back and did not stop until Georgia's whole body was covered, even her face, for Mendaline left only a small opening for her to breathe.

Lo wrinkled her nose at the paste. "What cure is this?"

"Crisis. It'll be a hard night, but that fever'll either break by morning or—well—we'll just pray it breaks." The old healer clanked pots and spoons together by the hearth. A crock dropped and shattered.

Georgia lay still. The herbs pricked and crawled along her skin in scalding lines, stinging especially over cuts, bruises, and at the edges of the bandage that protected the burned, flaking skin of her weeping ear. Worse, her feet and ankles began to twitch. After only the space of two paternosters, she felt nearly mad from the twitching. The long muscle on her thigh knotted and refused to release. In her heart, she desired none other than oblivion, yet her ankles tortured her with kicks and twitches. And memory swirled. She kicked up hurt and stems of memory. She saw again the three-year-old girl and the dogs. The child screaming.

The memory flickered and changed. Now it was her own body tied, her mouth screaming. The dogs snarled and tore at her. She screamed and thrashed, kicked out with her legs. Something grabbed at her shoulders.

"Georgia, Sister." Lo cooed to her. Her worry made Georgia want to weep. She felt so ashamed.

Mendaline clucked. "This may be harder than I thought." She held a leaf in her hand. "Here girl. Chew this."

Georgia tried to clamp her mouth shut, but Mendaline shoved the leaf between her teeth. She knotted her stomach against the expected bitterness, but found the flavor cool and sweet.

"Always remember," Mendaline said. "There are good things in this world, too."

The day passed into fits. The bed sank next to her, and Georgia could hear Mendaline snoring. The door opened and closed. She could taste the smoky oil of the lamps. Her fever boiled, though the aches lessened, perhaps overshadowed by the pulse that trenched her flesh. Voles swarmed over her, shrunk to the size of biting ants. They bit and bit and carried her away, piece by piece. Soon, there would be nothing left, just an empty hook to hang her rage.

The archbishop was right. She was nothing, a starveling, a cave dweller, a scum on the light. She had wandered too far and was stretched too thin. She was useless and too late.

Lo returned late but did not wake Mendaline. Instead, she settled quietly on the bed and talked softly, soothingly. She spoke of their early years together, of the priory and the well, of Eastertide and unpeeling chicken and duck eggs to eat one after the other. She filled a long silence with her knees curled up, rocking back and forth.

She left again, and when she returned, she picked at the gear and stoked the fire. Georgia heard water poured into the basin and thought she could smell rosemary. Lo then returned to the bed, smoothing the wrappings. She rocked herself to sleep.

Georgia thought she would never sleep again, not if she first had to pass through into her dreams. But finally, she slept. She saw the woman in the green dress. At first, Georgia tried to run from her, cursing and hiding under a water barrel. The lady brought a cooling rain, many drops at once. "See how they glitter?" she said. "So many of them." Lightning flashed and a roll of thunder followed. In the raindrops were the colors of lifetimes, her lifetimes, in images, memories. "The drops belong to you. Each of them. They are what they are, and to remember is your right."

The morning stirred, lifting the smell of rosemary even as the sun rose. Songbirds joined with the caw cawing of ravens, combining twitters into throaty harmonies. A goose trumpeted, followed by a chorus of indignant clucking. For the first time in days, the morning cold did not make her shiver, and although a blacksmith's hammer rang, his efforts did not echo misery along her bones. The fire under her skin had ceased.

Mendaline sat up, and Georgia pooled out from within her dream. It was as if she, too, were a drop of water. One of many and cascading with the rest, a round reflective jewel of lifetime.

Mendaline pushed the cloth away from Georgia's face. She opened her eyes and blinked, and the room cleared.

"And you feel?"

Georgia experimented with her throat. What had it been, seven days since Bishopsgate? Could she speak? "I am washed out," she said.

"Hm," Mendaline nodded. "Let's see your tongue, then."

Georgia stuck out her tongue, aware of a faint tingling low inside her belly.

"Ha!" Mendaline snapped her jaw closed. She slid from the bed and reached for her gown. "That's done it!" She tied on a clean apron. "I've never seen it fail yet, though Madgie Wheeler died on Saint Anne's day. Still! Such a tongue—" She catapulted back to the bed, patted Georgia's cheek, and winked triumphantly—"so pink it wants ale!"

☙

As Lo unwound the last of the bandages, Mendaline tipped the jug into a noggin. "Ah, see this girl? And bread, too. Lo, take that linen and burn it in the yard."

"We'll need to work quickly," Lo rolled the linen in a pile. "I've booked passage to Hull."

Mendaline almost dropped the cup. "Passage?"

"In the night. A wool merchant with a barge agreed to take us down river. He'll stow us for an angel."

"An angel? We've—" Coins jingled as Mendaline picked up the purse and shook it.

"And I paid the innkeeper."

Confusion drew Mendaline's brows together. "A merchant ship?"

"It's done."

"Six crowns for the innkeeper?"

"That is done, too." Lo took the purse and tied it to her belt. "There are more ways to pay a man than with money, Sister."

Mendaline stared at her, and Lo raised her chin in defiance, though she looked away. Mendaline sighed.

"We'd better send that letter to Sister Catherine, then." she said finally. "And hope for the best."

"That is also done," Lo handed her a sack. "It should reach the dock afore us." She continued packing.

"Well, up," Mendaline sighed, "you've heard the mistress. Go to."

Georgia shifted her legs and found that, indeed, her body moved.

"Come on, girl." Mendaline said. "You'll work all right. A might sore, but that can't be helped. By'r lady, there'll be no more talk of plague in this inn."

Georgia pushed her legs to the floor as Lo washed the remaining poultice from her skin and hair and helped her with a new shift, skirts, kyrtle, and cloak, combed her hair straight, and mounded it under a fresh scarf. Georgia winced as Lo tied a cloth around her arm to sling it.

"Come on," Mendaline waved.

Georgia tottered as she worked to control her shaking legs. Her body seemed better, but inside she felt queasy, as if there was something she'd missed. Something important. She balled her fists, and her right hand had no strength. Pain shot through to her elbow.

"I won't go to Hull," Georgia said, a whisper but audible, clean and steady. She feared to face the archbishop again, but she would not run. Not from the relic. Live or die, she would meet her doom in York.

Lo shouldered a sack. "The archbishop left for London yesterday. We cannot follow him with no money, a sick girl, and an old woman."

"Old woman!" Mendaline snorted. "Please yourself!"

"The boatman awaits. Be angry as you like, but steer yourself to the dock. As for me, I have a wish to live."

CHAPTER 41:
Holy Maid

Georgia knelt at the baptistery, the water drew her, and she thought of Lo's fountain, the clear water and the smell of hyssop. Here, between the font and the altar, she felt hidden and to a small degree protected. She opened her prayer book, but a woodcut of the passion, with its gruesome depiction of tortures and agonizing devices, led her to close the book with a shudder and a snap.

In the last two seasons, while the grinding bones in her arm and ribs had healed, the horrors of memory had receded only a little. They were imbedded in her now, like needles in her joints. When she wiggled, when she blinked or stretched, they would flash one after another. They were a constant reminder that the world was a terrible, despotic place. She recalled the finger of slime from the river and retched.

Yet there was the smell of hyssop, here, as well. The pedestal font gleamed a polished dark and was ringed with whitened fleury lilies and carved figures. Several leaded figures unwound from the basin. They told the story of Saint Winifred who, after refusing to submit to a would-be lover, was beheaded. From where the saint's head touched the ground, a well sprung up. The font showed the waters of that well pouring up the sides and into the basin. In the next scene, Saint Beuno restores Winifred's head and her life. In the last panel, Winifred wears the flowing robes of an important abbess as water from her uplifted hands flows up and into the basin.

Georgia tucked next to the fourth panel of the font, wedged between it and the southern altar. A stone-jawed lion leapt at her elbow, and a white linen cloth draped over the altar on either side. From the southern door, sunlight illuminated a wooden cross and warmed her right side, soothing the scarred, shriveled skin of her burned ear through a light veil. She wore a veil of enough weight to hide the scar. She was too young for a married woman's headwear and dared not wear one reminiscent of a nun. So she wore a maiden's veil instead, though that caused its own trouble.

She slipped the book into the pocket of her apron and turned to her rosary, counting out Hail Marys and Our Fathers and whispering prayers to Isela. "Forgive me," she whispered. And she pleaded, "let me free." As she counted, she kept watch. Rosaries were now forbidden, and though the village of Sutton was friendly to the old ways, she was careful to let the beads slide into the folds of her skirt and disappear as she worked her fingers along them.

When she came to the tiny carved virgin where the beads came together, Georgia whispered, "Pray, My Lady, heal Lo. Make her well again."

Lo had led them to Hull and persuaded Catherine to shelter them in a cottage nearby in Sutton. But since Georgia had risen from the sickbed, Lo was herself more often in it, fatigued and sometimes feverish. Mendaline suspected a wasting illness, fed her tonics of ripe figs, and powdered dillweed and clucked over her. But Lo worsened.

As summer passed, Lo's courses would first flood, then dry, with the bleeding coming in all phases of the month. The illness was a serious one, and Georgia knew she must leave and search again for the relic. For Lo must live. With the relic, perhaps Lo would be well again. And yet—Georgia pressed a bead too tightly in her fingers, and her thumb rimmed red, then white. Must they go? Could she not hope for a little more sleep? Or just a season to rest, a season to watch her garden bloom?

Georgia pressed the beads hard against her palm. Since that terrible night swathed in linen on the bed, her world was full of memories. She was afraid. Here, near Hull in Sutton, they were safe. Mendaline was skilled, especially at hurts of the womb. Surely, Mendaline could cure Lo without the relic. It would be better, Georgia told herself, to search for the relic once Lo was well.

Georgia thought of the autumn garden she had dared to plant. There was spinach and cucumbers and cabbage. What a joy to feel the soil in the webbing of the hand, to work the rot into the earth where it warmed into a rich bed ripe for seed—certainly a womb was not wholly different. Mendaline treated Lo with hot compresses of tansy and dung. Perhaps the rot just needed to warm and seep out, and soon Lo would be well again.

As Georgia counted prayers along the beads, the dark moons of garden soil under her fingernails made her pinch her shoulders together with defiance.

"Sweet Isela," her prayer spilled into the church. "Let us wait. Just a little longer."

A shadow fell across the nave. She bundled the rosary and shoved it into her pocket as a man came into the church. From the noise he made, this man wished to declare himself. He clumped loudly on the plank floor and sighed with a pained arrogance.

"The candle," he said. His voice was a clacking, pinch-nosed squawk, a noise that honked into the whitewashed walls and stuck there.

Georgia smelled frankincense, and she pushed her toes against the floor as a runner poised to flee. Frankincense was a scent favored by the Protestant preachers who wandered from parish to parish, preachers more zealous than even the Privy Council to keep the churches abiding the laws of the young king. The scent seemed to penetrate to the very corners of the sanctuary and squeeze her out.

A tittering response came from the parish priest, a former bond servant who had learned to read. "For the rood, a candle is allowed."

The preacher grabbed the candle and snuffed it before throwing it down. "It'll burn with the rest." He spun on his heel and glared at the spinet piano tucked into a corner by the altar, the polished walnut instrument decorated with dried petals and scrupulously clean.

"A spinet piano? Still? It, too, must be burned." The priest seemed about to protest but did not. The preacher picked up the rood and threw it down before taking old dusty prayer books from a stack at the end of a bench and throwing those down as well.

He spied Georgia in the baptistery and shuffled through the books to get to her. "You there, maid."

She drew her chin up, choking on frankincense. In his smile she saw paternal affection. "My daughter, I wish to commend you for your piety. More girls would do well to follow your example."

Georgia did not make eye contact with him. She held a picture of her garden in her mind, not as it was now, cooling seeds worked into the soil, but how it would look as it grew. It would be a winter garden, veiled in mist, fragile, and lush.

"Rise, maid, for I have come to preach." The man spoke loudly, throwing his voice so that it would carry outside the door where a number of village children gathered and a few villagers beside. The children cheered at his announcement. Wandering preachers brought the promise of lively entertainment. The lychgate just outside the churchyard that hosted bearbaitings would be his pulpit. There, regardless of weather, the travelling preachers unleashed a message of acid exhilaration.

"I am Father Lionel of York," he continued, addressing Georgia so loudly that everyone at the door could hear, "from the household of His Grace, the most excellent and gracious lord, the archbishop of York, who is even now in London with the king. By his authority, I can offer each of you God's favor."

Georgia's garden shrank away. She clenched her teeth to keep her mouth closed. She did not wish trouble. He would preach damnation and burn their spinet and pass on to the next town.

Her hands sweated as she smoothed the cover of her prayer book. It was not the right one. Her hidden rosary beads clicked, and a portion of the strand poked out of her apron. She quickly moved to hide it, but the preacher stuck his hand into her pocket to snatch the beads out, waggling the rosary in the face of the village priest.

"See how superstition keeps like a pestilence in the corners of England?" His sticky duck squawk rippled the water in the font. "A bonfire will purify the evil of this church." He threw the rosary on the floor and, with his heel, ground down on the small image of the virgin to crush it.

"Rise," he demanded.

Georgia bit her lip. Tonight would be a full moon. Tonight she could sow white succory.

"Rise when I speak to you, maid." The preacher's tone darkened, and as it did, the squawking muffled, and his mouth slanted. "Rise!"

Georgia rose. As she did so, her skirts swung down over her legs and smoothed against the contours of her body. The waist of her apron slipped up under her breasts with the combined effect to display her belly as it protruded large and round from under her ribs, an enormous ripe melon sinking deep between the bones of her hips.

The preacher stopped and gaped at her stomach. She gave him a defiant stare and then curtseyed. The bondsman priest fidgeted. At his twitching, Georgia pitied him.

The preacher kicked the broken shards of the virgin, scattering the remnants into the pile of books to be burned.

"With child! And a maid?" He stared at her, as if daring her to produce a husband. She lifted her chin and dared to look him in the eye.

The preacher recoiled. He wheeled toward the priest. "Has she yet been punished for her sin?"

The priest gabbled something about "mercy."

Georgia screamed. Perhaps it was that Lionel of York glared at her. Or perhaps it was the stench of onions on his breath as he grabbed her arm, or the sudden, shocking memory of writhing against a binding in the dark. If her scream shocked him, he did not show it.

"Tell me, temptress, who is to blame for this bastard child?"

Manwell. Manwell! She gasped, and he was there with her, solidly behind her. Shivers shot along her back as he spoke over her shoulder. "We are married. We are one." She blinked and imagined him lying on the ground, trampled by the riders as they rode through. Did he live, her Manwell?

The preacher spoke again. "The child's father? Pray you, do you know this at the least?"

Georgia refused to answer. Mendaline had confronted her with the signs and given her an amulet, an eagle stone, such as all pregnant women wore. But Georgia had flung it away. She had not wished it. She refused to acknowledge it. Her shame, so visible. That she had touched a man, had opened herself to him. She closed her eyes. *Manwell.* He faded away.

The preacher shoved her hard against the font. Water sloshed up from the basin over her back. The cold roused her.

"No." She threw out a hand to defend herself. She dodged around the font and away, catching the long muscle of her thigh against the side of a bench.

The folk in the doorway had multiplied to fill the windows and the doors. The preacher addressed them. "I put to you the question: What good can be said of this girl?"

Georgia screamed again. She picked up a discarded book and threw it at him.

"Even as a hellcat does she shriek." The preacher stalked her; she had nowhere to run. The townspeople crowded at the doorway. Their faces, even of those who had previously been friendly to her, were now lit with the excitement of spectacle.

"Behold the whore. The wanton!" The preacher rubbed his hands together as she darted again. "As a filthy swine to frolic in hell's delights."

The room grew narrow. The stinging odor of labored, unwashed bodies filled the nave as villagers streamed in. She fell near a bench and slid to her knees on the floor, the planks sending a thick splinter into her calf as her skirt raised up.

She rested her head in her hands and sobbed.

The rumpling skirts of village women quieted as people crowded the walls and whispered. Firm hands gripped across her shoulders. She leaned into them, and as she did so, she could tell they were his, the smell of the frankincense, the onions, and smoke.

"Do you regret your sin?" He knelt next to her, drew her in. Was kind to her.

Georgia nodded against his chest. There was so much to regret. Her illness. Her fear. Her cowardice.

He drew his arms around and embraced her, squawking at his audience.

"Let this maid be blameless, for the sin of fornication is not the fault of such a simple girl."

She relaxed her muscles and closed her eyes. Let someone else take charge; let someone else take the blame, Saint Cuthburga who was strong, or Saint Catherine, for it was her day.

The preacher took a deep breath. "It is no fault of hers. Women are by nature drawn to whoredom. It is why they must marry and be tamed, to prevent such a fall as this. They must submit to their fathers and their husbands in every obedience. And though they may beat her, yet it is done in love. For it is in her own good, to purge her of sin and licentiousness."

The preacher raised his voice. "All ye maids listen well, that you also must submit or else this be your fate. Sin. Debauchery. A woman whores easily."

Georgia quieted her sobs.

"It is only through punishment that we come to forgiveness. Who will help me punish this girl?"

Georgia stiffened. The wet patch on his chasuble felt clammy under her cheek. She drew back.

"I will be the husband. Who will be the father to punish this girl, as is right before God?"

Georgia blinked away her tears. She looked out over the congregation, men and women and children of Sutton; they stared at her, their eyes round. An old man looked away. She glimpsed the chalice and the font, where Saint Winifred had refused her lover.

She remembered an immense cathedral and the holy host. A swinging, smoking orb of incense and an honorable bishop. As the saturated bread touched her tongue, she fell into a fit of ecstasy. She drank the memory, not just in remembrance, but in whole-bodied devotion to the miracle of the host.

She snatched her hand away.

"I am a nun."

The preacher looked confused, but resumed his rising sermon, unleashing a sticky honk with a slanted smile. "She does confess her sin! The sin of nunneries—brothels—dens of viciousness."

She stood. She swung away from him, but the preacher struck her hard across the face. She staggered back into the altar table, knocking the cup back, splattering red wine across the altar cloth.

He grabbed her by the arms again, this time vicelike, shoving her before him as he yelled. "A sheet. Bring a sheet!"

She tried to wrench her arm away, but he held fast to her sleeve, shoving her out into the yard.

"Fornicator," his voice warm now and filled with zeal and purpose, "you will be stripped with only a sheet to hide your nakedness. For two days you will stand, except as I may serve as your confessor. I, as your husband in this punishment, will whip you on the third day. From bundled reeds for mercy's sake your blood will flow. I will purge you of your sin!"

Mercy's sake? Could she not have mercy without being beaten? Must she stand naked on a stool at the doorway of the church? Could he not have his bearbaiting without tormenting her?

His speech had pleased him, and the response also. The villagers were gathering in. He shoved her again, but his grip loosened.

She wrenched free, but the preacher grabbed at her, his fingernails catching under her chin and along her neck, leaving a deep scratch.

She whirled, but failed to compensate for the awkward weight of her belly and almost lost her balance. She remembered how the archbishop had grasped the relic in the moonlight, how his eyes had glinted with hate and satisfaction. They had taken all of it. She had nothing. She could not make Lo well, she had nowhere to go. She could not even save herself the shame of this.

He grabbed her again as she stumbled, holding her at the shoulders. "Tell me." He bawled in her face, his audience pressing in from behind, some uncomfortable, others flushed with the chase. "She is not repentant. Shall we cut off her ears for her defiance?"

He whisked aside her veil and grabbed her right ear, the same ear the archbishop had burned with the poker in York. Pain scored her jaw and skull where the scars ended in knotted muscle.

He recoiled, disgust and surprise at her deformity showing on his face.

She stumbled free and ran.

His condemnation followed her as the village crowed roared.

"The wanton. The whore!"

CHAPTER 42:
Mission

Georgia ran all the way home to the cottage, a stitch forming along her side that stretched from her hip to her neck and pulsed. Outrage drove her the entire way running even though her shoes slipped and stones protruded along the path.

It wasn't until she reached the garden that she felt the full point of the cruelty, that she should scrabble in the dust, slashing out with her fingernails in the hopes of slowing this latest pack who chased her. Or, was it that she should lie down in the grass and let them clamp their jaws around her throat.

A queasy nausea underscored her rage. It would not be until the full measure of her task was completed that she would ever be released. Until that day, they would pursue her, and she would run. It was a coward's ledge that she stood on now—she was a coward to run and a coward to stay. What a fool she was to lower her eyes and beg a simpler life. It wasn't a choice she was free to make; her doom was chosen.

She reached the cottage and stood with her hand on the gate gasping to catch her breath, for her lungs did not expand as she needed. She wanted to scream again as she had done in the church, scream at the gate and at the garden, at the woodruff-sweet smoke that curled from the chimney where, no doubt, Mendaline had laid branches over the fire—as if the smoke could ward away the evils of the world. There was nothing left but to get the relic and be done. They could not wait for Lo to be well. She might never be well. They must go now.

The gate latch whined, a thin, tired metal wedged from one beam to the next. Georgia shoved past it through the climbing roses and across the cottage yard, avoiding even an accidental glance at the fresh turned earth of her garden.

The door was propped halfway open by Mendaline's bronze kettle. Georgia charged in, the slamming door ringing the blackened pot like the bells of requiem.

Mendaline sat at the table where the light shone over rounds of dried bark. Using a rolling stick of walnut as thick as a forearm, she crushed the bark into powder, rocking the stick back and forth under her splayed, reddened palms.

Lo lay across the pillows on the bed spinning thread onto a brightly painted bobbin, the ivory thread seeming like dusk against her translucent skin. The day was fair and the fire warm, but still Lo was bundled against the draft. The whiteness of her cheeks was frightening. Maybe it was best to go. Georgia clutched at the nausea in her gut.

Georgia caught her breath as the kettle vibrated. "We leave now—for London—pack what you will bring. Three days' worth if the weather holds."

Mendaline shuffled chips of bark and rolled a walnut pin over the top, crunching and popping them.

"We must leave at once." Georgia kicked at Mendaline's feet. "Mendaline, hear me! We make for London."

Georgia snatched the distaff from Lo, separating the thread with her fingers. The distaff hung with the last of the thread, and she scooped it around the ox-horn carving at its top and tossed it aside, snatching the bobbin next and planting it into the basket beside Lo.

"Lo. Speak. It is three days' travel only." She seemed so frail. "Can you make it?"

Mendaline poured the crushed bark into a pouch. The air filled with a peppery dust, and Georgia coughed, her eyes watering.

The healer raised an eyebrow and handed the pouch to Georgia. "While you tie that, pray, tell us, what has caused this onslaught? I hope you do not seek simply to escape the caresses of some new plowman."

A light giggle escaped Lo.

"Laugh," Georgia said, turning to dare Mendaline to do the same. It was a sore point that Mendaline could not let go. Her words were meant as a rebuke, though a sarcastic one, for she was angry that Georgia would not wear the eagle stone, that she would not take the medicines made for her, and that she would not speak of her belly.

But Mendaline did not laugh. "When did you last eat?"

Flustered as she was, Georgia resented this question as well. She had left the house without bread in the morning, and Mendaline knew it. And she did not want the egg Mendaline would foist on her.

"I hate eggs. I want none."

"Bread then. Cheese." Mendaline left the pouch and brought a nest-sized basket up from under the table. "No eggs, see? I have made a cake of barley and honey and fig. Lo has eaten some, and we have saved some here for you."

In spite of her frustration, Georgia felt rueful. It was no small thing for Mendaline to make cakes to tempt her, though perhaps Lo had been well enough today to be of some assistance. Still, it was a kindness, and Georgia tweezed a cake from the sticky pile and took a bite. She could taste egg in it.

"There you go, easy as you please." Mendaline smiled, her face furrowed and now widely gap-toothed. A worm had rotted away two more of her teeth. "A sucking's sweet."

Mendaline babied her worse then ever since the sickness, and Georgia resented it. She did not feel like a child, but like a person dried out in an oven for too long. "There is egg in it, Sister. I taste it on my tongue."

"Only enough so it should hold together."

"Twelve hens could not produce as many eggs as you would have me eat." Georgia shoved the rest of the cake in her mouth and chewed. Swallowing proved harder, and she thought to spit it back into her hand, but Mendaline flattened her smile into a stern challenge of will. Georgia swallowed, hard, squeezing her eyes closed as if it would help. The cake went down.

Mendaline offered another, but Georgia shook her head. "There are things to do. We must leave at once. There will be no more rest for us here."

Lo sat upright on the bed as the straw crackled under her. Her voice was thinner, but still clear. "Did you have a vision at the church?"

"No." Georgia smoothed Lo's skirt where it bunched together. Old and new blood stains blotted her skirt and shift and bed linen. "Do you bleed today?"

Lo shrugged. "A little. But lucky for me I like eggs." She laughed as Mendaline snorted at them.

How thin Lo's face seemed. Georgia gave her a critical stare and saw that the joints of her elbows were visible even through her sleeves. The weather rash on her cheeks did not look so red as it had once been, but now more pink, as if she were a fine lady with the color painted on, an ochre thinned with talc. But she seemed too thin, too pale to manage a journey, even to ride a cart.

Georgia looked past her through the window, the shutters tied open. There were few houses along the lane to town, but over the rise lay the church and heart of Sutton. From where the church lay, a line of bluish smoke wafted up and blew north.

The books burned, Georgia thought, and likely the spinet, too. And after the preacher had wrought that destruction, he would likely turn his zeal toward her and rile the villagers to pursue, or else lie in wait and seize her on the morrow's Mass.

"Smoke," she said.

"What of it?" Mendaline stood behind her, and Georgia sensed that she was wary.

"It means we must go." They must all go; Lo must as well, for the relic must be found. The archbishop was in London, if the oniony preacher Lionel was to be believed, and Georgia must haul an old woman and a sick one across England regardless that her back hurt and her feet as well. "Do you have the succory seed?"

"In the pouch."

"Scatter it. Mayhap it will have a chance to take root." Georgia lifted a cloak from the hook on the wall. "Pack. We have tarried."

Lo shifted on the bed. "Where are we going?"

Mendaline grabbed the cloak from Georgia and threw it down. "Such a hurry! But I'll not go. There's a fine, old cemetery under that oak in the churchyard, and by'er lady I am content to see myself consigned to it."

Georgia snatched the cloak up again and shoved it into a long necked sack. "A preacher has come and promised the fine entertainment of a bearbaiting, but seeing as there is no bear, he has decided to slice off my ears instead." Georgia took up a blanket and rolled it. "London is three days only by cart, and the relic will cure her. We must go. Lo must bear a child. I am tired of running."

Mendaline's eyebrows shot up. She looked from Georgia's stomach to Lo's pale face and threw one hand on each hip. "Dame!" An old title that erupted of late when Mendaline thought Georgia inexorably bossy, stubborn, and foolish. "None of us are fit to go to London."

"We must. We all must."

"And you in that state."

"I am in no state. I am fit. I am young, see?" Georgia grimaced so as to show all her teeth.

"I may not have teeth so fine as yours, but I have lost none of my senses. I shall not go. I have aches! They switch from place to place and swell whatever they have a mind to."

"I can go." Lo slid her feet to the floor.

Mendaline glared at her before rounding again on Georgia. "I had forgotten what an inordinate fool you are at sixteen. Why does the saint not give you sense enough when she sends you back? And now you insist that we must cart across England to sleep on frozen pallets, Saint Dymphna!"

Georgia's muscles balled and poked under her skin. "I serve not myself here," though even as she said it, she cringed at the part of it that was a lie. She ran because she would not submit, because she was afraid that she would suffer if she chose to stay and fight. But there was truth as well. "I serve the greater happiness of all who come after us, all who suffer, all women, the fire of the mountain."

"Oh, make some sense," Mendaline stood her ground. "Saint Jude, preserve us!"

"You think I wish it that I don't remember? Or wish it that I do, and so horribly? That I am driven forth? Always forth, with the drover's dog biting at my heels?"

"I see no dogs, and it's hardly past the Nativity. There won't be drovers in Sutton for another cycle. Speak sense."

Georgia reached in her pocket for her rosary before remembering that the preacher had crushed it. Her fingers slipped instead over the smooth cover of her prayer book. The woodcut of the passion seemed alive within it, and she shivered.

"I am the Bearer of the relic of Saint Isela. I must go. The doom is laid." She gathered their money, opened another sack, and stuffed into it a hooded rabbit fur cloak for Lo. "We will bring only what we can wear or carry. We make for the crossing, for Barton."

Georgia cinched the sack. She picked up Lo's shoes and knelt next to the bed, slipping the shoes onto Lo's feet. "Lo, you are the Chooser. We dare not wait until winter makes the roads a trial, and we dare not wait even longer for spring. Do you feel anything in this?"

Lo wiggled her toes in her shoes. "I am fair to walk." At her declaration, the shadows around her eased. She whispered as if her soul, already leaking from her, could not be let loose. "The relic calls me, also."

Mendaline snorted. "I'll need help to pack this mess." She made a hearty jab at a bundle of dried asparagus leaves. "I'll never see the roots of that oak, then, I can tell. What with madwomen dragging me over every speck of England." She grasped a few pouches from where they dangled from the rafters and stuffed them into the bronze pot. She stamped as she spewed orders.

"Dame Georgia, take the eggs from the fire, please you. They'll not have time to cool. And mind you, you'd best start eating the shells with the meat and no complaint or I'll toss you from whatever ramshackle cart you might drag me onto. And I don't care what sort of fuss you make. There's a child in that belly of yours or I've been delivering mumps and goiters all these years. Hoy! You missed that cloth, and those loaves there."

As Georgia deposited the last of the food into the remaining sack, Mendaline stepped toward the north window. She paused her rant and whistled. "There's the drover and his dogs after all."

Georgia hoisted the sack over her shoulder and joined Mendaline at the window. At the top to the lane strode the preacher heading a group of villagers. Children skipped around them.

Georgia grabbed Lo and pushed Mendaline. "Away! We must away. To the woods trail."

She took a last look at the house, the hearth fire still burning, still laid with woodruff, and ushered them out.

CHAPTER 43:
Saint Eugenia

THE BARN WAS SMALLER ON THE INSIDE than it had seemed, and smoky, for it sucked in the smoke from the tanning fires when the door opened and the smoke lingered. The barn stank of tallow and horse. The straw smelled damp as well, and stale. Lo collapsed on a clump of it, and Mendaline unrolled a damp cloak over her. The journey from Sutton had at first energized Lo, bringing color to her skin and a happiness for adventure. But she had weakened, perhaps due to the ceaseless rain.

It was an October unseasonably, relentlessly wet and cold. For three weeks there was nothing but rain, and all they owned was damp with it. Georgia's cloak was saturated. She pulled it off and laid it over a beam, using it to shield their corner of the barn from others' view. For they were not the only travelers to seek work and refuge.

Georgia had too little money for this rain. The carters charged four pence each day they rode, and when the roads were impassible with mud, the innkeepers took their share at a sixpence each. After four weeks, they were no farther along than Bakewel. To make matters worse, there was a pestilence in England, a sweating sickness from Lincoln south to Norwich and as far east as Worchester. No carter would take the York road south to London, but pressed the longer way east, past Shrewsbury. All the while refugees swarmed north.

In the barn were a few of these southerners, and Georgia had seen them begging in the streets. One, a man known as King Hal, had stolen a full sack of apples. King Hal had ten people who traveled with him, men and women both, plus a girl, small, twelve years old perhaps. Georgia smoothed her cloak over the beam and watched him. He held out to the girl a dish of those apples, now stewed. Before he relinquished it, he caressed his palm across her cheek and whispered to her. She took the food but cast her eyes down. He smiled to the rest. There was a charm to him, no doubt of it, but Georgia thought that made him all the more dangerous.

The other person in the barn was a young apprentice tinker smith dressed in the customary blue. The young man was from the carter train. He led a hollow-eyed, galloway nag and splintery wagon through the mud. The boy looked healthy enough, but pale skinned and gray about the eyes. His ankles looked slender for his height, and his wrists and hands were delicate as well. As he polished a few small knives, his lips drew together and thinned, as if he ailed. Georgia wondered how old he was.

Mendaline seemed to have an interest in him, as well, and watched him with that look of hers that generally preceded a diagnosis. Too many days of thin barley gruel, Georgia decided. A boy needed more than that to eat. Mendaline settled her cloak before reaching into her satchel for a cup. She crumbled a stringy black powder, dry earth, or dung perhaps, into the bottom. The smell drifted into the air. It was tangy and prune sweet.

"What sickness?" Georgia asked.

Mendaline looked up, as if questioning, and then shrugged and went back to work. "Nothing I can't ease a little." Mendaline lumbered up out of the straw and went over to the boy and the wagon. She squatted with him, and they whispered together. He seemed alarmed, but then grateful. After adding ale to the powder, he drank it down.

When Mendaline returned, she nestled into the straw and withdrew pouches of celandine and hunks of dried angelica from her satchel. They had made a little money on the road selling amulets against the sweating sickness. Lo had been Mendaline's hands, tying the pouches and handling the smaller herbs as was needed. But tonight Lo lay watching, only moving to raise or lower the blanket.

Georgia removed Lo's muddy shoes and rubbed duck oil into her feet. The sooner the rain stopped, the sooner they could resume their journey. Meanwhile, it would be best to keep to themselves. The fewer to remember them, the better.

"Sweet Sister Lo," Georgia pinched some endive from Mendaline's satchel and worked it in with the oil, "shall I tell you of the day Isela set fire to the mountain?"

Georgia began it, but before the story was finished, Mendaline was snoring, an open pouch wedged between her knees. Lo was also fast asleep.

Though she was exhausted, Georgia took out her prayer book, but she was careful to keep the book hidden in her lap. She focused on the passion, on the knives and axes, the fire and the pokers. She could feel the echoes of hurt in her chest, in the core of her arm, and her ear seemed thick and dead, but she did not withdraw her gaze from the book. Suffering was part of life. If they were to survive, if she were to do the work of Isela, she must not be afraid.

The straw behind her rustled. King Hal's young beggar girl stood there, poking a toe in the pile. She picked at the wet cloak Georgia had hung for shelter and to dry.

"Good e'en." Georgia closed the book and slid it away.

The girl gave a polite curtsey. Her dress was of a decent cloth, though simple in design and now dirty. She seemed timid, as if afraid she would be turned away.

"Pray you, peace. I had not heard that story before."

"It is a story from the north," Georgia said.

Mendaline snorted into wakefulness, resuming her work as though there had been no pause in it.

"I am headed north," the girl said, her eyes brightening. "I am going to find my father." She knelt and, lowering her gaze again, twisted her fingers in the straw. Her gaze flicked where the corner of the prayer book protruded from under Georgia's skirt. "My father is a priest. He is called Father Thomas Moubray. Do you know of him?"

Georgia shook her head. What did the child want? Had King Hal sent her to rob them?

King Hal called from across the barn. "Ya, Brigitte!"

The girl flicked her eyes toward him and then back to Georgia. She smiled shyly and, after watching Mendaline for a breath or two, scooted up next to her.

"Can I tie the pouches for you, Mother?" she asked.

Using her hands like platters, Mendaline scooped up a set of pouches and plunked them into the girl's lap. "Indeed I would be glad of it." Mendaline resumed her work. "And how long've you been traveling?"

"A week."

"Your father's in the north, then?"

"So my mother said."

"And your mother?"

The girl blinked. "She is dead of the sweat."

"Have you no godparents?"

The girl shrugged. Her eyes flicked to King Hal again. "There are robbers on the road."

"Yes." Georgia slid her book under a blanket and kept her good ear trained toward the beggars. King Hal hoisted to his feet; she had expected that. No doubt he came to play the last part of this trick. But he stayed outside the dividing wall. He stopped short and then peed.

Georgia watched the urine foam and curl into the straw. She looked at the girl. Brigitte was focused on her work, her face pale. She tied the pouches with a timid resolution.

Georgia exchanged a look with Mendaline. There was more here than a simple trick, Georgia thought. Though it was trouble just the same.

"You may stay the night with us if you like, Brigitte—" Georgia spoke clear and loudly so the man would hear her, though her voice was unsteady. She imagined him striking her with his fists. "But you should know we are headed south."

"Oh." The girl sounded disappointed. She tied off another pouch and then smiled again. "I am from the south. From Everton on the Idle."

"Well, Brigitte of Everton, good to know you." Mendaline pushed another pouch in her direction.

King Hal fumbled back to his group. He threw himself down between two of the women and kissed them both. They laughed and clapped their hands.

☙

The next day, the next week, was the same, except eventually the rain stopped. Though the clouds lingered, the rainwater seeped under the mud, and the roads dried. With the weather changed, finally there would be work. Lo picked worms from soggy fruit, washed them, then plunked them whole into barrels of verjuice. Mendaline found a place in the kitchen. Her work there earned her a bit of ass's milk to add to Lo's washbrew fare.

But Lo ate little. And she worsened. Her body swelled below the waist, her belly bloating. Passing water became more difficult for her. Lo had to lean into Georgia and almost fully left before her urine would flow. Mendaline was convinced Lo suffered a resurgence of the putrefaction that had made her barren. She made her scrawl a prayer to Saint Anne on a slip of paper and watched as Lo sewed it to her shift.

Georgia worked as hard as any, though she made a penny less a day. She wanted to wield a scythe, but instead was made to crawl through the mud and pluck up beets and sunken pears.

Brigitte worked also in the mud, talking endlessly of her father.

"You may not find him," Georgia said. "There was much bitterness in the north."

"I have heard that there are priests who fled to France." The girl plucked a pear from the muck. "And monks, too."

Georgia thought of France, but her memories of late were crowded with the child and the dogs. "We go south," Georgia said.

"Brigitte!"

The girl shot an apprehensive look over her shoulder as King Hal slogged through the mud, grabbed her at the ankles, and dragged her backward. Her skirt lifted past the knee, and he insisted on a kiss before he released her. When she scrabbled away, a beggar women admonished her.

"Hal's just after a bit of fun, is all. Though you be too young to know it."

Another of the women pointed to Georgia's belly, laughing. "That one knows it well enough!"

*

After the next day's work, they were paid. Georgia counted out their purse, fifty-four silver pennies. That was forty-two in wages and another twelve pennies earned from the sale of amulets. It would be close, but they would have enough to get as far as Shrewsbury.

The next morning the sun broke through. Mendaline took a pouch of medicine to the boy apprentice as he stowed blackened tongs among the barrels in the wagon. Mendaline had done well for him. His skin looked better, and the dark lines that ringed his eyes had fleshed to pink.

Brigitte hovered nearby, plucking at Mendaline's sleeves. "You are moving off? Let me come with you."

"We go south, not north."

"But then to France?" She sounded hopeful.

Mendaline looked surprised. "Well, that's the first I've heard of France. We're not to be English anymore, then?"

"I have no plans for France." Georgia rolled the blankets and tied them.

Lo looked feverish, but when Georgia placed her hand at her neck, Lo brushed her hand away. "It's nothing. The day is warm."

"I can tie pouches," Brigitte said brightly.

From across the barn, King Hal stretched and splashed water on his face. He strode over and stood with his feet apart as if he were going to pee again—this time on their blankets.

"Brigitte stays here, with us," he said. "We're her family. Aren't we, girl?"

"I'd rather stay with Sister Georgia," she said. She added the "Sister" in an imitation of Mendaline, but Georgia cringed to hear it. She cringed all the more as King Hal looked at her belly and threw back his head to laugh.

"Sweet Brigitte," he winked at her. "You do not think to wander off with the likes of them? Without paying your debt to me?"

"For what does she owe you?" Georgia stood up. Here was another Romsfeld, though this one grew up hard and had known true hunger. She squared her feet on the straw, imitating his stance. The sounds of the child and the dogs raged from memory. She covered her ears, but the feel of the scar on her ear made her draw her hands away. Let this pony "King" strike her, then, she thought. It could not be worse than what SeVerde had done. "Go and piss on someone else. Leave us be."

Had he seen her fear? His cracked lips spread open to show teeth splayed in front. "She must pay me for her keep."

"She worked right enough, and now her pay is in your purse. Her debt is paid."

King Hal poked out his lower lip and sunk a wet, slimy tooth into it. "She belongs to me," he said.

The rest of his band began to gather. Several men, and the women were just as frightening. They backed him. Georgia thought there was little to stop them from doing as they liked.

"What do you care about her?" King Hal said. "Did she tell you she's a bastard? That her father's a traitor?"

"And you're a whoreson," Georgia said. "It's nothing to me."

"Brigitte is mine." He smiled, tucking his lip back in, though a line of saliva stayed across his mouth. "Come on back to old King Hal now, Brigitte. To your proper father, now." He opened his arms as if to welcome her. "We don't want trouble, here. Do we?"

Brigitte made a choking noise and burst out crying.

Hal took a step forward, but Georgia threw her balance to the balls of her feet and crossed her arms over her chest. She would not surrender Brigitte to such a man. "Brigitte is with us."

King Hal raised his fist, and Georgia countered by scooping up Mendaline's prized bronze cauldron and holding it up. "Strike me, and I will strike you back."

"Hoy!" Mendaline pushed a roll of bedding into Brigitte's arms and snatched the pot away. She waved it at Georgia then at the beggar band. "Enough! Name your price for her."

King Hal's lip curled, but then he grinned. "She's worth more to me than money. Maybe I'll sell her later."

Mendaline gave the pot to Brigitte and instructed her to pack it. "I've had enough of this fuss. She'll stay with us, and you can profit from that or not, as you will."

The beggar pack murmured, and King Hal spat at Georgia's feet. "I'll take an angel for her."

Georgia balked; an angel was ten shillings and far more than they had.

"One shilling," Mendaline countered.

King Hal glared. "Ten."

"Two."

"I am not a fool."

"Five then," Mendaline said.

"Five!" He waved his arms as if insulted.

"Five. A gold crown for a king, Sir Hal," Mendaline said.

"Sister Mendaline!" They only had the value of six shillings all together. To pay so much would set them back a full week.

Mendaline harrumphed. "A gold crown, and an amulet to ward off the sweat." Mendaline looped a medicine pouch over her finger and held it up. "Or," she pursed her lips and crossed herself. "Mayhap you'd rather take your chances with dishonoring this child, displeasing God, and bringing the plague upon you all together!"

King Hal scratched his chin. He eyed Brigitte and showed her his teeth, snapping them. He took the amulet. "She eats too much at any rate. Good riddance to her."

The beggar band nudged each other and guffawed, but turned away. No doubt, Georgia thought, to the alehouse down the road to spend *her* five shillings.

Brigitte hugged Mendaline but was contrite as she approached Georgia. "I'm sorry, Sister."

"You are not to blame. It is better done." Georgia looked around at the stale straw of the barn. "Unpack." Georgia felt the hollowness to say it. They had only seven pennies left. "We must work another week. We cannot go today."

From the corner, the apprentice cleared his throat. He spoke, careful to pull his cap low over his face. "You can travel with me if you wish, though only one can ride."

"You're going south?"

The boy nodded. "To London."

"But, we cannot pay you. We are too light." Georgia rattled her purse to show that it was almost empty. She felt like crying.

The apprentice shrugged. "At your pleasure. Though I can spare you cartage." He stroked the mare's nose and reached for the rope to guide her out of the barn. "Stow your sacks in the wagon, or stay, as you choose."

CHAPTER 44:
Signs

The trip to London took three more weeks and well into November. They lost six wheels to the road, three of them in a single day; the third time the damage marooned them between Pembridge and Webley. The repair took a full week.

Food, at least, was plentiful. The drovers wove their herds in and out along the road, and a goose could be bought for a fair price. Gil, as the apprentice was called, butchered them, throwing back his blue cape and drawing a well-sharpened bill from his coveted box where the shiniest of knives were well cradled in straw. He killed the animals quickly and skinned them easily. He refused to pluck the geese, instead throwing away their skins whole and all in a heap.

Mendaline clucked at the waste and groused about her hands. She instructed Brigitte to pull the feathers out one by one and collect them in a sack, and then throw the skin onto the fire to roast. It would make a fine display as the fat seeped into the fire, sizzling and sparking. Brigitte ate heartily, lingering by the spit to pick the bones clean of meat. Georgia understood a little more why King Hal had complained, for the girl ate easily twice the food of any other member of the party.

At night, Gil slept with the wagon and the nag while the women curled together under a lean-to or in a yeoman's barn. Georgia would tell the stories she knew from her dreams, of Isela and of the mountain, the pilgrims, and the well. She talked of the lost and crumbled priory, of Gotesind, of Sister

Agnes and her cell, and of the lifetimes she could remember—even the hard ones. Somehow, to speak of them made them easier.

She did not speak of the hope for fulfillment or of Lo's birth. To do so mocked their hope. Nor did Lo dispute details or harrumph as Mendaline did, but dozed under a fever that either heated her skin to ochre or left it as stale snow. When she peed now, it took Georgia and Mendaline both to support her. It was viscous, and it stank.

They came to London on Saint Margaret's day. Margaret had been blessed with six daughters, and Georgia celebrated the perfection of such an omen until Mendaline reminded her that Saint Margaret died of treachery. Yet treachery or no, they had arrived. As had countless others, for the crowd swarmed far and wide outside the city gates. Huts and lanes and dogs and goats and refuse crammed acre upon acre, all churned to mud and waste. Happy kestrels by the thousands were as a swarming cloud, darting in between what lived to eat what gave up living long ago.

Gil led them, pushing east to Leegate, a gate into the city that seemed as two hulking towers squatting over an arched tunnel. A steady stream of goods and men poured through under the watch of armed constables, a dozen, maybe more. It was they who determined who would be allowed to pass into the city.

Beggars were turned away and received a pike jab in the legs or back as well. Georgia picked at the mud and grease stains on her apron. Only Lo looked clean and respectable, for her gown, as well as being subjected to frequent washings, was of fustian cloth and had been protected from the rain and weather under layers of blankets.

Lo caught Georgia's eye and smiled. She sat up in the straw of the wagon, her eyes glittery with fever but alert, excited, euphoric, even.

"I feel it," Lo breathed. She squeezed Georgia's hand. "I feel it now as I have not before. You feel it, too? A thunderous ring."

Georgia shifted on the balls of her feet, suddenly hot and uncomfortable. "The relic?" She hardly dare say it for the disappointment if it were not true.

Lo's smile broadened. "We are in London, then?"

"At the gate."

"What's this?" Mendaline put a platter-sized hand onto Lo's forehead, first the palm, then turning the hand over to press the back of it against her neck.

Georgia tried to center her feelings, but everything raced across her mind at once. The constables at the gate, the mass of humanity, the stench of London, her tired feet—alive with elfshot, now, and twitching.

"No. I feel nothing." Her voice quavered; she was not sure what she felt, perhaps fear.

"She fevers." Mendaline sounded disappointed. "A dream."

Lo stayed smiling. "We are close." She sounded firm, assured, her eyes bright.

Brigitte pressed between them. Georgia twitched foot to foot, and Mendaline returned her hands to her apron to hide their deformity from the pushing crowd.

Brigitte asked, "Is it death she feels?"

Georgia thought to slap her, for whether or not Lo was dying, it was a subject unspeakable. Yet, though she should not have said it out loud, Brigitte had said no more than the truth. Lo was dying. Mendaline could not cure her or even slow the illness. Each day she worsened.

Mendaline clucked as Lo settled back into the wagon. "She shit her own water coming out, which is trouble in a birth. And she ate three clumps of wolfsbane like a great fool and should have had to explain to Saint Peter then what she had done." Mendaline winked at Georgia and eyed the gate. "She's a death cheater, this one. If she says the relic's there, I'll say she's set to cheat again."

Georgia smoothed her clothes and wished they had washed before trying the gate. She fussed at Brigitte. "Stand tall," she said, "for we are not beggars but have business in London. Chin up, Sisters. Gil, walk first with the nag. They will let you pass. We will follow."

The first constable waved them through the throng, but there were other constables to pass before the arch. Another, busy with a woman, waved them through. Only two wagon lengths from the entrance and Georgia could see the murder holes in the roof. She quickened her pace.

"Hold."

A squat constable waved a pike, and another stood next to him. They barred the way. A dyer and a cordwainer, Georgia guessed the men to be by profession, for one had fingernails of summer borage, and fibrous scars climbed across the knuckles and wrists of the other. Both had bushy beards and caps pulled low onto the center of their foreheads. Tradesmen and craftsmen took turns acting as constables in the city. These two, she wished, had not been called today.

Gil bowed. Georgia curtsied behind him, as prettily as she could, with Mendaline and Brigitte behind her, piling up like eager laborers to dinner, Georgia thought.

"Good sirs."

"State your business."

Gil adjusted his cap and kept his eyes down. "My master bid me come to London to learn pewtering." Gil lowered his voice and added a slight rasp. No doubt to sound older for he had not yet grown a man's beard.

"Who is your master, boy?"

"Gilbert of Netheringham."

"Is he known in the city?"

Gil nodded. "I am sent by his order."

The constable stared at Georgia, and she felt conspicuous, accused. "And these who travel with you?"

Gil looked over his shoulder. They had not planned in advance what they would say. They had not expected armed constables at the gates.

"Servants of my master's. Also sent to London. There is no harm in them."

The squat constable set his pike into the path. "That may be as I determine, bluecoat. London must be kept safe from the sweat. And quarrelsome beggars are to be hung, by order of the king." He pointed to the corbels that overhung the road. Two bodies swung from them, and a third rolled gently back and forth in a black iron cage. This third man was King Hal. Georgia kept her expression carefully still, but beside her, Brigitte gasped.

"King Hal! Sister Georgia, look—"

Georgia elbowed her. "Hush."

The constable trained a suspicious look on Brigitte. "You know him?"

Georgia curtseyed again. They must get past into the city. If Lo was right, the relic lay within. She struggled to control an impulse to fling herself past them and escape under the archway.

"He stole four shillings from us, good Constable. Forty-six silver pennies." It was, at least, the truth. And a robbery would help explain their ragged looks. "I would wish to have my pennies back, sir. As would my sister."

The second constable laughed, and the first then stepped back to let them on their way.

"You may pass. Make no trouble within." But as he lifted the pike, he caught sight of Lo in the wagon. Her flush had receded into white; she looked like a corpse.

"Stop!" He covered his mouth with a handkerchief from his belt.

"A minor sickness," Mendaline said, though the words seemed laughable when compared to Lo's complexion. "A few days rest, and she will be merry again."

"She cannot be brought into the city."

"She has not the sweat, good Constable. A simple ailment, a flux that has tired her."

The cordwainer brought out a chunk of stone the color of fresh cut ginger and placed it on Lo's hand before snatching the stone away.

"It pales." Both men took a step back and raised their weapons toward the wagon. "You shall not pass, by order of the Lord Mayor of London."

"Saint Mary!" Mendaline forgot to hide her hands and slapped them together. Her deformity did not help them.

Georgia felt a panic in the center of her chest. The relic lay in London. They stood just outside the gates.

"Good yeomen, have a care! We have traveled across England. We have business with His Grace, the archbishop of York, which is most urgent. He will not abide delay."

The men did not move from their stance. "His Grace is not in the city."

"Not?" Georgia pushed ahead past Mendaline, past Gil. She heard the horse whinny behind her and felt Brigitte by her side. She wished fervently the girl would step back and let her speak. She pushed her back. "I have heard he is in London."

"He keeps a house in Barking. Look there if you seek him."

"I seek him here."

The squat dyer snickered. "You won't find a yard of pizzle here, so push on."

She took a step toward them. Fools.

The men bristled. The dyer pointed the pike at her. "Draggle tail. Turn away or hang."

She clenched her fists and bit down. Isela best let her pass, she thought, or she would spend the next life, and the next, curled up against a boulder and refuse to budge.

"Do not refuse me."

"Another step will hang you." The squat one yelled back.

"I am on a holy errand!"

Neither man moved, but a third and fourth came up, the fourth smiling. Behind her Gil turned and backed away. Georgia felt Mendaline's hand on her shoulder.

Georgia thought again of the child and the dogs. She could hear the child screaming. She put her hand to her ear, to the burning there. She wanted to hold back the noise. The fool child, she thought, that she had cried for so many nights.

Mendaline lowered her voice to a whisper. "I cannot endure another prison. And Lo cannot. And what of Brigitte? They will harm her."

The screaming of the child faded. Georgia took a step backward. She cried, letting her tears fall. What did she care?

Gil led the retreat north, through the huts and lanes, back to grass and hills and into a sweeping cell of rain. Once past the city, Georgia threw herself down into the weeds. She could still smell the city in her nostrils. Curse Lo for her sickness. Curse Mendaline and Brigitte and Gil. Gil. She had allowed it, a boy, a man, to travel with them. He must be sent away.

She tried to curl her body but could not for her belly was too large. That, too, was something that could not be. Every step seemed harder than the one before. Isela asked too much.

She wiped her nose on her sleeve, greasy with goose fat and interlarded with mud and grime. She had not even had a bath or a change of clothes for months.

She closed her eyes and sought the relic, sought the river to open up and wash her away. There was no river. But she felt warmth, a warm breeze. It picked up around her, and a woman's laugh rang in it. The air filled all at once with rose petals. A woman strode up and sat down next to her. Georgia's heart rushed open. The mark on her palm tingled. More than anything, she wanted to put her head into Isela's lap and weep.

The vision faded, and she opened her eyes to the cold wind. She honed the feeling of warmth, digging it up out of her toes, through the cavity of her chest, and filling her ribs with it. And she found it. The relic. It was so; the relic was close. Close, yes. But not in London.

"What is east?" Georgia asked.

Brigitte and Mendaline both looked the direction of the sunrise, but Gil spoke. "Barking."

Georgia shivered. Lo was the Chooser, if for no other reason than that Georgia's own choices had long since fallen away. Georgia stood. "We go to Barking," she said.

CHAPTER 45:
Sepulchre

She knew where to go; the pull of the relic led her, one step after another to the grounds of Markham Manor. She went alone, without a bath, though she cleaned her face. Mendaline fretted, cajoled, and eventually threw up her hands, wishing her "Godspeed, then, that or a good kick, though I can't imagine that'd do much good with your head stuck in irons."

Georgia wondered if she was always driven against good sense. Perhaps she should learn deliberation over haste. But not today. Today it burned, the desperation, the desire that it must be done before it was too late, before the feet of the enemy closed in on her and stamped her out.

Markham Manor lay on the grounds of the old Barking Abbey at the end of a string of manor homes. Of the manors, Markham was by far the grandest. Its size gave her strength. Such a large manor would teem with servants. Likely she could slip in and out without drawing attention. And her task was a simple one. She must find the relic.

All the better, the day was sunny. That meant work. Georgia crouched by the hedgerow and watched as servants swarmed over the yard and grounds. Grooms of the stable brushed glossy palfreys and sent them cantering to pasture. Maids aired chicken cotes while matrons soaped, beat, and hung yards of linens. A group of dusty village folk rolled several wagons of dried herbs and strewing reeds up the lane and into the yard. Chattering housemaids clutched the crackling bundles against their aprons, all alike in whey, the color of well-scrubbed rouen's eggs, and disappeared into the house. The villagers scraped the old strewings from the floors and dumped them into waste wagons, picking agitated insects from their shirts.

Georgia kept her head down and slipped down the lane next to a trundling wagon. As she walked nearer to the house, she dared a peek at the windows. Behind one of them lay the relic, though she could not tell which. As she stared, it seemed the windows gaped back at her, multiple panes of glass, blank except for one. A shiver caught her spine. From the third window, something malevolent seemed to glint. The wagon stopped at the entrance as prickles cascaded along her back. This was the archbishop's house, and his viciousness hung over it. This place was food for kestrels.

"Girl!"

A maidservant in a whey apron chided her as she thrust a load of dirtied rushes into Georgia's arms. Georgia deposited them in the waste wagon and then took up a bundle of fresh reeds, hiding behind it as best she could, and followed the maidservant back into the house.

Once inside, she lagged behind, backing into the darkened corners of the hall, and farther back still where the wall opened to a dark nook. Mold wafted up from a spiral stair, slimy in the nostrils, a smell from the cracks of age-softened cider barrels. She could smell cinnamon and juniper and ale. Below her was the buttery. The kitchen must be nearby. There would be servants there.

She closed her eyes. She was so close now to the relic that she fell into prayer easily, the ground opening under her feet and the river pulling. Anger rose as the pain of separation was so acutely satisfied. She wanted to hold the warmth hard inside her where it could not do its own bidding but would instead keep her safe. And then she was afraid. She could see the archbishop as he picked up the poker and struck her with it. He struck again and again and again. She screamed.

Yet the scream stayed in her memory. She came back to the world on the buttery step, her mouth open but her throat tight, dry, and utterly mute. Prayer had not brought consolation. It had brought some other benefit, however. She could feel the relic like a beacon. It was above her, above and to the left.

She tightened her grip on the bundle and pressed against the walls of the great hall, skirting the kitchen with its clattering. At the end corner was a stairway painted smalted blue and trimmed in yolky yellow and vermilion green. She moved faster, but a door swung open in front of her.

"Ouf!"

The blow snapped the reeds in her bundle, and a woman, a laundress by her rolled sleeves and high-piled headscarf, rounded the door with a basket of greasy linen. Georgia collided again with the rim of the basket.

"Watch it!" The woman said.

Surprise elongated the woman's face and then a hint of doubt shortened it. Georgia bobbed a curtsey and cast her eyes down. "Fresh reeds, please you," she said.

Georgia kept down as the laundress trod past. She hurried to the dark of the stairwell, threw down the bundle, and took the stairs two at a time.

The stairway was cut in a corner recess and spiraled up to a second-story hall above. Though taller, the upper-level hall was smaller across, the extra space taken by a row of privy chambers, most with open doors streaming sunlight. She bore immediately left again, poking into the third chamber.

This chamber opened to two rooms, the first an office with a massive desk stacked with chests, books, papers, a vase of quills, and an open box of powder. The relic lay in the room beyond, a room that despite a wide window seemed darker than the first. This was due, perhaps, to a massive bed near the door, stained dark and overhung with velvet canopies cascading to the floor.

She gave the bed a wide berth, creeping to the window side and avoiding an imposing hulk as tall as she that stood in the center of the room, draped also in velvet, a looming thing that gave her a shiver as she passed it by. She looked over her shoulder for fear of being watched.

Beyond the bed, the sun shone unimpeded, illuminating a sideboard of glittering glass and glinting yellow and white metals. A hoard, the plunder of visitations across England, stood on the polished walnut shelves. Two gold chalices and a silver bowl of saints bones stood at the center; there was a tiny gold sepulchre, finely wrought, and a rood reliquary studded with jewels. There were coarser things, too. A broken stick, a finger bone, all colors of glass bottles, some lustrous, others age scarred, with stoppers of wood or twigs or bronze or gold. Five skulls were stacked neatly on a length of red velvet, several of them gilded, one so ornately that the bone shined gossamer as silk.

By contrast Isela's relic seemed plain, so plain that at first she missed it. She found it by sense, as a prayer reaching out. She took it up with the lightest touch of her fingertips, remembering the dark night among the ruined stones of the priory. As she clasped the relic to her breast, she heard Agnes's parting scream. She put the chain round her neck.

"Thief!" A shout from the hall.

Georgia spun to see a woman, likely the housekeeper, liveried like the rest yet well dressed besides, standing full center in the doorway, the laundress behind her.

"That's her, mistress."

Georgia shoved the relic into the bodice of her kyrtle and backed up slowly. Two menservants appeared—a farrier, one looked to be—and each with a cudgel raised and ready.

"Craving your pardon," she curtseyed, trying to think of what to do. "A misstep. I had the reeds, but got lost."

Her feet twitched under her. The archbishop would know her. He would beat her. The memory of York was too close.

"Catch her." The mistress blocked the doorway. "And in His Grace's privy chamber! A shame this day."

Two more men appeared at the door.

Georgia backed up again, but the window was shut tight, and she could not jump regardless. The door was blocked, and another door was too far to the right. She tried for it anyway, darting around the farrier. She saw the narrow stair behind her too late, for the men rushed her. They grabbed her hair and arm and held her backward; her bones twisted so she thought her spine would break.

"No!"

The mistress slapped her, and then she took the relic. Georgia struggled, but the mistress dragged it roughly back before searching for any other item that might be stolen.

"It's mine." Georgia twisted, and tears of frustration wet her face and slid down to her neck. "It was stolen from me."

"Stolen from *you*? Why you lying, little thief!"

"But the archbishop ..." Georgia felt her terror rise as her tears increased. She could not breathe from the onslaught of crying. Any footstep could bring him in.

"His Grace is at court," the mistress said, her eyes puffed and narrowed. "That's lucky for you, thief, or he'd have you turned into the pig cote to let the pigs eat you."

The mistress lied. He was there, somewhere, in the house. She could feel him all around her, the fear of him.

The mistress shook the relic in her face. "And His Grace a fine man, a man of charity. To be stealing from such a man as him. He would have fed you, though if that's a bastard you carry—" She poked Georgia's belly, hard. "Take her to the sheriff." She returned the relic to the sideboard and turned back. "Belly or no, I pray God they hang you."

CHAPTER 46:
Saint Agrippina

THE GAOLER'S ROD WAS ALREADY BLOODIED WHEN he brought the first stroke across her back. The blood belonged to the woman next to her, and before that a man with one leg twisted. Next in turn for the whip was a boy barely breeched, and although he had yet to feel it, he wailed louder than anyone she had ever heard. If he would not have grown up to be a man, Georgia would have pitied him.

All of them walked, stripped to the waist, with their hands tied above them to a cart beam. A mule pulled them along, so that if they did not keep up, they were dragged along the road. The man with the twisted leg fell frequently, jarring the beam into her shoulder sockets and earning a string of curses from the woman next to him. Those in town who gathered to watch threw garbage aimed most particularly at him.

Mendaline and Gil circled the crowd, though it was difficult for Georgia to keep track of them. Gil carried a blanket, and when the gaoler released them into the road, Gil was right behind. He placed the blanket around Georgia's shoulders, careful of her hurt. Georgia kept the blanket but shrugged the boy away.

"Stand off," she said. She did not want any man to touch her ever again. He looked quickly down and away, and stepped aside.

Mendaline clucked her tongue. "I don't like this thing you have become."

"Then go home," Georgia replied. She felt the unkindness of it, for there was no home either of them could return to. And for that, it was her own failure. "We will go to France."

"France? It is decided?"

"In France we will be nuns again." She thought of the priory, the orchard, and the garden, a chucking laugh from the kitchen. "Do you remember Sister Thomasine? How she scolded?"

"A grand nun."

"And I miss it. I miss the hours. In France, the bells still ring."

"And now you know so much?"

"There was a woman in the gaol. She spoke of this."

"A nun?"

"A whore. She laid with sailors."

Mendaline cocked an eyebrow. "Lo will not survive such a journey."

A stitch in her side made Georgia stop to catch her breath. Her swelling stomach rolled from one side to another.

"Does it pain you?" Mendaline reached to touch her, but she pulled away.

"No." She didn't say that her hips ached deep inside them, or that the pressure pinched and throbbed. Instead, she resumed walking, drawing the blanket tightly around her though it felt like salt against her back.

"You do yourself no good, nor the babe by this, to refuse my help. To refuse even the eagle stone."

Georgia shut out the words. What baby? She carried nothing. A tumor. A tumor, and in every way a mark of her failure. "When I have the relic, all will be made right."

"Made right?" Mendaline looked skeptical. "A belly full of child? What? Will it flatten all at once? Poof! Like a sailor's purse?"

"The relic is the answer. I will return tonight to Barking. I will take it, and I will use it how I will."

☙

Yet she could not leave that night. Filthy and covered in vermin, with her back split open from the rod, Mendaline insisted that she wash and submit to heal for a day at least. It was three days before she could go, yet she made use of the time in arranging for their escape to France.

There was a shipping berth at Wulwich on the southside of the Thames near Barking. Many larger ships docked there, avoiding the bend in the river. It was also a crossing point, and wherrymen, though fewer than in London, ferried folk across the river for a fee. Most passengers crossed from north to south, and of those, the richest veered to Greenwich, King Edward's favorite

London palace and where he currently held court, though it was rumored he was ailing.

Georgia planned that they cross the Thames there, taking what supplies they needed for the journey to France: boiled eggs, salted meat and fish, radishes, bread, and beer. But first, she would seize the relic. Once the relic was reclaimed, they would stay in England only long enough to see Lo well enough to travel. It would take only a few days, Georgia thought, for Lo to be made well.

Above the crossing point lay a small village abandoned since Henry VIII was newly king. The plague that struck then killed every soul in the village, earning the spot a reputation as cursed. The lanes had gone to weeds, there, and a few straw bundles still hung from shutterless windows warning all trespassers away. It was said that in the houses, peasants' bones mingled with rotted thatch.

They made it up among the weedy lanes, and Mendaline declared the houses cheerless and the hill to be avoided by anyone sensible. Nonetheless, she chose a cottage for shelter and instructed Gil to shore up the hearth with stones so she could set her favorite pot to warm cider on the fire. Georgia swept the floor with a handful of brush. Then, she and Brigitte stuffed linen with straw and laid Lo to sleep on it.

Lo would no longer eat, not even so much beer as Mendaline might mix with sugar and herbs. The liquid dribbled out of her mouth, even a spoonful at a time. Mendaline laid herbs and sheep's dung over embers and placed a pan to smolder near where Lo lay. She set Brigitte to waft the smoke, instructing, "Be sure Lo takes it up into her lungs."

Yet Lo seemed scarcely to breathe.

"Perhaps it is best to fetch that relic today after all, Sister Georgia, if you're well enough," Mendaline said. "If it can heal Lo." She rested a flat palm on Georgia's shoulder.

To Georgia, Mendaline's hand felt heavy, a weight as if to buckle her.

"Godspeed," Mendaline fumbled a pat. "I could not stand to lose you both."

A crack of thunder outside preceded a storm of hail that quickly changed to a heavy rain. Water dripped through the roof in places, but otherwise the thatch held.

Gil crouched in the corner and polished knives. Georgia did not look at him. Whatever Mendaline's sympathies were, thought Georgia, she would make sure that he did not follow them to France.

Brigitte lit candles, and she and Mendaline took up a vigil at Lo's bed, a unison of prayer said along the knots of a white corded rope. The words echoed into Georgia's chest: "So be it. So be it. So be it."

She had tarried. Taking up her cloak, Georgia ducked out of the hut and broke into a labored run. It would be dark before the sisters' first round of prayers would be sung and finished, and she wished to be in Barking before then.

☙

Georgia ran toward the river as best she could. She was fit, though her balance was an increasing challenge. A great gale swept up and soaked her utterly; her dress hung like a sponge, slapping against her legs. The wet wool was warm, but dragged her downward, and her knees popped and sometimes snapped. Her ankles felt stretched and bloated, and the joints would not bend properly.

As she came upon the manor, she slipped into the woods, shunning the road for fear of being seen. She discarded her white apron and headdress as she crouched behind a willow. She left her cloak, also. She would retrieve them after.

She stayed back from the house until the light behind the shutters had gone out. Only a few lamps burned in a house through the night, one in the hall and one for the latrine. Only when the smallest flicker in the windows remained did she creep out to the property.

As she passed under a cascading walnut, the deluge redoubled its efforts. She twisted her heavy overskirt to try to wring the water from it, but it only grew misshapen and then it would not smooth back to shape. Without her headscarf, her hair flattened over her eyes, and her nose ran. Without her apron to wipe it, she used her sleeve instead, then sneezed.

She needed a way in. There would be an outside entrance for the buttery, so the vintners and brewers could roll their barrels down into the cellar. She ran her hands over the brick, and in a breath or two, found a door, the wood slimy with rain. It was locked.

Near the door was a square window shuttered closed. The shutter lock at the center was weak and under pressure creaked and came open, with the smell of apples and juniper wafting up from inside. From the window, Georgia could reach the door inside, and from there, the latch.

She entered carefully, turning in a slow circle. Her burned ear was almost useless. She trained her left ear into the darkness. Above her she could feel the relic like a warm lamp, but she could hear no sound save her own breathing and the water dripping from her skirt.

She found the steps easily and took them up to the kitchen, opening the door just wide enough for a girl to slip inside. She did not fit. She had to open the door wider to fit her belly. She clenched her jaw and frowned to widen it as she passed through.

A dull, high pitch rang in her injured ear, causing her to strain to hear the noises of the house. All seemed well. From the hall came the crunch of straw trundles and the snores of servants fast asleep.

Yet even in the night, she did not dare go through the kitchen as the staff would be asleep on the kitchen floor. She chose the hall. But as she took a step, a chamber pot clattered nearby. She almost split her skin at the sudden noise, and her fright deafened her. She could hear nothing, now, but her own blood pounding and the now shrill ringing in her head. Then it was quiet again except for the noises of the storm. Yet someone in the lower hall was awake.

She took stock of where she was. She must get to the stair, to the door she remembered, where she had collided with the laundress. But she must avoid the hall, now, and whoever wandered there. That meant she must pass through the kitchen after all.

Georgia called to Saint Agrippina for strength, for she had held out even during torture. She called to Saint Lucy, too, so she could see better in the dark. And then Georgia stepped out into the kitchen. Soggy but silent, she picked her way slowly between the tables and the sleepers to the foot of the stair. She stopped when one of the maids turned in her sleep. A disgruntled neighbor cursed quietly and shoved the first firmly back with the flat of her foot.

Georgia waited for them to settle and then resumed her slow movements. But with her next step, she almost fell on the floor, for it was now wet and slippery where she had stood with her skirt dripping. She caught her balance on the wrought iron banister, but not without wrenching her back and ribs where she had been injured in York.

Fear accompanied the memory, and she dared not move. Saint Agrippina, after all, had died. She would have to climb the stairs carefully, for her dress still dripped rainwater, and there were no rushes strewn on the stairs to soak the water up.

Slowly, she made her way to the stairway at the end of the hall, glad of the storm outside that rattled the roof and windows and covered the slight creaking in the boards.

Fewer servants slept in the upper hall than the lower, and she was glad of that, too, as she inched along in silence. As she neared the third door, her nose prickled and began to drip. She rubbed it against her sleeve as her eyes watered. A shiver rolled down her back. She had to sneeze. She buried her face in her skirts to muffle the sound. While the sneeze subsided, her racing heart did not. She waited through three Hail Marys and an Our Father for it to quiet.

No candle burned in the third room. As she crossed the threshold, she felt a stab of horror that this was the archbishop's bedchamber. He was away, so the mistress had said, in Greenwich, at court, but even so the room felt full of threat. She thought of Saint Agrippina again, but rejected her. Agrippina had been tortured—she feared that above all other things. She would think of Saint Dymphna, instead, for she had run. Although, of course, Saint Dymphna also had died.

Georgia paused at the threshold. Her courage waned. Yet she needed the relic! How dare he have stolen it from her and destroyed everthing. She anchored herself with rage. Let them try to stop her fury; it would never stop, it never did. *"Saints be with me and demons flee,"* she whispered. And she stepped into the room.

There was no candle though the fire was lit and burned low, giving just enough light to make shadows. The large pane windows rattled with the storm, louder in this room than it had been in the kitchen or in the hall. Yet the room was not cold, and the drapes over the bed hung without even a stirring draft as she passed them.

The relic was exactly where it had been before; she could feel it, so close it made her dizzy. She fought the urge to grasp it and run, for her eagerness had caused her trouble before. No. She must now be deliberate, for she must get back to Lo.

She lifted the chain slowly, gathering the silver a little at a time to muffle it as she pulled the amber orb ever closer. And she had it! Its touch warmed her. The ringing in her ear changed its note, calling now joyful and sweet. She shook her head against the trance, her hair flinging rain droplets in all directions. She must stay alert. She must still get out. She must not make a mistake. She slipped the chain over her head and pushed the relic down between her bodice and her shift.

The desire to flee, now, was overwhelming. She stilled the urge; she must move with the same caution as before. But even so, she jolted forward to be free of the room, the house, the fear—

She turned more quickly than she meant, rotating on her heel, and she almost struck it outright. She threw out her arms to stop, for just above her, nose to nose, a hulking statue extended a tongue split over tooth and claw. Had she not been so desperate for balance she would have shrieked. The thing loomed there, its eyes protruding with one rolled backward into a head that jutted forward from a sinewy neck at the center of outstretched wings.

Georgia reached into her shift to lift the orb and ward the creature away, but she could not complete the gesture. Something struck her on the back of the head. She crumpled, flinging her arms wide. A dark shape grabbed her from behind, grabbed her arm and wrenched it, dug its fingers under her armpit and into her neck, and held her.

CHAPTER 47:
Furta Sacra

GEORGIA STRUGGLED. THIS NEW DEMON WAS A man, his eyes popping white and filled with loathing. He grimaced so close to her that she thought he would bite her in the face. Instead he whispered, "I've waited three nights for you."

Georgia had seen his face in the dark before, by torchlight, horsed. She had also seen it as she lay in a sack on a cold stone floor. Her enemy had found her—had lain in wait for her. This was Philip SeVerde, the archbishop himself.

He shook her, his tone loathful, insistent. "Where is she? Tell me. Where is the one they call Georgia?"

Georgia flicked her gaze through the shadows. She could see two men, one a priest, the other a guard with his arms folded across his chest. Both were armed but seemed content to wait; they stood one at each door.

She thought again of Agrippina. And then of Dymphna who went mad before they killed her. She felt the relic at her breast; she felt courage from it. "I am Georgia," she said. She felt the haughtiness in her voice. The hatred. Her triumph. She was Georgia. Let him think on it.

With a look of surprise, he released her.

She dug her toes into the floorboards, and another surge of hate made her gag. The tendons in her knees tightened, readied to launch at him. She thought to dig his eyes out with her nails.

He dodged her, grabbing her hands and twisting so that she could feel the ligaments stretch against her bones. He yanked a fistful of her hair, jarring her head down against her shoulder. Her belly stuck out wretchedly, an enormous tumor. He had to shift his balance to hold her.

He sucked in his breath. "So this is what it does, this demon. It has child after child, naming it always after itself. A line of wretches to torment me."

"I will outlive you." Georgia wanted to spit at him. She struggled, but he held her, his fingers puncturing her flesh.

He raised a long-bladed dagger and sunk it into the muscle of her upper arm. Her anger surged at the pain. She hated him, this man who had killed everyone, who had ordered the priory ransacked and supervised the killing at the cave.

He pushed the blade deeper. "Tell me. Where are the rest?"

"Murderer. Your grave will rot you."

He raised the blade and struck it down again, rotating it in the wound and pressing her so close to him that she could feel some ornament on his robe open the still-raw flesh on her back.

"Does the witch girl yet live?"

Georgia thought of Lo as he twisted her neck, her ear shrill with her own blood. His question echoed in her mind. She did not know. Lo, so close to death. *Did* Lo yet live?

He hooked the tip of the blade and sliced through her upper arm, his voice hushed and horrible. "Tell me, does she live?"

A sob puffed out her cheeks. The sorrow of it shook her. Lo would die, if she was not already dead, for the vigil had begun hours ago. And now she had failed. She was caught. She would be tortured to death. She felt again the weight of Mendaline's hand on her shoulder, a weight so heavy that her knees buckled, and she slid straight down to the floor.

The archbishop let her fall, shoving her with the heel of his foot.

"All are dead," Georgia wept. Let him kill her. It would be done.

"All except you? Or are there more? They say you drowned in York. They say they ran you through with a sword. They said they cut off your head. And now they claim you cannot die." He circled her and wiped his hand across the front of his robe, her blood staining it.

The guard at the door put his hand to the hilt of his sword and came forward, prepared to strike the final blow. The archbishop raised a hand to stop him, and he stepped back.

Her enemy crouched to face her, his face questioning. He grabbed her jaw and lifted up her chin; his eyebrows shadowed his eyes, which were already dilated black. He pinched her arm where he had gashed her. "Yet you bleed." He snatched at the hair covering her right ear. "And you burn, as well."

He slid behind her and wrenched his arm around her neck, pulling her against him. He brought the blade of the knife to the round top of her belly. "And now this."

He spoke in a whisper, his mouth pressed hard against her left ear. "Do you know what you have cost me? Do you know that the boy king lies dying, and it is Cranmer he seeks? They make plans for the throne, but Mary will be queen. And I, I who served the father faithfully will be rewarded. I will be Lord Chancellor. And you whom they say cannot die will finally be dead, by my hand, for this time I will do the deed myself.

"You think yourself a holy maid?" He forced her head in the direction of the sideboard, the skulls and powders there fervid with the ember glow of the bedchamber. "I will add you to my collection. And the child with you. For mark me, there will be no more of your line. Tonight you die. And your daughter with you." He raised his arm to plunge the dagger deep into the center of her stomach.

Even as he tensed to strike, his words echoed in the air, and she took them in: "There will be no more of your line ... And your daughter with you."

A daughter. Of course! How had she been so blind to the design of it? All this time she had been consumed by her own shame, had felt punished by her own failures—that she had lain with a man—that she had loved Manwell.

She shuddered, and he struck, plunging the dagger straight down.

"No!"

She twisted so violently that a string in her shoulder popped. The blade plunged down but slid across her belly, imbedding in the wet fabric of her skirt. It nicked her, but no worse.

A daughter. The joy of it swamped her, for in this child Isela had not condemned her, but instead had given her—all of them—a second chance. In this child, Lo would be reborn.

The hail outside returned, pelting the window panes like a burst of canon fire over the Thames. Her burden shifted. He was above her, but she could not fight with him. She could not imperil the child in her womb. She placed her hand on her stomach, for the first time feeling the child within her. A daughter. Lo! She must escape. She must not fail.

She scrambled up. Not Agrippina but Saint Marina—she remembered—it was Saint Marina who had defeated the demon and escaped. Georgia called to her now. She would flee. She would rush the door where the priest stood and be gone.

She ran, but the archbishop caught her by the back of her skirt. The jolt stopped her in midstep, and she fell flat on her face, the relic driving painfully into her breastbone.

He jumped on top of her, smashing her belly against the floor. She thought of how she had thrown the eagle stone away. She wished for it now. She must protect her child.

He raised the dagger to stab her stomach from the side, pinning her underneath him. He raised the blade, but she countered by crossing her legs at the ankles and forcing a turn, sending him heavily to the ground. She rose up and lunged straight at him, knocking the dagger from his grasp and throwing him back. She clawed at him. She would purge the world of men.

He shoved her, but she came on again. He grabbed her shoulder and spun her sharply. The relic swung wide at the end of the chain, and she grabbed it to shove it back into her bodice. Yet he struck her hard at the temple, and the chain broke.

The force of the blow knocked her off her feet and sent her sprawling on her back. She flung out her arms, landing at the foot of the pedestal with the gargoyle looming over her. The glass orb in her hand came down hard as she flung her arms out. It struck the marble at the corner edge. The bronze screamed and cracked, and the amber glass broke, a resounding, heart-wrenching, shuddering crack. The sound itself seemed to split her. She spasmed as the ground shook.

He came down on top of her even as she grappled with the shock, disbelieving what she had done. The relic was broken. It was not possible that it could break.

He did not let up, but clawed at her throat, his face lacerated with rage. Winding back his arm, he punched her stomach as if to gore her.

Georgia simultaneously wet herself and vomited at the blow. Her ears pounded with rage and hatred. He was nothing, a horror, a speck. He was no more than the gargoyle he paraded in his own bedchamber. She would not abide him.

She held the broken relic in her hand, her fingers bleeding, half the scrollwork missing. A broken chunk of bronze lay next to her, sharp and yellow in the light. She grasped it, a jagged, elongated point, and in one fluid movement swept her legs out. She moved to flip them both, and as she rose up she brought the shard around in a wide, deliberate arc, sinking it under the archbishop's chin, plunging it in between the cords of his throat. His blood spilled, but not enough to kill him. Enough only for victory and silence.

Her movement had been so quick that as she raised the final blow, he had not yet even registered his surprise. His eyes still burned with vengeance, as if he still believed himself the better of the two. As if he believed humans to be always evil and always in combat, one over the other, the witch or the knave, the whore or the bastard. Yet surely, if there were bastards, he was one. A true bastard—motherless.

He was weak, cruel, a child bereft. He was naked and alone.

She loomed above him.

Comprehension crept into his gaze. He opened his mouth, but no sound came out save a pitiful squeak.

She stared and knew. She could defeat him. She raised the shard yet higher, and tensed. But the desire to kill left her and the hate with it. It was a sin to kill a mother's son, even one so thin as this.

She lowered her hand and crawled backward into the shadows.

The archbishop's defeat had come so quickly that the guard and the priest even now seemed to disbelieve the outcome and hesitated. When they did run forward, the priest confirmed the wound with shock and surprise. He gave a shout to raise the house.

Georgia scrambled to her feet as the hall filled with the sounds of men. They poured into the room, some in shirts, others naked, clumsy with sleep, and armed.

"Find the girl and kill her," the priest screamed as the men advanced.

∽

Georgia had been trapped in this room three days ago. She was blocked from the doors then, just as she was again. But tonight she remembered the back stair in the corner. Between the stairway and herself, the room lay in shadow. She needed only to move quietly and quickly, and she would not be seen.

But the fight had upset her balance and drained her strength. She stumbled.

At the sound, several men turned at once, but it was the guard who saw her. He jumped, sword outthrust. She ran, gained the stairway, and took the steps two at a time, the broken relic still clutched in her palm, her arm aching, her whole body aching.

She landed in the kitchen, catching her balance on the wrought iron banister as she reached the bottom, the same banister she had leaned on earlier in the night. She prayed that the door to the buttery was still open as she had left it.

The kitchen staff staggered from their sleep as the hue and cry resounded in the house. Lamps were now lit. Two of the kitchen servants spotted her as she came down the steps. Georgia tensed, trapped between the servant women in front and the men behind. She tried to breathe over the echoing pain in her chest and belly. Her own vomit stank in her nostrils. She dodged them.

They might have caught her, but they slipped on the water that had dripped earlier from her skirt onto the floor. They slid into it, slamming their heads together and pitching full tilt into Georgia's pursuers, tumbling all together on the stairs.

Georgia leapt, slammed the buttery door behind her, ran down the buttery steps, through the smell of apples, and out the cellar door. She made a break for the trees, for that part of the grounds was darker than the rest. Stumbling, she pushed forward, her legs a ruin of bruises and fatigue, her breath all but gone. Her legs shaking. The rain had stopped, but the grounds were slick and wet. Hail crunched under each step as she rounded into the lane, and when she hit the woods, she slid into slick mud and fell flat on her face, jarring her shoulder on a tree trunk.

As she lay, she heard the dogs. She did not dare to rise; she did not have breath to rise, and the pain in her shoulder eclipsed all the other pain she felt. She could not move and lay wheezing, unable to find any strength in her hand. Slime from her nose coated her face, and she sneezed again.

She closed her eyes. She focused her thoughts only on the baby, her baby, the daughter who would save them. The daughter who must be born. She felt a warm liquid seep from between her legs.

She willed herself to get up, rolling to her side. The bone in her shoulder rolled. It clamped as if one bone snapped into another. The pain lessened, and she almost wept with the relief of it. She drew her knee under her, raised herself up, and leaned against the bark, gulping air.

She could hear the men and then see them. They swarmed over the grounds with lit torches. A triumphant cry went up from a man in the woods to her left. He ran into the open and waved a white cloth over his head; it was her apron. She made the sign of the cross over her heart. *Praise Isela, she had left it there*! He called to the others to follow him. They descended en masse toward the spot.

She sucked in breath and, her legs still wobbly, slogged from trunk to trunk. With the relic sharp and broken in her hand, she found her breath and ran.

CHAPTER 48:
Saint Margaret

When her breath caught, or when a stitch doubled her over and forced a break, Georgia rested. But then she would run again, and still it took until daylight to reach the country lanes, and longer still before she neared the Thames and started up the hill toward the cluster of cursed cottages.

All the time she held tightly to the relic. When she stopped, she ran her fingers over the shorn side where the rolling break made the surface ripple. There was a separate chip as well, but otherwise there were no other cracks. The chain was broken but had not been lost; it tangled in what scrollwork remained.

Georgia took the last of the steps to the cottage, fighting again against a stitch. She sneezed as she entered the house so that Mendaline jumped and Brigitte gave a little shriek. Lo lay with her head and chest raised on the mattress, and when Georgia came in, she blinked and swallowed, but did not move otherwise. Yet she was alive.

"*Sweet Mary!*" Mendaline left off wafting smoke to gape. She picked at Georgia's bloody clothes and tilted her head, peering at the bruises on her face, her cut lip, her scarred ear now crusted with blood. "By Saint Margaret, I'm never letting you out of my sight again. Every time I do you come back to me looking like you've been tied to a pig's tail and trod over by a barnyard." She poked at her muddied, torn skirt. "And by Saint Jude, not another apron gone?"

Georgia submitted long enough to wipe her nose on her sleeve before she pulled away. Limping, she went over to the broken table where Mendaline had spread out her pouches and medicines. Her satchel lay open, and Georgia rummaged through it.

"Hoy!" Mendaline tried to snatch it away, but Georgia found what she was looking for and drew it out. It was a thin strip of leather secured to an amulet of worry-worn blue. The walnut-sized stone of the amulet had been hollowed out and a pebble placed inside so that it rattled.

Georgia shook it to hear the noise. "You kept the eagle stone for me."

"One of us needed sense." Mendaline folded the satchel closed and laid it back on the table. "It's a true lapis, that. My own mother's, not that you minded when you sent it sailing."

Georgia put the amulet around her neck and then knelt next to Lo.

Mendaline squatted beside her and fussed with Lo's blankets. "There's water in her lungs, now. She'll not be able to talk to you."

Very gently, Georgia reached for Lo's hand. Lo's fingers were frail as morning ice in a winter basin, with the tips of her fingers a gentle blue. Across her palm was the ruin of what Romsfeld had done to her. Georgia laid the broken side of the relic onto the scar.

"We are as life makes us," she said. "Scarred, broken, yet we persist. We are the shards of the promise. Yet the light!" She held the relic up; broken though it was, golden rays burst along the walls of the small hut. "The light shines through us." She placed the orb again on Lo's palm, closing her fingers around it. "Even now you must remember who you are." She laid Lo's hand and the relic together into the blankets. As she did so, a line of blood oozed from Georgia's palm where the broken glass had cut her.

Mendaline sorted out a clean linen rag. "Brigitte, your hands are quick. Come child, bind this wound," Mendaline plucked at Georgia's blood-saturated sleeve—"though I have no idea where to start with the rest of her."

"Food," Georgia said. "I am hungry." She ignored Mendaline's openmouthed gape and submitted as Brigitte tied the bandage. As the girl worked, Georgia watched Lo breathe shallowly. How could she have let death come so close? She took the slice of bread Mendaline held out to her. It smelled of summer rye. She took a bite and wiped her eyes with the fresh bandage on her hand.

"It is no fault of yours," Mendaline used scissors to cut away the bloody linen of Georgia's sleeve. "Lo will go to God in peace. Last rites are said, for we feared to wait. Unless there is a miracle—"

Georgia took Mendaline's hand and placed it on her own stomach. "This daughter I carry; this is the miracle!" She closed her eyes and felt the child within her, the heartbeat, the curling feet and folded elbows. "This baby is Isela's gift. Lo will live again. The promise will renew."

She opened her eyes and thought she saw a flicker of hope in Mendaline's expression, and then pity.

Lo lay without moving. Brigitte laid a moistened cloth to wet Lo's lips.

"This sickness is not your doing." Mendaline cleared away the shreds of Georgia's sleeve and grimaced at the wound underneath. "I always said she had her own path to take. It cannot be helped."

"You are an old woman." Georgia wrenched her arm away. "You know nothing."

Mendaline blinked, and her lashes were wet. "If I had the hands to slap you I would, for you deserve it. You forget that you are sixteen, and with child, and a tyrant. You are Mars-born this life. You know only how to fight."

Georgia turned away.

Brigitte rinsed the cloth in a bowl of muddied water. She kept her eyes down and spoke timidly. "Sister Georgia, you should crave pardon when you hurt someone."

Georgia wanted to give some retort, but sneezed instead, convulsing with a jolt that sent a painful spasm through her shoulder. And then a pain she did not expect wrenched deep inside her back, a pain as if a heated rod of iron seared below her gut, gripping through her hips and down her right thigh before embedding itself in her knee.

She recoiled forward and cried out.

Mendaline placed a hand on her back. "Georgia?"

Georgia writhed. The pain was unlike any she had ever felt. "Mendaline! I die!"

The healer clucked her tongue, a gentle noise. She took up the wet linen from the basin and wiped Georgia's face. "There, there," she crooned, "you're going to live fine as ever. I suspect you'll have this baby, now. That's all. It's a hard thing. Be a brave girl, now. I'll be with you. All will be well. You'll see."

***

Mendaline set the cottage in motion, sending Gil for water and for wood. Brigitte unpacked straw from the mattress and laid it down to make a birthing bed that would catch the blood and fluid. Together, Mendaline and Brigitte stripped Georgia of her kyrtle and underskirts and covered her in the remaining blankets.

Georgia closed her eyes and reached deep into the swoon of prayer to escape the pains. She prayed for a straightforward birth and to survive it. She prayed for Lo, and to be worthy of the task ahead. Then pain pulled her into the world with a gush of fluid as she soaked the straw between her legs.

"I bleed."

Mendaline cocked a brow. She ran her hand along Georgia's calf and drew her hand away wet. "The waters only. And clean. Lie back now."

Georgia lay into the thick straw, and Mendaline lifted Georgia's shift to poke her belly. "You are near enough to your time." Mendaline ran her fingers over a fresh bruise. It darkened at Georgia's navel and spidered out over the ridges of skin and muscle.

Georgia grimaced at it. "The archbishop held me down. He tried to kill her."

Mendaline traced the bruise and the shallow cut that curled around into her hip. "He did not succeed," she said. She raised both eyebrows. "And neither did you, though I worried you might." Mendaline nodded toward the eagle stone. "Brigitte, take the amulet and tie it round her thigh, for it will draw the baby out."

Brigitte hurried to do as she was bid.

Breath and prayer and smoke drifted into a cloud that dispersed into fire when the pains came. Once, after Georgia cried out, Brigitte pressed a stone into her hand.

"Jasper," Brigitte whispered. "Sister Mendaline says it will speed you."

Another pain came, and another, with no break. At the third Georgia struck out with her fists, trying to release the pressure that built in her hips, her back, and across her chest.

"Oh, I cannot. Sister, I cannot." Georgia wailed outright and threw her head backward. "It is too much. How can Isela ask so much?"

Mendaline put down the almond oil and grasped Georgia's belly with both hands. "Already? That is good. It is a good sign when they come quickly."

Brigitte pressed her forehead into wrinkles. "She says she cannot."

"She should have thought of that before." Mendaline huffed as she stood up, but Brigitte burst into tears, and the old woman gave a nod of reassurance. "It's a hard thing, child. There's most of them wish they hadn't before they're done. And yet most of them up and do it again! Now, let's up with her, for she's set now to push that baby out."

Mendaline summoned Gil who worked in the shadows rinsing cloth to reuse for cleansing. "Bring that chair. It'll do, and we'll need help to hold her."

Gil complied, making sure the chair was sturdy before taking one of Georgia's arms to haul her up. The movement brought another pain, but Georgia's indignation rose above it. Men were forbidden to attend a woman's confinement, even doctors, even boys.

"I'll not. No man shall touch me!" She tried to tear her arm away, but

Gil held her near the dagger wound, and everything hurt more than she had imagined possible.

"Oh for mercy's sake," Mendaline rubbed her hands in almond oil and lifted Georgia's shift. "If you haven't sorted it out by now, I think mayhap you're too thick to bother with. Gil, Brigitte, haul her up."

"Leave me." Georgia struggled to snatch her arm away from Gil as Mendaline guided the lifting. She kicked her legs against them. "I have had enough of men!"

"Georgia, but you are an uncommon fool. Gil is not a man. Still yourself now." They set her on the edge of the chair, and Gil supported her as Brigitte shoved folded sacks behind her, giving cushion for her back. "Do men have courses?" Mendaline continued, her voice short. "What did you think, the medicine I made was to breed a beard? Gil's no boy."

Georgia stared into Gil's face. She felt blind and stupid, and she hurt, every part of her hurt.

"I am nine and twenty," Gil said. "But there's none as will hire a woman for a smith. It's safer in a blue cap. My name is Gilberta, though I am used to Gil, now."

Brigitte pressed down on the top of Georgia's belly, putting her hands on either side where Mendaline showed her. Brigitte looked up at her. "In truth, Sister Georgia, you did not know?"

Georgia screamed. Pain swept her, and her frustration exploded under it. Nothing was as it seemed or as it should be. A sharp tearing in her knees moved down along her shin and caused her foot to throb wretchedly.

"Push," Mendaline commanded.

It took a breath to sort it out, sort out the feelings in her body, the shift in how she felt. Then a raw desire filled her from all sides at once. For the first time since the pains struck, she found she could meet them force for force. She buckled over herself, bearing down with a strength that pulled through her entire body, every cell pulsing to meet this child on whom she hoped so much would be restored—this daughter who would make it as it was before, when it was Johanna who had pushed and wept.

Mendaline clucked her tongue and rubbed her hands first together and then against the fabric of her skirt. She opened and closed her fingers as she massaged between Georgia's legs.

"That's a girl, then," she said. "A good, strong girl you are Georgia, for an owl pellet, all hair and bones. Good wide bones, though. See how easily the baby comes?"

Easily? Her tissues stretched, burning and widening, drawing her into the hardest work she had ever done. Yet it filled her with an overwhelming passion for birth.

Mendaline took a length of linen and wrapped it tightly around her wide, flat hands. She could not tie the ends, and they flapped loose until Brigitte could tie them. She rubbed her hands together but seemed no more pleased with them.

Georgia felt her body stretch open. Soon, soon the baby would be born. She looked over toward Lo.

Lo's breath stilled. She took one last slow swallow, as if tasting the world a final time and then sunk downward into the blankets. Her hand twitched and was still.

Georgia fell into a half world. She felt the eddy of it and knew it when it touched her. It was the crossover, the path that took you to the next world or delivered you back into this one.

She could hear Mendaline's encouragement. "Push, at-a-girl-now. A little push again. Easy, Saint Margaret! Easy, Saint Anne! Let the child glide a bit. That's just fine. All is well. Easy now." And she could feel warmth course along her legs and up her back.

She tried to grasp for Brigitte, but Mendaline pulled the girl down, instructing her as they crouched together to watch the child descend. Georgia grasped for Gil instead, finding it hard to speak from one world into another, "Tell Lo … she must come quickly to the babe," the sound swirled like pollen, "without the soul … the child will die." She gazed into Gil's face, so pink at the jaw. How had she believed her to be a boy? She shoved Gil toward where Lo sunk further into the blanket. "Tell her—or it will be too late!"

Lo's eyes glazed. She closed them. Her soul lifted free, awkwardly at first, a limb at a time, rising.

Georgia called to her. "Do not tarry. You must not come too late."

The baby descended. She could feel the stretch between her legs; her privy parts burned as if the world pushed out.

A circle formed near Lo, a swirling blue, and then another. Both circles spun open, widening into channels, like misty undulating funnels that poured away. One poured into a misted, radiant white. The other poured toward the baby, swirling blue and misty pink. Georgia knew this path. It was the way back to life, the path she herself would always take. This path would take Lo back into the world. To their new chance.

Yet Lo hesitated, as if she did not quite understand or perhaps was not quite sure which course to take.

"Do not tarry!" Georgia felt desperate. She could feel Mendaline's hands on her thighs, her body heavy with the pressure that exploded from within.

From somewhere outside of herself, she could hear Mendaline coaching Brigitte. "It'll be slippery when it comes. It might come all at once, or it might stick. And there might be water with it. You have to catch it. Hold your hands out. I need your hands, girl. Hold them like this. That's it. That's a girl."

Lo floated above herself and gazed around the cottage. She looked over, and Georgia saw the depth in her eyes, her suffering gone, yet a deep sorrow remained in them. The world was a cruel place. Who else but Lo could know this as she did?

Gil knelt next to Lo's body, checking for a heartbeat, for breathing. Gil did not see past her own world.

Georgia flung her arm out. "Lo! It will be too late!" For if the soul did not enter the baby at birth, the baby would die. If Lo went too slowly, her daughter would be dead. Lo would be dead. The baby must not come from the womb before the soul stirred within it. Without a soul, it would be stillborn.

Another pain rolled up across her body, but now Georgia fought it, wanting to give Lo that extra heartbeat chance to slip into the channel back to life, to be reborn, to live.

Lo reached out a finger and swirled the mist. She smiled so sweetly, an infant's smile, and Georgia remembered a winter day at the priory when Lo had tottered through the dorter after prayers. She had worn a tiny woman's dress, her first, and it made her seem impossibly small. Her little skirts caused her trouble, and Elizabeth laughed at her. Uncertain, Lo had stopped to think of what to do, putting a chubby finger in her mouth to suck it.

Lo held that smile now, and then she chose the second swirl, the one that poured upward and away. As she stepped through the circle, she turned with a final look at Georgia. "Things must change," she said. And she dissolved into mist.

Georgia's throat constricted as she tried to call out and to breathe at the same time; she managed only stuttering. The cottage darkened to firelight, the crossover closed as if a hinge had snapped the edges shut. "Lo! Lo!"

But Lo was gone.

CHAPTER 49:
So Be It

Georgia fought the birth, refusing now to submit to pains that were for nothing. Lo was gone; she slumped and was dead. Gil knelt over her and prayed. Light broke through the niches in the shutters where the slats had cracked and fallen away. A hawk screamed.

Mendaline did not look up from her task, instructing Brigitte. "See the crown there? How it bobs a little out and back? Those are the last heartbeats a child takes in the womb. And now the oil, there, and your hands ready."

Georgia relinquished herself to defeat as another swell of force doubled her over. In a final crush, she delivered the baby, head and shoulders all at once.

"Ah. Ah, catch it. Hold it." Mendaline grunted as the baby slid into the world and into Brigitte's arms, the girl's face pale and terrified. "That-a-girl!" Mendaline said.

But Lo was gone. Georgia had lost all, her chance, her child, and Lo, for Lo was all of those at once, sweet Lo who as a child had cried because she could not follow the ducklings into the pond.

"Well caught." Mendaline laid out a white cloth like a bleached sail, and Brigitte laid the baby into it. Yet Mendaline's smile faded quickly as she wrapped the baby up. There was no sound of an infant's cry, and its skin was dyer's blue with no sign of pinking.

Mendaline rubbed the baby's back and limbs with a handful of straw. "Brigitte, the amulet—" Brigitte snatched the stone from Georgia's thigh, and

Mendaline laid it on the baby's chest. She sucked the white cream from its nose and mouth. Yet still it made no sound.

Georgia could see the top of the child's head. So tiny. To have struggled so hard to put things right, only to have the child born dead.

Another pain tightened cross her back, the afterbirth yet to come. Brigitte took hold of the cord, but Mendaline stopped her. "Hold. Easy, not to pull. Let it come as it may."

Mendaline returned to the baby, upturned a pouch of dried, crushed mugwort, and, sprinkling it, chanted a prayer. "Breathe! *Placebo Domino.* I blow the poison from you." She filled her lungs and blew her breath over the baby, the blankets, her own hands, and the straw surrounding them. The mugwort wafted over everything; Georgia could feel it brush her ankles and knees. Mendaline added a chant to bring the soul, to fix it. *"Matthew, Mark, Luke, and John—bind, bind, bind."*

Another pain loosed the afterbirth, and Brigitte placed it into the basin on the floor.

Mendaline kept at the work, rubbing the baby with the straw again. "Wee one," she cooed softly. "Come on, love. Give a cry, little love."

It's no use, Georgia thought. They were too late.

But a tiny stirring cry followed next, and then a great wail. The baby's skin colored purple and then pink.

Mendaline shouted gleefully, and her smile pushed up all the furrows of her face so that she had the look of a wild rose. Clamping the cord at four fingers width, she instructed Brigitte to cut and bind it.

Georgia did not believe the sound. Lo had not been in time! Lo had not taken the right crossing.

"Lo is dead." Gil lifted the blankets from under Lo's body and used them to cover her.

Mendaline made the sign of the cross in Lo's direction and kissed her thumb, her index finger placed across it. "It is done then. Her suffering at least is ended. *So be it.*"

"So be it." Gil raised the blanket over Lo's head. As she did so, the relic tumbled out onto the cottage floor, the broken scrollwork reflecting like a scar in the firelight. Gil took it up and examined the raw edge. "I can fix this."

The baby cried again. Georgia wet her lips, her mouth sticky from breathing wide open. Lo was gone, yet her daughter lived. Isela had given her a daughter, a daughter swaddled in linen and wrapped over in a cap and blankets.

Mendaline put the baby in her arms. "You can speak to baptize as well as I."

Georgia poked to widen the blankets around the baby's face, the child's skin so new and wrinkled pink, and the cheeks round. "Then I baptize you, my daughter, in the name of—"

"No. It is a knave child," Mendaline corrected, "a son."

Georgia withdrew her gaze from the baby's perfect face. Instinctively, she made a sign of warding.

"Yet it is not so bad as that, Georgia!" Mendaline said. "You do not risk a third breast as did Saint Whyte."

"You jest, then."

Mendaline grew serious. "You have a son, my girl. And a fine healthy boy at that."

Georgia fought the impulse to throw the baby back. She ripped the amulet from where Mendaline had tucked it into the blankets, and threw it. It bounced into the fire, sending up sparks in every direction, and then bounced again, hitting the far wall. Fires sprung up in the straw in several places, and Gil rushed to stamp it out.

Mendaline slapped at the sparking hay. "There now, watch that you don't burn us all with your peevishness."

Georgia unwrapped the baby; it could not be true. The child wailed as she jostled it to take the last strip of linen from around its middle. It lay naked. There was no doubt it was a boy. She shoved him away.

Mendaline scooped the baby up, handing him to Brigitte to help her as she rewrapped him, rolling him in the girl's lap as she wound the linen and placed a wool blanket over all.

"Georgia! The weather is not so fair, nor your son so very sturdy, as to risk the cold. And the fire burst open. You are a tyrant still."

"A son! To grow up to be a man! What good can come of this? The promise is broken. My term is over."

"Surely it is not so dire as all of that?"

Georgia scraped at her hand and screamed now at Isela. "Take your mark. Take your mark! I bear nothing." She clawed at it, but the mark would not erase.

Mendaline put a hand on her hip. "You are not the woman I knew."

Georgia closed her eyes and pretended to be dead.

Mendaline poked her with her foot, but she refused to budge. The baby cried. The span of eternity passed. She lay there, refusing to be alive. Mendaline nudged her again, harder this time.

Georgia rolled over and wept. Mendaline was right; she was not who she was supposed to be. She had failed utterly. What brighter mark of her failure than to bear a boy child from her womb. Not a daughter, but a boy who would grow up to be a man.

Sobs stole through her, taking with them every shred of herself and mocking it. She, who had been an abbess. Who had traveled to the holy land, had been reborn and reborn to hold open a space for hope. And it had all come to mockery. To villainy. A knave child.

Mendaline sat next to her and placed the baby between them. He fussed a little. She rocked him with one thick, spade-shaped hand, while she smoothed Georgia's cheek with the other.

"Before I cut the cord, I read the ridges on the baby's navel," Mendaline soothed. "It said you will have two more children."

Georgia sobbed harder. Saint Christina the Astonishing had been repulsed by the smell of all humans. She had been thought dead, but then she had jumped from her coffin onto the altar, spinning tales of purgatory that had terrified any who dared listen.

"Sweet child Georgia." Mendaline's voice was kind, though Georgia felt she deserved no kindness. "In each life, you have to make what you can of it. You are not the only woman to have a child you did not expect. And you are not the first woman to have a son."

Georgia looked up, and Mendaline smiled at her, not so wide as rose petals this time, but unkempt and haggard and beautiful. The room smelled suddenly of warm, ripened rye, as if the floor were strewn with it—sheaves of it.

"And now that you've got him," Mendaline continued, "think on what it is that made him. Perhaps Isela—perhaps God—knows something here that you do not?"

Georgia watched her son as he fussed, then calmed, and then hiccupped. He looked like every other baby she had ever seen. He looked like Manwell.

A prayer opened inside her, between her ribs, expanding as she breathed. Her heart stirred. Georgia thought of all the struggle she had known, all the anger and the hurt, where was love? Was not love the most perfect gift of all? She remembered the archbishop, how he had hung over her. Yet in the end, he had been a child as well. He had been a baby such as this.

"My son," she whispered it.

"Yes, child! He is not mine, surely!"

Georgia buried her face in the blankets and felt the baby root toward her, seeking her, her smell, her touch. Mendaline scooted him closer with her strong, flat hands, tucking Georgia and the baby together.

"You'd best suckle him."

"Yes." Georgia whispered it. And then she laughed. And then the tears flowed again. A fountain.

"Mendaline?" she said.

"Yes?"

"Mendaline, I am free."

"Yes." Tears spilled over the old woman's cheeks as her face again transformed into roses. "Oh yes, my sweet Georgia. It is a new day. Hold him safe and raise him strong, and he will be a fine man."

Gently now, she lifted the baby to her breast. Sliding her nipple across his cheek as she had seen mothers do, she waited for him to root into her touch. His soft cries turned to suckling, and a tiny hand kneaded her breast. She drew him close. She felt the warmth of his skin—and loved him.

"Yes," she said. "So be it."

ACKNOWLEDGMENTS

THANK YOU SO MUCH TO ALL THE people who have supported me during the writing process, especially to Marci Dehm and Kat Richardson, my dearly beloved writer compadres. Thanks to my family, to my kids—who endured their mother's love of history—and to my husband who learned under fire to be a good listener when a draft wasn't going well. Thanks to my mother, Rev. Isabel Gardner, and father, Jim Gardner, my first readers and supporters. Finally, thank you to those at iUniverse for their democratized vision of book publishing.

This project was sparked by a dream in 2002, a dream that challenged me to ask questions about women and faith, gender, culture, humanity, religion, and with all my research into the "Hero's Journey," an unmanageable question bloomed: What is the hero's story for women? What does it mean for a woman to struggle and to sacrifice and *to believe*? And how might that manifest itself in a lifetime? The questions would not let me go, and the result was hours of research—and a gift I did not expect, a pathway toward the reclamation of my faith.

This is my first novel, but I have previously published two regional history books, *Washougal* (2006) and *Fishers Landing* (2008), both local histories of early communities on the Columbia River. I also maintain a Web site, http://www.historyfish.org, and I invite you to drop by. If you are new to monastic or medieval history, I invite you to explore these subjects. The world of Joan of Arc and Joan the Meatless alike is absolutely fascinating. And whether you were born in 2008 or are as old as Moses, the stories of our human history are well worth the telling. After all, history is part of how we know who and what we are.

Though this is a work of fiction, I wanted to ground it as firmly as possible in the historical world. When I began this project, I knew nothing of medieval piety. As such, I consulted many sources in my research—far too many to list. The following books in particular, however, helped me to imagine not just what it might have been like long ago, but, more importantly, how those born in another time and place might have understood their world. I am very, very grateful to these fine academics for their painstaking research and informative books: *Medieval English Nunneries* by Eileen Power (1922); *Forgetful of Their Sex* by Jane Tibbetts Schulenburg (1998); *Holy Feast and Holy Fast* by Caroline Walker Bynum (1988); *The Art of Cookery in the Middle Ages* by Terence Scully (1997), especially for the banquet scene; *Thomas Cranmer: A Life* (1998) and *The Boy King: Edward VI* (2002) both by Dairmaid MacCulloch; and *Female Monastic Life in Early Tudor England*, edited by Barry Collett (2002), for its edition of Richard Fox's *Benedictine Rule for Women, 1517*. Thank you especially to JoAnn McNamara, for her book, *A New Song, Celibate Women in the First Three Christian Centuries* (1983), which helped pique my interest in the subject altogether. In addition, thank you to Glenn Gunhouse for his parallel Latin/English Vulgate Psalter at medievalnet.com and to all those who created, maintained, and contributed to the ORB Internet archive. Two other fabulous volumes, *The Stripping of the Altars* by Eamon Duffy and *Medieval Popular Religion, A Reader* edited by John Shinners (1997), inspired or informed many of the prayers recited by the characters in this book. As for medical information, I appreciated these two books in particular: *Leechcraft, Early English Charms, Plantlore, and Healing,* by Stephen Pollington (2000); and Eucharius Rösslin's *The Rose Garden for Pregnant Women and Midwives*, translated by Wendy Arons and available in her book *When Midwifery Became the Male Physician's Province* (1994). Another fine book that explores the phenomenon of anchorites is Rotha Mary Clay's *Hermits and Anchorites of England* (1909). This book is now in the public domain, and a digital copy can be found on my Web site, www.historyfish.org.

LaVergne, TN USA
02 January 2010
210711LV00004B/30/P